THE NORTHERN
PALMYRA AFFAIR

BY HARRISON E. SALISBURY

FICTION

THE NORTHERN PALMYRA AFFAIR

NONFICTION

TO MOSCOW—AND BEYOND
THE SHOOK-UP GENERATION
AMERICAN IN RUSSIA
STALIN'S RUSSIA AND AFTER
RUSSIA ON THE WAY

THE NORTHERN PALMYRA AFFAIR

Harrison E. Salisbury

HARPER & BROTHERS
PUBLISHERS · NEW YORK

THE NORTHERN PALMYRA AFFAIR
Copyright © 1962 by Harrison E. Salisbury
Printed in the United States of America

FIRST EDITION

A-M

LIBRARY OF CONGRESS CATALOG CARD NUMBER: 62-9923

THE NORTHERN
PALMYRA AFFAIR

1

Georgi Alexandrovich Morozov sat almost motionless in the straight chair with its faded purple upholstery and intricately carved back. Just behind his head the carving rose to a triangle from the center of which protruded a lion's head. Sometimes, when he leaned back carelessly, the small, slightly projecting teeth of the lion's jaws caught him at the occipital point of his skull. When Ludmilla, his secretary, saw this happen a smile would come over her usually serious face.

"Comrade Director," she would say, "why don't you put that chair out for visitors and take the good black leather one for yourself?"

"How can I do that?" was the reply. "It's my seat of authority. No. The lion is my protector and my guardian. He is there to remind me that uneasy is the head upon the throne. So it is and so it must be."

Tonight there was no danger that Morozov's head would collide with the lion's jaws. He was leaning forward, both elbows resting on the desk and his long, rather gaunt face propped between his hands. So deep was the train of thought touched off by his unexpected visitor that the strong tea which Ludmilla had brought him

1

after the departure of young Michael Galin—as he insisted on calling himself—remained cold and untouched on the desk.

The truth was that the sudden appearance of Galin and the news which he conveyed had struck Morozov one of those careless yet deadly blows which life sometimes deals out as casually as stones fly from the wheels of a passing cart. Morozov had not yet had time to ponder the full effects of the blow but instinctively he knew that the wound was not one from which recovery was likely.

His hand automatically reached toward the glass of tea but he did not complete the gesture by putting it to his lips. The spoon still stood in the glass, two sturdy lumps of sugar lay in the blue china saucer and the burnished helmet of the *bogatyr* which decorated the German silver glass holder reflected in miniature Morozov's profile. It was a profile marked by high facial bones, rather sunken cheeks, a slightly crooked nose and broad forehead with receding hair, still black but strongly peppered with gray. In the shadowed room the blue of Morozov's eyes could only be guessed. He was a man of middle age, thin, with something military in the line of his shoulders. He wore an olive-drab military blouse without insignia, dark blue military breeches and soft, worn but well-oiled and polished boots.

Morozov had been staring unseeing into space for fully fifteen minutes when the door of his office, heavily padded with winter felt, opened slightly. His secretary started to enter but seeing his rigid, unmoving figure she quietly withdrew. Morozov gave no sign of noting her intrusion but, perhaps, it was perceived by his subconscious, for in a moment or two he stirred from his reverie, sighed deeply, picked up his glass of tea, strode over to the high windows which gave onto Hertzen Street and pulled back the heavy velours curtains.

The January cold had painted arabesques on both the inner and outer windows and the lamps on the street cast brilliant aureoles, which were, in turn, diffused by the intricate geometry of the frost, depriving the scene of perspective and breaking it into a prismatic complexity beyond the power of human optics to resolve.

2

Yet, so often had Morozov stood at the window and gazed out on the winter scene that, blurred and distorted as it was by the ice crystals, to him each aspect was fully recognizable. The distortion did not prevent him from perceiving the twin yellow lights of the trolley-buses as they came down the street and the elephantine shadows they cast in passing. He knew that the sputtering trail of electric blue was the trolley, whining around the corner. The whorls of crimson succeeded by amber and followed by green were the traffic lights, the succession of their colors as unvarying and reassuring as the waves lapping at the granite of the Neva Embankment. Morozov could not see the passers-by on the sidewalk, leaning into the wind, heads bent, fur collars turned up, a succession of black beetles scurrying against the snow which steadily sifted down, carpeting all the city in white velvet. Nor could he actually see the wan and fitful lights of the frosted windows across the way. But long since his eyes had captured every detail, every cornice, the precise division of each window into panes, the decoration of the second-story windows (more ornate than the simple copings of the third and fourth stories). Indeed, he could easily have drawn from memory each cracked pane of glass, each *fortochka*, each jar of herring tucked between the double windows, each newspaper-wrapped package, each variation in winter weather stripping. Nor was this a memory trick or personal idiosyncrasy. Morozov was an engineer and an architect and he had an eye for detail, precise and trained.

Thus, for all his preoccupation, had someone suddenly said: What is it that you see from the window? Morozov would have started a bit and then replied in his ordinary tone of composure: "Nothing much . . . just the evening traffic on the street . . . the buses . . . passers-by . . ." And he would have added: "It's still snowing, you know."

Yet this would not have been an entirely accurate answer. For while Morozov saw the snow and the lights and the wind moving the lights he was not at the moment seeing what existed outside his window on this specific January evening in 1949. He saw

3

Hertzen Street, all right. But it was on another winter night, a winter night of the distant past. How long past it was! The force of the passing years suddenly hit him like a blow in the body. You did not realize how the years flowed by until an evening like this when a few halting words spoken by a nervous young man with ragged fingernails, haunted eyes and parchment skin released their full, evocative force. It was like being caught by a sudden turn of the tide. He remembered a summer spent at the house on the Baltic not far from Reval. He must have been eleven or twelve. Not more. He loved the waves, the salt taste of them, the power of them as they smashed at his thin legs, the suck of the water as it tore the sand grains from under his feet. He learned to wade out into the blue sea and brace against the current. When the big waves came he leapt upward, breasting them full force, letting them bear him back but keeping his head in the clear sunshine. Sometimes they knocked him down but he was up in a flash, scrambling out of the surge of water as it rushed back to the sea. And then this grew too tame. He learned to time the waves and to dive just as they were about to break, emerging sleek as a seal in the quiet trough beyond the breaker. He could remember the feeling this gave him of mastery over a power so much greater than his own. It became a battle in which his slim, wiry body was pitched against the overwhelming might of the sea.

"You see, Georges," his father had told him. His father always used the French rather than the Russian form of his name. "You see how physical skill and the use of the mind enable man to cope with the most elementary forces of nature. The sea is a million million times more strong than you. And yet, by the use of your mind and your small muscles, by correct timing and judgment, you make it your slave. You rob it of terror. You command it."

"Like King Canute?" he interjected.

"Not like Canute," his father replied. "Canute was a fool. He tried to command forces over which he had no power. But you, correctly assessing your own strength and correctly assessing that of your thousand times more powerful opponent, bring him to his knees."

4

This was the kind of philosophizing in which, Georges knew, his father delighted. And yet it was true, too. He did possess the power to master the sea. But one day his timing was off. Or perhaps he did not leap high enough. Or he failed to note a change in the tide.

One moment he was diving cleanly, smoothly into the oncoming wall of water. The next he was overpowered. Borne down, whirled in every blue-green, terrifying, murky direction. His head pounded the sand with stunning force. Everywhere the water rushed and tore at him. He clawed and fought but he did not know which was up and which was down, where was land and where was sea.

Then, just as suddenly, he felt himself thrown violently to the sand and scrambling like a crab as rivulets of sea water swirled backward, sucking under his body.

"You're all right, Georges?" It was his father, instantly by his side, lifting him with a strong arm, beating him on the back as he choked the water and sand out of his lungs and nose.

And later, as they walked up to the bathing house at the edge of the beach, his father spoke.

"You see now," he said, "that was a good thing. It frightened you a little, Georges, just for a moment. And that was right, too. Because now you will always remember the real power of the sea. You know your ability. And you know that of the sea, as well. It is an old tiger. You can tame it and you can tease it. But you must be on your guard. Because one blow of the tiger's paw . . . that is the finish."

There had been times, Morozov admitted, when he had not thought of this incident nor of his father's words for years. And yet, sooner or later, they always came back to him. They came back at moments like this when he felt the rush of the tide surging around his legs and when he knew that its force was stronger than any skill that he might oppose to it.

"Never forget, Georges," his father had said, "that the tide turns. Sometimes it is with you. Sometimes against you. The danger is when it is turning."

The danger of the turn. Yes, this surely life had taught him. Sometimes the turn was swift and unexpected—November, 1917, or

5

June, 1941—and sometimes it was slow and imperceptible, turning with such tiny steps and stages that for a long time you could not really be sure which way the current was running. This was what you learned in Russia. You learned to know the tides and to fear them. For a long time you did not think of them or you thought you had mastered them. Or perhaps you just put all thought of them out of your mind. Until . . . until . . . Until such a night as this. Morozov shrugged his shoulders imperceptibly. There would be no forgetting from now on. The tide was turning. Indeed, the tide had already turned and it would carry him with it. Sometimes Morozov called himself an optimist. Given two alternatives he liked to believe the better of them. But now there was going to be no alternative. The die had been cast. Precisely how it would happen, precisely how much time was left he would not try to guess, although he felt certain that he could postulate the circumstances without much difficulty. The time? Soon. Very soon. Fantastically soon. A matter of days at best. Even of hours. Yet, considering the years that had passed, considering what those years had brought, the wonder was not that time was running out. The wonder was that it had not long since expired. Perhaps some would say he had no reason for regret, for sorrow, for fear. What was the slogan of the Putilov men and women? "We do not fear death—death is afraid of us." Well, slogans were bright and brave but he had lived a long time, often in times of danger, and he had never learned how to put fear aside. He could thrust it away in his mind, perhaps, but he knew no way of keeping that hard, tight ball from forming in his stomach like a stone of granite.

He pulled back the curtains again and looked down into the street. One of the window panes was hardly frosted and he saw in the corona of light from the street lamp a young couple hurrying by. They were holding hands and the lamp cast a great double silhouette of their heads and shoulders as they passed beneath it, two lovers hurrying homeward on a snowy evening.

2

It was Shrove Tuesday—Maselnitza. Nina Petrovna and Tatiana Struve were giving a pancake party and "You must come, Georges, there will be a special surprise for you—a very special surprise." The year must have been 1922, Morozov thought. It was the time of NEP, the New Economic Policy—a time of wildness and looseness and craziness. Not a pleasant time really, as you looked back on it. And yet when he thought of some of the later times he wondered. You never really can be certain when you are living through a given period in life exactly how it will seem later on. He could not have imagined in those difficult, difficult years of the early 1920's that later on they might seem in retrospect almost like a golden age. But so it had turned out.

Certainly he had gone to the party. It must have been February, 1922, all right because he was still in the Army, still in the Engineering Corps. The girls were artists, and somehow (actually, he could guess how) they had managed to get an enormous room in a fantastic old building just off the Nevsky. Before 1917 the building had been the headquarters of a big export firm and the room the girls had acquired for a studio was on the top floor, with great skylights

7

and high ceilings with windows that ran right up to the roof.

It was very late by the time he got to the party—midnight or close to it. How clearly he remembered the evening! He was working in the old offices in the General Staff Building, and when he came out under the arch the wind was blowing a gale, whipping the snow past him on the street. It blew him along, jostling him forward with an invisible hand. He had never been to the apartment before and he wasn't quite sure where it was. He went through a passageway into an inner courtyard and there were several entrances, dimly lighted. He tried the first at random and inside there was no light at all. Finally with the help of a match he made out a faded list of tenants. The last name on the list was Struve. The flat was on the top floor.

Once he had climbed the three flights there was no question where the party was. The hubbub beat on his ears. A phonograph was blaring a tango and someone seemed to be playing the piano at the same time. He was tempted not to go in. It didn't sound like his mood at all. In after years he had sometimes wondered what would have happened if he had turned on his heel and marched back down the stairs and straight home to the little room he then had just off the Haymarket. It was a question which came to him again tonight as he looked down on the gradually thinning traffic on Hertzen Street, so blurred and distorted by the deepening whorls of frost. Suppose he had not met Irena on that Shrove Tuesday night. Suppose he had not met her on the evening of her return to Petrograd from Paris. Suppose the meeting had been delayed—for a week, a month, six months—as so easily might have been the case in those turbulent, uncertain years. Would they then have ever really met again, and if they had would it not have been merely a chance encounter, a brief blur of sentimental feeling evoked by childhood memories? Once—well, perhaps it had been more than once—they had discussed this question. Not that it was a question for Irena. To her it was fated that they would meet again, that they would meet as they did, and that everything which followed would follow. This, she said, she had known from the very

8

beginning, and for a long time he had not challenged her judgment because he believed almost superstitiously in the validity of her instinctive fatalism. But there had been moments later when he wondered deeply about this and tonight the question inevitably arose. And again remained unanswered.

For, despite his momentary impulse, he had not turned away from the door. He had knocked, and, knowing that his knock could not be heard in the noisy room inside, had tried the door and pushed it open. The moment he did this the noise was really deafening and his nostrils were assaulted by an overpowering smell—the smell of wet, steaming wool which arose from a pile of coats and scarves which was heaped on the floor of the entryway. Morozov found himself in a very small passage which gave onto the extremely large and high-ceilinged room, whose vastness was lost in gigantic shadows. It was lighted only by two or three candelabra fixed to the high walls, and to Morozov's confused eyes it was completely filled with people, swirling and moving, talking and laughing and drinking. Once again the impulse to flee swept over him, and probably he would have turned blindly back down the stairs had it not been for the fact that he was desperately hungry. He had not, he suddenly realized, eaten anything since morning. He had been working over a complicated problem of structural stresses for the past week. His calculations stubbornly refused to come out. Then, suddenly, the solution of the problem came to him, and once he was in the final stages of it he was driven, as always, by a fury to complete the solution, heedless of time, food or any other consideration.

He stood for a moment trying to get his bearings in the confusing room. As his eyes grew more accustomed to the play of lights and shadows he looked for his hostesses. He did not know either of them well. He had flirted with Tatiana Struve, but they were really not attracted to each other and each quickly recognized this. She was several years older than he, the widow of the famous artist Struve, who had been accidentally killed in a railroad wreck during the Civil War. In her painting she was inclined to cubism, making up in the vigor of her contrasts and the boldness of her colors for what

9

Morozov felt was a basic lack of imagination. He did not know Nina Petrovna's work at all. She was several years younger than Tatiana—a creamy blonde with golden hair combed back tightly in two tresses which she wore braided over her forehead in classic Russian style. The women, Morozov had heard, were lovers, but whether this was really so or merely Petrograd gossip he was not prepared to say. If they were lovers it seemed clear from his experience with Tatiana that she was by no means faithful to her sex. Whatever their relations they were friendly, good-hearted, generous women who enjoyed parties, conversation, drinking and laughter.

Neither of them seemed to be visible, and although Morozov had now been standing in the doorway for five minutes no one had paid him the slightest heed. The reason for this was that the attention of most of the people was now fixed upon a scene being enacted on the far side of the room, where a tall curved window was let into the upper quadrant of the wall. Around the window was a small interior balcony overlooking the room to which access apparently was gained from an inside staircase. On this balcony stood a woman who wore a black silk dress with extremely low décolletage, a black Spanish mantilla around her shoulders and a tortoise-shell comb in her hair. She was leaning far over the balcony and because her décolletage was so low and her breasts so abundant they kept slipping out of her dress and dangling like great pendulous udders over the dark railing of the balcony. Each time this happened she nonchalantly and with a gesture of resignation stuffed them back into her gown, only to have them pop out again a moment later. Morozov recognized her instantly. She was Agripina Antonovna, still the star of the Musical Comedy Theater although she was said to be in her mid-fifties, renowned for her boldness, her periodic drunkenness and her enormous but rather coarse voice. She was, Morozov deduced, playing the role of a wanton and debauched Juliet to a cynical young man who wore Spanish tights and a white shirt with open collar and stood on a heavy table just below the balcony, pantomiming a serenade, interrupted by gestures of catching, fondling and milking each time the great round breasts of the soprano made their appearance. Morozov had never seen the young man before but he knew that he must be the latest juvenile star of the Musical Comedy Theater and, ergo, Agripina Antonovna's current lover.

Revolted by the obscene pantomime Morozov turned his eyes to the crowded room and noted that at least half of those present were in costume of one form or another. He was now able to make out the hostesses. Struve, wearing a rather mannish embroidered Ukrainian smock, had appeared beside the young Spaniard and spoke briefly to him. Whatever her words they had instant effect. Throwing a kiss to his drunken Juliet the Spaniard leaped from the table and vanished in the throng. A moment later the soprano withdrew from the balcony. The phonograph began once more with a very scratchy American foxtrot. Conversation sprung up on all sides. Half of the people were dancing. Morozov could see the playwright Spingarn dancing with his beautiful blonde wife, the leading lady of the Drama Theater. The poet Maxim Voronsky, his hair thrown back like a lion's mane, was laughing in the corner with a man in army blouse and breeches who looked very much like the Commissar for Propaganda—and probably was. If there wasn't a scandal about that ridiculous Agripina Antonovna it would be a holy wonder. A girl came dancing past with a small green cut-glass *rumka* full of vodka.

"Drink this," she said, handing him her glass. Automatically he raised it to his lips. As he did so he realized again that he was fiercely hungry. He also perceived that he was still standing in the doorway, just as he had entered, still wearing his heavy leather coat with his gray caracul hat in his left hand.

"I must get something to eat," he said to himself, turning to find a place for his hat and coat. As he did so he heard a soft, fresh voice almost in his ear, saying: "Thank God, you have come. I have been waiting and waiting for you to take me away from here."

Irena! He knew before he turned. He knew with the first soft musical tones of her voice. This was why he had come. This was why he had not gone away. This was the surprise that Struve had

11

promised him. "Irena!" He was swallowed in the depths of her gray-green eyes that glowed in the half shadow with a kind of golden fire.

"Don't talk," she commanded. "Don't say a word!"

Her arm was through his and he saw that she was wearing a fur *shuba* that swirled up and around her neck, which gleamed like a white swan against black velvet. Her eyes did not leave his as they walked through the door, closing it against the noise and moving in the complete blackness of the staircase. It did not seem that their feet touched the cold marble of the steps as they sank through the darkness, and suddenly their lips were touching and they were thrusting the courtyard door open with their shoulders and stepping out into the snow, lips against lips, cheeks on cheeks, body leaning to body, and the snow falling, falling, falling like diamonds as they moved to the beating of their hearts and the velvet of lips on lips, moving and moving through the snow of the Petrograd night.

3

It was a miracle. Morozov knew then that it was a miracle just as he knew it now. It was a miracle upon a miracle because that was what their life had been. Their life! It made him grimace. Their life! Not a life, certainly. A series of miracles, separated in time and space. He remembered the time he had tried to tell Maxim Voronsky about it. Why had he done that? He was drunk, of course. That is, both he and Voronsky were drunk. But perhaps he was more drunk than Voronsky. They had run into each other by chance—quite by chance. He was in Moscow on business for two or three days. What it was he no longer had the faintest idea. But there had been a delay in the Commissariat. There was always a delay in the Commissariat. It was summer. Possibly 1929 or 1930. One of those stifling Moscow nights when a Leningrader dies for a cool breeze off the Gulf of Finland. He was completely at loose ends. Out of sorts. The business, whatever it was, going badly. He had dropped in at the Hermitage for the concert and, afterward, went out on the veranda of the café and ran into Voronsky, Voronsky sitting with a blonde—a cheap, whorish-looking blonde. Voronsky must have been bored, and perhaps he was depressed, too, for he insisted on Morozov coming and sitting with him. They drank cherry brandy and then vodka. At first the conversation was desultory. It was Voronsky who brought up the subject of Irena and it was only after the blonde had gotten up and vanished (he remembered Voronsky slapping the blonde's chunky buttocks and saying: "Take it away for tonight, *golubushka*. I'm bored") that Irena's name came into the conversation.

Suddenly Morozov shuddered. Why wasn't Voronsky here tonight? Why were they all gone? Why had he survived? Not that much future lay ahead of him after this evening's encounter. But for what reason should he be living and they be dead? Were all the people of the twenties gone? Undoubtedly. Some had disappeared within a few months—either from typhus or the Cheka. Others lived into the 1930's and died after Kirov or in the years that followed. And those who survived these terrors lived on to die in the hunger and ice blockade. The band had grown smaller and now the time had come for the last survivors to join those who had gone before. Morozov sighed. It was lonely and even terrifying to be a survivor. How he wished that Voronsky, at least, were here tonight! Not that he could have made sense out of it all. But it would have been good to talk to somebody—to a man who had blood in his veins and who bled when he was hurt.

He had tried to tell Voronsky that night at the Hermitage about Irena. But it was hopeless. Perhaps they had had too much to drink. And yet if they had not drunk they would not have talked at all.

He had tried to tell Voronsky about his first meeting with Irena but it dissolved in his hands. It was like one of those gold-and-blue butterflies in his father's specimen case. They looked like beautiful jewels, and one day his father opened the yellow wooden cabinet with its slanting glass top and the dazzling specimens, each in its little nest of cotton wool. How carefully his father lifted out the small nest and how breathlessly he watched.

"Now, Georges," his father said. "Pick up the butterfly. But be as careful as you can."

His hand trembled a bit in the solemn moment. As carefully as he knew how he grasped the beautiful wing with his two fingers.

He could still feel on the surfaces of his thumb and forefinger the imprint of that incredibly soft texture. One moment he grasped it and the next second before his eyes it dissolved into chrome and ochre dust.

Tears started in his eyes and he looked at his father in sheer horror.

"There, there, Georges," his father said. "Don't cry. I'm sorry it shocked you so. But I wanted you to remember this. I wanted you to have this lesson. Not just about butterflies. But about life. Try to measure the possible consequences before—not after—you act."

"But," he told his father, choking through the tears, "I didn't mean to hurt the butterfly."

"No, Georges," his father said. "Of course you didn't. The butterfly was beautiful. You just wanted to touch it. You wanted to hold it. You wanted it for yourself. And there was nothing wrong in that. But you did not understand how delicate was that beauty. How careful we must be to preserve what nature creates. Not knowing, you destroyed it. Beauty is so rare that when we try to possess it we often destroy it."

Today, Morozov supposed, his father would be considered a dull and prosy person. And yet what truth there was in those simple little experiments, those homely dramas which he employed to demonstrate to a youngster the principles of life.

When he had tried to tell Voronsky about Irena the beauty and singularity of the experience crumbled into grains of dust. Perhaps such an experience was like those gossamer wings. Too fragile to touch. And yet that could not really be so. How real that day in the Summer Garden still seemed. He had taken a book with him that afternoon—certainly it was Pushkin. He was just at the age when every phrase of Pushkin's suddenly becomes meaningful, pulsing and throbbing with the emotion of life. He had slipped the volume into his jacket pocket and gone over to the Summer Garden. It must have been toward the middle of June—school examinations over and his parents still in Petersburg, not yet gone to the seashore or, as sometimes happened, to Germany or France.

So he had gone to the Summer Garden. It was a cool June day,

15

one of those June days when Petersburg had outdone itself, the sky blue with scudding high white clouds, a gentle breeze which brought just a touch of sea to the Garden, the golden spire of the Admiralty like a rapier reaching for the sun, the Neva blue as the sky and the embankment gray and granite and the Garden peaceful but not entirely quiet. There was the murmur of the *nanyas* as they sat beside the carriages of the infants. There was the murmur of the young men in uniform and women in stylish dresses as they slowly strolled the allées, arm in arm. More distantly there was a dim sound of traffic on the boulevards. The air was heavy with the June scents, the odors of the phlox and nasturtiums, the clover in the grass and from somewhere the faint smell of wild roses.

Of all this Georgi was vaguely aware, sitting on a bench under the row of lime trees which shielded the sun from the pages of his book. He was not actually reading—he was devouring the poetry which, like the atmosphere around him, was fragrant with the scent of youth and hope and romance. What was he reading? *Eugen Onegin*, of course, and his head at twelve was filled with dreams of Tatiana.

So he sat there, his nose buried in the book, his legs just beginning to stretch out before him and the sun just beginning to cut through the green leaves and pass a golden hand across his pages. Suddenly, he was aware that someone was standing before him, looking at him, and had been there for some time. He knew this before he raised his eyes from the page. He could not have said how he knew it but, as he thought about it in later years, he was certain that it was not just some trick of sight or sound. It was a presence, an aura. Indeed, had he seen no one at all he would still have known that someone unseen was there.

He looked up and into her gray-green eyes, with their depth as deep as that of the sea, and he felt them search right into his soul. She was perhaps eight or nine years old, with sunny chestnut hair flecked with gold; thin; her neck long, but white and slender and so beautiful in its gentle inclination from her shoulders that it brought his heart up into his throat.

16

"My ball is under your bench," she said. "My red ball. I rolled it there so that you could get it out for me."

He reached under the bench, his eyes lost in hers, and with one blind hand brought the ball out and up, placing it in her extended palm.

"My name is Irena," the girl said, "and I want you to read to me."

She seated herself, lightly, smoothing her white schoolgirl's apron and moving so close to him that he felt the tremor of her body as she breathed, a tremor like the feathery flutter of his pet finch when he held it in his hand, her eyes not leaving his and her face turned to him with an intensity which shut out all of the world.

"I don't play with balls, really," she said. "I only brought it to roll under your bench."

"How did you know I was here?" he asked her, not understanding anything that the girl had said.

"You have come every afternoon for three afternoons," she said. "I knew you would be here this afternoon so I brought my ball. Read to me, please. We don't have much time. My governess will be finishing her gossip soon and then I must go."

He turned to his book and began to read, just where his eyes happened to fall. He read no more than three or four lines, with no notion of what the words might have been, when he felt his eyes turning from the book to the girl beside him.

"I can't," he said, half choking. "I can't read any more. Your eyes won't let me."

She slipped from the bench almost immediately, stepping backward, and not turning her head from him. "Come tomorrow," she said, then turned and ran, long-legged, her short schoolgirl's skirts skipping about her knees, down the allée to a little crosswalk, where he saw her bend over a middle-aged woman, deeply engaged in conversation with another governess. A moment later, she had disappeared down the crosswalk, lost behind the fresco of leaves and shrubbery.

That was how it had begun, but when he tried to tell Voronsky

17

about it it had turned to gray and brown ashes in his hand.

"Don't play the sentimental idiot," Voronsky had said, bringing his great peasant's fist down on the marble-top table with a blow that knocked one of the vodka glasses to the red-sanded floor. "Irena is steel and fire. Why, there's more strength in her body than there is in yours and mine together."

Strength . . . yes. He remembered one night after a concert. Voronsky had been reciting his verses. He was in flaming spirits. They had gone to a restaurant, Voronsky talking on and on about peasant blood, peasant strength, peasant roots. That was what gave Russia her soul and body. The peasant. The earth. This was Russia. The rest was nothing. The cities and the intelligentsia—nothing but manure—manure under the strong feet of peasant Russia.

Irena was teasing him. She loved Voronsky's force and power but she was strong, too.

"All right, muzhik," she laughed. "Let's test that Russian strength of yours."

She hunched her chair forward and put her elbow on the table, clenching her fist. "Let's see who's strongest here—the peasant from Penza or the Pietersky aristocrat."

Voronsky put out his arm and they clenched their fists in an Indian wrestling grasp. The veins on Voronsky's forehead stood out. The muscles on his forearm bulged. But the woman's arm was like supple steel. It bent slightly and then slowly, precisely, relentlessly forced Voronsky's arm toward the table—almost but not quite to the table, because as his heavy arm with its black hairs neared the dirty, wine-stained linen, she suddenly broke off her grip.

"Let's not be children," she cried. "This is stupid. Let's get out of this place. I'm stifling!"

4

They had come down Hertzen Street that midnight Maselnitza of Irena's return. Of course, it was not Hertzen Street in those days. That was before they had taken to changing the names all around. It was Bolshaya Morskaya then and Morozov had never really got used to the change. They had come down this street, passing under this very window and going on across St. Isaac's Square, with the cathedral black and heavy against the snow-filled sky, and all this time they had said not a word, nor could they, for their lips had not left each other's since they had come together in the infinite darkness of the descending staircase. Indeed, he could not say that he was aware of anything at all except Irena and, perhaps, the crystals of snow which sifted down their warm cheeks, melting as they touched the skin and wetting their cheeks and necks and running down inside the collars of their coats.

A guard looked at them curiously from his sentry box outside the Marie Palace, and finally their feet slowed to a halt beside the Moika and Morozov saw with amazement that they had almost come to the Kissing Bridge and the turn into Opera House Square.

"We'll never stop," Irena said. There were snow diamonds on the

19

long lashes of her eyes and in the nest of hair that bulged over the wide collar of her *shuba*. "Never. Never. Never."

"No," he replied. "Never."

And so it had been, too. It had never stopped. Not to this moment. There was not going to be much time left. That was obvious enough, and in a sense, perhaps, he should be glad or relieved that it would be ending soon. But he did not feel this. Instead, he felt a hot white flash of anger suddenly burning through his body, and he turned from the window, giving the heavy curtains a powerful tug as he did so, and strode back to his desk, the heels of his boots sounding solidly against the worn crossweb of the once beautiful carpet, the remaining tea in his glass splashing dangerously close to spilling.

"Excuse me."

He looked up to see his secretary standing in the doorway. Her broad face with its smooth white cheeks and wide forehead was expressionless—so carefully expressionless that an iron might have been passed across it. Preoccupied as he was with the deep and powerful train of thought touched off by the words spoken to him by young Galin, Morozov was still perceptive enough to realize that the woman had sensed the seismic nature of his mood and was herself instantly and reciprocally shaken, not alone, no doubt, by reason of her love for him (for they had been lovers for two years— for her the wide, yielding, bestowing, sacrificial love so natural to a Russian woman and for him a tender, thankful and welcoming emotion, by no means as deep as hers, but generous and responsible) but also by an inevitable premonition of the nature of his disturbance and its probable consequences. He frowned and attempted to simulate mild anger as if irritated at her interruption.

"What is it?" he said, passing his hand across his forehead and slightly rumpling his hair. "The meeting, I suppose? I wish you wouldn't interrupt me like this."

"Excuse me," the woman repeated, looking at him, or so he thought, a little curiously. "But it's past eight-thirty and the meeting is at nine."

"How time flies," he sighed. "Yes, it's time I was getting off. Just bring me the *papka* on the Narva project and I'll study it a moment. Yes . . ."

Ludmilla pressed her lips anxiously and seemed on the point of a question but suppressed it and silently left the room. A moment later she was back and placed a liver-colored paper folder on the desk. This time he saw that she had steeled herself.

"Excuse me, Georgi Alexandrovich, for asking," she said, nervous concern deepening and enriching the low timber of her voice. "But you are so pale. Is there something wrong? Are you not feeling well?"

Morozov managed a wry smile. "God knows," he said. "I guess you are right. Something at lunch disagreed with me. Perhaps that fish was a bit off. But it's nothing serious. Tell Andrei to go down and start the car. I'll be right along."

Morozov turned his eyes abruptly to the folder on his desk. He did not feel at this moment like meeting the half-puzzled, half-worried frown which he was certain had now appeared on Ludmilla's placid face, a mirror of flesh so clear and quiet that one could read in it without trouble every shadow which fell across the simple and usually sunny corridors of her mind. What to do about her—what he could do about her—he had not yet even dared to begin thinking. Again, he passed his hand across his forehead and opened the folder. Not that there was a single figure, fact, diagram or proposal in the bulging file which was not fixed in his mind like a living blueprint. Still—he hated above all things even an accidental slip. Hardly had he begun to run down the opening paragraphs of the presentation when the telephone on his desk buzzed—buzzed sharply, emphatically and with a curtness that brought his hand to the nickel-bound receiver like the stroke of a lash. The lightning thought swept through him—not already! And even as he automatically mouthed the words: "Morozov here!" he felt the flush of his pores and a thin but clammy sweat break out on his upper lip and temples. Even as he spoke his name he knew that his fear was idiotic and childish and he cursed himself, although he realized that he was physically powerless to halt this conditioned reaction.

His shame deepened as he heard the warm and familiar voice of Leonid Schapiro, architect of the Narva project.

"Georgi Alexandrovich," Schapiro was saying. "So glad I caught you before you got away. Will you bring two or three extra copies of the original variant of the Narva project—you remember—the one Professor Slansky prepared during 1941-42. I want to make certain that the historical record is complete in case any question arises about honoring his role."

"Gladly, Leonid Natanovich, gladly," said Morozov. "I will see you shortly."

As he hung up the receiver Morozov took a white handkerchief out of his coat pocket and mopped his forehead.

"What a child I am," he said with loathing. "I who have gone through three wars and two revolutions. Not to mention the hunger blockade. What a coward!"

5

The house in which Morozov's offices were located had once been the residence of Michael Borin, a merchant who had made a fortune out of manufacturing and selling brick tea—those black, iron-hard, pungent blocks on which Siberia and Manchuria supported a life of hardship. Borin had tea plantations in the Caucasus but he also imported bulk tea from China and India. In his factories at Irkutsk and Petersburg he blended his tea bricks, mixing in as much manure and straw as the trade would allow, and sold his product by caravan and bazaar all over Asia, bringing back gold nuggets from Siberia, rhubarb and ginseng from China, mandrake from Mongolia, and amassed a great fortune. When the Revolution broke out Borin was in Persia. He never returned to his mansion on Hertzen Street, which was duly confiscated, furniture, lackeys and all, for revolutionary use. The lackeys soon went their way and the mansion was turned over to one Soviet institution after another. It was dark, uncomfortable, unpleasant and filled with decayed relics of grandeur. At the outbreak of World War II it accommodated two Soviet offices, the planning and design bureau with which Morozov had long been connected, and a small institute engaged in climatological research. The design bureau was immediately incorporated into the Army, but the climatological institute was not considered important enough for any special measures. Younger members of the staff went into military service. Five elderly men remained. One was killed in an early air raid. The other four died in the winter of 1941-42. It was not possible to say exactly what was the cause of death—cold, starvation, disease or a combination of all three. A young woman, looking for another office but having been given the wrong address, stumbled upon the four in the arctic-frigid building, in December of 1941. Three of the old men were dead. The fourth died a week later in the hospital.

This melancholy history was recalled anew to Morozov as he emerged into the upper corridor of the Borin mansion. Lined up against one wall were packing cases and brown wooden filing cabinets, the remnants of the climatological institute. After years of bureaucratic feuding it had only now been decided to consolidate the Leningrad institute with a similar organization in Moscow. The packing cases awaited shipment and the space occupied by the institute—the former ballroom of the mansion, ornate with tarnished gilt angels and a rather pornographic but scarcely visible frieze of satyrs and shepherdesses just under the ceiling—was being turned over to Morozov for a drafting studio.

The décor of the house had not been touched since the Bolsheviks commandeered it in 1918. Morozov walked down a lavish staircase of cream and amber marble, past the figure of a Mongol warrior with breast armor and bow and arrow, and emerged into the street. The snow was still falling as he entered his car. The chauffeur, Andrei, had run the motor long enough to warm the decrepit machine, and it smelled richly of strong naphtha and *mahorka*, the black, pungent tobacco which the chauffeur smoked in paper twists which he tore from *Pravda*, having gotten into the habit of smoking newsprint during the war.

"To Smolny," Morozov said, as the springs of the front seat groaned under him. The thrust of the snow in his face, the tug of the wind at the skirts of his gray military overcoat, the icy stab

of the fresh air in his lungs—all of this brought back with fresh
vigor Morozov's musings of a few moments earlier. The car started
down Hertzen Street toward St. Isaac's Square with a complaint
from the gears.

Yes, it was such an evening when Morozov and Irena had walked
down the street, past the sentry box at the Marie Palace, and on
toward Kissing Bridge. He did not think they had exchanged a
single word. He could still feel the rhythm of their hips as they
slowly walked, the two bones working against each other with each
slow, each desperately slow step, the bones flat-sided and close-
pressed.

Their feet carried them up the slight incline of the bridge across
the Moika. Slowly they came to a full halt, leaning against the low,
snow-cushioned parapet.

And now Irena was speaking, her lips moving like snow roses,
caressing his cheek as she spoke.

"You were so long, Georges," she said. "I waited and waited and
waited. I thought I would go mad, and then, finally, I saw you
standing in the doorway. You were so tall and pale. You were like a
ghost. You frightened me."

"I didn't know you were there. No one told me you had come
back from Paris," Morozov said. "Three times I almost turned back.
I couldn't bear the thought of going in to those people. But something pulled me there."

"It was me, Georges," she said, her breath making quick clouds
of frost. "It was me. I pulled you. I pulled and pulled and pulled.
And finally you came."

A whirl of snow seemed to surround them, blotting out the slow
curve of the canal and the swinging yellow lights.

"Take me somewhere, Georges," the girl said. They turned and
crossed the bridge at a swifter pace.

"I live just down here near the Haymarket," he said.

"Hurry," she said, taking his hand and running ahead, her *valenki*
crunching in the snow under her flying feet. Suddenly both of them
were running through the snow, she ahead and he following with

25

long strides, laughing at the snow pelting their faces, the ice slipping beneath their feet, and the wind that filled their eyes with tears. They turned into a half-open iron gate that set off a small courtyard, skirted a pile of sawed logs and entered an ancient doorway, heavy with the smell of age, decay and winter-rotted potatoes. There was a dim light and they climbed the worn staircase, still hand in hand. Georges' room was on the top story, a wing of the attic among the chimney pots. They halted at the door as he fumbed for a big iron key.

"Wait a minute, Georges," the girl said. She was breathing rapidly and she pressed close to him. "Kiss me. Now."

His arms slipped around her and he pressed her so closely that he felt her breasts soft and round through the heaviness of their overcoats.

She broke away quickly, exclaiming: "Please let's go inside and turn on the light. I want to look at you."

The tiny room was cold and the dim yellow bulb emphasized its smallness and the clutter of books, papers, dishes and tobacco on Morozov's work table. There was a straight-backed chair and a small leather-covered divan, badly worn, springs sagging, which served him as a bed. They sat there and Georges moved to embrace Irena, but she held him off with one hand, passing the other swiftly over his high cheeks, the bone ridges over his eyes, and the line of his nose and chin. She smoothed back his hair, mussed by his fur cap, and her fingers ran down his neck, across his shoulders, over his breastbone and along the cage of his ribs.

An intense, serious look held her face and her eyes remained on his, devouring and drinking them in, as her hands explored his body.

"You're thin, Georges," she cried, tears suddenly starting in her eyes. "Why are you so thin? Why? And your face is so tired and so old. Oh, Georges, already we are getting old!"

"But, little one," he smiled gently, "it has been almost four years. Much has happened since you last saw me. And you have changed, too. You've grown up. You are so beautiful that my eyes ache, just at seeing you."

She ran a finger down the lines which extended from his mouth and suddenly began to sob.

"Georges," she said. "We're getting old already and we haven't even begun to live. Oh, Georges, why have we waited all these years? You have lines around your mouth and crow's-feet around your eyes."

"Now, Irena, now." He tried to halt the rush of words.

"I feel old, Georges," she said. "Life has run away from me. I used to be able to catch it in my hand and hold it. It was bright and glittering and beautiful—just like quicksilver. Remember how you used to say that? And now—what has happened to us? Why have we been so stupid? Why did you let me go away to Paris? You are so smart and you're older than I. You shouldn't have let me go."

She was crying now, inconsolably, tears brimming from her eyes like the dark tides of the sea, crying and running her fingers again and again over the muscles of his face and down the tendons of his neck to where the cords vanished within his shoulders.

Each tear fell on Morozov's heart like hot wax from a candle, bitter and sweet, tender and piercing. He began to talk, softly, quietly, earnestly, talking at random, telling what he had done since she had gone away with her parents after the Bolshevik coup d'état, telling her how empty the long years had been, how wasted the days, and how he had filled them with work and then more work, going on with his engineering studies in the Army, picking up where he had broken off when the war caught him in Paris, serving in the Engineering Corps during the Civil War, preparing defenses for Petrograd, first against the Germans, then against Yudenich, working, working, working, through crisis, through danger, through hardship and loneliness.

As he talked he grew interested in what he was saying and so did Irena, for he was passionately devoted to his profession and now, as he told her, while still in the Army he had begun to work on dams and canals and breakwaters, on plans for making good the damage of war, revolution and destruction, on new projects for building the country.

"Now," he said, "I'm studying architecture as well. We're going to build houses and parks and roads and streets and squares. We're going to transform Russia. Just think, Irena, how wonderful it will all be!"

Suddenly Irena laughed, a clear laugh like the tinkling of silver sleighbells from a troika. She clutched Georges' shoulders with both hands.

"Of course you are!" she said. "You're going to transform Russia. I just know you will. I believe you, Georges. You will do it because you are smart and brave and honest. And Russia needs you, Georges. You aren't like those people I saw this evening. What are they doing—transforming Russia, too? I don't think I like very well what they are doing with our country."

"They are scum," Georges frowned. "That is, many of them. But not all. That's what's curious about it. You've been away, Irena. Away from Petrograd. You don't know what these last years have done to people. The weak ones, particularly."

"Maybe I know more than you think," she said, a strange shadow passing over her face. But Georges hardly saw it as he hurried on with his explanation.

"No," Georges said. "No one who was not here can understand. You take some of the weaker people. They haven't known how to live. They have done anything. Anything . . . You saw that drunken woman—the one who was playing Juliet. If you asked her what she had done these last years—she would tell you: I survived, what else? And so she has."

"But, Georges," she said gently. "You should see the people in Paris. I have been busy, too. Like you. I have been working night and day. Learning the sculptor's trade. But I have seen the people —the lost people. I've known them—some of them, at any rate. What is happening to them? Has everyone lost his way?"

He smiled grimly.

"Here it hasn't been so much a matter of losing your way," he

28

said. "It has been a matter of life and death. Bread to keep you alive for the day. A bit of milk for the baby. People have died here in our Petrograd. Starved to death. We've been hungry in Russia. We still are."

Another grim smile crossed his face. His own hunger, which had gnawed so fiercely, came back to him momentarily and then receded to a dull distant ache.

"Oh, Georges," Irena cried. "I understand. That is what I see in your face. So thin. And your lovely strong bones. I feel every one of them."

"We've been cold, as well," he added. "The war . . . well, it hasn't been much fun. Thank God it is over now. You will never see such times as we have been through. The black bread. God knows what it was made of. But we were glad to have it. Sometimes there was none. Girls sold themselves to anyone for—for what? A tin of sardines. A cake of soap."

"Georges, Georges," she cried, pulling him to her. For a moment he thought the hysteria was coming back. "Hold me, Georges. I want you to hold me very close."

She pulled him down on the broken couch, pushing back their coats so that he felt her body, warm and tender and soft against his, with only the thinness of dress and shirt between them.

"Thank God," he murmured, "that you have been away during these terrible times. And thank God that you have come back."

"Things will be better now," she said. "Now we will be together and never again will be apart."

They lay for a moment with the soft hush of their breaths coming and going like the rustle of a spring wind in the white birches.

"Hold me closer, Georges," she said. "Hold me very, very close. I want you to feel me. I want you to know me."

He felt the tenderness of her body close against his own and the faint trembling of her legs and arms, and he felt the play of muscles in her arms as her hands passed over his face, molding it to them and then swiftly and sensitively coursing down his shoulders.

They did not become lovers that night although they lay until

29

morning in each other's arms.

Many years later Irena spoke to him about this. It was in the spring after the terrible winter of 1941-42. He had not seen her for many weeks, and then he found himself in Leningrad near her studio in the rambling old building near the Fontanka, which he knew as well as the lines on his hand. It was mid-April and the sun was hot enough to warm his shoulders under his gray army overcoat. The door to her studio was off the street under a half-moon passage that led into an interior courtyard. The snow and ice and refuse which had jammed the passageway were gone. He knocked at the door and almost instantly it was opened by Irena herself, thin, drawn, with sharp lines on her face. She was wearing her overcoat and a dark wool shawl over her head.

She looked deep into his eyes as always, not speaking for a moment, simply grasping him by the wrist and clutching his hand to her breast.

"Thank God," she said. They stood a moment by the door, possessed again by the unbreakable bond which held them, the bond of the years, of the emotions, of the duality of their long years, the fears, the tragedy and love of their existence.

"I was just going to sit in the sun," she said. "We will go together."

They walked very slowly, saying nothing to each other, to the Pantelemon Bridge. The Fontanka was still frozen, its ice dirty and gray with street rubbish. But the water was melting and ran in dark pools and channels around the icy hummocks.

Across the Fontanka they entered the Summer Garden and sat down on the first bench. Just beyond them was a cluster of antiaircraft guns, half-hidden by a torn camouflage net, and a handful of dirty, tired girls, their faces as gray as their greatcoats, trudging back and forth from half a dozen trucks to a big dump of tarpaulin-covered supplies.

"Do you remember the day I rolled my ball under your bench?" Irena said suddenly. "Do you remember how I stood waiting for you to look up from your book?"

He remembered.

"I've thought about us this long winter," she said. "Sometimes, when it was very cold. It made me warm again. Do you remember the night when I had just come back from Paris?"

He remembered. He took her hand, which had been twisting a button of her heavy black cloth coat, and crushed it strongly in his own, surprised as he always was at the strength of her hand, at the steel firmness of her fingers, strengthened by years of work with a sculptor's hammer and chisel.

She was silent for so long he thought she had lost herself in reverie. He felt the muscles of her hand tremble a little and was surprised to see a wry smile on her lips.

"I have never told you this," she said. "But our history almost ended at the very beginning—that night in your cold little room back of the Haymarket."

He looked at her in wonder.

"Men are so stupid," she said. "Even you, and you are less stupid than any man I have known."

He squeezed her hand and smiled.

"But that night," she said, "I asked you to hold me. I told you I wanted you to know me—as I wanted to know you. I wanted to know your body, to know the feel, the touch, the wonder of it. And I wanted you to know me. But you didn't understand that. You thought I wanted you to make love to me. I was so shocked. Because I thought you were not like other men. That you would understand the difference."

She broke off, frowning.

"Oh, it's so hard to tell you and I don't think you understand even now," she continued. "It wasn't that I didn't want you to make love to me. I did. But first I wanted to know you. Do you understand the difference? To know the bone and muscle of you. The way your poor pathetic ribs felt under my hands. And I wanted you to know me exactly the same. I wanted you to know the softness of my breasts and everything—first. But you nearly spoiled it all. I wanted to run away. I almost did."

31

And so she had. They were lying together on the old sofa so close he could feel her heart beating through the soft breast that pressed against his chest. And with the rising of his feelings he began to draw her closer when suddenly her hands drove against him strongly and she pushed away, saying: "No. No. No. You fool! You fool!" And burst into wild and uncontrollable sobs, crying: "Men are all fools. Fools. Fools."

He lay shaken and bewildered. One moment they were one, alike in feeling and mood, hardly knowing where one began and the other ended or if they were one person or two. And now a sharp knife had torn them apart. He felt that he clung to the edge of a mountain precipice. At any moment he might slip into the abyss. The hand which had helped him, the comrade with whom he was climbing, had hurled him to the margin of the cliff. He felt his body shivering uncontrollably and knew that it was not with cold but with fear—fear that he had lost what he never had, the world of his dreams, the world of Irena in which he had lived every day since he had felt her presence at his side on that summer day so long before. In years to come he was to know terror well. It was to become his constant companion, sometimes hardly making itself noticed, sometimes clutching at his breast with the claws of a beast. It was to be his bedfellow in the years of the middle thirties. It was to be his alter ego in the hunger and cold of the blockade. And now it once more was sitting by his side in this old car, its skeleton pressing against his chest and making his heart beat more rapidly.

But never had the edge of the knife touched more coldly against the pulsating walls of his heart than on that night in the shabby attic room with the broken springs of the sofa softly sighing and the moan of Irena's sobs in his ears: "No. No. No."

6

The snow seemed to be slackening as the car turned past the Admiralty and headed for Palace Square. Morozov could see the Admiralty spire, slender and golden, and the gray-green bulk of the Winter Palace that loomed like a dark menace against the snowy sky. Never could he cross the vast wastes of Palace Square without a faint, undefinable moment of terror. From whence it came he was not certain, but he thought that it must go back to that January Sunday when Father Gapon led the dark thousands of Pietersky workers into the hollow square to present their respectful petition to the Czar and the assembled Guards in panic opened fire and mowed them down by hundreds. He had been just a child but he never forgot his father's face as he came back to their house, long past nightfall, ashen and shaken, and, taking his wife into his arms, said: "Julia, I cannot live in a world where such things happen. I saw them lying there in the snow. Lying like dirty bundles with blood coming from their mouths and making little puddles on the gray stones of the square."

Suddenly his father broke off. He went to the sideboard and poured himself a glass of brandy. Georgi watched and listened in horror.

33

"I cannot live in a country so cruel, so senseless," his father said. "I am ashamed to be called a Russian. I am ashamed to have brought into the world a son who must call himself a Russian."

"Please, Sasha," his mother said. "Please restrain yourself. If not for me—at least for Georgi."

"*Dushinka*," his father said. "Dearest, I want Georgi to hear this. I want him to know the cruelty, the stupidity, the ignorance of our Russian land. If I and my generation do not have the courage and the strength to change all this, perhaps his will."

Morozov could not remember much of what his father said that night. The words poured out of his lips, like angry waves dashing against the shore. But for all time to come he would see in the eye of his mind the gray, torn bundles of men and women and children lying on the stone paving blocks of the Palace Square, the blood forming blackening pools in little depressions, the people running and crying madly, the grunt of the command, the sharp crack of the rifles and in the air the faint smell of powder smoke, drifting with the wind.

Morozov had not been present in 1917 when the Winter Palace was stormed, but even had he witnessed the shelling by the cruiser *Aurora* he did not think this would have replaced the image etched in his boyhood mind by his father's horror on that evening of January 9, 1905.

As the car spun across the broad square he felt, as always, the grandeur and the mystery of the city which Peter had built on the Neva. These great buildings, these grandiose ensembles which he loved with an artist's passion, these piles of granite hurled up on the swampy banks of the Neva, these palaces, these monuments, ornaments of man's powers of creation which loomed out of the fog and snow like the elements of a fantastic nightmare—how could they, he thought, fail to arouse in the Petersburg soul emotions of fear and fantasy? There was blood mixed into the very mortar that bound the great stones, block upon block. The titanic caryatids which held upon their powerful, weary shoulders the portals of the Hermitage on the street called Millionaya—were they the symbol of Petersburg? Or was it the poetic spire of the prison fortress of Peter and Paul which he could just make out across the icefields of the Neva, silhouetted against the cloudy sky? Or was it great Peter on his bronze charger, rearing over the city, the sharp and dangerous heels of his stallion pawing the air as Peter negligently paused a moment, letting the people wonder where next the iron hoofs would strike? Was this Petersburg a city of stone? Had it heart as well as spirit? Was its soul possessed by the demon, the Great Whore, as Blok had said? Was this, indeed, the city of the Apocalypse?

Morozov was not a man of superstition, but he confessed that the strange city on the Neva aroused in him feelings whose source he did not really wish to investigate. Its beauty was another thing. Where in the world, he asked himself for the thousandth time, as the car moved along the embankment (not the most direct or swift way to Smolny, he noted, yet somehow it was the route he had hoped Andrei would choose), was there a city of such terrible and tragic beauty as Leningrad? The Northern Palmyra. . . . How well the name suited her. The aura of mystery, of the Orient, of the past, of conspiracy. For of all cities it seemed most made for conspiracy.

How he loved it! The sphinxes and the great lions guarding the Naberezhnaya. The great Klodt horses at the Anichkov Bridge. The lovely allées of the Summer Garden. The childish fantasy of the Engineering Palace. A city of beauty, of passion, of mystery. He thought, inevitably, of old man Ilyn. Not a brilliant architect, perhaps. Not a great man. Yet how he had loved the city. He remembered the meeting on that January day in the midst of the hunger blockade. The very worst days. A small knot formed in his stomach even now when he thought of that time. A meeting had been organized. God knows who had been behind it. Irena had a hand in it. The Artists' Committee, perhaps. The Party section of the Institute. The City Soviet. It didn't make any difference whose idea it was. The real purpose, of course, was to sustain morale. To give people a sense of doing something. Anything. To show each other they were still alive. Still strong enough, still vital enough to carry out a

35

task. Even just to get about the streets.

It was a clear, frosty day—one of those rare Leningrad winter days when the sun was a disc of gold in a blue sky and the frost so hard the snow screamed under your boots. Morozov was in the city then. In those days he was back and forth constantly between the fortifications at Pulkhovo and the city itself. He arrived at the hall early. The meeting was in the beautiful little chamber of the Academy Choir at the Pevchinsky Bridge. The sun turned the snow into diamonds and blazed against the blindness of the boarded and sandbagged windows. Within the hall it was dim and cold. The red velvet chairs seemed to have turned to ice and the velvet drapes were like shrouds. In the dimness he saw Irena, her lips blue but her eyes burning with some secret fire. He took the seat beside her.

"Thank God. Thank God. Thank God," she said, putting her ungloved hand on his. It was blue as her lips and cold as marble.

"Yes," he said. "We're alive."

"We will live," she said. "We will. We will."

They sat silently, their breath coming from their mouths in little puffs of frost. He watched the room fill. The men and women walking slowly, carefully, conserving each movement. They lifted their *valenki*-clad feet cautiously, not quite shuffling, not quite walking. They sat with care, looking straight ahead, and then, moving their heads only enough so their eyes could see at oblique angles, began to peer about. Not all of them, however. He saw old Zoskind, the satirical writer, author of the famous unpublished play *The People and the Power*, sink into his seat and his head slump forward onto his chin. He seemed to be in a coma, his breath hardly coming. And Olga Kartova, the biologist whose husband was head of the Botanical Institute, almost fell as she sat down. A coarse brown wool scarf over her face was white with hoarfrost. She must have walked several miles. There were white frost spots on her cheeks. All around him there were faces with skin tight-stretched against the bones, purple and yellow and green colors in their cheeks, eyes sunken and leaden (except for a few like Irena whose eyes burned in fever). They sat silently, holding themselves together, holding their coats tightly around them so that not a bit of body heat might escape, holding back the shivering which exhausted more strength than they possessed.

The meeting was late in getting under way. Finally, a slight, elderly figure, a small man in black overcoat with black caracul collar, neat white academic beard and fine aristocratic features, slowly made his way to the platform. He hardly lifted his feet from the floor as he walked. But he stood erect and his blue eyes behind his gold-rimmed pince-nez were clear, although tears dripped from the reddened corners of his eyes. He mounted the four steps of the platform with the care of a tightrope walker, slowly approached the podium and grasped each side with his gloved hands. For what seemed to Morozov like an eternity—but perhaps was not more than five minutes—he stood there, a tiny, erect figure, a man of perhaps seventy, so slight and frail that you wanted to rush to help him except that a cold fire in his eyes held you back. He stood, gripping the sides of the lectern and letting the slender reservoir of his strength refill, like a small spring in a mountain crevasse.

Finally he spoke.

"Comrades," he said, speaking slowly but distinctly. "I must apologize for my lateness. But I could not come more rapidly."

On some of the faces watching him there appeared expressions of sympathy.

"No," Ilyn continued. "Not because of my age, which, I admit, is great. Nor because of my strength, which, I admit, is feeble. No, comrades. I could not come more rapidly because I could not leave the streets of Leningrad this morning. I could not leave the sight of our beautiful city with the golden sun shining on its winter beauty."

He had, Ilyn said, left his home in ample time. True, he had to walk more than two miles, but he could have gotten here on time. Had it not been for the city.

"I could not come faster," he said. "I could not leave the beauty of the city—the arches, the domes, the golden spires. Oh, I know they are green and gray with camouflage. But to me they are still golden."

Irena's hand which had lain like a marble glove on Morozov's began to tremble. He turned to her and her eyes were melting in his. The poetry of the old man's words, the beauty and nobility of his thought seemed to have illumined the hall. Everywhere people were sitting straighter. Even old Academician Strumkin—the Fat One they had called him in academic circles. He was no longer fat. His skin hung in sagging yellow folds and his overcoat fell around his collapsed belly and narrowed shoulders like a wind-blown tent. Even this pathetic ruin of a man somehow had become infused with grandeur. His face took on the look of an aged eagle, not that of a dying buzzard.

Ilyn's voice, cracked and halting when he began, had deepened and assumed a richness and vigor which it had not possessed before.

"I confess," he said. "I love this city. I love the gray stones of which it is built. I cannot walk down the Nevsky without my heart beating faster. I cannot pass through its gracious squares, my eyes cannot view the perfect beauty of its curving canals, nor the rich façades of our palaces, without tears springing to them. If this be weakness let me confess this weakness."

It seemed to Morozov as Ilyn spoke, his neatly trimmed spade beard gently moving with the quiet motion of his jaws, that the frigid hall was growing warmer, that light was flooding into the murky corners. Months later when Morozov heard that Ilyn had been killed—killed by a chance shell that sent a sliver of steel into his heart as he walked down his beloved Nevsky—Morozov could not grieve. He was certain that Ilyn had died as he wanted to die, strolling down the most majestic street in this city of majesty.

"The Germans have tried to destroy our city," Ilyn went on. "They have tried to turn the Winter Palace into a heap of ruins. Their bombs have torn holes in the Summer Garden. Their shells have scarred the face of the Hermitage. We have had to hide the treasures of the Anichkov deep within the earth. They have killed our husbands and wives. They have burned our houses. Our children starve in the schools and freeze to death in our streets. But they have not broken the spirit of the city of Peter. They will not break it. It is they who will die on the gray stones of our city. The Northern Palmyra will survive. The present is tragedy but the future belongs to us."

Ilyn strode down the steps like a monarch from the throne. The feeble hands of the audience rustled a tattoo of applause and from Irena's lips burst a fierce "bravo" which somehow surprised her so much that she buried her face on Georgi's shoulder.

Other speakers told of the plans they were drafting for the new Leningrad which would arise after the war. One of them was the Mayor. He read a message from Zhdanov, the Party Secretary. Another speaker was Morozov, for it was his drafting bureau which was specifically concerned with the plans for reconstruction. He displayed some of these plans. One was a scheme for a beautiful park in which residence apartments would be placed. It was designed to be erected not far from the Narva Gates in the very region which had been turned into fields of rubble by the Nazi bombardment. The co-author of this plan was Professor Slansky, Morozov's close friend and associate. Only the day before this gentle elderly man had died in the emergency station to which he had been taken in the last stages of distrophy.

"The city of Peter will rise in new glory," Morozov had said. "The Nazis have not wounded our spirit. They have strengthened it. We will emerge from these terrible days tempered and strengthened. Our city was founded by a great emperor as the capital of a great nation. The tradition of Leningrad is the tradition of empire fused with the tradition of revolution. Out of the ashes of war the Northern Palmyra will arise anew—stronger, more glorious, more imperial, more revolutionary than ever."

They had all shaken his hands—the Mayor ("Comrade Zhdanov will be proud of your remarks, Georgi Alexandrovich"), General Orlov ("The city and the Army are one, Georgi Alexandrovich"), Secretary Ivanov ("Leningrad is the crucible in which Soviet steel is forged, Comrade Morozov") and even cold-eyed Dmitri Chaikov-

39

sky, the State Security chief, who alone among all who were present did not seem to have lost his piggish jowls ("I will never forget your words about the Northern Palmyra"). And finally Irena, who simply said: "Only Leningrad can save Russia, Georgi Alexandrovich. And save her we will."

They emerged from the cold hall into the crystal world of a sunlighted city of ice. The snow on the streets was packed shoulder high and they walked as though they were crossing a glacier in Antarctica, up and down ravines and across icy crevasses. Around a steaming manhole women were letting down pails for water and setting them gingerly on ice-crusted children's sleds. The water slopped over their coats and turned them into crackling sheets of mail. Two girls pulling a sled came toward them. A middle-aged man huddled on the sled, bundled in a woman's fur coat and a down comforter. He hunched forward, his head practically on his knees, his eyes open but vacant. The sled slipped from side to side and his body swayed and fell off. This happened every few yards. As Morozov and Irena approached one of the girls wearily lifted the slight figure of the man back onto the sled.

"*Dedushka,*" the girl said in a voice so weary the words were like lead. "Grandpa. Please hold yourself on the sled. I cannot pick you up again. I am sorry, but if you fall off again this trip will end in the cemetery, not the hospital."

The girls went slowly past, the man no longer slipping from side to side but holding himself rigid as a scarecrow on a crossed stick.

Irena turned to Morozov with a strange light gleaming in her eyes.

"Georgi Alexandrovich," she said, spitting the words out like stones of fire. "Georgi Alexandrovich, when this war ends . . . when we crush the Nazis . . . as we will . . . then the new war opens . . . the war against war. Do you understand? The war against war!"

He stroked her shoulders as he had so many years before in the little room off the Haymarket on the night of her return from Paris.

"I mean it, Georges," she said, holding his arm with a grasp of steel. "I mean what I say. I will put all my strength into that war.

Just as into this one. And if I die—well, you can erect a small plaque which says: 'Here lies Irena Galina. She survived war but died fighting it.'"

They were approaching Smolny now. He could see the big gates and the sentry boxes. And as his car swept up to the entryway and he reached inside his greatcoat for his red-covered internal passport and party card Morozov could hear Irena's words echoing in his ears. He could see the flecks of golden fire in the deep pools of her green eyes and he could feel the steel clasp of her fingers on his arm.

"I mean that, Georges," she said. "I have never been more serious. Say that you will do it."

She was not joking. It was no whim of emotion. This he knew. Irena never joked about serious things. He had given her his word and tomorrow, as he had told her son, young Michael Galin, not more than an hour ago, he would carry out his pledge and his promise.

The guard at the gatehouse returned the documents, stepped back one pace and saluted. The chauffeur put the car into gear and it moved around the circular approach and up to the entrance. Morozov bundled his liver-colored folder with the papers on the Narva Gate project under his arm and entered the building. It would be, he surmised, the last time he would visit Smolny and the last meeting of his official career.

7

Standing in front of the mahogany pier glass, Simon Smirnoff
nervously ran a comb through his abundant iron-gray hair, deliberately fluffing it up. There was no doubt of it—his hair was his most
distinguished feature. He shuddered a bit as he pulled the comb
through his locks. Why had he ever let that dreadful Galin boy into
the flat? And what was he going to do now? For the thousandth
time he cursed the name of Galin. Nothing but evil had it brought
into his life—and now this! Not only evil but danger. Real danger.
He knew the smell of it. My God, yes! He was an old sparrow when
it came to danger. You did not pursue a writer's career in Russia
for twenty-five years without knowing the smell of trouble. But
what on earth had possessed him to let the boy in? He squinted
more closely at the glass and carefully removed a long gray hair
which had attached itself to the lapel of his dark velveteen lounging
jacket. Finally, he turned away with a shrug of the shoulders and,
going to the massive pseudo-Russian sideboard which was one of
the proudest items of décor in what he liked to think of as a luxuri-
ous but not ostentatious flat, poured himself a small glass of cognac
—good Armenian cognac it was, too, although the label on the

bottle said Hennessy. But this was only designed to make some slight impression on his guest of the evening, Natalie Petrovna, a young and quite possibly talented poet who was bringing some of her verses to read this evening. Of course, as he admitted quite frankly, he hoped to determine whether she did not have talents in other than poetic lines, and had he not been on edge about her impending arrival and, indeed, had he not leaped to the hasty conclusion that it was she who was ringing his bell, a full hour early but unable in her anxiety to wait any longer for the rendezvous, he would not have romantically thrown his velveteen jacket over his shoulders, pulled back the heavy bolt and opened wide the door. He had been startled when, instead of Natalie's dark brown eyes, her cushiony breasts, her blondined hair and her impression of youthful eagerness, he found standing at the doorstep this fierce youngster with his worn sheepskin jacket, hawk's face and expression of taut-strung passion.

"Are you the writer Simon Simonovich Smirnoff?" the strange apparition demanded with the tone of the State Prosecutor.

"Who are you? What are you doing here?" Smirnoff responded, stepping back in confusion. He felt that had he confessed that he was, indeed, the writer, Simon Simonovich Smirnoff, the young man might well have pulled a knife—a *kinjal*—from the sleeve of his greasy sheepskin and plunged it then and there into his breast.

That backward step, however, had been a fatal error. Because as he stepped back the youth stepped forward. Then Smirnoff stepped back again and by this time the young man was inside the apartment and closing the door behind him.

What had the boy said next? "Yes, I recognize you now, Simon Simonovich. You're older and fatter. Your hair is gray and your cheeks have jowls. But I recognize you."

Smirnoff pirouetted quickly and returned to the pier glass, automatically whipping his comb into his hair. What rot! Gray—yes, his hair was salt-and-pepper. But it gave him a most distinguished appearance. So Natalie had told him the first time they met. "I knew you were a poet the moment I saw you," she said, clutching

43

his arm with a nervous hand. "Your hair. It's so distinguished, Simon Simonovich. The moment I saw you I knew I saw before me a man of passion and a man of genius."

She was a gushing young girl. But she was not the only one. There had been Masha, too. How she loved to run her hands through his hair. Sometimes she would gather it up and hide her chin in it, saying: "Look in the glass, Simon. . . . Look at the bearded lady." What a pity that she was such a flirt. Why on earth she had ever gone off with that young playwright, Serov, was more than he could understand. "You'll come back," he told her. "You'll come back to me. Have your fling with that whippersnapper." And she would be back, too. In the not distant future—if what he had heard about Serov was correct. It was not for nothing that he had suggested that Comrade Ivanov take a good hard look at Serov's plays. Apparently Ivanov or someone had done just that. Ideological distortions. That's what they were saying about Serov's work. Well, that would bring Masha running back to him. Not that he would open wide his arms. No indeed. Let her cool her heels a bit. The wine didn't spoil for the aging. Let her simmer. Meantime, he would be helping Natalie to discover her talents. That is . . . a shudder came over him as his mind turned back to the terrible interview with young Galin. What *was* he going to do? He would have to call the Party Secretariat. But what would they think there? Wouldn't they think it strange? How could he put the question, after all? They would be bound to ask why he had talked to Galin. Indeed, they would want to know why Galin had come to see him—him, Comrade Simon Simonovich Smirnoff, chairman of the Writers' Union, a Party member since 1933. Why should this guttersnipe, this product of all that was revolting in a decadent and drying past, come to talk to him? Wasn't that a suspicious circumstance just in itself?

Smirnoff began to pace the floor from the mirror at one wall to the ornate sideboard at the other. Step. Step. Step. Step. It was eight paces long. He had known that for years. This was how he got his exercise and solved his problems. He had done it the night Irena walked out of his flat. He had paced the floor—eight paces up and

44

eight paces down, again and again and again. He thought the night would never end.

She had stretched out on the green-covered divan like a princess, her head high on the stiff pillows, her skirts tucked around her legs and the pointed toes of her shoes close together. In one hand she held a rosy wine glass, which she lifted from time to time to her lips. He sat cross-legged on the floor, reciting the poem which he had written to her. Later on he had published the verses in *Novy Mir*. It was a daring thing to do but he had calculated well. They won him a special fame among young people and a mild and rather fatherly rebuke from the Kremlin. Stalin's remark that these were the kind of verses which one whispered into the ear of a woman in bed rather than printed in a public journal gave him an éclat which he had never had before, and when his big war novel, *Smoke and Flame*, won the Stalin prize it was apparent to all not only that he had the favor of the court but that he was a bold and passionate man in the great Russian tradition of Pushkin, Lermontov and Mayakovsky, a man ready to dare all for the woman of his heart, a man who loved madly, oblivious of the consequences, a romantic figure in an age of socialist realism. Women flocked to his apartment like flies to honey. Not that he did not acquire enemies— powerful ones, too. But it had been some time now since they had dared raise their voices. Not since he had demonstrated to Irena that he laughs best who laughs last. It had been a long time since anyone had repeated the old story that he had fled Leningrad at the height of the siege—a wanton lie since the Writers Union had ordered him evacuated so that he could work on *Smoke and Flame* —and certainly no one had repeated that calumny since his speech about Irena in connection with the Party decree on art in 1946. Yes, indeed, that had put a stopper on a good many lips. The gossips had shut up. It was fairly certain that no one, even in private, would dare at this late date to retell that ridiculous story of the hedgehog. Over the years he had learned to take care of himself. There were not many opportunities that he missed. Take the verses he had written to Irena, for example. Actually, until this day no one to his knowledge had known that they were, in fact, written to her. It had been assumed because of the affair in which he was involved with Tatiana Pless at the time the poem was published that he had written them for Tatiana. To be sure he had presented them to her and, naturally, she spread the story all over Moscow. All through the years there had not been a word from Irena. He presumed she too wanted to forget the incident. Then, tonight, this creature out of the darkness, this drowned rat from the cellars of Siberia, this hatchet-faced delinquent appeared on his doorstep with a copy of the poem in his breast pocket, or so he said, the very copy Smirnoff had given to Irena herself, the one in his own handwriting with the ink spots and the stain where his tears had fallen—all right, he would admit it. He did rub his eyes to make them water. But he felt like crying when he wrote those words.

My God, what was he going to do? What had that fiendish boy said: "Do you want to read the poem, or shall I?"

"You are a madman," he told the boy.

"Perhaps," the young man said. "But I think my mother would have liked to hear you read the poem. She once told me that your words had left an indelible mark in her mind and I should not want to betray her memory."

For a moment Simon Simonovich had thought of throwing himself on the young man. But the look of desperation in the boy's eyes, the hardness of his lips as he spoke, and, above all, the overwhelming conviction that there was a knife (if not a gun) concealed in that ragged, grease-stained sleeve held him back.

Simon Simonovich had asked his housekeeper to prepare some tidbits in honor of the young poetess—a little herring, some caviar, cheese, sweetmeats—and these had been set out on the big sideboard. Suddenly, he found himself with his mouth full of herring. How it had gotten there he did not know. He cursed. Of all things, he did not want to smell of herring when Natalie arrived. Hastily he strode to his bathroom cupboard, took the bottle of eau de cologne and swished some around his mouth.

To his horror he saw that it was almost nine. Natalie, far from being early, was late. This was annoying. But it gave him, perhaps, a few minutes to talk to the Party Secretariat. For there was no doubt in his mind. He must tell them about his visitor. What happened after that depended on the reaction. Thank God, he had a telephone of his own and need not go to the corridor and speak in Aesopian language while his neighbors listened in.

Fearing at any moment that a knock at the door would interrupt him, Smirnoff dialed the number of the Secretariat. Ivanov's secretary answered, an officious woman whom Smirnoff hated with a deadly hatred but whom he treated like a countess.

"Good to hear your voice, Galina Petrovna," he said, striking just the rich baritone note which he had hoped he might achieve. He was well aware that certain chords in his voice were not without influence upon the female sex.

"I am so sorry to trouble you," he continued. "I know how busy Comrade Ivanov is. But I wondered whether I might have his ear for a moment. Just for the tiniest of moments."

He sighed with relief. Apparently Galina Petrovna, dragon that she was, was in not bad humor this evening. She asked him to wait and almost instantly he heard Ivanov's businesslike voice.

"Well, Simon Simonovich," boomed Ivanov, "what's on your mind."

"Excuse me for troubling you," the writer said. "But something extraordinary has come up which I thought best to bring to your attention without delay."

"Never mind the apology, Comrade Smirnoff," Ivanov broke in. "Just what is it?"

Now came the plunge. "I've had a most unusual visitor, Comrade Ivanov," said Smirnoff. "How shall I put it—like a voice from the grave. Young Galin, as he calls himself, the son of Irena Galina."

Smirnoff could hear Ivanov draw his breath in.

"Yes, Smirnoff," Ivanov replied after an almost imperceptible pause. "Yes, indeed. I have heard about young Galin already."

Smirnoff was so taken aback he hardly knew what to say.

47

"I'm sorry, Comrade Ivanov," he replied. "I thought I should report it."

"Very well," the Party Secretary replied. "I shall consider that you have reported it. Until tomorrow."

Smirnoff put the receiver back on the stand, a cold chill descending his spine. He sank into a chair, his heart racing like a motor. Only one thing registered in his mind from the conversation—only the important thing. Ivanov had greeted him as a friend, calling him "Simon Simonovich," his name and his patronymic. He had shifted to the official form, calling him "Comrade Smirnoff," as soon as Smirnoff hinted what was on his mind. And then—and this was crucial—when he had been told of Galin's call the Party Secretary switched from "Comrade Smirnoff" to plain "Smirnoff." No longer was he a comrade. Already he was beyond the pale, excluded from the Party.

My God, said Smirnoff to himself. What can I do now? The last words of the Secretary echoed in his mind: "Until tomorrow." This was not trouble. This was disaster! He did not dare to think what might be implied in those words, normally so conventional, now so pregnant with sinister significance.

Suddenly, Smirnoff sat bolt upright in his chair. His bell was ringing. In fact it had been ringing for some time but in his terror he had been too distracted to hear it. He rose hastily, crying: "Moment. Moment." Straightening his velveteen jacket with one hand and running the other through his hair, he went to the door and drew back the bolt.

"Dear Simon Simonovich, I fear I'm disturbing you." It was Natalie, her big brown eyes rolling under the heavy kohl of her eyelashes and her bounteous breasts moving in and out, in part because she had just climbed three flights of stairs, and in part to show that she was a young girl, breathless at being in the presence of genius.

Smirnoff stood a moment in the door as though he had not quite recognized his caller, and the girl looked up at him with what she obviously intended as wide-eyed wonder.

"Oh, dear," she said. "I'm afraid you were in the throes of some great creation and I have intruded at a moment which is not appropriate."

With the last shreds of his composure Smirnoff caught himself.

"Please," he said. "Please come in. I've just been sitting here waiting for you. I particularly want to hear your new poems."

8

Smirnoff watched with sheer relief as Natalie made her way, somewhat unsteadily but determinedly, toward the bathroom. Not even the rather extravagant movement of the well-developed haunches of the young poetess, sleekly emphasized by the tightness of her black silk skirt, evoked the usual quick response in him. The truth was that the state of his agitation was so great that the liberal quantities of vodka which he had drunk (he would have preferred cognac but the girl insisted that they drink "red-and-white"—red wine for her and white vodka for him) seemed to have had not the slightest effect upon the gnawing in his heart. He had done his best to carry off his role with accustomed style. He had listened to her verses and then treated her to some of his own more romantic poems. The glasses of red wine which he poured for her were large and quickly refilled. They had drunk *do dna*—bottoms up—she in wine and he in vodka. The effect on the young woman had been notable. In other circumstances he could not have been more pleased. That her talents were extensive, that she was experienced in their use, that she was not only willing but eager that he put them to the test—all of this was quickly apparent in the way she had flung herself on the couch, insisting that he seat himself (as he fully intended) at her side, leaning repeatedly over him to knock the ashes from her cigarettes and, in the process, caressing him more and more openly with her full breasts, turning her large brown eyes upon him in wide-eyed adoration as he read from his poems, clutching his hand (clammy with what she may have thought was passion but what he was only too well aware was fear) to her breast in ecstasy at his romantic lines ("The wounds which you have inflicted upon me will never heal for the blood that flows from my heart issues from my soul and not from my body"), encircling his arm in hers and drawing him ever closer to her lips with each glass of red-and-white, drunk in "Brüderschaft," and, finally, struggling to her feet with the cry: "My God, my God, why are you putting me through this terrible torture?" and then with a sob, half-romantic, half-dramatic, saying that she must leave him for a moment and walking, unsteadily but with a calculated rhythmic movement of her hips, toward the bathroom.

Yes, thought Smirnoff, the scenario was unrolling only too well except that one of the actors, himself, was incapable of playing his role. A half dozen times he had been on the point of ordering this miserable girl from his apartment but each time let the moment slip, unable even to carry out this simple affirmative act. All that he could hear ringing in his ears were the terrible words of the Party Secretary: "Until tomorrow." And the echo of that demonic young man's question about the poem to Irena. The poem—this was the most horrible thing of all. It was fatal evidence which could destroy him, evidence that his association with Irena had been deep, intimate and complete. How could he possibly escape its fatal implications? How? How?

What in God's name was he to do? He was right back where he had been on that awful night with Irena—that night when he had paced the floor and told himself that if there were a revolver in his drawer he would put it to his head and draw the trigger. But there had been no revolver in the drawer that night and there was no revolver in the drawer on this night, either.

51

"Why don't you shoot yourself, Smirnoff?" Irena had said to him as she rose to leave, and the contempt in her tone touched his breast like frozen steel. A tremor shook him, and though he pressed his shaking thighs until they were white he could not halt the trembling.

"You can pull your trousers up now, Smirnoff," she said. "Consider my curiosity professional. We sculptors, you know, have an interest in anatomy. Even the anatomy of freaks."

Of course, he had known that she hated him from the start. And he knew why. It was because he had brought the charges against old man Bardin, whom she adored. But he had actually not realized the strength of her hatred until much later. It was certainly true that she had remarked once to Voronsky at a reception when Smirnoff was seated at the same table and she was aware that he could hear her remark: "Aren't you rather tired of Russian writers who, as soon as they have a few thousand rubles in royalties, order a tweed jacket from London, start smoking a brier pipe and profess to a fondness for Hennessy cognac?"

And, of course, it was like that peasant Voronsky to laugh uproariously and say in a voice loud enough for everyone to hear: "Smirnoff—did you hear what Irena said? She cut you down—and she didn't use her chisel, either."

For months thereafter he had not dared wear his new tweed jacket (for which he had paid no less than five thousand rubles to the rascal Klepov, who worked for the British Embassy) and the brier pipe (which cost him two thousand, together with a year's supply of Bond Street tobacco) had gone unused for even longer. As for the Hennessy cognac—well, the bottle stood on the sideboard this very day.

This, of course, was after the success of his first important novel, *Steel Is a Russian Word*. (How he had sweated over that title. But it had been worth it a thousand times over. The book dealt with the building of the steel mills at Magnitogorsk. But the play on Stalin's name was not lost in the proper quarters.) It was this success which caused the Writers' Committee to propose that Irena do his bust.

Naturally, this request was the same as an order. Nor had that been any accident, since with the modesty fitting to a young and newly successful author he had dropped a hint to the committee that Irena Galina had asked him to pose for her and, therefore, that it might be appropriate if the committee made a formal request. He felt it would serve the sarcastic bitch right if she was compelled to do his bust—and he thought that it would mark one more forward step in his career. Everyone knew that Irena Galina was rapidly becoming the foremost sculptor in the country. The Kremlin had shown her special favor, and to have his bust done by her would set a seal of a special kind upon the reputation which Smirnoff was beginning to attain.

But what a fool he had been! When he called first at her studio butter wouldn't melt in her mouth. She had taken him around the cluttered room, showing him some of the work she was engaged in. He remembered how she flung up a plaster-spattered canvas and said: "Here is Commander Cheprikov—handsome, don't you think?" And when he agreed that the famous airman was certainly good-looking she had said: "But, confidentially, Simon Simonovich, he is not quite so handsome as I have made him." And they had both laughed as though it was a conspiratorial secret. She had flung back another gray canvas and shown him the sensuous figure of a young girl which she was doing in clay. "How would you like to hold her in your arms, Simon Simonovich?" she asked playfully, and when he had hesitated and then ventured: "I would rather have you," she had fixed him with a strange look from those witch's gray eyes of hers and the flame had suddenly leaped up inside of him, and he thought: "My God, she does like me. I've set a spark inside of her."

The first time he went to pose she had made him take off his jacket. In fact, she had removed it herself, coming so close to him that he could see the deep cleft of her breasts and smell the faint violet fragrance of her perfume, and he felt himself tremble when her strong hands swept his shoulders. She drew away from him with a penetrating look that seemed to strip his clothes from his body,

53

and he thought: "That is how she sees me—naked and holding her in my arms," and the surge of passion mounted in him so swiftly that he was startled when she said: "Please, Simon Simonovich. Please. Remember, you're posing for me."

He had been puzzled for a moment.

"That expression on your face, Simon Simonovich," she said. "Do you really want me to mold it in bronze?"

He felt a hot flush suffuse his cheeks.

She gave a little cry. "I must make you blush again," she said. "Your cheeks are so beautiful and red and you are no longer a serious man—you are a little naughty boy."

He blushed even more deeply and did not know what to say. She laughed gaily for the first time.

"Now, let's go to work," she said.

It did not seem to him that she had worked for very long before she said: "Enough for today. I don't want to work too fast until I get the feel of you."

He asked her to come out for tea or even just for a walk. But she put him off, teasingly, in a way that set his heart pounding. She insisted that she was far too busy.

"Easy does it," she said. "Let's not rush things."

He left her studio and walked out into the raw fog of a November afternoon. The mist had turned the city into a gallery of grotesques. The mushroom tops of churches were lost in haze. The canals vanished and bridges loomed up like iron fences across cotton-wool wastes. He walked down the Nevsky without the faintest idea of where he was going and was surprised to find himself a little later seated at a small marble table in a shabby café, eating a dish of ice cream and sipping a glass of not very good cognac. It was then he realized that he was completely in Irena's toils. Later, he angrily told himself that she had deliberately cast a spell over him for her own savage and cruel purpose, but at that moment he could only think of the promise of her words and the unutterable good fortune that had befallen him—to stand on the brink of a love affair with this woman for whom Voronsky had cut his throat (well,

54

perhaps, he had not cut his throat for her—but he had undoubtedly been her lover and he had undoubtedly cut his throat), for whom it was said even the greatest of living Russians had shown a personal interest and who was rumored to have had affairs with some of the most prominent artists and writers, a woman, moreover, of exquisite beauty, of features so haunting, of passions so smoldering that she even set afire the blocks of stone from which she carved her statues.

It was that night, half in a daze, that he began to work on the famous verses—"Make me your slave, beat me, humiliate me, strike me where you will but I shall love only you until my heart lies still."

Smirnoff's nostrils twitched. His room was suddenly filled with the overpowering scent of eau de cologne—his eau de cologne! That woman!

He raised his eyes to see approaching him, arms outstretched, eyes gleaming, walking slowly and carefully, straight to the couch where he sat, his poetess of the hour, naked as God had made her, and softly murmuring as she approached, closer and closer: "Simon Simonovich . . . make me your slave . . . beat me . . . humiliate me . . . beat me . . . make me your slave."

9

Smirnoff awakened with a start. He had heard the knock sharply and distinctly and he was in terror. They had come. He had no doubt of it and yet so transfixed was he that he could not force himself to rise immediately and go to the door. My God, he thought, here I lie naked and they will take me off without even clothes on my back. He lay trembling, his ears awaiting the next blow at his door. But it did not fall and gradually he realized that the knock must have come to him in a nightmare. Yet so strong was his conviction that someone was there that he forced himself to his feet and tiptoed silently to the door, put his ear to the crack and listened intently. He heard nothing but the sound of a broken toilet, running interminably, and, finally, slapping his hairy chest in frustration, he went back to the divan and sat down on its edge.

He looked with cold hatred at Natalie's full body. The woman (she certainly was no girl, he now realized) lay on her back, one hand passed over her face, her mouth open with a rivulet of spittle coming from its corner, her breasts creased by the weight of his body, her legs sprawled carelessly apart and naked except for the green baize cover which she had grasped with one hand and which was flung over her left thigh. He had to get her out of his apartment but it was not going to be easy.

He felt a wave of nausea rack his stomach and he thought he was going to be ill, but the moment passed and he lifted himself to his feet and went to the sideboard. There was still brandy in the bottle and he poured himself half a tea glassful and downed it, sputtering and coughing. It was cold in the flat and he picked up his trousers and started to draw them on. As he did so there returned to him—as had returned to him a thousand times since that terrible evening—the hot humiliation of the shame to which Irena had subjected him.

How she had led him on. The half-promise of intimacies each time he went to the studio. The little caressing gestures. Always she must remove his jacket. And then her decision that she must remove his shirt as well. "I want to feel the play of your muscles," she said, "so I can translate them into bronze."

She had slipped off his shirt and run her hands over his shoulders, over the pectoral muscles and across the bulge of his hair-grown chest. And with each touch he trembled. He could still see the cryptic look that veiled her eyes as her fingers touched his quivering flesh.

Once when he could not hold himself in check and his arms reached out to grasp her she slipped beyond his reach so swiftly that he almost lost his balance.

"Careful," she said, reaching out a cool hand to steady him. "If you lose your balance—who knows what might happen?"

He thought he had planned with masterly caution. Not until the final session of posing did he suggest that she come to his apartment.

"You have created something beautiful out of cold clay," he said. "I can never repay you. But let me make a small offering in exchange."

"Are you sure you really want this?" she asked, and her green eyes seemed to have hidden flashes of fire.

"Yes," he said, and he knew that he must sound like a schoolboy

57

because he felt like one. "Oh, yes. I do want it. Very much."

"Very well, if that is the way you feel," she said. "I think it is fair. You have come to my working quarters very often. I will come to yours."

He had arranged everything about the evening with the most precise care. He had decorated the room with a small white lilac bush. It cost him 800 rubles but it provided the note of purity and exoticism which he wanted to strike. His Hennessy bottle was hidden and he would offer nothing but Caucasian wine—not ordinary wine but a special Tsinindali which he got through one of the Georgian writers. And he set out no *zakuski*—just some Antonov apples and blood-red tangerines on a table near the divan. Simplicity and imagination—these were the leitmotivs. He wore dark blue corduroy trousers and a pure white silk shirt with wide collar and ruffled cuffs. The shirt came from the costumery of the Marie Theater. He was afraid that its theatrical quality might strike a false note but finally decided that the touch of flamboyance was merited. He placed a single candelabrum on the sideboard but, finding that it left most of the big room in darkness, managed to borrow another. The two gave the room a certain subdued brilliance. He possessed an excellent gramophone and a good collection of records. But he decided against anything so obvious as Rachmaninoff. Better, he thought, to play Offenbach and Strauss—music which would only be a background for the mood of the moment.

Finally, of course, there was the poem. He had, it was quite true, labored over this for weeks. First, polishing and perfecting it and then deliberately introducing here and there a few calculated roughnesses, to simulate those excesses of passion which cannot be confined to iambic meter. He had committed the verses to memory and had prepared the inky, tear-spotted copy which he drew from his breast pocket and handed to her in the moment of silence which came at the conclusion of his recitation.

She took the poem in her hand, lying back against the pillows of the couch. She looked at him as Cleopatra must have looked at Anthony, fire in her gray-green eyes, her breast moving gently, her shoulders proud and her arms like the marble of a goddess.

"My slave . . ." she said. "Yes, Simon Simonovich, you are my slave . . . I am your mistress and you are my slave. . . . My serf . . . Tell me again, Simon Simonovich, that you are in my power."

"I am your slave," he said, humbly, his voice breaking. "I am in your power."

The sheer horror of what followed Smirnoff had tried again and again to eradicate from his memory. But he was powerless to erase the image from his mind—how, acting at Irena's hypnotic suggestion, he had stripped, first his shirt, then his trousers, then the remainder of his clothing and stood nude in the cold blaze of her eyes, nude beside the small puddle of his clothing. Then, like some animal trainer, she had put him through his paces. How could he have subjected himself to such humiliation? She had read the lines of his poem to him . . . humiliate yourself, Simon Simonovich . . . humiliate yourself . . . crawl at my feet . . . lower, lower . . . crawl like a dog . . . like a snake . . . pray to me, Simon . . . pray for mercy . . . you slave . . . pray that I permit you to live . . . pray for my smile . . . pray that I favor you with the sound of my voice . . . the sight of my eyes . . . pray, Simon Simonovich. . . . And he had prayed, shivering and shuddering like the meanest monk in a medieval monastery. Then she broke the spell.

"Get up, Simon Simonovich," she cried, her voice hot with anger. "Get on your feet. Stand before me!"

He stood dazed, as the peal of her laughter struck like cold steel in his heart.

"You fool," she said. "You slave. Look at yourself in the mirror and tell me why you dare to call yourself a man. . . ."

And with his head reeling she had risen slowly from the couch, contempt covering her face like a mask, and strode out of the apartment, crying to him: "Why don't you shoot yourself, Smirnoff? . . . You can pull your trousers up now, Smirnoff. Consider my curiosity professional. We sculptors, you know, have an interest in anatomy. Even the anatomy of freaks!"

He pulled his dressing gown tightly about him as the dreadful words echoed through his mind. What would she not have given to know that to this day he could not see his body without a flush of abysmal shame. He was no better than one of Pavlov's dogs. The reaction which the fiendish woman had established had left him her prisoner. More than a year had passed before he was able to sleep with a woman again, and it was only after he had hired an imaginative and able prostitute that his powers began to recover.

What had been hardest was to preserve his outward calm. To appear unshaken toward the world and, particularly, to maintain a light but cynical tone toward the sculptress herself. He well knew that she was beyond his power to damage, at least for the time. But he knew that if he lived he would see her in hell. And so he had—except that now she had reached beyond the grave and clutched his coat tail with her bony hand.

What was he going to do? What could he do? He found himself pacing back and forth, back and forth, just as he had that first terrible night. One thing he could do. One thing he must do. That was to get rid of this horrible female who lay stupefied on his couch. He went over and shook her vigorously. Her head wobbled, one eye opened but she fell back on the divan, burying her head in the pillows like a child. He shook her more vigorously and slapped her tentatively on the cheeks.

"Darling," she said. "Darling." And groped for him with her arms. The last thing which Smirnoff wanted was to be encased once more in her bovine embrace. He strode resolutely to the bathroom and returned with a pitcher of water. He began to slosh it on her back and neck.

The reaction was immediate and vigorous.

"Goddamn it!" the woman said, suddenly fully conscious. "What the hell do you think you are doing?"

"Get dressed and get out of here," he said. "It's almost daylight."

"What's the big idea?" she said, her face red and resentful. "Can't you wait for daylight? You weren't in such a hurry for me to leave a little while ago."

For an answer he picked up her dress and slip and threw them at her.

"Get your clothes on and get out," he said. "Or I'll throw you out as you are."

The anger in his voice reduced her to squirming sobs. She pulled on her clothes in a blur of drunken moans and made her way to the door.

"You rat," she said, "that's the last time you get under my skirts. You fake poet."

"You got what you wanted," he said coldly. "Get out before I kick you out."

"You bastard," she cried. "You . . . slob . . . you . . . pimp . . . you . . . hedgehog . . ."

The door slammed behind her before she could see Smirnoff blanch at the word "hedgehog."

"Oh, my God," he said. "My God!"

He walked slowly to his bathroom. His eau de cologne bottle was almost empty. He opened the medicine chest. For a long time his hand stood poised over the razor that lay there. Then, he turned quickly, almost running back to the couch, where he flung himself down, crying: "Oh, my God! My God! My God!"

10

It was not possible to say that Zoskind's story called "The Hedgehog" was widely known or even well remembered in literary circles. To be sure it was one of his works which had been singled out for mention in the Party Decree on Art in 1946, together with his novel *Wild Acorns* and his never-produced play, *The People and the Power*. But only a handful of people had ever read "The Hedgehog." It had appeared in a badly printed almanac called *The Northern Palmyra*, which was gotten out, late in 1942, in an edition of less than one thousand copies, the first literary volume to be published in Leningrad with the easing of the siege. The almanac contained a letter of congratulation to the writers and artists of the city by Party Leader Zhdanov, a brief introduction by the Mayor, an authorizing decree by Secretary Ivanov and contributions from Leningrad writers who stayed in Leningrad during the siege. Smirnoff was represented by his war poem, "I Will Live," containing the memorable lines: "I will live while you believe in me—I will live so long as you are true to me. Forget me, and I perish." Not all of the material was literary. There was a brief article by the architect Morozov on plans for a new and greater postwar Leningrad. Irena

Galina had contributed a sketch for a war memorial but, unfortunately, the reproduction was so blurred and the paper so shoddy that almost nothing could be made of it. Since the city was still under siege not more than a handful of copies of the almanac had ever gotten to Moscow. Thus, while most literate Russians were familiar with the satire of Zoskind's *Wild Acorns* and the savage humor of his play (which had been published by one of the leading literary journals), the nature of the "subjectivism" represented by "The Hedgehog" as well as its "decadent fatalism" was hardly known.

Smirnoff had never been certain whether he was the first to draw the attention of the Party to the ideological perversion of Zoskind's work just as he had never been entirely clear whether the letter which he had written about the concealed counter-revolutionary symbolism in Bardin's fairy tales had been the major factor in the purge of the old man. However, in the case of "The Hedgehog" he was reasonably certain that he was the first one to suggest the affinity of its author for formulations linked with the rotten past.

Some might have thought Smirnoff well advised not to draw attention to "The Hedgehog" but he believed that the way to disarm suspicion was to meet it head on. There was no way in which the case could be proved or disproved but Smirnoff believed that "The Hedgehog" was a study of himself. It was the story of the moral struggle of a man against temptation set in Leningrad during the most terrible months of the hunger blockade—those days when the ration was only a slice of bread a day, bread made largely of sawdust and rye. A writer, something of a fop, something of a womanizer, something of a sybarite, is caught in blockaded Leningrad. A bachelor with a bachelor's selfishness, the only real affection which he permits himself is for a pet hedgehog, which he keeps in his apartment. The timid little beast has come to trust the writer completely. He sits at his feet while the writer works at his desk. From time to time the writer casually caresses the animal. As the food pinch becomes tighter a struggle arises in his conscience. Shall he continue to feed the hedgehog or shall he preserve every scrap

63

of food for himself? Day by day he wrestles with the problem. Some days he does not feed the hedgehog until late at night when the mild little animal comes and begs beside his table. Finally, he hardens his heart. For the first time a whole day passes in which he gives the hedgehog no food. The next day he breaks down and feeds it a few crumbs. But the day following he again deprives it of food. When the second day without food has passed he knows in his heart that he has sealed the fate of his pet; already, although he has not admitted it, he has decided that the hedgehog shall get no more food.

It is cold—icy cold—in the apartment. The writer had been in the habit of putting the hedgehog in his lap as he sat, wrapped in his fur coat, fur hat on his head, writing. The little animal is warm-blooded. It was like having a lap warmer. Now something prevents him from putting the beast in his lap. The animal senses that it is being abandoned and becomes bolder and bolder in begging for food. But another thought is overcoming the writer. The hedgehog represents food. That is, the hedgehog is potential food today. But if left to perish of hunger or disease this will all be wasted. And so a new struggle begins. The writer realizes that he is not simply going to let the hedgehog die. He is going to kill the animal and eat him. The thought of eating his pet nauseates him. Still, once the notion enters his mind he cannot rid himself of it. He reaches down and strokes the animal. The beast, thinking it is finally to be fed, rubs fondly against his leg. Involuntarily the writer notes how thin the hedgehog is. Already it is losing its fine padding of fat. He tells himself that since the die is cast there is no point in further temporizing. He might as well do the deed. It is only torture for both the animal and for himself to put it off. But the hedgehog senses its fate and retreats to a favorite hiding place—the place where it sought refuge in the old days when callers came to the writer's apartment. The writer gets down on his hands and knees and peers under the sofa. He sees the glitter of tiny eyes. The little beast is in the farthest corner. He reaches for the animal but his arms are not long enough. He has to crawl under the lounge. Suddenly, fear comes over him. Suppose the animal turns on him. It has sharp quills and claws. It might inflict a nasty wound. This could be a dangerous business. He hesitates, then steels himself. Under the couch it is dark, dusty, cold. The hedgehog is in the back corner in a nest made of old straw and rags. The writer extends his hand and the hedgehog weakly claws at him. He grabs wildly, catching a leg, and pulls the beast out as it whimpers like a sick kitten. The writer hurls it savagely against the floor but the animal whimpers more loudly as blood spurts from its mouth. Half-frantic, the writer strikes the beast again and again until it lies silent and limp on the floor.

Looking at the small corpse, the writer asks himself: How could I have done this? But even as he asks the question he feels the saliva start in his mouth at the thought of the savory little body. He takes his slain pet in his hand and goes to the kitchen. Two hours later, his stomach filled, a few grease stains on his lips, the writer sits belching contentedly at his desk, composing some lines about the soul of the city—the human hearts which formed a living wall against German steel and flame.

The reason why Smirnoff thought that "The Hedgehog" dealt with himself was simple. He had kept a hedgehog, called Bobby, as a pet at the outbreak of war. It used to sit in his lap as he wrote. As in the story he was a bachelor and he was aware that his way of life might be described as sybaritic. But the resemblance did not halt there. As the blockade tightened Smirnoff had done exactly what the writer in the story had done—he had killed his hedgehog and eaten it. The truth was he had undergone psychological torments much the same as those described by Zoskind, although he preferred to think that his actions had a simple logic about them. If a choice had to be made between the survival of a hedgehog and the survival of a man Smirnoff felt that no moral judgment need intervene. Logic dictated that man survive and that hedgehog perish.

The circumstances being so parallel and the fact that he kept a hedgehog being well known in Leningrad, Smirnoff could not but feel that Zoskind had him in mind. Curiously, however, Smirnoff had never said a single word to anyone about the destruction and eating of his small pet. He had left Leningrad soon after the event—having, with a stroke of genius, convinced the Union of Writers that if *Smoke and Flame,* his novel about Leningrad's heroic battle, was to be finished quickly and published, he would have to get out of the blockade, where it was not possible to carry forward sustained literary work.

So the question arose, how could Zoskind have learned about the murder of the hedgehog and actually was it not sheer coincidence? Smirnoff knew in his bones that somehow Zoskind had guessed (understanding Smirnoff's character entirely too well) what the fate of the hedgehog had been.

Such subtlety on Zoskind's part was too dangerous to be permitted. Smirnoff vowed the moment he read "The Hedgehog" that Zoskind must go. He did not know how or when this would be accomplished. But he knew that it must be done. The danger of a man with that kind of instinct was entirely too great.

Zoskind's satire and talent had already won him many enemies. It was not difficult for Smirnoff to pour a little gasoline on the flames, to drop a hint here and there of Zoskind's unhealthy influence on Leningrad morale in the worst days of the siege, of his affinity for western things. ("Naturally, I'm not saying that he has the slightest sympathy for the Germans. No man who was in Leningrad during the blockade could have anything but fierce hatred for them. And yet it does seem strange to find him so often utilizing German forms and models. His passion for Freudian analysis is curious. There is something definitely non-Russian about Zoskind. And what Russianness there is in him—is not that of our Soviet Russia, it is the Russia of Dostoyevsky. It is the Russia of Nicholas, perhaps, but not the Russia of Stalin.")

It was no great trick when the turn came in 1946 to make certain that Zoskind was one of its main targets along with the poetess Margerita Morova and the sculptress Irena Galina.

Smirnoff recognized that logically his sensitivity concerning the hedgehog was not justified. After all, life in Leningrad during the blockade had not been a fancy-dress ball. It was not accidental that he himself had written one of the first attacks on Margerita Morova, in which he held up her poem "Not the Least of Sparrows" to scathing ridicule. Perhaps it was true, as Margerita had indignantly contended, that she should not be criticized for not having been in Leningrad during the siege. Perhaps it was entirely true that she had been directed to go to Tadjikstan to work with the Tadjik poet, Abbas, on a translation of his works into Russian (and not, as Smirnoff had insinuated, in order to escape from the city because of fear of impending doom and, moreover, in order to carry on the passionate but disgusting love affair of an older woman for an ardent young man which was hinted at in her lyric sequence *My Lover, Asia*). Nonetheless, it was certainly true that she had not been in Leningrad during the siege and she should not have had the temerity to describe what life in the city was like or if she did she should have been shrewd enough to get an accurate report of what conditions actually existed. Had she done so she would never have committed the inexcusable error of picturing her young heroine, Nadezhda, a beautiful and idealistic Komsomolka, finding a sparrow on the steps of Kazan Cathedral, its wing broken by a shell fragment, and the young girl's vain and pathetic effort to save the life of this tiny victim of the Nazi horror. Because, as everyone who had been in Leningrad well knew, there were no more sparrows on the steps of the Kazan Cathedral, nor pigeons around St. Isaac's, nor birds of any kind anywhere in the city by New Year's of December, 1941, the date on which Morova had fixed for her story. By that time every bird in the city, including pet canaries and finches, had been eaten. Even the pair of lovebirds which Academician Strumkin, the Fat One, had presented to his wife on their twenty-fifth wedding anniversary, had gone into the stew pot, a fact which the old couple grimly but frankly told about themselves.

So that Morova could hardly have committed an error more dramatically designed to emphasize her ignorance of what life in Leningrad was like under the siege. "For an authoress who prides herself on being known as a 'Leningrad poetess,'" said Smirnoff in his critique, "the least she might have done (since, perhaps for personal reasons, she chose not to spend those critical and historic days in the city of her birth) was to acquaint herself with the real nature of the ordeal through which passed our Northern Palmyra."

The destruction of Morova was foredoomed from that moment. There was nothing she could say in her own defense. No amount of explanation would ever restore her reputation. She died not long after her denunciation—of pneumonia, it was said, although since the death had occurred in Stalinabad or somewhere even more remote in Tadjikstan the actual circumstances had never been precisely known in Leningrad.

All this being true, as Smirnoff had often told himself, there was no reason in logic why he should cringe at the word "hedgehog" nor why in his heart of hearts he should harbor a guilt complex about the little animal. He could have adopted half a dozen suitable attitudes. A shrug of the shoulders—so what? Or a wry grimace—tough, but what can one do? A pensive frown—yes, that is the kind of hard decision which war brings. A quizzical response—and, by the way, whatever became of that big Siberian cat of yours? Or downright cynicism—not such bad eating, my friend, try one sometime!

On the half-dozen occasions when anyone had made a remark to him about the hedgehog he had responded in one of these fashions. But he was certain that his face betrayed his inner feeling, his feeling that this was a chink in the armor which he had so carefully constructed to protect himself against the dangers of the world in which he lived. He had never been able to analyze his emotion accurately. All he knew was that he felt an acute sense of danger and had struck back at Zoskind as hard as he knew how. It was quite different from the calculated blow he had aimed at the fairy-tale writer, Bardin. That was designed to establish his own firm orthodoxy in a time of heretical challenge. He had nothing against Bardin. In fact, he felt sorry to have been the instrument of the old man's destruction. But, as he told himself at the time, Bardin had lived his life. It was only a matter of this year or next. But with Zoskind the case was quite different. With Zoskind he felt a sense of personal jeopardy from a man who could so acutely read his mind, his actions and his conduct (for he was convinced that Zoskind had simply drawn upon the knowledge which he possessed of Smirnoff's character and, by a process of pure ratiocination, had been able to understand not only what Smirnoff had done with the hedgehog but what was far more dangerous—the interplay of Smirnoff's motivations, hesitations and vacillations). This kind of prescience constituted danger of the first order.

But even after Smirnoff had analyzed his feelings in this fashion, even after he had begun the insinuations and machinations which ultimately destroyed Zoskind, Smirnoff still experienced a moment of panic whenever the hedgehog intruded upon his conscience. Why this should have been so he did not understand. It was ridiculous to suppose that the hedgehog story or any variant of it could at this late date be turned into an effective weapon against him. Zoskind had been relegated to some unknown point in distant Siberia (if he still survived, which was doubtful). Yet the sense of fear survived. It was a baffling mystery which Smirnoff could have solved only if he had been prepared to face the cold truth—that the timid, inoffensive, affectionate little hedgehog; the fuzzy creature which liked to sit on its haunches, delicately opening up sunflower seeds and extracting their oily, nutty centers; this small inarticulate beast, so defenseless against Smirnoff since its teeth and claws were so small and it had long since ceased to bristle in Smirnoff's presence (thus depriving itself of the one weapon in its natural armory) because of a complete and total confidence in Smirnoff's good will; this curious animal was the only living thing which had aroused in the heart of the writer genuine warmth and affection. It was the only living creature which had ever placed itself wholly and totally in Smirnoff's power, submitting completely to whatever fate he prepared for it, and by this submission the small beast had won what none of Smirnoff's women had ever succeeded in arousing—real love. Was this because of some psychological affinity between the writer and the hedge-hog? Did each feel fundamentally weak and defenseless against the world? Was this why Smirnoff struck out so ruthlessly, so swiftly, so mercilessly at anyone and everyone whom he conceived to be an enemy or a possible enemy? Did he, like the hedgehog, bristle and stick out his quills because he felt that if he did not do so he would be defenseless and impotent in the face of the strong? No such questions ever passed through Smirnoff's mind for he never saw himself in such terms. But he did know that there was some dark secret buried within his breast, some secret to which the hedgehog was a clue, some secret which he hoped would never come to light, even though he did not perceive its nature.

11

Smirnoff had been dozing again and he noticed with a start that it was nearly 6 A.M. It was, of course, still pitch dark outside but he could hear the first sounds of the awakening city—the beginning rumble of trucks and the distant whine of trolley buses. Within the apartment building there were recognizable groanings of the water and sewer systems, the clanging of steam in the radiators and the muffled outcry of alarm clocks.

Smirnoff told himself fiercely that it was time to shake himself out of his fatal despondency and begin to think in terms of plan or action. To continue to sit, half-dozing, half-brooding, was to accept inevitably the fate which seemed to lie just ahead. Perhaps, of course, there was no means of escape. He felt with a heaviness of heart which he could not ignore that, indeed, there was little chance of saving himself. More than ever the desperate and dangerous eyes of young Galin seemed to him to have been sent back from beyond the grave by Irena, determined to accomplish his destruction, determined to grant him no respite, to permit no possible salvation.

And yet . . . and yet . . . he was an old sparrow. He had passed through times of danger before. To every situation there

71

always must be a key. But what the key to this one might be he could not imagine. His fuddled mind could not invent any tale which would adequately explain the circumstances with which he would shortly be confronted. The situation would have been bad enough without the copy of the poem. But with it in young Galin's hands, it was hopeless.

He was pacing the floor again and his feet led him inexorably to the great baroque sideboard; the next moment he was squatting by its side, fiddling with one of the huge walnut whorls with which it was decorated. Quickly a small panel slid back and he put his hand into the shallow compartment and drew out of it a slender sheaf of documents. This was what he referred to in his mind as his "life insurance policy"—the small and secret hoard of papers of one sort and another which he had put away over the years—the papers which might give him some hold or leverage over this individual or that; the little bits of evidence which, in time of need, might serve either as blackmail or testimonial for a man hard pressed and driven into a corner.

For the life of him Smirnoff could not think of any document or memorabilia contained in his collection which would be of the slightest value in this crisis. He knew the contents well. There were, bound by a rotted rubber band, three notes he had received at various times from Irena, none of them of the slightest value. In fact, potentially dangerous should their existence ever come to light. There was a letter from the Kremlin—personal congratulations on *Smoke and Flame*—no use to him now. There was a faded snapshot of a well-known writer standing beside Trotsky, a relic of the early twenties. No good now. The writer (actually, it was Bardin, the famous writer of fairy stories) was long since dead, executed in the purge of the mid-thirties. Why he had kept it Smirnoff did not know. There was a rather ample collection of indiscreet epistles from various women, including one from the wife of a very prominent Party official. But the letter was neither indiscreet enough nor the official powerful enough to save Smirnoff in the present situation. There was his copy of *The Northern Palmyra* almanac, which had once proved so valuable to him. But he could see nothing in it which could be of service this time. Still, he leafed it through. You never knew. Things sometimes sprang at you from the strangest sources and at the most unlikely moments. He looked again at the smudged and murky design of Irena's war memorial. There was an example—a prize example. Looking at this sketch one could make nothing of it. And yet he held in his hands the very source of the terrible woman's downfall.

It had not come about as a complete accident, to be sure. When he accepted the assignment from the popular magazine *The Torch* to do a sketch on Irena Galina and her plans for future work he did so in the secret hope that this might in some way give him a weapon to use against her. But he had no notion that he would find her delivered into his power. It was a hot summery day when he arrived at her studio. The month was July and the war had been over just two months. The old woman, Shura, Irena's housekeeper, let him into the studio. He had deliberately come a few minutes late but Irena was not there. She had gone somewhere—the housekeeper was uncertain just where—and there was nothing to do but wait for her.

Smirnoff amused himself strolling about the studio. He had not been there, needless to say, since he had posed for his bust. And he had not spoken to Irena except to greet her formally on public occasions since the night of his humiliation. He could not have spoken to her before—he would not have had the courage. Now, armed with this assignment, he had, as it were, put himself to the test. He had telephoned her for the appointment and had steeled himself for a sarcastic response. But, as always, she caught him off guard by a quick acceptance, given in warm and friendly tones as though nothing had ever been between them. He had been prepared for coldness, rudeness, even a refusal. So, as always, she had put him off balance. Now that he was in the studio again he was, he had to admit, jittery as a cat and wishing that he had never taken the assignment. He had good nerves. But whether they were strong enough to face up to Irena—this was an open question.

73

As always, the studio was a clutter of wooden stands, mounds of clay, blocks of marble, castings, charcoal sketches, plaster of paris, platforms, easels and bric-a-brac. In one corner Smirnoff saw a beautiful nude, cast in green bronze, and was startled to realize it was the very statue which Irena had shown him, not quite finished in rough clay, so many years earlier. Between two windows which gave directly onto the street stood a desk, heaped high with magazines, newspapers and a jumble of books and papers. It looked like a magpie's nest. Smirnoff picked up a newspaper and blew the plaster dust from it. The date was June, 1941—just before the start of the war. For lack of anything better to do and, perhaps, he admitted later, out of some ulterior curiosity, he riffled idly through the papers. Mixed among the newspapers, art journals, clippings, photographs there lay a slender volume of poetry—one of Tsvetayeva's early collections. He opened it and a letter slipped into his hands. Acting on God knows what impulse he quickly tucked the slender book into his pocket and walked away from the desk to the north end of the studio, unaccountably excited. He felt (with every reason) like a thief. But once on the other side of the room, somehow, he felt that he was safe, that his crime would not be discovered. He stood by the north windows with their sloping skylight for some time. Irena still did not make her appearance. Old Shura came in to ask him if he wanted some tea and, apparently certain of a positive answer, set down a glass and a plate of small cookies. He sipped the tea idly and began to pace about the studio. He wished Irena would come. The longer he waited the more nervous he became. He inspected busts which were in various stages of completion. Here was an old one of Cheprikov, the famous aviator; here one of Marshal Tolbukhin; here one of Svetlana Tetlov, the famous girl guerrilla fighter; here one of Comrade Ivanov; here one whose features Smirnoff did not recognize—possibly, he thought, it might be Morozov, the architect with whom she had had a love affair many years ago. There was a plaster model of her famous full-length statue of Voronsky, the one which had been put up in the square which was named after the poet following his tragic death.

74

There was also a model on small scale of a full-length statue of General Orlov in his military greatcoat with a pair of binoculars around his neck. And in one corner was the plaster model of her well-known group showing Stalin, Voroshilov and Büdenny on the parapet of Tsaritsyn.

Next to the Tsaritsyn group there was what appeared to be another group over which a much-spattered canvas had been thrown. It was the most massive work in the studio. Smirnoff tugged at one end of the canvas, trying to get some idea of what lay underneath. The canvas was heavy and because the work rested on a wooden platform it was difficult to toss it back.

He was struggling with it when a voice which caused goose pimples to rise on his neck said behind him: "Perhaps I can help you with that."

Smirnoff turned to find Irena Galina standing in the doorway, looking at him with an expression which seemed to compound curiosity and menace. The confusion which he had hoped would not overpower him at the sight of her swept over him, reinforced with a feeling of guilt. He did not know of any reason why he should not look under the canvas but something in Irena's expression suggested that he stood on the brink of new catastrophe.

"How do you do, Irena Mikhailovna," he said. "Excuse me for disturbing your work. I was amusing myself by looking at the statues while I waited for you to arrive. Forgive me."

"On the contrary, Simon Simonovich," said the woman, advancing into the room, her head thrown back, her eyes flashing and reminding Smirnoff somehow of a ship breasting the steel-gray waters of the Baltic. "On the contrary. There is no one whom I would rather have see this work than you."

As Irena came up to him he involuntarily drew back. It seemed to him that the same force which had enabled her once before to cast him powerless at her feet was again throwing a spell about him. Irena apparently sensed this.

"You needn't be afraid," she said scornfully. "I have no great love to see the past repeat itself."

75

She clambered up on the platform and, grasping the heavy canvas with her steel hands, quickly began to strip it off.

"I had not intended to show you this," she said, pausing a moment in her effort. "But on second thought I know of no one I would rather view it."

He started to help with the bulky cloth.

"No," she said imperiously, towering above him on the platform. "Don't interfere."

"Let me help you," he insisted.

"No, Simon Simonovich," she said. "I will not permit it. Go across the room and turn your back to me until I tell you to face around."

Reluctantly he crossed the room and turned his back, involuntarily patting the pocket in which he had secreted the book of poetry.

Presently she said: "All right. Now you may turn around."

He slowly turned. The platform had been fully exposed and Irena stood at one side, grasping a corner of the canvas with her hand, like a magician who has suddenly produced a full-grown woman from a silk hat. She stood, her eyes ablaze with green fire, her breast slightly heaving, her face flushed and a kind of lightning emanating from her brow. Slowly he turned his eyes from her to the group of figures exposed before him—he looked and his eyes started in horror. He could feel the hair on his head rising like a dog's and an involuntary cry sprang from his throat. The horror smashed into his brain like the blow of a rough fist. Here was a young woman, pinned against a rough bench or table by the powerful arm of a figure so primitive and brutal that it was impossible to say whether it was man or ape. Flinging her skirts back with a powerful paw, the half-naked monster stood on the edge of an act of rape, his body crouched, his loins ready. The horror was heightened by the look of pure innocence and pure fear which Irena had captured not only on the girl's face but, somehow, in the virginal mold of her limbs. She was about to suffer a degradation which her soul had never known existed in the world. But this was not all. Under the feet of the anthropoid lay an infant, a child of three or four, its body hideously smashed by the monster's jackboots. This was what Smirnoff grasped at first glance. Then he became aware that there was another figure in the group —a heroic female figure, possibly the mother of the child, stripped to the waist, with powerful hips, arms of a peasant and the breasts of a goddess. In one arm she brandished a rifle butt which was about to crash down upon the ravisher.

"Look well upon that figure, Simon Simonovich," said Irena in resounding tones. "Look well. I want every man in the world to stand in meditation before this statue."

His voice half-choked, Smirnoff asked: "What do you call this group, Irena Mikhailovna?"

"I call it 'The End of War,'" she said. "And I mean to make it the end of war. We women will halt the rape of humanity if we have to drag every male in the world, screaming and kicking, to stand before this statue."

Smirnoff cast his eyes to the floor. He could not bear to look at the scene of horror. But he could not keep his eyes from it either. They were drawn back to it with the irresistible fascination of a powerful magnet. He was drawn again and again to the look of innocence captured in the girl's face, the animal paws which crushed her shoulder, the ape's bestiality of the attacker, the frozen horror of the trampled-upon infant, the majesty of the valkyrie and the savage brutality of the monster's loins as he pressed toward the virgin maiden.

Smirnoff felt that he could not stand there another moment without hysterics. He could feel the screams stifling in his throat, but somehow he controlled himself and forced himself to ask the pedestrian questions and hear the pedestrian answers which the editors had sent him to ask. He knew that there was no point in concealing from Irena the titanic effect of her sculpture. All he could do was to ask his questions and get away as soon as he could. Finally, he found himself outside in the golden sunshine of the afternoon, almost running down the broken cobblestones of the street which led to the Fontanka and the bridge toward the Neva.

77

He kept on until he found himself up against a great iron chain which swung along the granite embankment at the side of the wide blue river, sparkling in the late sunshine, the delicate needle of the spire of St. Peter and St. Paul rising across the stream, and a tugboat chuffing past him with a line of coal barges. As he looked out on the familiar and peaceful scene he felt that for the rest of his life he would bleed internally as if from a physical wound. It was not only the savage power of Irena's concept which left him gasping. It was something more—something so terrible and personal that it left him weak. For what he had seen in the moment of supreme horror was himself, standing in the jackboots of the beast, his hairy chest bared, his loins ready to ravish the virgin grasped by his coarse paws.

He walked the streets of Leningrad for hours before he went home that evening. What thoughts had passed through his mind he could never have told. But when he finally reached the sanctuary of his apartment one thing was clear beyond a doubt. Irena Galina must be destroyed and he knew how this would be accomplished. Perhaps she had inflicted upon him a mortal wound. But she had, in her blind passion, exposed herself to retribution. Granted that she had the most powerful of supporters; granted that the Kremlin itself approved her work; granted that high figures in the Party respected her; granted that she numbered the elite of the land among her friends and lovers. None of this would save her. She thought, no doubt, that she had constructed a supreme weapon against war. She thought that by conceiving this horror in stone or bronze she could turn man's revulsion against man's bestiality into a passion for peace; that she could rouse womankind to stand against the bayonets and bugles. Perhaps she was right. But she was never to get a chance to test her power. He, Smirnoff, would see to that. For what she was preaching was not Communism, not the triumph of Socialist society, not the militant force of Marxism which would prevail against a decadent and dying capitalism. No. What she preached was heresy. She was preaching the horror of war—of all war, not merely imperialist war. Her figures had no nationality.

They were male and female of any nation, any age. The hand which was striking down the ravager was not a Russian hand striking down a Hun. It was not a Communist striking down a colonial despot. It was Woman striking at Brute Man, the eternal Female striking at the eternal Male. And this was heresy. This was preaching against all war, all armies, all uniforms. It was a blow at the Red Army; at the Party; at the state; at Stalin himself. Irena had crossed the bounds of Soviet art. She had crossed the bounds of Soviet society. She had trespassed beyond the freedoms of the Soviet state. This was not just heresy. This was treason. This was incitement against the power of the state itself, against the dictatorship of the proletariat and its armed forces.

Smirnoff sat down at his desk, dipped a scratchy pen into the rusty ink of his inkwell and began to write: "Dear Comrade Zhdanov: There are certain facts which I deem of such supreme importance that I must bring them to your personal attention. They concern one of the best-known and most honored figures of our Soviet culture and they are facts of such revolting and such subversive nature that I think they clearly call for decisive action. . . ."

As Smirnoff wrote through the night, his pen sputtering from time to time but never at a loss for words, he felt the bulk of something in his pocket and automatically reached in and drew it out. At first he could not recollect how he happened to have the little volume of Tsvetayeva's works in his hand. Then he remembered and shoved it into a corner of his desk, out of sight and out of mind.

The document which Smirnoff compiled that night became, as was widely known, the foundation of the Party's famous 1946 Decree on Art, citing Irena Galina, not merely for artistic deviations, not merely for foul distortions of the doctrine of Socialist Realism but for what were called creative crimes against Socialist humanity. It was nearly a year before the whole case was documented, elaborated and prepared and Irena was summoned before the Union of Soviet Artists to hear the indictment and to offer such defense as she might have. Smirnoff spoke at the session, emphasizing the full unity and support of the Writers' Union against what he called "the obscene and ignoble" distortions of a woman who owed everything —her life, her creative talent, her opportunities for its development—to the Socialist state. "Like an animal which devours its young," Smirnoff had said, "she has turned against all that she by ties of blood and passion should have held most dear and near."

Oh, it was a fine, passionate speech all right, the finest of his career; and he had not failed to pledge that the Soviet Writers would purge their own ranks of every alien voice and taint—the opening gun, of course, in the campaign which destroyed Zoskind and Morova. It was only a matter of days after the ideological indictment of Irena Galina before she was summoned to the State Prosecutor's office and quietly sent into exile.

12

The little volume of Tsvetayeva's verses had long rested in Smirnoff's "life insurance" vault. He opened it now, as he had occasionally in the past, and glanced again at the inscription written in strong black ink on the fly leaf: "To a woman of beauty and courage—with deep affection—C. C. Orlov." The date was October 14, 1940. October 14, Smirnoff happened to know, was Irena's birthday. There was nothing to be made of this. Orlov was a great figure—the savior of Leningrad some called him. In any event he had been an important leader in the city's defense during the war and was today the military commandant of the Leningrad region. In this inscription there was nothing which might threaten the security of Orlov or which might compel him to take some action in Smirnoff's behalf. Actually, what could Orlov do, even if there was some reason for him to intervene? This was a Party matter at best and a police matter at worst, or at the very worst a combination of Party and police matters. Not much that Orlov could or would do, even in the best of circumstances.

Smirnoff unfolded the letter which had fallen from the book on that summer day in 1945. He read it through again. It had been written in January of 1944. It was, essentially, a love letter, yet so restrained was Orlov's language, so respectful his thought, so careful and rather old-fashioned his manner of expressing himself, that (as Smirnoff had long ago decided) it really could not be utilized effectively as a mechanism of pressure or blackmail. On the contrary. It was evident from Orlov's calm and purposeful style that he would repel any attempt at pressure by simply squashing the author of such an attempt between his powerful fists.

Smirnoff reread the letter with a feeling of despondency. It had been written a few days after the Leningrad armies had finally and completely lifted the blockade of the city—nearly nine hundred days after it had been imposed by the Nazi forces at the end of August, 1941. And it obviously was in response to a message from Irena.

"I do not deserve your kind words, dear Irena Mikhailovna," the General wrote, "although I value them more than pure gold. This is not my triumph. It is a collective victory and the most important factor has been the moral superiority of our forces. No matter how they tried, the Nazis could not quench the flame of Leningrad patriotism, the flame of Leningrad bravery, the flame of Leningrad spirit which lights a beacon not only to the fatherland but to the whole world."

The General wrote that his headquarters was moving up rapidly following the advance of the troops but that he hoped within the next few days to be back in Leningrad briefly. He would see Irena then. He would press her hand and again look into the purity of her eyes. It would be a short meeting because, of course, he would have to return to the front, which, if it continued to move so rapidly, would soon approach the frontiers of East Prussia.

"Soon," he wrote, "we will no longer be fighting on the blood-soaked soil of our native land. We will for the first time be carrying the war to that of our enemy. Thank God when that day arrives."

He thanked Irena again for her kindness. Assured her of his best wishes and constant thoughts, expressed his hope for her continued health. "With undiminished love and affection," he signed his name, characteristically in strong, bold strokes.

There was a P.S. "Your letter about M.M. has just reached me. Believe me I will do everything within my power to help Michael Maximovich. I assure you that I love your son, as if he were my own. I will personally request his immediate transfer from the punitive battalion."

Smirnoff reread the postscript carefully, blowing his nose as he did so. Was there something in this which he could use? It seemed to him that there might be. But he could not immediately put his finger on it.

The reference to young Galin was entirely clear to him. The boy had been only a youngster at the outbreak of war and had been evacuated in August, 1941, on one of the last boats that got away across Lake Ladoga. He had been sent to the Urals with thousands of other evacuees and wound up in a school, Smirnoff believed, in Sverdlovsk. But he had the fiery temperament of his parents. He was not Maxim Voronsky's son for nothing. Despite his youth, within a year or so he had managed to enlist in the Red Army and was fighting on the central front, not far from Kursk. One night he was sent out on patrol. He did not return. He was listed as missing in action. His mother did not despair. Like thousands of others, she was convinced that Michael was alive, possibly a prisoner who would return at the end of the war. And, unlike most cases, she was right. In late autumn of 1943, as the Soviet armies advanced, young Michael did indeed turn up, as a member of a band of partisans. It was weeks before his mother learned of his rescue. Finally, he was permitted to write. He had been, as was the Red Army custom, placed in a separate camp. He was interrogated again and again as to why he had not returned with his patrol; how he had met with the other partisans; precisely what they had done during the long intervals behind the Nazi lines and, again and again, sometimes being waked up in the middle of the night and subjected to hours of interrogation, he was accused of deliberately deserting; of having gone over to the Nazis; of having entered their service; of

83

having returned to the Red Army only to act as a German agent and spy.

Of this, naturally, there was nothing in his letter. Only a few lines to say that he had been a partisan; that he had been in a special camp and that, finally, he had managed to win permission to rejoin the Red Army and was being assigned to a special battalion in which he would have the opportunity of showing again his dedication to his motherland.

Irena knew, of course, like every Soviet mother, of the punitive battalions. She was well aware that assignment to such a battalion was almost (if not quite) equivalent to a death sentence. The young men were not put up against a wall. No. They were simply given the most dangerous, the most difficult of assignments—night patrols to cut barbed wire ahead of the advancing troops, mine-scouting parties, surprise flame-throwing attacks on pillboxes. And so on. They were the most expendable of the Red Army's expendables.

All this Irena knew. And it was in this crisis that she had appealed for help to Orlov.

As Smirnoff puzzled over the fateful lines he began to sense the germ of an idea. Suppose he could reach Orlov—now, immediately, this morning. Suppose he were to tell him that young Galin was in the city; that Galin was armed with a letter in which Orlov promised him every assistance; that the young man in revenge against his mother's fate had set out to destroy everyone who had been close to her; that the only way in which he might be prevented from accomplishing his purpose would be to intervene before the boy had had a chance to present his evidence to the security forces; that—though the hour was late—he could still be seized by a detachment of special military police (on suspicion, let us say, of being a deserter); since he was known to be armed it would not be surprising if he had to be killed, resisting arrest.

What of this? The idea seemed unreal to Smirnoff even in his fevered condition. He had no confidence that it would succeed. And yet—what other card had he to play? He could, perhaps, strengthen the case with Orlov a little. He could hint that he knew of the charges that young Galin was going to present (that he had, for example, persuaded the young man to show him the evidence); he might, delicately, make it apparent to Orlov that if Galin were not seized, that if Galin went ahead with his intention, he, Smirnoff, certainly had no idea of keeping to himself the nature of the boy's evidence; that to save his own skin he might be forced to implicate Orlov by denouncing him as an associate not only of the decadent and traitorous sculptress Galina but also of her son, a known Nazi agent and escaped criminal and possible spy. A desperate tactic! But it was a moment for desperation.

Yes, he thought. That might do it. And, if it did not—well, the alternative was too black to contemplate. Invigorated at least slightly by the decision to act, he rose from his desk and went into his bathroom. The eau de cologne was still there where his stupid and boring poetess had left it after spraying it so liberally over her breasts and buttocks. His mouth felt absolutely terrible. He pushed the cologne to one side, turned on the water and put his head down under the tap, letting the ice-cold current run over his fevered temples. He might be in a corner, he conceded grimly. But if he went down he would bring some fine heads rolling alongside his own.

13

The truth was that Party Secretary Gregory Ivanov was considerably more alarmed by the appearance of Michael Galin than he had given hint of in the telephone conversation with Smirnoff. He clenched his teeth as he replaced the receiver on the cradle. He would have to move fast. If only he did not have this meeting on the Narva project he would put in a call immediately to Dmitri Chaikovsky at the State Security office. When Smirnoff had telephoned to him Ivanov had acted largely on instinct. There were few men in Leningrad, if the truth were told, whom Gregory Ivanov despised more deeply than the posturing, venomous writer. He had known Smirnoff much too long and much too intimately to respect him either as a man or a writer. But at the same time he harbored an awe of the man's quick wit, of his extraordinary talent for intrigue and his unerring nose for danger. He was poisonous as a cobra—and as swift to strike. The moment Ivanov's secretary told him Smirnoff was on the line he sensed there was trouble and he knew that if it were not serious trouble Smirnoff would never have telephoned him in this unexpected fashion. Smirnoff was far too clever for that. No. Something must have thrown Smirnoff off balance and caused him to let his guard down momentarily. And, since young Michael Galin had left Ivanov's own office not five minutes before, it had not required an act of genuine precognition to put two and two together and to suspect even before Smirnoff spoke Galin's name that this was why the writer was calling.

Instantly Ivanov had concluded that he must disassociate himself from any connection with Smirnoff—though at this moment he, Ivanov, did not by any means perceive what lay behind the Galin affair.

He rubbed his hand across his close-shaven head and pressed his thumbs hard over his almost naked eyebrows. Something serious, something dangerous was afoot. He was not even certain that this Galin boy was mixed up in it directly. You could never be sure. Everything was so fantastically confusing. So seldom was anyone what he appeared on the surface. Nor for that matter even what he seemed to be at the first level below the surface. No, indeed. Everyone these days played a triple role or a quadruple role. If a man said something the possibilities were almost infinite. What he said might be true. This was the rarest possibility. Or it might be untrue. This was also rare. Or, it might be partly true and partly untrue. This was the most frequent possibility. But that was just the beginning of the game. The game was to ascertain which part was true and which untrue. And then to figure out why the man had made the statement and what his real motive was. Sometimes, Ivanov thought wearily, the man himself could not in honesty tell you precisely what the motive was. Sometimes you said things largely on pure instinct—as he had spoken to Smirnoff a moment ago.

It was time that he went to the meeting but he could not bring himself to leave his desk. Let them wait a bit. It did not matter and what he had on his mind was extremely important. It could be—although he did not like to think of it in such terms—it could be a real matter of survival. He had cut Smirnoff off because instinctively he knew Smirnoff was in trouble and he was afraid Smirnoff would bring him down, too, just as a heavy tree in the forest sometimes falls, carrying a whole train of trees along with

87

it. Only too often he had seen this happen in the Party. He was a battle-scarred veteran and he knew how to protect his flanks. But he had been nervous for some time. It wasn't merely the fact that with Zhdanov's death there had been shifts in the Party structure. He had anticipated this. Like any prudent Party man he had reinsured himself. That is, he had tried to protect himself so that even if Zhdanov went down he would be able to survive through his alternate ties to other Party leaders.

There had been the usual shifts, the usual rumors and indications of change. An order for a transfer would not have surprised him at all. But these past few weeks something else had started. There had been little things . . . the way Moscow talked on the telephone . . . the fact that the Kremlin did not telephone quite so often. He slept in his office. Every Party leader whom he knew slept in the office and had for years in case there was a 3 A.M. call from the Kremlin. He had gotten plenty of late calls. Often two or three an evening. But not lately. He had caught Dmitri Chaikovsky looking at him speculatively at the last meeting of the plenary—a cold, appraising glance which seemed to say: Well, I wonder how much longer he will be around.

Had it not been for his inner sense of uneasiness, for his antenna-like exploration of the environment for clues to what was going on, he might not have received young Michael Galin. His secretary, a fish-faced functionary named Pupin, obviously had been of two minds whether even to report that Galin was asking to see him.

"What is the nature of his business?" Ivanov asked, toying with a crumpled bit of white paper, torn from a student notebook, on which the name Michael Galin had been scrawled.

"He would not say, Comrade Ivanov," the man replied. "All he would say was that he was the son of Irena Galina and that you would remember her."

"Obviously," snapped Ivanov. He had recognized the name instantly and his antenna told him he better see the young man, but he did not intend the secretary to understand this. He let the silence lengthen a bit and then told the man: "How many times have I told you to find out a caller's business before you present the name to me?"

"I'm sorry." The secretary cringed. "I tried, Comrade Ivanov, but he flatly refused to state his business."

Ivanov sighed. It was a ceremonial, official sigh.

"Very well," he said. "Let him wait ten minutes. Then send him in. Once again I shall have to do your business for you."

Ivanov narrowed his eyes in thought. Perhaps young Galin had no connection with what was going on. Sometimes the instruments of intrigue had no notion that they were acting on anything more than their own motivation—never realizing that they had been granted the freedom to act only because certain forces saw in them a useful tool in a complex and insidious scheme.

The Party Secretary could not recall having ever seen young Galin. He knew of him, to be sure. Everyone knew of this child of the tempestuous love affair of Maxim Voronsky and Irena Galina. And everyone knew of the tragic history—how Voronsky in a fit of passion had left Irena; how he had eloped with an actress from the Moscow Circus to the Crimea and how, a few days afterward, he had locked himself in the bathroom of the suite he occupied with the actress (the so-called "white suite" with a great balcony overlooking the sea in the hotel which had once been a villa of the Czar); and how, while police vainly battered at the heavy door, Voronsky had bled to death from the jagged wound he had slashed in his throat; and of his last distinguishable words—"Hurry, hurry" followed by mumbled syllables which the romantic insisted was the word "Death" while the cynical contended it was the word "First aid."

All this Ivanov knew well, just as he knew that the boy insisted on calling himself Galin after his mother rather than Voronsky after his father. He knew, too, that the boy had been in trouble of some kind and that, even before tragedy befell his mother, he had been banished to Central Asia. As for Irena, he had known her well but not intimately for many, many years. During the blockade days he had come to respect her as a brave woman of inextinguishable

89

spirit. He would never forget the terrible night of September 8, 1941, the night of the first great Nazi air attack; the terrible night when the Baldaev warehouse burned and with it those priceless stocks of grain and sugar whose loss condemned the city to suffer from hunger so quickly and so sharply; the night when the whole of Leningrad seemed to be going up in flames; the night when the Nazis rained down fire bombs by the thousand and explosive bombs by the hundred.

The attack had started in late afternoon and at 2 A.M. it was still in progress. Everyone in the city, it seemed, had turned out to fight the fires, everyone except the military staffs—Zhdanov, Orlov and the others who were combatting the even more deadly peril of the land assault—German tanks had penetrated that day into the outskirts of the city and some had been destroyed within the very limits of Leningrad itself. Perhaps it was not the worst night of the war. There were so many bad ones to come. But because it was so horrible and the horror was so new it had impressed itself more vividly on his mind.

Shortly after 1 A.M., when the firemen had finally gotten the Baldaev blaze under control, he had turned back to the center of the city, intending to make his way to Smolny, which, he had been told, had been hit a number of times earlier in the evening. However, as he neared the center his car was engulfed by a flood which swept down the street. He managed to get out of the machine and up a flight of stone steps above the water level where he learned that a heavy German bomb had pierced the principal water main, flooding a whole block of buildings and cutting off access to them. What was worse, fire bombs had been dropped and people were trapped in the blazing buildings. Every effort to get through the flood waters had failed. The residents faced certain death—either by fire or by water.

Ivanov organized a group of firemen, soldiers and ARP members. They tied ropes around their waists and plunged into the water. In some places it was over their heads. But not everywhere, and they found the currents not so swift as they seemed. Half-swimming, half-floundering, half-drowning, the rescue party managed to cross the water to the burning buildings and form a human chain across the torrent.

The first floor was flooded, but above, flames garishly illumining their faces, appeared at the windows women and children, white with terror, gasping for air and screaming for help.

Ivanov fought his way into the building, up the flooded staircase. Here he came on a weird scene. In a large room, lighted only by the glare of the fire, filled with acrid smoke, was a group of twenty or thirty children. They were sitting on the floor quite calmly, their heads bent over their knees, and above the roar of the flames, the rumble of falling masonry and screams outside, he could hear a voice, reciting calmly, quietly and firmly: "Heads down. Breathe quietly. Hands at sides. Inhale. Exhale. Heads close to floor. Breathe in the pure air. Breathe out the bad air. Quietly. Quietly . . ."

The voice was that of Irena Galina. The building was a children's school to which she was assigned as an ARP worker. As long as he lived he would hear those calm, quiet words, rhythmically easing the children's fears and distracting their attention from the peril. Ivanov's men with no little difficulty managed to convey the children and the others in the building across the flood to safety. Irena was one of the last to leave, just as the fiery walls began to fall, hissing and sending into the air tremendous clouds of steam.

Ivanov had not recognized in this self-possessed, smoke-smudged, flame-seared woman the famous sculptress. Before he left the scene he shook her hand. "My name is Ivanov," he said. "May I know with whom I have the privilege of speaking?"

"Certainly, Comrade Ivanov," she replied with a wry smile. "My name is Galina. Irena Mikhailovna. We have met before."

And they were to meet many other times. As the siege of the city grew tighter and the suffering greater the spirit of this slender woman seemed to carry her everywhere. There was a day in October when the Putilov works was under particularly heavy fire. The great steel plant lay on the outskirts of the city, close to the German

91

advance lines. The Nazi guns were only a mile and a half from its sprawling shops. Many of the Putilov workers and some of their machinery had been evacuated. But not all by any means.

On this day the Germans seemed to have zeroed in on the plant. Shell after shell smashed through the broken roofs, exploding with a deadly whine in the machine shops. So heavy had been the fire that in the evening Ivanov himself went to the works to assess the situation. In an improvised hospital, lying on blankets spread out on the cold masonry floor, were twoscore youngsters, mostly girls. A dim electric bulb cast enough light to show that many of their bandages were soaked in blood. Some of the wounded moaned with the endless cry of the dying but, as Ivanov learned, there was no more morphine to ease their pain. Beside one girl, sitting on the cold concrete, resting the head of the youngster in her lap, a woman was murmuring quietly an old Russian lullaby . . . "Sleep, my baby . . ." the very one with which Ivanov's peasant mother had sung him to sleep. As he came nearer he saw the woman lift the girl's head from her lap and place it tenderly on the floor. Then she drew up the blanket over the youngster's face. The woman rose now, turning toward him, and Ivanov saw that it was Irena Galina, tears streaming from her face. She came up to him and silently put her head against his breast.

"Comrade Ivanov," she said, "I am sorry to be a weakling. I am sorry you find me crying. But I cannot help myself. That girl—so beautiful, so young—died with her head in my lap. One moment her blue eyes were watching me as I sang. Then, next moment she was gone."

This was only one of many, many visits Irena was to pay to the Putilov girls. She took the young factory girls under her personal protection. No matter what her other duties—and they were many —she managed somehow to get to the plant several times a week.

Yes, indeed, Ivanov had respected Irena Galina, and more. He had loved her as one loves a comrade in wartime. He loved her as one who stood staunch in those cruel days. Nor was he alone in that. Everyone who knew Irena Galina knew that she was all heart and spirit and flame. A real woman of Russia. A real woman of Leningrad.

And so, he said to himself, how did we reward her? How did we serve that courage, that spirit, that heart? We destroyed her. It was just as simple as that. He did not believe in telling lies to himself regardless of what he said to others. They might think him a tough old sturgeon who talked in nothing but Party clichés, who bowed his head whenever the Kremlin called, who toed the line, who spoke what he was told to speak. He preferred it that way. By far. Far less dangerous and far easier to live like a thick-shelled turtle than a thin-skinned hare.

Had there been any moment of doubt in his mind when the blow fell on Irena? He did not think so. Of regret—yes. But of the necessity for the action—not a doubt. After all, it was like a war. He had sent his closest friends on assignments from which he knew they would not return. He sent them to their deaths. He knew this. But the sacrifice was necessary if Leningrad was to survive. He did not know how the others had felt about the Decree on Art and the purge of the Leningrad intelligentsia which followed. For himself he knew perfectly well that it was directed against some of the finest, bravest men and women whom he had ever known. But he also knew that had they not been sacrificed it would have been worse. Not only would the *intelligents* have gone to the wall but along with them the whole Leningrad apparatus. By sacrificing some the rest had survived. Cruel? Of course. But life was cruel. He was a peasant and no one knew the cruelty of life better than the peasant. It had been a dangerous and delicate moment and another such moment was approaching. He could feel it in his bones.

It was time now that young Galin come in. He pulled out the side drawer of his desk slightly and felt with his hand to see if his Nogin was there. It was. He drew it out swiftly. Loaded and cocked as usual. There might be those who would call him old-fashioned and melodramatic. But you never knew who a man was in these times. *Kto kovo?* Dog eat dog—who gets whom? Who will be master, who will be victim? These were the questions which had crucified his whole generation in the Soviet Union. He did not suppose that when Nikolayev was admitted to Kirov's office on December 1, 1934, the Leningrad Party Secretary had felt there was the slightest danger of attack from a young man so obscure and so confused. But this had not prevented Nikolayev from drawing a gun and shooting Kirov dead. Ivanov did not believe Galin was a Nikolayev but he took no chances.

His secretary opened the door and announced: "Michael Maximovich Galin."

No, Ivanov thought, he had never seen this young man before. He eyed the boy closely as he walked with an air of defiant pride to the exact center of the room and, squaring his sagging shoulders almost like a soldier reporting for duty, stood before Ivanov. The Party Secretary did not rise and he kept his hand on the revolver concealed in his drawer. There was a wild gleam in Galin's eye, and the stained sheepskin, the worn *valenki,* the gray fur cap had the smell of Siberia all over them. Ivanov directed a piercing glance at the boy and did not speak. Galin stared back a moment, then dropped his eyes in confusion.

"Excuse me, Comrade Ivanov," he said, betraying his nervousness by twisting his cap in his hands. "I am carrying out a mission in behalf of my late beloved mother, Irena Galina."

He hesitated, obviously uncertain as to how to proceed. Ivanov saw that the boy was not only nervous, he was also half-dead with fatigue. There were harsh lines on his face and a muscle in his jaw quivered intermittently.

"I'm sorry, Michael Maximovich," Ivanov said, not unkindly. "I did not know about your mother."

"We are burying her tomorrow," the boy said. "At the Volkhov cemetery."

"I'm sorry," Ivanov repeated. He actually was sorry and he was embarrassed. He was a blunt man and the impulse was strong within him to tell this boy that his mother had been a brave, fine woman. Such a remark, of course, was out of the question. This youngster was not play-acting—of that Ivanov was certain. But this

94

did not mean he might not be the unconscious pawn of some hostile force.

The boy was speaking again: "My mother once said that she respected you and that she never had forgotten those moments during the days of the blockade."

Ivanov cleared his throat. There were many questions he would like to ask young Galin but the quicker he could get him out of the room the better. He must put the matter in Chaikovsky's lap—and swiftly. He supposed the young man would have to be arrested. He could see no other alternative.

"We would be pleased if you felt that you could attend the funeral, Comrade Ivanov," the boy said. "But we understand how busy you are and all that. . . ."

His sentence trailed off uncomfortably because the secretary, in response to Ivanov's hidden touch of the buzzer, had appeared in the doorway and was saying: "Comrade Ivanov . . . the meeting is about to start."

Young Galin looked at the assistant, then back to Ivanov and began to edge uncertainly toward the door.

Ivanov cleared his throat, gestured vaguely with one hand and said: "Yes . . . yes . . . As you see I'm very busy."

Not five minutes later the telephone was ringing—Smirnoff's call.

Ivanov rose and started down the corridor to the room where the meeting of the Party Bureau was to consider the Narvo project. Yes. His antenna had not played him false. Something was up. And, if he were any judge, the Galin boy had no more idea than the man in the moon what was going on. In a way he was sorry that the meeting would delay his call to Chaikovsky but in another he was not. He had not the faintest doubt that Chaikovsky knew all about Galin already and, as for himself, he could use a little more time to order his thoughts and try to figure out from which direction the danger was likely to strike.

14

The meeting had been under way for nearly half an hour when General Orlov arrived and took his place beside Secretary Ivanov. In one sense his arrival was not a surprise since his aide-de-camp had appeared and said that he would be slightly delayed and to go ahead without waiting. What was surprising—and here Ivanov's antenna immediately picked up unusual vibrations—what was surprising was that the General himself had decided to be present. To be sure the interests of the Leningrad Defense Command were deeply and directly involved in the proposed housing development. As Schapiro, the architect who had prepared the detailed plans, was just beginning to explain, the project could only be carried out with the approval and the collaboration of the Leningrad Command.

Orlov murmured an apology as he took the chair at Ivanov's right at the head of the long table with its cover of green baize. There was a brief pause. Schapiro halted in his presentation. Orlov's aide hurriedly whispered in the General's ear, briefing him on what had gone before. The General was a rather tall man with a figure which was growing somewhat more angular with age instead of filling out in the classic beefy pattern of the Russian General Staff.

He wore rimless pince-nez, and with his iron-gray hair, his erect and intelligent appearance could have passed as an academician had he not been wearing his uniform with its broad shoulder boards and embroidered collar. Like most military men of high rank he was accustomed to the fact that his appearance invariably caused a slight stir, and if he even noticed this he no longer paid it any heed. He had bowed stiffly in a military way on his entry and had said good evening to Ivanov. Now he was toying with a cigarette box as his aide rapidly spoke to him, checking off points on a small pad of paper with a red-colored lead pencil.

Ivanov looked around the table, adjusting his antenna again and rechecking his impressions. No, he was not mistaken. Each of the men present was precisely the man he had expected to see—except for Orlov. There was Morozov, who was the chief architect of the Narva project; there was the Party Secretary of the Narva Gate region; there were the two other Party Secretaries, one for construction and one for political affairs; and there was the deputy of the Security department for political questions. The chief of City Construction was present, in an advisory capacity—he could speak but was not permitted, at this point, to vote; there was Schapiro, who was, of course, the appropriate man to make the detailed presentation; there was Ivanov's own special assistant and there was the editor of the Leningrad *Pravda*, who was a member of the Party Bureau.

Everything was as it should be—except for Orlov. He was a member of the Bureau. His military command was directly involved in the project. And yet, by custom, he ordinarily would have sent his Chief of Staff to represent him.

"Excuse me, comrades," the General said. "Please don't halt on my account."

The General turned to Schapiro: "Please continue."

Schapiro went back a few paragraphs in order to begin again with the question of the involvement of the military. Actually, it was a simple matter but an important one. The proposed project was considerably more elaborate than most. It was, indeed, an innovation in Soviet practice. What was suggested was the creation of a large park in the center of which would be located a series of low-rise apartment buildings on a site which would follow the natural contours of the land. By damming a small stream, a series of ponds and park areas, following the water course, would be created. The opportunity to construct such a project of beauty and architectural unity within the city boundaries of Leningrad was unique. It arose from the fact that the entire region had been pulverized by German bombardment and had lain untouched up to this time, awaiting a decision on how it should be rebuilt. In the interim the military had taken advantage of the vast rubble fields to install a large, important and permanent unit of the city's defenses, incorporating not only antiaircraft and radar units but also some underground installations of very secret nature. The existence of the underground installations, Ivanov was well aware, was known to only two persons in the room, or possibly three—himself, Orlov and perhaps the Security representative. If the Narva project was to be erected according to the plans drafted by Schapiro and Morozov the military installations would have to be removed to some other location. This would be expensive and complicated. It was most desirable that they be located as close as possible to the great industrial complex which adjoined the Narva Gate region. But where they could be shifted to Ivanov himself just did not know. It was possible that Orlov had come to the meeting because of concern over the installations, but somehow, watching the General listening to Schapiro's presentation, the Party Secretary felt certain this was not the case. He had sat through numerous meetings with Orlov. He knew his mannerisms as well as he did his own, and when he saw the General take off his pince-nez and tug soberly at the lobe of his ear he knew beyond peradventure of a doubt that the General was under some secret inner tension, and it suddenly occurred to him that he should be able to guess precisely what it was. How stupid he was not to have realized it before! If his mind continued to work on such a level of dullness he certainly would not survive very long. After all, he knew perfectly well that Orlov had once been Irena Galina's lover. He knew more than that. He knew that the sculptress had personally extracted from Orlov his pledge of honor not to intervene at the time of the Party decree and her banishment to the East and he suspected that Orlov had come very close to violating that pledge because of his love for Irena.

Ivanov sat completely motionless at the head of the table. His eyes seemed to have retracted into his skull. The dull light of the heavy chandelier (half of its bulbs missing) cast a shadow over his almost bald pate. His hands, perfectly quiet, lay on the green baize in front of him, one on either side of the pad of white paper placed geometrically before him. The half-dozen red-colored pencils, freshly sharpened, stood untouched in the glass holder. He did not make a habit of scribbling on scratch pads or of taking unnecessary notes. Every little gesture was apt to give away something to someone. In public as in private he cultivated a Buddha-like appearance. He knew that it was said he did not possess a nerve in his body and he also knew that this was not true.

So . . . he thought to himself. This is beginning to work out although where it will lead God knows. Orlov was nervous. Orlov had been visited by the Galin boy. Was that why Orlov had unexpectedly shown up at the meeting? Yes, Ivanov thought. Almost certainly yes. He had come, the Party Secretary felt certain, in order to have a private and seemingly casual word with him. Something about Irena Galina. The plot was thickening.

Ivanov looked around the room. There was no reason to expect to encounter any other abnormal phenomena within this group. And yet you never knew. The ramifications of the unknown led in unknown directions. He studied his companions closely, well aware that none of them realized that his eyes, now narrowed to gimlet width, were upon them. Schapiro had outlined the military problem (as he envisaged it—knowing nothing about the secret installations) and was proposing a substitute location. Ivanov glanced at the Security man—an Armenian named Sarayan with bushy eyebrows and a shaved skull that looked blue-black in this light. The

99

Armenian had learned well the lesson of self-control. He kept his eyes on the pencil holder in front of him and did not look up or show the slightest special interest as Schapiro offered the substitute military site. Ivanov could make nothing of him. Sarayan was the kind of man who could rise and tell the whole company that it was under arrest and not betray the slightest sign that he was about to act. What of his own subordinates, Ivanov wondered. When something was in the wind they were likely to be the first to pick it up— they had to be to survive. He had been watching the Party Secretariat with the closest attention in recent days. And he studied each of the Party Secretaries present with careful concern. It might be that he was mistaken but he thought he detected a bit of inner nervousness in his own deputy—the way he tugged at his coat sleeves. Granted he had done this a thousand times in Ivanov's presence. He was a nervous man and this was his characteristic mannerism. But wasn't he a little more nervous tonight? Ivanov could not decide. He listened to the editor, who had interrupted Schapiro with a question. The editor wanted to know what plans there were for housing the people who would be displaced from the proposed new defense site. Schapiro carefully explained that the persons on the site were not actually occupying housing. They were still living in the cellars of destroyed houses which had been fitted up for temporary occupancy with stovepipes aboveground, and since the numbers were small he felt certain housing at least as good—if not better—could be made available by the City Housing Bureau. Had Schapiro asked the City Housing Bureau about this? the editor persisted. No, Schapiro confessed, he had not. This was not really within his sphere of competence, but he would see that the proper inquiries were made. The editor subsided, a gleam of triumph in his eye. He had made his point. A small one, but one which, should he choose, might be magnified. Bureaucratic laxness. Failure to pay attention to communal living needs. Ivanov could write the editorial in his mind he had read it so often. Was the editor's questioning a bit sharper than usual? Did he bore in for the kill a little harder than was justified? No, not really, Ivanov told himself. It would not do to make mountains out of molehills and it was just as dangerous to see shadows where they did not exist as to fail to observe them when they were present.

He passed over the others. None of them was close enough to the source of power to possess clues of tangible value. His eyes, still hooded, went over the room again carefully. Had he missed anyone? Suddenly he gave an almost audible grunt. In fact, to cover himself he cleared his throat and coughed slightly. For some reason, perhaps because Morozov was sitting just at his left, he had not included the Chief Architect in his survey. What a mistake! Morozov was obviously controlling himself with difficulty. He had a handkerchief balled in his hand and occasionally he passed it over the back of his neck and around his forehead, on which, as Ivanov saw, light perspiration was standing. This was puzzling—why should Morozov be nervous? Could it be that some aspect of the Narva project touched on a politically sensitive nerve? That is, some aspect other than the secret installations? Did Morozov know of the secret installations and did this guilty knowledge (for even though Morozov was a military architect the security restrictions were so strict that he should not have known of the installations) cause him to be nervous? Was the nervousness connected in some way with Orlov's presence? The Party Secretary could not say for sure but he had certainly seen no signs of tension in Morozov until after Orlov appeared. Had Orlov's nervousness in some way been communicated to Morozov? The Secretary studied both men carefully. Yes, it was something about the General which was linked to Morozov's condition. Now that his attention was alerted he could see Morozov's gaze returning to the General, again and again. Why, the man could hardly keep his eyes off the General! And unless Ivanov was greatly mistaken the two men had in some way exchanged a secret look of recognition—or sympathy. His eyes blinked. Yes. That was it, sympathy. Mutual sympathy. And why not? They had, Ivanov realized, good reason. For certainly Morozov had been as close to Irena Galina as the General. Of course, it had been years earlier at a time when Ivanov was still an obscure Party worker, slugging his way up through the factory schools out in the Urals. But he knew of it as he knew or tried to know of every little nugget of gossip or information about his people. So . . . that was how the wind blew. They both knew of Irena Galina's death. But neither of them knew that Ivanov knew. When the meeting ended, he was certain, as certain as he could be of anything, Morozov would have a quiet word with Orlov. And he was just as certain that Orlov would have a quiet word with himself. And then what? Ivanov wished he knew.

Schapiro had finished his presentation. The construction men spoke briefly, chiefly about financial costs, materials and labor availability.

Then it was Orlov's turn. He was not prepared to give a final reply but he spoke warmly and well. The concept of the project was creative. It was typical of the Leningrad spirit. Leningrad, as always, must give the lead to the nation. The military was ready to do their part. The military would never forget the aid the city had rendered during the days of the blockade. The bond of unbreakable unity had then been forged. The city and the Army were one. The project presented some difficulties. Certain technical difficulties. But he hoped they might be overcome. After the sacrifices which Leningrad had made for the Army the Army must repay the city in kind.

There was a polite and pleasant murmur after Orlov ceased. He spoke in cultured tones and his words were as gracious as they were sparse. Even Ivanov, old bear that he was, felt warmer.

It was up to Ivanov now and he picked up where Orlov left off. The Party had carefully considered the Narva project. The design was sound. It combined practicality with beauty. The cost was not, on the whole, excessive. Naturally, housing must be found for anyone displaced. There were, as the General noted, certain technical difficulties. If these could be overcome he felt certain that Party approval could be given. He would so recommend to Moscow.

He paused and Morozov spoke up, a little embarrassed.

"I'd like to present one more aspect of this project," he said, "one which Comrade Schapiro touched upon briefly. As you all know this project had its origin in the dark days of the blockade. The first design was placed on the drafting board by the late Architect Slansky who died in January, 1942. We would like to honor Architect Slansky in some way, to memorialize his courage and imagination in those darkest of days."

"Your proposal is entirely admirable," Ivanov said. "Did you have something in mind?"

"Yes," Morozov rejoined. "Architect Schapiro and I have been discussing this matter. Of course, the simplest thing would be to erect a statue or bust. But we believe another approach would be more suitable. You will notice that in his original plans Architect Slansky gave the project a title. We would like to incorporate his title in the contemporary version."

"What is the name which Comrade Slansky attached to the project?" Ivanov asked.

"He called it," Morozov replied, "The Northern Palmyra project." Ivanov pondered a moment.

"Very well," he said. "If there is no objection I suggest that we accept Comrade Morozov's suggestion. I propose the tentative approval of the Northern Palmyra project with the understanding that General Orlov and I be detailed to work out the technical difficulties and, in event of successful solution of these problems, we will present it to Moscow. Do I hear any objections?"

Ivanov looked about the room. Morozov smiled with pleasure. Orlov looked grave. The other faces—like Ivanov's and the Security man's—were expressionless.

"Be it so ordered. The Northern Palmyra project is tentatively approved," Ivanov said. "Meeting adjourned."

15

By the time Ivanov returned to his office it was close to 10:30 P.M. The secretary followed him in and set on the desk a glass of tea and two irregular lumps of sugar on a saucer.

"Has anyone called?" Ivanov asked. The question was pure formality. Had anyone important, that is to say, had Moscow called, he would have been interrupted at the meeting.

There had been no calls of consequence, his secretary assured him. Ivanov sat down at his desk, put a lump of sugar in his mouth and began to suck his tea through it. He did this a little noisily. He was aware that this was not the most cultured way of drinking tea but this was the way he had learned to drink tea in the *izba* of a small gray village not far from Smolensk where he had been brought up and he did not mind advertising his peasant parentage and his closeness, despite his role of Party Secretary in a great and sophisticated city, to the Russian soil of his birth.

It was time that he was talking to Chaikovsky but he wanted to think things through a bit further. Haste was not a virtue in a world of cautious men. He sat sideways in his chair and gazed up at the colored portrait of Stalin in generalissimo's uniform on the wall behind his desk. This was the only decoration of his severely formalized office, an office exactly like ten thousand other offices in Russia. Ivanov had been at substantial (but carefully concealed) pains to make certain that there was not one aspect of it which a visitor would ever be able to recall as revealing the slightest trait of individuality. His desk was of some kind of dark wood, possibly mahogany, with a green-colored desk pad, a rather elaborate desk set made of mottled Urals stone—an inkwell, a stand for pens, a stone blotter, a little covered jar (God knows what it was for—but it was included in every one of the sets) and a shallow tray for pencils. There were two telephones on the desk, one with an old-fashioned nickel-plated receiver and one of a conventional bracket design. The bracket phone was the direct Moscow line. His desk was clean of documents and papers. Before he admitted even the most casual subordinate every paper and file was carefully replaced in his drawer. In front of his desk was a table covered in reddish baize with curved leather armchairs on either side and a larger chair directly facing him. On the table there was a single bile-colored ash tray of the same soft Urals stone as his desk set and a water carafe on a glass tray and two glasses. There was no other furniture in the room except for a big Soviet safe, which was painted dark green precisely like at least a hundred thousand other safes in the offices of Party secretaries, collective farm chairmen and factory managers throughout Russia. This was always locked and closed and not even his secretary had ever been in the room when Ivanov opened it. Actually, there was not much in it. Some of the intra-Party reports which were circulated only for the eyes of secretaries like himself but which he was required to preserve for reference (unlike the numbered reports which had to be returned to the Kremlin under special seal), Party membership and dues statements; a petty cash box; the Secretary's large rubber stamp (the most precious possession of a Soviet office) and a few confidential files—but nothing of a personal nature, for Ivanov knew perfectly well that the Security services possessed a key to the safe and he assumed they checked its contents periodically just as he assumed they checked the contents of his desk, of his overcoat pockets and every inch of the plain and ugly apartment in which he lived with his plain and ugly wife.

There were lemon-hued draw curtains at the windows of his office and heavy drapes with a kind of paisley pattern (not that Ivanov would have known what a paisley pattern was had he been asked) which were drawn as soon as night fell. Ivanov did not use his office for conferences—the conference room was next door. His room was paneled to shoulder height in Karelian birch and finished in eggshell plaster above that. There was a center chandelier, somewhat complicated, with insets of blue glass as well as crystal, the product of the Leningrad porcelain factory. Similar chandeliers illuminated most of the larger offices in Smolny. There were two bracket lights on the wall and a small desk lamp with a green shade on his desk. The carpet was of a standardized Turkey-red pattern which was supplied to Soviet offices from Tadjikstan to Brest-Litovsk.

It was, Ivanov felt, the perfect office for a Soviet official. He did not flatter himself. There were, he knew, men far more clever than he in the Party. But he did not suppose many of them had acquired greater skill in blending into the background, in effacing their personality, in robbing enemies of any easy hold or lever. As for his personal appearance—he could walk down any street in Russia and everyone who saw him would know that he was a Soviet official and to each person he would seem somewhat familiar but a moment later if you asked them if they had seen Ivanov pass they would look up puzzled and uncertain. He was as familiar to them as log huts with thatched roofs, as dirt roads leading off through the forest into nowhere, as the goats tethered beside every village in Russia.

Ivanov was sixty-four years old, but with his shaved pate, his smooth skin, his expressionless face, his placid yet powerful physique he could as well have been forty-four or fifty-four. Unless you knew him you would not be certain precisely how old a man you were dealing with and he would offer you no clue in his conversation. He had been thirty-two years old when the Revolution broke out, a member of the Bolshevik party since he made his way to Petersburg not long after the events of 1905 and got a job in the railroad yards. Even then he was steady, cautious, conservative, careful, determined, ambitious and clever with the cleverness of peasant Russia. He knew then the basic lesson of the peasant— never say "No" to your superior, always tell him what he wants you to tell him, never fail to demonstrate that you are clumsy and not too bright—but never seem too stupid—and in general you will be able to do things pretty much your own way. Ivanov never attracted the attention of the Czarist police and he attracted very little attention from his more dynamic Party comrades. But, as the years wore by, he became known first in his own little circle in the railroad yards and then in a gradually expanding sphere as a man who seemed able to carry out tasks at which others failed.

He got his first real education in the Party factory schools out in the Urals after the Revolution and gradually began to rise in the Party industrial apparatus. He was nearly fifty at the time Kirov was assassinated and had recently returned to Leningrad in a position of local importance. In the rapid shifts and purges of the 1930's he moved rapidly up the ladder and by the eve of the war had become a wheelhorse of the Zhdanov organization—one of the Leningrad secretaries on whose broad backs fell the task of getting the city through the peril and suffering of the hunger blockade.

He was now, as he fully realized, as far as he was likely to go— and, indeed, he had no real ambition to go further or higher. His ambition was much more modest. It was simply to survive. And for the moment this ambition was specifically focused on getting through, perhaps, the next forty-eight hours. All the protective coloration in the world was not going to preserve him if he did not succeed in discovering what was involved in this Galin affair.

As yet, he was not much further along than he had been. Orlov and Morozov, as he anticipated, had exchanged a few private words as the meeting broke up and then Morozov had departed with an air which Ivanov described to himself as one of determined resignation—or resigned determination—the look of a man who is going to do his duty but knows that the consequences are likely to prove fatal. In this, he thought, cynically, Morozov was not likely to prove mistaken.

The General had then approached the Party Secretary.

"This is only for your ears," Orlov had said. He spoke soberly and seriously. "We have been comrades for many years."

"That is right, Constantin Constantinovich," Ivanov replied, adding the conventionality he was certain the General expected. "We have come through some tight places together."

"Because of that," the General said, "I want to tell you something in strict confidence. Irena Galina is dead. Her son has brought the body back to the city and she will be buried tomorrow."

"Ah, yes," sighed Ivanov. The sigh was as far as he would go, even with the General. There was not a more steadfast man in Russia, Ivanov knew. But even with Orlov he kept his real feelings, his real opinion of Irena Galina, to himself.

The General was now tugging at his ear and then, a clear sign of his inner disquiet, he almost dropped his pince-nez.

"You must know, Gregory Ivanovich," the General said, "I am going to attend the funeral. I realize there may be a certain fuss over this."

"A certain fuss." Yes, Ivanov thought, there surely would be. The only question was what kind of a fuss. There was no point in trying to dissuade Orlov. He knew the General perfectly. This was a matter in which Orlov felt his honor—his honor as a man and as a Soviet officer—was involved. He would attend the funeral if he had to crawl on hands and knees across a minefield.

Ivanov sighed again. "Yes. Yes. Of course. I suppose there may, as you say, be a certain fuss. Yes."

Orlov hesitated. There was apparently something he was going to add but he changed his mind. "The funeral," the General said, "will be at the Volkhov cemetery at noon. I've told no one else. But I wanted you to know—just, well, just in case . . ."

"Thank you, Constantin Constantinovich," the Secretary said, pleased to see one of the Party Secretaries coming toward him and utilizing the other man's approach to turn a little abruptly from the General, thus avoiding the necessity for shaking hands with him—an act which might well be subject to misinterpretation as the "certain fuss" developed.

Now, Ivanov told himself, the question was how to put the matter most effectively to Security Chief Dmitri Chaikovsky. First of all, it was absolutely certain that Chaikovsky knew everything that Ivanov knew. Chaikovsky would know that young Galin had been to see him. He would know that Galin had seen Orlov and Morozov. He would know that Galin had talked to Smirnoff. He would know— or at least suspect—that both Orlov and Morozov planned to attend the funeral. What more might he know? On the operational level he would have a complete report on Galin's activities. But even Chaikovsky might not know who had set Galin in motion or what the motivation was—but perhaps he might have a considerably better idea of this than Ivanov. Chaikovsky should know, for instance, whether this was a scheme aimed directly at Ivanov or whether there were other victims on either a higher or lower level.

There was no use trying to trick Chaikovsky or wheedle information from him. Trickery he would recognize and resent. Wheedling merely demonstrated weakness at a moment when weakness could not be afforded.

No. The only approach must be direct, blunt and a little stupid —precisely in what Chaikovsky would consider to be the "Ivanov manner."

He asked his secretary to get Chaikovsky on the wire and a moment later picked up the receiver to hear the Security Chief's high-pitched and rather pedantic voice.

"Good evening, Dmitri Trofimovich," Ivanov said. "Tell me— how is this Galin affair being handled?"

"The . . . the . . . Galin affair, you say?"

Ivanov smiled inwardly. This had worked better than he had anticipated. Chaikovsky had been caught off guard. Ivanov deliberately said nothing, letting the silence build, letting Chaikovsky real-

109

ize that he, Ivanov, knew perfectly well that Chaikovsky was fully apprised of the Galin affair.

The pause was portentous but Chaikovsky was finally compelled to break it.

"Yes . . . well, Gregory Ivanovich," Chaikovsky said. "Of course, I was going to telephone you a little later about the Galin matter."

Chaikovsky paused and Ivanov grimly listened silently. He was going to make that bastard Chaikovsky come to him if he had to drag it out of him. Obviously Chaikovsky realized that Ivanov had retreated into one of his characteristic bull-like silences, for he now went on: "I've been in touch with Moscow, of course, and they have just come through with instructions."

I'll bet they have just come through, Ivanov thought. I'll bet they came through a week ago and you have been sitting there on your stone ass waiting for the case to develop.

"They've just advised me," Chaikovsky resumed (as though, Ivanov thought, Chaikovsky had read his mind, a quite likely possibility. If he, Ivanov, knew Chaikovsky's character so well it was reasonable to assume that Chaikovsky knew Ivanov equally or almost equally well). "They've just advised me that they regard this as a state matter of the first importance."

"Obviously," Ivanov permitted himself to say, and then fell silent to compel Chaikovsky to go on.

"Moscow has requested, Gregory Ivanovich, that we exert extreme care not to reveal that the matter has attracted special attention," Chaikovsky said. "They wish it to be carried out without interference. Thus we can observe the full ramifications, participation and sentiments of those involved."

"I see," said Ivanov slowly. He did not like the sound of this at all.

"For that reason, Comrade Ivanov," said Chaikovsky, "I was instructed to convey to you the opinion that it would not be wise to indicate in any way a negative attitude."

"Yes," said Ivanov, aware of what Chaikovsky was driving at but somehow trying to halt the train of his thoughts.

"What is meant," Chaikovsky continued, "I believe, is that we are not to discourage participation in the ceremonies. Treat the whole thing normally. In other words it is thought best that those of us who have been invited should not raise the alarm among others by failing to show up."

The son of a bitch, Ivanov thought. The bastard!

"Good, Comrade Chaikovsky," he rejoined, his voice as blunt and expressionless as it had been at the start. "You know best, of course, and if that is what Moscow wants that is what will be done."

His voice booming in most comradely style, Ivanov added: "With you on the scene everything will be in good hands."

"Thank you for your confidence," replied Chaikovsky. "Until tomorrow."

Ivanov replaced the receiver with as firm a hand as he had taken it off the hook. He noted this, particularly, because, if the truth were told, he was badly shaken. That bastard Chaikovsky! He had really broken it now. If he had ever heard of a gold-plated, triple-jointed provocation this was one. The effrontery of it was simply dazzling.

"Until tomorrow!" That did it. The very words he had used earlier this evening on the spur of the moment to that unspeakable rat Smirnoff. A lot of good it did to disassociate himself from Smirnoff when he had just been politely told to put his head into the very same noose that had been constructed to fit Smirnoff's throat. And as for his clever maneuver of not shaking hands with Orlov—hell! He might as well have clapped him on the back and invited all present to join them tomorrow at the funeral.

He looked at his big paws before him on the desk. Big they were, and strong, and tough. They had shoveled a lot of manure in their day. Cow manure. Horse manure. And human, too, if you want to come down to it. They had dug coal and they had dug potatoes. They had wiped engines and, a few times during the Revolution, they had killed men. And there was one other time, too, during the war—but he had no special desire to think about that tonight.

Kto kovo? Who was behind this machination anyway? Who was plotter and who was victim? By the way, he did not even know to this moment what kind of a plot it was.

What good was his peasant brain to him anyway? Was there a way of escape? If so the path certainly lay through stupidity and not through cleverness. Through peasant boobery. Carrying out orders. But doing it in such a blundering and imbecile fashion that when the net was closed you were branded a nincompoop, a tool rather than a prime mover. Better a thousand times to be called a fool; pilloried as an idiot for the delectation of the clever; subjected to the most painful humiliation—better all this, better to lose job, Party privilege, even Party membership; better to be compelled to make your way back to the deep provinces again; or even in a pinch to taking Kazakhstan or Siberia—better all of this than going to the wall.

And, by God, Ivanov knew in his bones that the wall was what was involved here. There was too much devilish ingenuity about it. It smelled of those dark and evil minds that populated the Kremlin. Ivanov hated to think of such things. He had a peasant's superstition about the Kremlin. Better not even to think about what went on there. Yet he could not keep his mind off the horrible possibility, the horrible suspicion, that actually it might be Stalin himself who was involved in this.

He tried to halt the chain of thought. But it was irresistibly carrying him on. After all—who had really been responsible for Kirov's death? Ivanov had heard all of the old whispers, the half-voiced insinuations. Who could have been behind it? Certainly the police had had a hand in it. And certainly the Kremlin knew what the police were doing. And, once you started thinking in that direction, what about those strange things that happened in the first months of the war? He had seen them. He knew that Zhdanov and the others had, too. Why had it taken so long to get the civilian side of things organized in Leningrad? Why had the Kremlin blocked the plans to organize the people for a siege, a blockade, a long street-by-street defense? Why had the orders come in as late as September—

September, mind you, when transport with the Great Land, the Big Earth, as Mainland Russia was then known, had already been cut off? Why did Leningrad keep getting orders: ship food, ship meat, ship grain, ship munitions? Why? Why? Why had Leningrad been forced to send by plane from out of the flaming circle of the siege special guns, special arms for Moscow in October? Why had Leningrad been forced to fly troops out to Tikhvin to break the Nazi stranglehold on the rail line which would have choked the city to death within three weeks? Were all these things sheer chance? Or was there someone in Moscow who deliberately was planning the destruction of Leningrad—who feared Leningrad, who hated Leningrad?

Why had Kirov been killed? Was it sheer chance that he had been the Leningrad leader—and popular as well? Ivanov knew as well as anyone the deep roots of hostility between Leningrad and Moscow; the eternal fear in Moscow that Peter's city might once again become Russia's capital; the special fears of the Party about the "Leningrad question," the intellectual ascendancy of Peter's city over the traditional peasant center of Moscow; the ever-recurring Moscow worry at the "Western" orientation of Leningrad.

Not the least of reasons why Ivanov had always been at such pains to advertise his peasant origin, his muddy boots, his closeness to the Russian village and the Russian soil was his instinctive knowledge that the Kremlin did not trust anyone who was too closely identified with Leningrad. Nor was he the only one. Why had Zhdanov, to put it openly, made a public sacrifice of Irena Galina if not to blunt any insinuation that he, too, had acquired the special Leningrad taint?

Now Zhdanov was dead. And now the specter was rising again. The menace was clear and present and Ivanov could feel it. The conviction was overwhelming. Someone feared Leningrad. Someone hated Leningrad. Someone was ready to go to any ends to satisfy that hatred and quench that fear.

Ivanov found himself suddenly shivering—an actual physical chill had gone down his back. It could not be! And yet when you went back over some of the things which had happened there was more than enough to make a peasant wonder.

But, he told himself, this was no time for looking back. This was a time for working out every step of his action for the future. Blind, stupid obedience to orders. That must be the line. The first thing to do was to call in his secretary and tell him to cancel the meeting of the regional Party Secretaries which had been set up for noon.

The buzzer brought the secretary on the run.

"Advise the *raion* Party Secretaries," he said. "The meeting for tomorrow noon is postponed to 4 P.M. I've got to attend a funeral. And tell the other members of the Secretariat, too. Moscow's instructions."

The man gasped. "A funeral, sir?"

"Yes," Ivanov grunted, "a funeral." He hoped it would not be his own.

16

Dmitri Chaikovsky narrowed his eyes in concentration. There was something about his conversation with Party Secretary Ivanov which did not ring true. What could it have been? He ran over their brief give and take. Not Ivanov's bluntness. Not his tactic of silence, which forced Chaikovsky to take the lead in speaking of the Galin matter. Not that. This was Ivanov's copyrighted technique. Chaikovsky had known the Party Secretary for more than fifteen years and had been through that routine again and again. No. It was something else, but for the moment he could not quite put his finger on it. For that matter there was something about this whole Galin case which made him nervous. His instructions were clear and simple enough but what lay behind the affair was another matter. He had thought of hardly anything else since the call had come in from Moscow only a little more than twenty-four hours ago. One of the Deputy Security Chiefs told him that young Galin was arriving on the Leningrad section of the Urals interconnection express and that he was accompanying the body of his mother. The train was due in Leningrad at 8 A.M.

"I see," Chaikovsky had said. "I presume you wish me to take

Galin into custody and make appropriate disposition of the body."

"No," said the Deputy Chief quickly. "No, Dmitri Trofimovich. The matter is a little more complicated than that."

In essence his instructions had been to place the young man under surveillance, report quickly to Moscow on precisely what he did, with whom he met and, if possible, the nature of his conversations and, by no means, to give away to anyone that Galin was under observation.

The instructions had not proved difficult to carry out. If only, Chaikovsky sighed, he could comprehend Moscow's intentions so easily. He himself had been waiting in a dark corner of the icy train shed when the express pulled in. He had half a dozen of his best men on hand. Two of them with white porter's aprons had been assigned to assist in moving the coffin when, as inevitably he would, young Galin sought assistance. The train arrived in a cloud of hissing steam and Chaikovsky took advantage of the confusion to draw nearer to the baggage car. He recognized young Galin immediately, with his hawk's face, his nervous scanning of the platform, his impatient leap from the open baggage door and his tug at the rope handle of the plain pine box which contained his mother's body. Chaikovsky also caught a flashing grimace of recognition from one of the baggagemen and knew, as he had correctly anticipated, that regardless of what Galin might think his trip had not been unattended.

Chaikovsky's two porters approached the car and began to barter rudely with Galin over their fee. Chaikovsky was not close enough to follow the argument but he could see the hard, desperate look which came over the young man's deeply lined face and noted the ominous movement of his right hand to the worn but bulging pocket of his sheepskin jacket. The porters apparently sensed Galin's mood for the argument suddenly broke off, Chaikovsky saw the flash of a fifty-ruble note as Galin's hand emerged from his pocket and the two men with much tugging and straining began to pull the coffin from the car and onto a small hand truck.

It had been three years since Chaikovsky personally had sent young Galin to the East. The sentence was an extremely mild one, one year at labor to be followed by four years of forced residence. The other members of the gang of currency speculators had gotten terms of seven and five and the ringleader had been sent out for twenty-five years. The comparative leniency with which the boy had been treated was, of course, due to the prestige and influence of his mother. There had been intervention at a fairly high level in that case, as Chaikovsky well remembered. Indeed, the surprising thing about the Galin matter was not the short sentence but the fact that the boy had been implicated and tried in the first place. The truth was that there had been no very convincing evidence touching on his participation. To be sure when the plainclothesmen went to Irena Galina's studio they had found in Michael's room $50 in old United States gold notes, a small book of Indian pornographic drawings (which Chaikovsky still kept behind the collection of official statutes in the green-curtained bookcase in his office) and a pair of American-made women's silk stockings. Michael had readily admitted that he obtained the bank notes from the leader of the gang, a certain Sasha Schmidt. He said he had gotten the American money in return for a pair of fur-lined flying boots and a heavy British flight jacket which had been given to him by his mother. She had received the clothing, he said, from an American friend.

Chaikovsky happened to know that this was the literal truth. To be sure such transactions were against the formal letter of the law. But if everyone in Russia who violated the law about trading in clothing, foodstuffs and currency had been arrested there would have been no one left to serve as jailors. It had been quite a different matter during the days of the Leningrad blockade. Chaikovsky remembered with physical satisfaction arresting a fat red-cheeked woman in November, 1941—a time when to be fat and red-cheeked in Leningrad was prima facie evidence of violation of the cruelly inadequate rationing. This woman worked in the bakery storehouse and she with four others had regularly been carrying out of the storehouse in their fat *sumki* a kilo or more of wheat flour a day.

The woman and her comrades were tried before a people's court. It was an open trial but so cold was the day and so weak and preoccupied were the people that not a handful turned out to witness the proceedings. The five women were sentenced to death, and within two hours under Chaikovsky's orders the sentence had been carried out and the five bodies were cast into a common grave just beyond the municipal burying ground. It was one of the last graves that was dug until the spring of 1942. From then on the bodies piled up like cordwood around the cemeteries, mortuaries and, indeed, as Chaikovsky well knew, even in the frozen, cluttered courtyards of the old houses.

It had been, then, somewhat strange that young Michael Galin had been arrested and even stranger that he had been sent off to the East—to a camp not far from Tashkent, as it developed.

Chaikovsky had never discussed the case with anyone. Instinctively, he knew it was in some way sensitive; the kind of case in which it was better not to interest oneself. He had let it follow the prescribed routine. Trial was before a troika—a three-judge court made up of three officers of the Security service. Sentence had been determined before the boy came before the trio. In fact, the order for the sentence had been sent from Moscow.

Moscow's motives were often so complex that it was better simply to let matters take their course. When, a year later, the affair of Irena Galina broke like a bombshell Chaikovsky thought he understood why her son had been sent out to the East the previous year. It had been in the nature of a warning—a warning, obviously, which the famous sculptress had ignored.

The denunciation of Irena Galina and her subsequent exile to Tashkent had not been handled by Chaikovsky although he had directed some of the technical details—her arrest, sentencing to forced residence and transport to the East. However, in all of this he was merely acting as an agent, carrying out orders transmitted to him by Moscow. He had, naturally, made a very careful inquiry into her associations, her friends, contacts, past history, etc. This was standard police procedure, but the case against the sculptress was not what he would describe as a police or security case. It was a political-ideological case and it was not really so much a matter of her being the target as of her being a figure on a very complex chessboard, a queen's knight being sacrificed for a purpose which only later would become apparent.

Not that anyone had told this to Chaikovsky, nor if you searched the security files would you find one atom of evidence to support this thesis. But Chaikovsky knew the dynamics of Soviet power better, perhaps, than he knew the rhythm of his own pulse. No one had to tell him when so prominent, so talented, so important a personage as Irena Galina was struck down that the blow was directed not, actually, against her own comparatively nonpolitical self but against the political structure, the political environment, the political arrangements which had permitted her to flourish. Nor was he one whit deceived by the fact that the author of the blow against Irena Galina was Zhdanov himself, and his wheelhorses of the Leningrad organization: Smirnoff, head of the Writers' Organization; Ivanov, the city Party Secretary, and all the rest. Perhaps better than almost any other man in Leningrad Chaikovsky understood the interaction between Leningrad and Moscow, for while he had lived and worked in Leningrad for years his big boss was in Moscow; in any conflict (and conflicts, no matter how well disguised, did invariably arise) his loyalty inevitably and absolutely was to Moscow.

Thus he knew that whatever ambiotic responsibility might appear to exist between Moscow and Leningrad in the Irena Galina case that the move had been forced upon Leningrad because of the crushing competition of factions within the Kremlin; and that, in essence, the Leningrad group was seeking to demonstrate by the public sacrifice of one of its most beloved idols that it was, in fact, more catholic than the Moscow Pope; that the sword of the inquisition would cut deeper and the flames of the execution pyre would rise higher in Neo-Orthodox Leningrad than in Old Orthodox Moscow.

True, Chaikovsky did not put his thoughts in precisely such

119

language. But this was their essence, and it was because of the existence of these high-level political interrelationships that his role in the Irena Galina case had been little more than that of an interested, a deeply interested observer.

The truth was that Chaikovsky admired Irena Galina—not as an artist, not as a sculptor (although she had done his bust and he was secretly proud of this fact and proud of the tough and sturdy appearance which she had given to his slightly doughy physiognomy), not as a woman of talent. No. Chaikovsky's admiration was direct and primitive. He admired her as a woman. He admired her body, her deep breasts, her heroic carriage, her strong hips, her straight back, her firm legs, the steel clasp of her hands.

Looking at her made him excited, made his breath come quicker, and she knew it—devil that she was. She knew it and enjoyed it—and laughed at him.

"What's the matter, Dmitri Trofimovich?" she asked him once when she was doing his bust. There was a gleam in her eye and the hint of a smile on her lips.

"You know perfectly well what the matter is," he said doggedly. "I'd like to throw you on the bed right now."

She laughed—a silver peal that tightened his throat and sent quivers down his back.

"Oh, Dmitri Trofimovich," she said. "You're too sensitive. Don't excite yourself so."

And when the bust had been finished she threw her arms around him one day and kissed him on the lips—the warmest, softest lips he had ever felt.

"You're such a bulldog, Dmitri Trofimovich," she said. "Such an ugly bulldog."

He had not resented that. In fact, he had felt proud to inspire any reaction from her. He knew very well that she was not for him. But he felt, too, that she liked his being excited; that she was a real woman; that she expected men to react to her sex; and enjoyed it when they did. She was honest and frank with him and (within certain limits) he was honest and frank with her.

When Michael had been arrested she came to see him.

"We've been good friends, Dmitri Trofimovich," she said. "You know that if you can help Michael I will never forget it."

Chaikovsky knew what she meant. She meant that if he could get her son released she would sleep with him. It was as great a temptation as he had ever encountered. He looked at her for a moment. He saw a vision of her white breasts, the red-brown nipples, the white strength of her arms, the roundness of her belly and the fullness of her hips. He felt her for a moment in his arms and a shudder came over him. For a moment he blinked his eyes closed and then sighed.

"Dear Irena," he said, the affectionate term escaping him before he could call it back, "I wish that I could shake your hand and tell you that we had made a bargain. But I must be honest. There is nothing I can do."

Her face flinched as though it had been struck by a whip. Then she stretched her hand to his.

"You are a good friend," she said. "You are the best kind of friend because you tell the truth."

"I'm sorry," he said. He felt a blush creeping over his face. God knows how many years it had been since he had experienced this sensation.

"So am I," she said. "More sorry than you know."

She turned then and walked swiftly out of his room, a tall, sinewy figure in black coat, small black hat and black gloves. As she passed through the door he glanced down at his hands to see his fists clenched and white, his nails digging into the palms of his hands until they almost drew blood.

"More sorry than you know." The words had echoed through his mind again and again. "More sorry than you know." To Chaikovsky they meant, they could mean, only one thing. She had not been proposing a cold, commercial exchange, a transaction of alien bodies, a trade of favor for favor. It had been an offer made in the warmth of her woman's body, her woman's heart. She had *wanted* him. And because of that and only because of that she had made the suggestion. But Chaikovsky knew that it was a suggestion which never would be renewed. That the moment once passed never would recur again. That as long as he lived he would endure the pang and ache of a longing which could never be satisfied. So it had been, too. He had not seen her again. Not even when the charges were brought against her, when the public demands arose for her shaming, when the flames of the auto-da-fé began to rise higher and higher.

He had done one thing—but only one. General Orlov had come to him with a request that she be permitted to go to Tashkent as her place of forced residence so that, at least, she might be near her son. He had looked at the orders for her deportation and found that no specific area had yet been designated. The next day in casual conversation with his deputy he managed to raise the matter in such an oblique fashion he was certain the deputy never realized when he wrote down "Tashkent" as the place of exile that the suggestion had come from Chaikovsky.

Now Irena Galina was dead. The wheel had come a full circle but it had not halted. A new and strange chapter was opening up. What kind of chapter? What would be its conclusion? Chaikovsky wished he knew. He had gone back over every facet of the case of young Michael. He had studied the charges against Irena. He had reread the investigators' reports of the associations of each.

What could one make out of it all? The young man obviously was of no political consequence. Shortly after his mother arrived in Tashkent he had been permitted to go and live with her there. Not all his friends and associations were politically reliable—but what did you expect in Tashkent, where half the Russian population had been exiled from one place or another—and many, many of them from Leningrad. What of Irena? Of course, her friends and associations read like a bluebook of Soviet aristocracy. There was literally almost no one in high office or position in Leningrad (or Moscow, for that matter) with whom she had not been associated. So far as the time in Tashkent was concerned—a blank. It was quite plain that this last episode, the scandal, the denunciation and exile, had finally done what nothing else had been capable of—broken her heart and spirit.

What of his instructions to give young Michael his head, to permit him to go about the city freely and without interference? Chaikovsky turned through the reports of his plainclothesmen with frustration. He had it all there. He had every movement the boy had made —the carrying of the coffin over to the morgue on Marat Street; the visit to the cemetery; the arrangements for the burial; the hectic trips around the city to invite people to the funeral; the calls on Morozov, Ivanov, Smirnoff, Orlov, himself, on all of the others (and, as far as Chaikovsky knew, the boy was still at it this evening). What did it all add up to? His instructions were to give the boy complete freedom, to report every movement to Moscow, not to interfere in any way so that the full scope of the affair could be exposed. But what was "the affair"? This was where Chaikovsky ran up against a blank wall. What "affair"? Naturally, he could not ask since this would be an indictment of the most damning nature against himself. It would be the same as signing his own death warrant. For if there were an "affair" certainly the chief security officer in the city was the man of all men who must know its nature. Yet, as he studied the lists of persons whom young Galin had visited, as he thought back through what he knew of each, he could not, for the life of him, see any common denominator, any link which bound them together, other than association of one sort or another with Irena Galina.

It was possible, he had to admit, that there was something about young Galin that he did not know. That Galin had associations which put quite a different aspect upon the whole matter.

He thought again of the old man, Secretary Ivanov. He thought he understood now what it was that he had sensed in Ivanov's conversation. The old man had his wind up about this matter but he was going to enormous pains to indicate that he was in no way disturbed; that he was just his usual bluff, uncommunicative, walrus-hide self. That was it, Chaikovsky felt certain. And if the old man had the wind up it almost certainly was because he, too, could not see exactly what was involved in the case, and if Ivanov couldn't puzzle it out then certainly something very deep and very sinister must be at work because that peasant brain of Ivanov's had a ratlike ability to gnaw right through to the marrow of a secret, no matter how thick a bone of security surrounded it.

He must, of course, advise Moscow of the call from the Party Secretary. He rang the Deputy Chief in Moscow on the direct wire and in a moment was listening to his quiet, curiously musical voice.

"Ah, very good, Dmitri Trofimovich," the Deputy said. "Everything is in good hands. That I can see."

"What are your instructions for tomorrow?" Chaikovsky said.

The Deputy paused. "Tomorrow, yes, indeed, that is a very good question. What would you propose?"

Chaikovsky was certainly not going to commit himself on that.

"I'm at your service," he interjected quickly.

"Hmmm . . ." The Deputy seemed for a moment to consider. "Well, yes. I think we will proceed in the following fashion. No move before the funeral service. None whatsoever. But we must be ready to act at any time."

"Certainly," said Chaikovsky. "I have my best men already assigned."

"Be sure that you do," the Deputy said, a little iron coming into his voice. "We will send a small party, too. In fact, they are already on their way. On the night train. We will join hands, then, in the morning, and be prepared for any eventuality."

Chaikovsky replaced the receiver and began vigorously to rub his right eye. When he was nervous this eye had a tendency to twitch and this was precisely what it was doing now.

He should be prepared for any eventuality. Very well. Apparently arrests were going to be made after the funeral. But whose arrests? And on what charges? He must confess he could not even at this late moment predict with any feeling of assurance.

17

Morozov had been walking with General Orlov through the snowy Leningrad streets for almost ten minutes. Both men were silent, apparently lost in their thoughts, but presently, Morozov knew, the General would begin talking in his laconic fashion. Orlov was not a man of many words. Stone Face he was sometimes called in the Army although Irena had smiled when, once, Morozov had asked her how she managed to carry on a conversation with him.

"Words aren't everything, Georgi dear," she replied. "You know that. Some men talk with their eyes. Some with their hands. Some, well . . . in every sort of way."

"Of course," he said. "But don't those long silences get a little boring?"

Irena chuckled in a recollection of shared intimacy.

"Georgi," she said, "silence can be more eloquent than all the words in the language."

Morozov agreed but he had reservations where Orlov was concerned. Orlov was a man whom he respected, a man whom he admired. But, still . . .

"The difference between Constantin Constantinovich Orlov and every other man whom I have met," Irena once said, "is that he is the only man whom I completely respect and completely trust. If he promised to bring me the jewels of the Kremlin I know that he would do it—even if he had to burn down Moscow. His real distinction is that he never speaks a word which he does not believe and he never makes a promise which he does not know he can carry out."

There had never been the slightest doubt in Morozov's mind of what had attracted Irena to Orlov. He was the symbol of security in a world which seemed to be founded on quicksand. The passionate, dramatic and tragic culmination of her romance with Maxim Voronsky, Voronsky's spectacular abandonment of her and his subsequent suicide, had shaken her to the depths. Morozov was often at her side in those days. He had held her in his arms and heard her say in a voice, small as a child's: "I am going to die. Very soon. Why should I live in this terrible world?" He had tried to comfort her but nothing which he said seemed to make any difference.

"Let me go, Georgi," she said to him. "Don't try to keep me here. I know you mean well. But it is not kind of you. To go on living is to suffer more than I can bear."

He had talked of her boy, so slender, so serious, so handsome. He had talked of her work—of the magnificent group which she had conceived for the Paris exhibition, of her forthcoming trip abroad. He had even talked of himself.

"Dearest Irena," he had said at the end of one long despairing evening. It was October, the rain had been pelting at the windows since five o'clock and Irena was lying in the great mahogany bed of her chamber. The only light came from a small candle which illumined the ikon of the Virgin Mary in the corner. He could hardly see the face of the Virgin and the Mona Lisa smile which the ancient painter had bestowed upon her.

"Dearest Irena," he had said, "I know that life means nothing to you. Not now. I understand. But if life no longer seems worth living to you—please, please think of others. Think of your son. Think of me. What would my world be without you?"

She lay silently against the pillows, her eyes staring lusterless into the gloom. Her pale face was shadowed and if she had heard or comprehended his words there was not the slightest sign. He took one of her cold hands and stroked it gently.

"Dearest Irena," he repeated. "Don't go away from the world. We need you. I need you."

Quietly Irena began to cry. The tears formed in the corners of her eyes and dropped one by one to her cheeks, slowly coursing downward like the first drops of a spring shower. Outside, the wind moaned in low tones and the branches of the old linden tree in the courtyard creaked and scraped against the cornice of the roof.

"Believe me," Irena finally said in a voice so low that it was almost a whisper, "believe me, Georgi dear, I don't want to hurt you. I don't want to hurt anyone in the world. I never have. But I don't know how . . . I just don't know how to live any more. I can't go on."

That night Morozov had stayed with her until nearly three in the morning; until finally she had dropped off into a sleep of exhaustion and her breath came in deep, long draughts. He watched for a while at her side. It was a troubled sleep. Sometimes she moaned and once he was surprised to hear her chuckle—the close, intimate chuckle he once had shared with her.

Finally he had risen, stiff and cramped, and tiptoed out of the room. Old Shura, her housekeeper, was cradled in a sofa. She awakened at Morozov's footfall. He put a finger to his lips and she nodded acknowledgment. Then he silently emerged onto the street. It was still raining and, of course, there were no cabs. He walked all the way home.

It was not long thereafter that Constantin Constantinovich Orlov appeared in Irena's life. It was one of those providential meetings which, in retrospect, seem inevitable but which actually arise out of sheer chance. Orlov, just back from the Civil War in Spain, was walking one afternoon with young Cheprikov, the aviator, just back from his famous flight to Alaska. Irena had done Cheprikov's bust after the young airman's rescue, a year previous, of the Swedish explorer Hansen from a drifting ice floe.

As they walked down the street Cheprikov suddenly exclaimed: "Good heavens, here we are at Irena Galina's studio. Let's drop in and say hello."

Orlov declined. He was shy and the prospect of meeting a famous sculptress terrified him. But the airman insisted.

"Oh, come on," he said. "She is a wonderful woman. It's only proper to call on her now that we are at her house. We'll just stop a moment and then go on."

Reluctantly Orlov agreed and they knocked at her door. Had either of them any notion of the emotional crisis through which Irena was passing they would never have dreamed of visiting her. But they knew nothing of her affair with Voronsky and, indeed, only had vaguely heard of Voronsky's tragic death.

Old Shura answered their knock. She saw before her two handsome officers—Cheprikov, blond, snub-nosed, cheerful-faced, of medium height and typical Russian countenance, and Orlov, tall, slender, very tall, indeed; grave-faced, dark-haired, already marked with an air of quiet confidence and command.

It was Cheprikov who spoke: "Excuse me," he said. "I am Commander Cheprikov and this is Commander Orlov. We would like to pay our respects to Irena Galina."

Shura did not hesitate a moment.

"Please come in," she said, and before Irena quite knew what was happening Shura was ushering into the bedroom the two officers, the one gravely handsome and shyly silent and the other gay and jolly with bubbling spirits which seemed to fill the room with sunshine and against which the dark shadows of Irena's soul could not contend.

The afternoon sped by like lightning. Shura brought in tea and some of her own strawberry jam, "the best *varenye* in the world, if I do say so myself," as she assured the company; twilight began to fall, and when the two officers finally excused themselves, Irena was surprised to hear herself telling them they must drop in again.

That was how it all began.

When Morozov called later that evening he found Irena more at peace with herself.

"I do feel better, Georgi dear," she said shyly. For the first time Morozov felt that she was not going to succumb to the miasma of her emotions.

"She told me once that I had saved her life."

It was Orlov speaking, breaking the long silence of their walk through the almost deserted winter streets of Leningrad. Morozov looked up at the tall figure, striding with military precision, his boots snapping down on the snowy pavement as regularly as if he had been drilling on the Champs de Mars. Morozov was tall himself but he felt small beside this straight-backed military man, his six-foot-two figure topped by a gray caracul general's shako on which a ruby star dully glowed. It was as though for a moment Morozov was a boy again striving to keep pace with the long strides of his father. And, as sometimes when he knew that his father had something difficult on his mind, something hard to talk of, Morozov felt a sense of embarrassment, a desire, somehow, to help this silent man to say what he wanted to say. Orlov had suggested that they ride back together from the meeting at Smolny and then had dismissed his car almost outside the Smolny gates, telling his aide that he and Morozov would walk a bit together.

"A little exercise never hurts you," the General said, as they descended from the long black Zis limousine. "Keeps you fit."

And now at last the General was speaking of Irena. For "she," of course, was Irena. As a matter of fact, Morozov believed that Irena's statement was almost literally true. The General had saved her life.

"I believe," he said thoughtfully, "that Irena was not exaggerating. I saw a good deal of her at that time. I did not think she was going to get over the shock of Voronsky's desertion. She could not seem to get hold of herself."

Orlov looked at Morozov swiftly and then walked on, increasing his pace a bit. They were going straight down the Litenny Prospekt,

129

directly into the snow, which slanted into their faces like small pellets of lead. The night was growing colder. Only a rare food store, here and there, was still open, its lights burning feebly behind opaque windows. Occasionally, a lonely streetcar whined down the center tracks, its windows too frosted for them to know whether it was empty or filled with passengers. Morozov could feel his ears beginning to smart. He hunched up the collar of his coat and tugged his fur cap a little lower.

Suddenly Orlov was speaking again: "Voronsky didn't desert Irena. She sent him packing."

If the General had struck Morozov across the face with his black-gloved hand the architect could not have been more amazed.

"What do you mean?" he said in bewilderment.

There was a long silence. Pace by pace they walked. Finally Orlov began to speak.

"I gave Irena my word of honor never to mention this," the tall man said slowly, each word coming out syllable by syllable.

"It is not easy to speak," he said, "but I think that tonight Irena would want you to know. She said once that she would respect my judgment; that the principal thing was that the boy was not to know."

Morozov listened in wonderment as Orlov's explanation poured out. There had been a fearful quarrel between Irena and Voronsky. It had been in the making for a long time, for several years, in fact. It had its roots in the great purge of the mid-thirties, in the charges which began to be brought against persons near and dear to Irena. Politics had never concerned her. Nothing, she thought, was more dull. When the trouble had begun, when political figures began to fall, she had been almost uninterested. But, later on, it was different. Persons whom she knew, writers, artists became involved. With the passionate intensity of her soul she wanted to help her friends. Voronsky, normally so rebellious, normally so fiery, urged caution. No doubt he was much more politically sophisticated than Irena. He knew the dangers whereas she was prepared to flout them. They quarreled repeatedly but each time she finally deferred to Voronsky's superior wisdom. He assured her that he was doing what he could: that it was better not to make a public protest; that by working quietly with "the right people" much more could be accomplished. She was restive and uneasy, but absorbed as she was in her great figure group—the one which became the central theme of the Soviet exhibit at the Paris fair—she did not press the matter to a conclusion.

"It was the case of Boris Bardin which brought things to a head," the General said. Boris Bardin was a children's author. His fairy stories had been recited by two generations of Russians, for he had been a well-known writer long before the Revolution. Irena was devoted to him. He was a friend of her family's. Not only had she been raised on Bardin's fairy tales but one of her first big successes was the famous group, based on Bardin's story, of a little girl leading an animal orchestra, the bear playing the bass fiddle, the fox on the flute, the rabbit at the drums and the bragging wolf on the trumpet. The group now stood in Moscow's Central Park of Rest and Culture. To Irena, Bardin was like a beloved grandfather.

When Irena learned that an ambitious young writer named Smirnoff had denounced Bardin, that the old man had been arrested and held for interrogation, she flew into hysterics, demanding that Voronsky go to the Kremlin immediately. He refused. He said it would do no good. He had been drinking and his tongue was rough.

"Keep your shirt on," he snarled. "Any move now would only do harm."

"Harm to whom?" Irena stormed.

"Harm to you and harm to me," Voronsky growled carelessly.

"Then let it do harm," Irena said. "Better be whipped as a man than kicked like a dog."

"It's too late," Voronsky said.

"What do you mean—too late?" Irena flared. "It's never too late to act like a man."

"I mean—like the virgin said—it's too late to do anything about it," Voronsky retorted.

"Why?" demanded Irena, a gleam of fear in her eyes.

"Because," said Voronsky, tossing back his shot of vodka, "because Bardin's dead. That's why. The old man's as dead as a stuck pig and there's nothing you or I or any other person can do about it."

Irena was silent a moment. Then she faced Voronsky. "Get out!" she cried. "Get out of this room, you peasant! You coward! I never want to see you again so long as I live."

When Voronsky tried to protest, she opened the door, clutched his shoulders with her powerful hands and physically hurled him across the threshold, slamming the door in his face.

"She told me about this in Paris," the General said. "She considered that she was morally and physically responsible for Voronsky's death. Nothing I could say ever changed her opinion."

No, Morozov thought. Nothing would have changed Irena's mind on that question. She was brutally honest with all persons and equally brutal with herself. Now, for the first time, he understood the depth of her emotional turmoil over Voronsky's death. Of course, she would have been upset in any event. This was only human. But it could have been no surprise to her or anyone else if Voronsky dashed off with a circus actress. Voronsky had not been physically faithful to Irena during the years of their love affair. She had not expected him to be. He simply was not so constituted. He loved to drink, he loved to carouse, he loved to pick up women and carry on wild drunken orgies, orgies which might last three days or a week. This was part of Voronsky, part of his flaming temperament, the wide expansiveness of his Russian nature. He was a man of the soil and he had the coarse tastes of the soil, as well, of course, as passions much finer. All of this Irena knew. All of this she accepted. He would not have been Voronsky without this. She had wanted him like this and because of this. He supplied something necessary to her. She herself was a product of sophistication; of gentle parentage; of artistic talents; of cultured background; of the drawing room and nuances. But she was something more eternal too, a woman, with all the earthy and primitive quality of woman. And Voronsky was the man who complemented her character. This was what he brought to her and this was what she wanted of him. It was she who had wanted the child, not Voronsky. She wanted it to be his child because she wanted it to have his strength and his passion as well as her quality and her fiber. He thought her naïve when she asked him to give her a child. But he was flattered, as well, and, for all his wild parties, for all his whoring and carousing, he loved her as he loved no other woman.

So, Morozov thought, it was a nearly fatal thing for Irena. And it was fatal for Voronsky. He simply had not been able to face existence without Irena or, what was probably even more fundamental, he could not face existence in the knowledge that she despised him as a man; that to her, no matter what he might do in the future, he would be a coward and a weakling. That would have been the insupportable thing for Voronsky. And so he had brought his life to an end in what he deemed to be the appropriate manner. Perhaps he was not even conscious of what he did. Perhaps it was just accidental . . . picking up the circus girl in Moscow . . . an acrobat, she was . . . starting out on a round of drinking . . . hitting the small cafés . . . the Metropole . . . boarding the train for the Crimea in an alcoholic glow . . . champagne bottles hurled out the windows as they roared across the Ukraine . . . the arrival at Yalta . . . the finest suite in the finest hotel . . . more drinking . . . the bedroom door locked all day and all night except to admit fresh relays of waiters with vodka and champagne . . . and chocolate cake . . . Voronsky was passionately fond of chocolate cake . . . and then that final morning . . . waking up with a hangover . . . ordering the girl out of the room . . . locking himself in the bathroom . . . the girl, worried at his strange conduct . . . coming back to find the door locked and the futile effort to break it down as Voronsky moaned . . . Hurry . . . Hurry . . .

What had he really said, Morozov wondered. Did he call for Death to hurry or for first aid? And did it really matter now? Perhaps not. Perhaps it only meant that Voronsky with his child's instinct, his child's cunning, had found a way to get quicker to the place where they all soon would be.

Morozov looked up at the General walking ramrod straight beside him. He felt tired. Very, very tired. It had been a long walk and the pace was swift. He touched his ears. The left one, as usual, had lost all sensation. It had been impossible to keep it from freezing ever since the time during the blockade when he came so close to losing not only his ears but his life, the time he had fallen on the long walk across the ice to Kronstadt and twisted his ankle.

"Yes," he said to Orlov. "I am sure you saved her life. I thought so at the time. And now I know that it is true."

They were approaching the Nevsky. Morozov lived only a stone's throw away in one of the big old blocks just beyond the Fontanka. He dearly wanted to go on home, to rest a bit, to collect his thoughts, to try to order his mind for tomorrow. But looking at the tall silent man beside him he was swept by a feeling of compassion. He knew with a sure instinct that Orlov wanted to be with him, wanted to talk more and yet hardly was able to articulate what was in his soul.

Morozov suddenly smiled at Orlov.

"It's been a long walk, Comrade General, and the air is crisp," he said. "You know, I live just on here. Won't you come up and have a glass of brandy? Something to ward off the frost."

"That's very good of you, Georgi Alexandrovich," the General said with a shy smile. "Very good, indeed."

They turned down the Nevsky, walked across the Anichkov Bridge, guarded as always by the great Klodt stallions, and then made their way along the canal and into a small *pereulok*. It was dark and filled with snow.

"Mind your head, General," Morozov said, as they entered the long passageway which led to Morozov's quarters. Stamping his boots and squaring his shoulders to shake the snow from his broad shoulder boards, the General followed closely behind the architect.

18

Morozov poured the brandy into two water glasses, good stiff drinks that glowed with an amber fire in the soft light of the room.

Orlov lifted his glass and stared deeply into it. He was silent for a moment and when he spoke it was as though he had returned from a long journey.

"Let us drink," he said. "Let us drink a toast to the bravest woman we shall ever know."

"I join you," Morozov said, lightly touching his glass to that of the General. As he drank he could not help thinking that in another's mouth the words of the toast would have sounded ceremonial, almost pretentious, and yet uttered by Orlov they had the dignity of simple truth. The reason for this, thought Morozov, lay in Orlov himself, for if ever there was a man whose life had illuminated the meaning of bravery it was that of this tall, inarticulate General.

There were those who gave to Party Secretary Zhdanov credit for saving Leningrad from the Germans. It was said that his single-minded doggedness, his total conviction that the city would never surrender, his insistence that Leningrad would not and could not fall, no matter what the cost in lives, no matter what the cost in suffering, no matter if every house should be shattered in ruins and every man, woman and child should perish of cold, hunger, disease or bullets—that this had provided that fateful margin which spelled the difference between victory and defeat.

Morozov of his own knowledge knew this was but the simple truth. And if, perhaps, he was more inclined to credit that fanatic determination to the people of the city at large, rather than to the man who led those people, this was, at best, largely a matter of emphasis. Because everyone who had lived and fought and survived in Leningrad during the ice siege knew that the stubbornness of Zhdanov was merely a symbol of the stubbornness of the people as a whole.

But what many did not know was that none of this courage, none of this stubbornness, none of this confidence would have availed Leningrad had it not been for the quiet bravery of the tall figure in a general's uniform who now stood in Morozov's tobacco-scented apartment, staring once more into the brandy glass which he held in his hand.

All the world had heard Zhdanov's flaming proclamation of August 21, 1941: The enemy is at the gate. . . . The question is of life or death. . . . Either the working class of Leningrad will be transformed into slaves and its brightest figures executed . . . or we will clench our fists . . . answer with a crushing blow . . . and dig for Fascism its graveyard in Leningrad.

But few, even in Leningrad, were aware of what actually had happened within the next twenty-four hours. Morozov did not know the whole story himself. He doubted that anyone knew it all. But he had heard parts of it at firsthand from some of the survivors.

It had begun on the evening of the next day a few hours after the "enemy at the gates" proclamation. At Kolpino, just outside Leningrad, stood the Izhorsk factory—one of the oldest, one of the most famous, a monument to pre-Revolutionary Pietersky capitalism. Like the workers of all the Leningrad factories the Izhorsk workers had formed their defense units; many had already gone to the front. That evening a meeting was in progress. The Party Secretary was reading to the workers the Zhdanov proclamation.

Suddenly, a tall, slim officer appeared in the hall and interrupted the meeting.

"Sorry," he said quietly, "for the interruption. But the enemy actually is at the gates . . . almost at the very gates of your own factory."

The hall stirred. The officer raised his hand for silence.

"Those who are ready to fight for Leningrad—please come with me. I think I can guarantee that we'll give the enemy a good fight. And if we die, well, we die in a good cause."

There were shouts from the workers: "Let's go. Let's go."

"Just a moment, comrades," the officer said. "Let there be no misunderstanding. If there are any of you who are afraid to die— just stay behind. I cannot promise that anyone will come back from this battle alive."

The calm seriousness of the officer's words gripped the men. Quietly they followed him out of the hall. The arms which had been assigned to the factory were distributed. Through the hot August night the workers marched forward, taking their places around a perimeter assigned them (as chance would have it) in an old cemetery, hastily throwing up barricades and tank traps across the highways. Behind them, luridly illumining the sky, great fires rose around Leningrad as Nazi planes attacked. Sometime during the night other officers appeared and the Commander vanished for a time. A few other units took positions beside the workers. At 5 A.M. the first Nazi scout cars appeared, silhouetted against the gray line of the sky. By 7 A.M. patrols of Germans were pushing into the cemetery under the rattling machine-gun fire of the Izhorsk workers.

By this time the quiet Commander had come back, taken stock of the situation, disposed the forces a little differently and then gone on his way again.

"I'll be back, lads," he said. "Don't let me down. Remember there is nothing between you and Leningrad. Nothing. Only you can hold the Germans out."

The officer, of course, was Orlov. Every word he spoke to the

137

Izhorsk workers was true. Nor was this the only hole in the line. The whole eastern approach to the city was wide open. There were gaps of a mile or two in which there were no troops, no defense dispositions. Nothing. The gates of Leningrad lay defenseless. The path to the Neva was clear. All the Germans need do was to keep moving and the Northern Palmyra was theirs. But as the advance guard of the panzers crawled up to the city's approaches that morning of August 22, they were met at Kolpino, at a dozen other points by determined clusters of men, training their fire upon the advancing armored columns. The momentum of the attack was slowed. All day long the armored columns probed and thrust. Here and there a machine broke through. But the main bodies did not penetrate. Not many of the workers who took up their posts in the Kolpino cemetery that morning survived to celebrate Leningrad's victory. But two and a half years later—nine hundred days later—when in January, 1944, the forces of Leningrad now commanded by Orlov himself finally rose up and hurled back the Germans, lifting the greatest, longest and cruelest siege which any modern city had ever endured, one of the jump-off points for the attack was the Kolpino salient. In two and a half years of fighting the Nazis had never managed to drive across the cemetery. The barricades thrown up that morning under Orlov's quiet precision had never been breached.

"I remember that morning well," one of the Kolpino workers had told Morozov. It was a year or so later and they were whiling away a long night in one of the snug cement blockhouses which had been built in the Kolpino sector at Morozov's direction.

"Commander Orlov was leading us down the road to take up our positions," the worker said, shifting his goat's leg cigarette to the corner of his mouth. "The sun was just coming up. We knew it was a pretty tough proposition. But I don't know. Somehow, we all felt this commander would manage to pull us through."

Just at that point, said the worker, "who should we see coming down the road but Yuri Danilov—as bright a lad as you would ever find, a great one for the girls, he was. He was wheeling down the road on his bicycle and he had a blue towel folded around his neck. You see, he had a big date for that evening and he was planning to go to the baths after he got off the shift and get slicked up before he picked up his girl.

"'Where are you going, lads?' Yuri asked. He was surprised to see us marching down the road so early in the morning with our guns and all. 'We're going to fight the goddamn Germans,' we shouted. 'Come on along if you're not afraid of dying.' 'I don't mind if I do,' Yuri said. 'The only thing is I haven't got a gun.' 'Never mind that,' one of the lads said. 'First one of us gets hit—you can have his gun.'

"'That's a deal,' Yuri exclaimed. He turned his bike around and began to follow us. It wasn't an hour later that the skirmishing started and he got his gun."

The worker sighed. "He was a great fighter, Yuri was. He never stopped for three days. Then he got it. Bit of a grenade came across and sliced him in the belly. We buried him there in the cemetery. Right convenient it was. That's where our lines were. We put his blue towel under his head for a pillow. Seemed only fair. After all, he never did get to take that bath."

How many Yuris there had been, Morozov thought. How many of those brave lads, so generous with their lives, so cheerful in the face of death, riding out on their bicycles to a shell-torn grave; strolling down the streets to a rendezvous with a burst of machine-gun fire; waiting patiently in the cold for reinforcements that never came; falling in the snowy fields, really never knowing what had brought death to them—a bullet or the silent frost or just a sudden weakness of the heart.

For them, for the Yuris, there had been just one Kolpino. For this serious, solemn man still pondering over his brandy glass there had been many Kolpinos, one after another, and each of them, as Morozov knew, he had faced with the same quiet determination that what must be done would be done.

"Bravery is not an uncommon quality in our city," the General said, finally breaking the silence.

139

Morozov nodded agreement.

"I think," the General continued, "that we expect soldiers to be brave. This is our training. Our tradition. But we expect ordinary men and women to be afraid, to show fear in the face of danger. Yet this was not true of Leningrad. In our city the people were as brave as the soldiers. Braver, I think. And the bravest of all were the women."

Morozov nodded. "In part," he said, "I believe that was because of the siege. After all—we were all in the boat together. Where else did the same streetcars run to the factory, to your apartment and to the front? I mean, of course, as long as they ran."

"True," said Orlov. "But excuse me for saying that I think there was another factor involved—the tradition of our city. I am a Russian and I have the pride of a Russian, but I know also that many of us, for all our pride, have the habit of deference, or submission, of bowing to a superior—let us say to a Czar, or perhaps to a German or some foreigner from the West. But we of Leningrad, we of Peter's city, if you will, we do not bow our heads. We do not have that habit. Our people of Leningrad have a pride, a special pride, and they did not betray it during the blockade days."

The General squared his shoulders.

"We have our principles," he said. "We know what we live for. And we know what it means to die. We know how to value our lives. And, to be sure, this was the special gift of the woman we both loved. She knew what was important in life."

And what of yourself, General Orlov? Morozov thought. You have your principles. You know what it is to die. Do you know what is important in life? Do you know—do you really know— why you fought so bravely? Do you know why a million men and women, a million living, breathing, loving, hating, suffering, enjoying men and women, boys and girls, lovers, friends, fathers, mothers, sons and daughters, babies whose mothers' teats shriveled up in their mouths, women who reached out in the night and found their husbands' shoulders turned to eternal marble, do you know,

General, why they all died? Do you know why all this happened? Do you know the reward of Leningrad's courage? Do you know the price your country sets upon your bravery and in what coin it will pay that price?

"Perhaps," said Morozov, "she knew better than we."

"Perhaps," said Orlov, "she did. She knew more about most things than anyone I ever met."

The General fell silent again and Morozov sipped his brandy reflectively. He wondered whether his companion even now really understood the implications of what had happened and of what was about to happen.

"You know," Orlov said suddenly. "At the time of Irena's trouble. I mean, in 1946. I wanted to go with her. I told her that I was resigning my commission. Indeed, I showed her my letter of resignation. It was ready to be sent."

"She refused to let you send it in," broke in Morozov.

"That's right," sighed the General. "I am ashamed to say this—we never had quarreled. But we quarreled bitterly over that. She said that it was not any use. That they would not permit me to go with her. That if I did resign I would either be arrested or forced to live in retirement at some designated place."

"She was right," Morozov said.

"I suppose so," Orlov said sadly. "She told me I was being quixotic. She said that everything was at an end. That she would die. That nothing could save her. That they had made up their minds to destroy her and that she would be destroyed."

"I know how she felt," Morozov said.

"Of course," Orlov said. "Excuse me. I know that you do. The terrible thing is that she was right. I did not admit it to her then because I could not help hoping that she was wrong. But she was not. As always, she was right."

Morozov nodded. He remembered suddenly the evening he had come back to Leningrad after spending the summer of 1926 on the railroad project, surveying the sites for coaling stations along the Turksib. It had been his first long absence from Irena in the four years of their idyll, the first separation except for an occasional week in Moscow. He had written her almost every day. God knows how some of the letters had gotten back—or if they had. Some of that Asian country had been God-forsaken indeed. In the back areas he would have sworn that the dark-faced tribes, the Kirghiz, the Kazakhs, the Tadjiks, whatever they were, had never heard of the coming of Soviet power.

Wherever he had been he had written faithfully and entrusted the letters to whatever route he could find. Once they piled up for two weeks before he finally gave them to a tough-faced, swaggering cavalry lieutenant who loved to boast how he "cut those Cossack officers right down to the ass" with his saber during the Civil War.

During all that period he had gotten exactly three letters from Irena—hectic, scribbled notes, a glitter of burning words, scattered across the page. And then he was back in Leningrad, sitting across the table from Irena, at the little outdoor café near the Finland Station, watching her serious face and listening to her grave words. They were both in their overcoats. It was September and the wind was so cold that no one else was sitting outside and the white-aproned waitress had retreated indoors. They sat over small glasses of green liqueur and he listened to Irena tell him that their love affair was over, that she would always love him and that he would always love her, that whatever happened in their lives each would always be first in the other's heart, but that she had fallen in love with Voronsky, that it was not the same and never would be the same as with Morozov.

"Dearest Georgi," Irena said, "you know that you are in my heart and you know that I am in your heart and you know that nothing can ever change that and nothing ever will change it."

"But, Irena," he had protested, tears in his eyes. "I love you. I can't live without you."

"Of course, Georgi darling, I understand," she had said. "And all our lives we will love each other. A deep, tender love. But for now and for some time we will have other persons in our lives, too.

142

And this will not spoil anything that we have had together."

"That's not possible," he protested hotly.

"Yes, Georgi," she said. "It is possible. And you will see that I am right. You think that if I love Voronsky I can't love you. You are wrong. I can and I will always love you. I will love you just the way I did that first afternoon when I threw my red ball under your bench in the Summer Garden. And you will love me as well. But there will be other women in your life, Georgi. I know that—even if you do not."

And again he had protested, angrily, fiercely, crying, almost hysterical. And she had looked at him gravely and said: "Georgi, dearest. You know it isn't true. You know that I am right."

And he had not admitted it. But inside of him, deep inside, he had known that she was right and, even more, he realized that he had known this even before he had gone away from Leningrad. But how he had known it he could not say.

"Irena was brave," the General was saying. "And she was very wise. Wiser than we men, and, I think, more gallant."

"She was a woman," said Morozov. "And women—when they are wise—have a wisdom which is deeper and sounder than ours."

"Tomorrow," said the General, "I will say a word or two in her memory. It is time, I think, that someone spoke for her and what she believed in."

He rose.

"Thank you," he said. "Excuse me for imposing on your hospitality. But sometimes a man has things within him which he must say. Until tomorrow."

"Until tomorrow," Morozov said. He stood a moment at the door. The wind had dropped but the snow was still falling lightly and the low-hanging clouds glowed luminously with the reflection of the city's lights.

Yes, Morozov thought. It was time that someone spoke. After all, life was not an empty gift that fell from heaven. It was not a free ticket on a summer's excursion. Life was love and honor and friendship. He had fought for his country and his city and for his belief.

143

And so had his comrades. Some had died of hunger. Others had fallen on the ice and never risen again. Some had bled to death on the street crossings and some had perished as a surgeon massaged their hearts. Some had died in the war. And some, like Irena, had lived on to die in peace. There had been much death and there would be more. There had been suffering and there would be more. But was this all to be as accidental as the casual life of animals in the jungle? Were some to live because they were strong and some to die, merely because they were weak? Did not the living carry on the banner for which the dying had shed their lives?

Yes, Morozov said to himself. The only meaning which life had was that which you gave to it. If you believed in life you must speak for it, just as you must, sometimes, die for it. He did not know whether General Orlov had thought of the penalty which he might incur in speaking for Irena. But he knew that this would have not the slightest weight in Orlov's decision.

Morozov suddenly thought of the Izhorsk workers, marching off down the road toward the cemetery with Orlov at their head on that hot and dusty August night. They knew the chances were they would not return, but somehow they had felt that with this quiet officer at their head even death would not be an ordeal. Morozov smiled. It was curious, but he felt very much the same himself.

19

Morozov had never married and now, reflecting on that thought, he was more than ever glad. His only tie was to Ludmilla, his secretary. He would try to spare her in so far as he could the consequences which were certain to flow from the events of the next few hours. In truth there probably was not a great deal he could do except to keep her in entire ignorance of what was about to happen. This gave his conscience a cruel twist. Yet he knew that Ludmilla's innocence was best protected by a lack of knowledge so basic that it could not help but impress an interrogator. Any words of parting, any words of caution, any special gesture which he might make would be paid for not by himself but by this faithful, guileless woman.

The apprehension that had swept over Morozov after his talk with young Galin had been dissolved by the evening's events and in its place was a mood of quiet acceptance of the sudden turn. The hour was late when Orlov left, but Morozov had no particular desire for sleep. The feeling was strong within him that he would not soon again have a moment for peaceful contemplation and there was much that he wished to think about. It had been his habit over the years, periodically, to sit down and review his life; assess his accomplishments; analyze his feelings; draw up some kind of balance sheet of his own private affairs. He had often done this at New Year's time.

The thought of New Year's brought a smile to his lips because it brought to him the recollection of the first deliriously happy New Year's Eve Irena and he had spent together.

The had gone to a little café on the Nevsky with some friends, had drunk champagne, had walked home through the snowy streets, singing songs, arms about each other's shoulders. Now, back in their little attic room, they were looking out the dormer window at the silvery roofs of the city, phosphorescent in the soft light of a late moon.

"Oh, Georgi," Irena said, clasping his hand in hers. "You don't know how happy I am tonight—here with you where I have longed and longed to be."

He softly kissed the nape of her neck. As always her hair smelled like fresh-cut hay.

"And, Georgi," Irena continued, "you don't know how unhappy I was a year ago in Paris. All I could think of was: will I ever get away, will I ever come back to Petrograd, will I ever see you again?"

She had spent her last New Year's with two other Russian girls, art students like her, daughters of good Petersburg families who had gotten out of Russia about the time of the Revolution or soon thereafter.

"We were so unhappy—all of us," Irena said. "One of the girls' sweethearts had been killed, fighting with Denikin. The other had just quarreled with hers. And as for me—well, you know what it was with me."

The girls amused themselves in the traditional Russian way. They told each other's fortunes.

"First," Irena said, "we sat around a table. On the table was a sheet of paper with the letters of the alphabet in a circle. Then we put a saucer on the paper and our hands on the saucer. The saucer was supposed to spell out our fate. But nothing came out right. The words got all mixed up."

Then the girls lighted a candle and let the melting wax drop into cold water. Each twisted shape foretold a different future. A round ball meant a happy marriage. Many tiny droplets—children. Grotesque designs—unhappy love.

"The trouble was," Irena said with a wry smile, "none of us really knew much about telling fortunes. Always before we had some old aunt or governess to do it for us. We weren't good at all. It seemed as though each drop from the candle doomed us to a more tragic fate."

Finally they took a cut-glass bowl, filled it with water, put a diamond ring into the water, set a candle on either side of the bowl and peered into it intently.

"We stared and stared until our eyes were bulging," Irena said.

"And what did you expect to see, dear stargazer?" asked Georgi.

"Why, our future husbands, of course," said Irena. "Everyone knows that."

"And did you see me?" Georgi asked impishly.

"No, I didn't," Irena said. "And that was the end of the fortune-telling. All I saw was the diamond ring lying there in the bowl and little bubbles of air, tiny bubbles that had collected around it."

Irena had squinted and squinted, trying to make the image of Georgi's face appear on her retina. And when it did not appear she fell into despair. She began to think of the old superstition—if you do not meet a person on New Year's Eve, you will not see him the whole year out. At least she might have seen Georgi in the bowl! Another year without him, separated from him in distant Paris, began to open out in front of her.

"We went out on the streets after that," Irena said. "Paris is so gay at New Year's. Something like Petrograd—only gayer. It wasn't cold at all. Everyone was in the street. They were singing. Men and women were walking together, sweethearts were kissing on the sidewalks, in the cafés, everywhere. I was never so lonely in all my life. You don't know how unhappy I was in Paris. You can't imagine."

147

How had it happened? Morozov asked himself, as he so often had when in a philosophical mood. How could his golden romance with Irena have come to an end? True, they had remained close, dear friends throughout their lives. But the fairy tale of childhood had turned imperceptibly into the comradeship of an adult man and woman. Was it just a matter of maturity, of growing up? Morozov had never been able to analyze it exactly. But he thought that the seeds of the change had been sown in the four years, or nearly four years, in which they had been separated.

From that June day when they met in the Summer Garden Irena had been the princess and he had been her devoted courtier. Indeed, she had so called him. While she was four years younger than he she had from the first moment ruled his heart with a royal hand. Nor had this ever struck Georgi as in any way unusual. He had submitted to her sovereignty as though it was a law of life.

Their meetings were not long confined to stolen moments in the Summer Garden. Their parents were acquainted and if Irena was not quite so unchallenged a mistress of her home as she was of Georgi's heart she was far from being without influence. Not that she was a demanding child or spoiled by her parents. Rather, she was a reasonable, logical person, even as a youngster. She spoke with her mother and, more particularly, with her father, in serious and adult terms. Since both families spent the summer at the same seaside resort Georgi and Irena soon were meeting in each other's houses as well as on the sandy dunes of the beach.

Morozov's heart warmed as he thought of those distant and cloudless days. He saw himself strolling along the beach with his student's cap and schoolboy's jacket. Irena was sitting primly on the bench near the hotel, her auburn hair in plaits.

"Sit beside me, Georgi," she greeted him. "Tell me something interesting."

"Did you ever wonder how the gulls know that you are coming out on the beach to feed them bread?" he replied.

"No, Georgi," she said. "Not about the gulls. Something interesting. Something about us."

He knitted his brows and then began solemnly:

"We are going to grow up very quickly. Almost before you know it. Maybe before anyone even guesses—we will be grown up. And we are going to be married. I am going to come one night to your window. I will be riding a coal-black horse with silver harness. I will whistle—a low, quiet whistle. And you will leap over the window sill into my arms and we will ride away in the night. Across the steppe and deep into the forest to the far mountain, and there we will find a small house, all made of wood, with food and all furnished to live in. And no one about. Not for miles. And I will carry you over the threshold and take you in my arms and tell you that you are my wife forever more."

And while he told this story Irena looked at him with eyes that saw nothing but him, blotting out all the world—both for him and for her.

They had played and walked and talked and looked into each other's eyes all that long summer, and when fall came and they were back in Petersburg again, back to school, they found ways and excuses for seeing each other surprisingly often.

So it had gone—fetes, name days, holidays. Easter, Christmas. Shrove tide and visits to the country. There was never a question of another person in either's life. Irena liked to flirt—but only with Georgi. She liked to tease—but only Georgi.

"Tell me something funny," she would say. "It's so *skuchno* . . . so boring."

Georgi would dutifully relate an anecdote. He was very poor at remembering jokes and worse at telling them.

"You tell such bad jokes, Georgi," Irena would tell him. "Now tell me something sad. Tell me something terribly sad."

"But I don't want to tell you something sad," Georgi would reply. "It always makes you feel so bad."

This was true. Once he had yielded to her begging and told her of a terrible dream which he had had—a dream of how they had been in a small boat at sea. A great storm came up. Huge waves. Terrible lightning. The boat overturned. He reached for her hand. He could not grasp it. He touched it, white and gleaming in the dark water, but it slipped away from him and he felt himself going down, down, down into cold, black depths.

"Oh, Georgi," Irena had cried. "How terrible! I can see it all. The terrible black thunder clouds. The boat. The waves and you going down into the inky waters."

And she burst into tears. They were sitting in the large formal drawing room of her parents' home—a room with mahogany tables, big, dark, uncomfortable chairs, a French tapestry on the wall and some rather worn Oriental carpets on the floor.

Irena's mother, a quiet woman with rather severe manners, entered the room and exclaimed in some astonishment: "Irena! What is the matter?"

"Oh, Mother," she cried, rushing to her side. "I just saw Georgi drowning in the ocean. It was so terrible."

How could it have been, Georgi had often wondered, after a childhood so close that they ever had separated? The reason, he felt, must lie in those Paris years. True, he had gone to France himself but it was earlier and both of them were younger. When he had come back the war was on and Russia stood at the eve of the Revolution. Yet Irena and he seemed never to have been parted. The pace of events, his military service, the gathering political storm clouds, none of this affected their closeness, their dependence upon each other.

But the turmoil left its mark on their world. His father did not live to see the overturn of the Czar. He perished of typhus on the Galatian front in the autumn of 1916. His mother, already in bad health, survived only a few months. She was ill when the February Revolution occurred but she told Georgi: "How I wish your father could have lived to see this day. How proud he would be of Russia. Thank God we are finally beginning to emerge from the Dark Ages!"

So Georgi himself felt. He welcomed the February Revolution and cheered the October coup d'état. He was not a Bolshevik but he had no quarrel with Lenin's program. Not so Irena's family. Her father was a member of a good Petersburg banking family—not wealthy, not noble, but of the well-to-do bourgeoisie. The Galins were liberal but it was a liberalism of the Kerensky pattern, the Cadets, the Constituent Assembly. Bolsheviks, Lenin, Trotsky, Communism—all this to them was anarchy—wild and impossible.

At the first opportunity they made their escape to Paris and, of course, Irena was compelled to go with them. Already she was deep in the study of art and her parents, by no means wishing to sever the bonds which linked Irena and Georgi, advanced the idea that the journey to Paris was more or less a temporary one; that they would go to France and spend a little while, as the winds of Bolshevism blew themselves out; that in the meantime Irena could pursue her studies in Paris (as, in fact, had been planned all along) and then when the future was somewhat more clear the young people and, actually, the whole family could make plans of a more permanent nature based on a better understanding of the situation.

The project was too reasonable to argue against.

"After all, Georgi," Irena said, on the night before her departure for Paris, "after all, it is only for a little while."

The time was June. It was the month of the *bieli nochi*—the white nights, the season of the year when in Leningrad there is no real night; when at midnight you can read a newspaper in the street, and when at two-thirty in the morning a wafer-pale sun rises in a colorless sky and suffuses the sleeping city in mysterious illumination. Except, of course, that half the city is not asleep. Like Georgi and Irena it is strolling the wide boulevards, sauntering under the lime trees in a dreamlike state somewhat akin to sleepwalking.

Georgi and Irena were walking along the embankment beside the Neva, which lay quiet and as pale as the most distant horizon under the oblique refraction of the rays from the nocturnal sun.

"It will not seem that we are apart, Georgi," Irena said, "because each day will bring us closer together again. Each night we will come together in our dreams and I will kiss you."

Irena was braver than Georgi in that moment. He was oppressed with a feeling of separation, with a feeling that he was losing Irena before he had really found her, with a feeling that she would vanish into the distance and that all that would remain of her would be the echo of her low-pitched voice, the image of her slim figure, so erect, moving with such grace across the earth, the soft warmth of her shoulders, the tender molding of her breast and the faint, fading scent of new-mown hay which always lingered in her hair.

From across the water came the low sound of music—possibly students singing on a barge. Along the embankment there was the quick, bright clatter of horses' hooves and an open carriage swept up behind them and on ahead, the horses' feet moving in rhythm that echoed lightly against the wall of the palace and out across the water.

"Do you remember my crown?" Irena asked suddenly. Her eyes were more gray than green in the light of the pallid sun. She was wearing a dress of white and she looked like a young Ophelia against the dull granite of the embankment. She had worn white the day he made her the crown from golden dandelions. They were sitting in the later afternoon sunshine on the broad green lawn just outside the little Greek summer house at Gatchina. The lawn was yellow with dandelions and he had woven a circlet of them and placed it on her chestnut head. Then he had taken more dandelions and made bracelets for her arms and a necklace for the thin arc of her throat. She had made him a crown as well and, placing it on his head, said: "I crown thee my prince."

"I'm still wearing my crown," she said to him, her gray eyes full on his. "Do you see it? I'll never take it off. Never."

And he had looked into her eyes and promised that he would wear his crown as well.

It was nearly seven in the morning when they finally returned to her house. The luggage was already packed and waiting to go to the station.

Irena turned to him in the doorway.

"Please, Georgi, don't come to the station," she said. "Say good-by to me now. I could not bear it to stand on the train and feel myself being carried farther and farther away, seeing you on the platform, growing smaller and smaller in the distance."

He embraced her, pressing her lips so hard that she cried. "Please, Georgi. You're hurting me." Then he had wrung her hand and run down the step and up the street. He did not look back. He could not bear to.

So they had parted, and when they met again, when she returned to Petrograd after a fearful quarrel with her mother and father (her father had died soon thereafter but her mother, as recently as the end of the war, was still living in Paris, very old but still in good health), it was as though they had been separated only through a long night or a bad, interminable dream. And still, Morozov thought, perhaps there had been something else. Something in Paris. It never occurred to him in the time when Irena returned to him. He was too happy, too completely happy in the childhood dream come true, in seeing the fantasy world of the Summer Garden, of Gatchina actually come to life. He had not questioned Irena's return, had hardly asked her how it came about. And she had said little—beyond the fact that she had insisted on coming back; that there had been a terrible family row, her father declaring that if she came back she would cease to be his daughter, and other things too frightful to repeat or even think about.

"But, Georgi," Irena had said to him, "I had to come back. I knew you were waiting for me. And I knew—I had learned in Paris if I had never known it before—that there were only two things in my life which had any value. You and my work, my art."

There had been times when he had found Irena deep in thought, brooding, over what he could not even imagine.

He had asked her once when he came upon her in such a mood.

"What is it, dearest?" he asked.

"Oh, Georgi," she said. "Nothing real. Nothing that exists. But sometimes the devil catches my soul and gives it a twist."

He put his hands on her shoulders and held them firmly, their eyes meeting. Then hers turned away.

"You are so good, Georgi," she said. "You don't know how good you are. Shake me a little so I'll know that I'm not dreaming."

153

He gave her a little shake and she nestled in his arms.

"That's right," she said. "You are real. Nothing else is. That's what I dreamed in Paris and I didn't make a mistake."

Had those moods been a reflection of some profound event in Irena's life about which she had never told Georgi? Later on, after they had separated, after Voronsky had entered her life, he sometimes had thought about the question but it had been a futile speculation. The very first night she returned from Paris a terrible shadow had fallen over her face—something about her experience there. What might it have been? Now, he realized, he would never know. It was a mystery which would go to the grave with him along with other mysteries. It was surprising how many things in life never did really become clear to you. He had thought while talking with Orlov tonight of asking him whether Irena had ever spoken of her years in Paris. It was possible, after all, since it was in Paris, at the time of the Exhibition, that she and Orlov had become good friends. It was curious, yet he had always thought of them as good friends rather than lovers. Friendship seemed much more the foundation of their relationship than romantic attraction or the kind of flaming passion which had brought Irena and Voronsky together. But somehow, although he had been on the verge of asking Orlov about Irena's early years, he had drawn back. What, really, was the point of it now? Irena Galina was dead. Her life had ended. It had ended pointlessly, stupidly, in a manner that made no sense and contained no reason. Just as Russian lives so often had ended for so many years. As for himself—if he were to be honest—his own life had ended sometime in the past. It had not ended so suddenly nor perhaps so dramatically. It had been a piecemeal death. A part of him, he knew, had died when Irena left him, but in the warm relationship of their later years this had been obscured. Now it was quite evident. And, of course, these last few years, these years of Irena's disgrace and banishment, had drained his existence of meaning. In the morning Irena was going to be laid to rest. If there was any logic about life, it seemed to him, there would be two graves and a joint ceremony, for surely his existence had come to an end as well. It was only a curious Jovian jest that let him go on walking about in human form when the real spark long since had been extinguished within his body. Well, he thought, no doubt the gentlemen from the government's Security Department will do their best to make amends for this oversight at the earliest opportunity. And with such a quizzical thought in his mind Morozov lay down on his bed. The fear which had touched him earlier in the evening had vanished. He sank immediately into a deep and dreamless slumber.

20

The young man stumbled on the icy steps, almost falling, but catching himself just in time by clutching the iron railing. He was overwhelmed with weariness, so bone tired that the muscles of his knees trembled with each step. The flame of anger that had carried him so far seemed to be flickering out, leaving a void in his breast. For one terrible instant he felt himself on the verge of collapse. Then his hand went to his face where the blow he had just been struck still burned like fire. God! What strength the woman had —greater than a man's. He shook his head. It was clearing again and he could feel a little life flowing back into his exhausted muscles. There was no stopping now. He must go on. And on. He must. No time for weakness. He had come far but there was so much yet to be done. It was late and he had another visit to make, a distant one for, as he had learned, Nadya still lived in the old studio. A walk of several miles through the bitter night faced him unless he was fortunate enough to catch a bus. The likelihood of finding a taxi in this remote and already sleeping part of Vasilevsky Island was beyond the realm even of speculation.

Michael Galin walked through the dark street between the two rows of apartment houses, which seemed to press in upon the ill-lighted, ill-tended pavement. Snow stood in great mounds on either side and he picked his way down the center along an icy path worn by the procession of many feet. It was cold and the snow was falling steadily but he was hardly aware of his external physical circumstances. His thoughts were on the blow he had received and the tremendous anger of the woman whom he had just left. What a woman she was!

"She cradled him in her arms like a baby." He had never forgotten his mother's phrase, describing Katerina Kuzmin. The symbol of Russian woman—so his mother had called her. The strength of Russian woman. The fortitude of Russian woman. The patience of Russian woman. All these qualities Irena Galina had found in the broad-shouldered, sturdy-hipped Katerina, whom she had met entirely by chance during the ice blockade. Irena, so she had told Michael, had gone one day to the Hermitage. All of the works of art, of course, had been evacuated—all that could be. There were only a few of the heaviest pieces of sculpture left, the Rafael loges and the Italian wall frescoes which could not be moved. But it was not art which had brought Irena Galina to the hulking palace that hunched beside the Neva like a fortress. While the works of art had been sent to places of safety the same was not true of the personnel of the gallery. Many, of course, long since had joined the defense forces—all of the able-bodied men and some who would not have been so classified in ordinary circumstances. Most of the women were gone, too. There remained a handful in the enormous empty galleries. Here and there a Nazi shell or bomb had pierced the roof of the building, letting in snow and ice. In this arctic citadel the few remaining workers kept a lonely duty, on guard against the chance that fire bombs might hit the building and cause an even worse catastrophe.

The month was December. The rations of the city had been cut to the lowest ebb—to the death mark. It was literally true, as Michael well knew, that Leningrad lay dying. Each day thousands quietly turned their faces to the wall and expired—of what? No doctor ever came to give a death certificate. Why should he? There were not enough doctors to attend a city in which a million persons stood on the margin of death. And what was the point of a death certificate when everyone was dying of the same cause? Let it be called the "Leningrad disease." Such was as good a name as any.

This was the time when Irena, herself gaunt and hardly able to get about, paid her visit to the icy chambers of the Hermitage. The Director, or rather acting deputy Director, was a pale, golden-haired woman with eyes that seemed to reflect the faded gold of her hair. Her skin was transparent with the waxy transparency which was so common in Leningrad at that time. She sat huddled in a small office in her heavy coat and heavy woolen scarf. There was no heat and the temperature was ten degrees below zero. She did not rise when Irena entered the room and sank exhausted into a chair.

"We cannot complain," Irena was told. "We have our work. Of course, it is very difficult. But no more difficult than for everyone. Every day a few more people are not able to come to work."

The two women talked quietly for a few moments.

"One thing worries me very much," the Director said. "We have been able to do nothing with Professor Hippius and his wife. They are still here. Living—if you can call it that—in one little room, his old study, off the west gallery. There is no heat—but, of course, we all have that problem. What is more important, there is no light, except for, perhaps, an hour or two. They are in darkness almost twenty-four hours a day."

Irena walked through the frigid corridors of the empty museum. It was like walking through a cavern in the mountains of the moon. The windows were boarded up. Here and there a faint flicker of light came through. They crossed one gallery where the roof had been smashed by a German shell. There was a gaping hole in the floor and an ice hummock which rose halfway to the ceiling.

The Professor and his wife were lying in a small iron bed, completely clothed. On the bed was piled a goose-feather comforter, their overcoats and the Professor's fur cap. The only light in the room came from a thin crack in the boarded-up window. The Pro-

158

fessor was terribly embarrassed. His wife, however, lay apparently in a coma.

"Please forgive me," he said to Irena, slowly rising from the bed and nervously smoothing the little tuft of white hair on his bald pate. "We were just taking a small nap."

"This is no place for you, Professor Hippius," Irena said, speaking as she might to a small child. "I think that you and your wife could be cared for much better in the hospital."

Whether there was any way of getting them to a hospital was another question. But Irena could not see this tiny, ancient man— one of Russia's most brilliant scholars, a member of the Academy since 1912, the finest specialist on Italian Renaissance painting in Russia, or, in all probability, in the world—and his wife, herself a distinguished scholar, sink, as inevitably they must into endless sleep in this hovel of a room.

"Thank you, dear Irena Mikhailovna," the Professor said. "But you see it is quite impossible to leave the Hermitage."

Irena tried to interrupt but the Professor raised a thin hand and continued with the patience of a lecturer explaining a rather complicated point.

"You see," he said, "I am getting on in years. In fact, tomorrow will be my eightieth birthday. I do not have much time left and I have so much to do. So very much to do."

He turned around to his desk, which, in the deep gloom, Irena could see was covered with papers, folders, small collector's boxes and such a jumble that she could not make out what it all consisted of.

"I'm afraid," he said, "this looks like a terrible mess. But I am working on the cataloguing of my personal collection of antiquities —medieval coins and medals. It is my own fault, but they have never been put into proper order. And there is no one to do this but myself. So you see it's quite impossible. . . . Although, of course, it's very hard on my dear wife."

Professor Hippius added the last words sotto voce, as though to keep them from the frail, haggard form which lay on the bed

159

motionless and apparently oblivious of what was going on.

Irena pressed the Professor's hand silently and withdrew. Something, she said to herself, must be done. But what? If the Professor and his wife stayed a few more days in this leaden chamber it would be the end. Indeed, his wife seemed already to have entered that fateful and final withdrawal from the world which, Irena so well knew, presaged physical extinction.

As Irena walked out of the Hermitage and started down the embankment, slick with ice from the procession of women and children who with small sleds and pails were drawing freezing water from the Neva, she encountered a detachment of sailors. They had made their way across the ice and now were finishing the task of chopping away some of the heavy encrustation which had turned the staircase leading down to the Neva into an ice cascade. The men from the submarine *Speedy,* which lay down the embankment three hundred yards, firmly frozen in the ice for the winter, were collecting their ice picks and axes, preparatory to returning.

Suddenly an idea occurred to Irena. She approached the sailors.

"Are you going back to your submarine?" she asked. "Is your commander now aboard?"

Thus the great project had been put in train. The *Speedy* was one of the few remaining sources of electric power in Leningrad. The Commander had agreed that, if cable could be found, he would run a line along the embankment to the Hermitage, to Professor Hippius' room.

"We'll give him some light," the Commander said. "Of course we will. After all, he is one of the great scholars of our country. And, you know, I shouldn't wonder if we could give him a bit of heat, too. Hitch up a small reflector there in his room. We'll never miss it. Only problem is where to get the cable."

The cable did not prove to be an insuperable obstacle. With several sailors Irena went to the factory where the Commander thought some line might be had. It was a fiercely cold day. The sky was heavily overcast but no snow came down, only a searing wind from the Baltic. When they entered the factory grounds it seemed completely deserted. There were shell holes through the roof and the approaches were deep in unbroken snow. The door to the building stood open, snow drifted so high that it could not be closed. They walked through a long corridor, their feet echoing on the floor and icy winds chasing them down the hall. Finally, they found a room where the acting Director sat in his overcoat, drinking a glass of pale-colored liquid which presumably passed for tea.

"Of course," he said. "We have the cable. We have thousands of meters of it. Tens of thousands, I might say. Getting it is another matter. It lies out there. . . ."

He made a wide gesture of his hand, beyond the boarded-up window.

"It is under the snow and ice," he said. "How to get it out is a problem. There are not many of us left. You see, we are not working—just now. No power. No fuel. And not many of our workers are strong enough to come to the shop any more. We try to help them. But you know how it is. . . ."

The Director's words trailed off into space and he seemed lost in thought.

One of the sailors said: "We'll help get the cable out. That's what we came for."

"Well," said the Director, looking more tired and distressed by the moment. "Let's see what we can do. Perhaps Katerina will have some idea."

They passed out of the building into one adjacent to it and found a small room in which there appeared to be about twenty persons, sitting or lying on temporary cots which had been placed along the walls. The room was small enough so that the body heat of those within it had slightly raised the temperature.

A young woman, broad-shouldered, deep-hipped, clad in a man's sheepskin jacket and man's sheepskin cap, rose immediately and came to them.

"This is Katerina Ivanovna," the Director said. "Just tell her what is needed. If there is a way of doing it she will know."

Irena looked into the calm blue eyes of the young woman. Her

161

face was broad, Slavic and a little heavy—wide forehead, high cheekbones, firm jaw. She looked tired, weary beyond measure, yet there was more vitality in her appearance than in all the others. She moved with a kind of muscular determination which spoke of grit and strength.

As Irena told of the project to save Professor Hippius and his wife the eyes of the young woman began to melt.

"Of course," said Katerina. "Of course we can get the cable out. With your lads from the submarine and two or three of ours. You bet we will."

And they did. Late the next day the cable, hacked out of the ice, had been swiftly run along the edge of the embankment, in through one of the boarded-up windows, and now Katerina and two sailors were carrying it down the corridor toward the Professor's room.

In a few minutes a connection was made. Then the little group approached the room. Nothing had been said in advance. It was to be a surprise—a birthday surprise. Irena knocked at the door. The others waited in suspense. There was no response. She knocked again. No response. In a sudden panic she thrust open the door. In the darkness nothing could be seen. One of the sailors lighted a match. In its brief glitter the forms of the Professor and his wife, huddled in the bed, could be made out. With a gasp Irena stepped closer. The forms were still. Had they come too late? A sailor touched the switch of the lamp on the Professor's desk and a soft light diffused within the room.

Katerina stepped over to the bed, thrust her strong arms under the Professor's frail body and lifted him up. "She cradled him like a baby," Irena Galina had said. As Katerina held the old man in her arms his pale blue eyes opened and he smiled gently.

"I don't know who you are," he said, "but unless I am mistaken a small miracle seems to have happened in our little room. I hope it is not too late for my Anna to share in it. We were so weak. . . ."

His eyes closed again like the gentle closing of a child's eyes in the warm and comforting arms of his mother. It was not too late—

so it turned out. It was close, very close, but the Professor and his wife began to draw strength from the light and the warmth which, as Irena Galina had always said, "was the gift of Katerina."

So had been founded the deep, rather inarticulate bond of friendship between the sculptress and this strong Russian woman, a friendship that was almost physical in its basis. For just as the warmth and strength of Katerina had attracted Irena so the purity and courage of Irena attracted the younger, simpler woman.

When his mother had come to compose her "End of War" group she had turned to Katerina for the figure of the avenging woman, immortalizing her great body, her commanding presence, the power of her shoulders and strength of her arms, her sturdy torso with its magnificent breasts and strong belly, her dynamic thighs and oaklike legs.

"She is Russia," Irena Galina had said one evening, talking with someone. Michael could not remember who it was now. Probably Morozov. It was with Morozov that she liked to discuss her ideas and concepts.

"You have only to look at her," his mother had declared. "You can see in her the physical strength of Russia. Her feet are rooted in the soil. They are dirty with cow dung. Her armpits smell of the smell of Russia. Her hand can fell a man and her breasts can nourish a whole village. She can live without man. But man cannot live without her. And man can lose himself in the deepness of her thighs. She can squeeze him dry and cast him aside. But she will not. For she has the compassion of Russian womanhood. She knows what it is to be a man, to be small, to be feeble, to be afraid in the night. And she gathers man to her arms and nourishes him and gives him comfort. She is a woman and she is man's mother."

Yes, thought young Galin. She is a woman. A fierce and powerful one. She has not lost her strength and had she wanted she could have knocked me across the room. But why had she been so angry?

After all, he had done just what his mother would have wanted.

163

It was puzzling but he felt hovering on the edge of consciousness an explanation which his tired mind could not quite grasp. If only he were not so tired. He could not really think straight. The arches of his feet ached and the pain ran up along his tendons into the calves of his legs. The pain in his hip was severe. His head had begun to ache dully from the blow he had received and he caught himself several times, half staggering on the icy pavement. Suddenly he saw the dim headlights of an autobus. There was a stop station a hundred yards ahead. He began to run wildly, shouting: "Stop! Stop!" although he realized the driver could not hear him. His heart sank. Then he saw the bus slow down at the stop. It came to a halt and the door opened. An old woman slowly began to get out, drawing a half-paralyzed leg after her. Michael plunged up to the door, almost knocking the old woman down, and thrust himself inside. The air was heavy—so fetid that he could hardly draw it into his lungs. He slumped into a seat, wondering whether the machine was going in the direction of his mission.

21

Michael swayed from side to side in his seat. The windows of the bus were so frosted over that the machine seemed to be moving through a long gray dim tunnel, passing over an endless succession of obstacles which tossed its wheels up, then brought them down with a crashing jar that smashed at the bases of his skeleton and set each bone vibrating dully, like the broken ends of a saw. The air was thick with the odor of matted fur, sodden boots, brown floor polish, petrol fumes, smoked fish, unwashed bodies, human sweat, stale exhalations of lungs, garlic, old leather, pungent tobacco—and the smells that go to make up the smell of Russia. His head ached with a dull, dull ache that compressed each segment of his cranium individually, and he could feel his brains quiver like jelly with the torturing jerks and jolts of the bus. He found it harder and harder to sit upright. His head was going around in circles. Where was he being taken? Where was he going? What was his destination? His mind felt raw and his thoughts were telescoped one into another. Suddenly he felt himself shudder. It seemed to him that he was alone, careering through an endless night, blindly, unable to see where he was going, driving in a direction he could not guess toward a destination at which he would never arrive.

Once before he had suffered this sensation. When was it? His mind simply would not work. Yes, it was when he was being driven up to the front. After he had been put in the special battalion. It was a night like this. They were in a bus. A blue-painted one. The windows were barred with iron bars and the door was locked from the outside. But he had not been alone then. There were a score of them packed into a converted truck with straight wooden benches that ran down either side. Two small barred windows were glazed with frost. The truck was bitter cold. The road, if it was a road along which they were being driven, was an endless corduroy. They were thrown up and then smashed down on the wooden benches. They had packs but no rifles. Not trusted with rifles. The packs rose at a different speed from that of their bodies. Their bodies fell first. Then the packs bashed down on their feet and shoulders. The bus went on and on through the night. None of them spoke. They had been smashed and beaten beyond talk, beyond sensation. Their bodies rose and fell, twisted and shifted like half-filled sacks of grain. Once there had been a tremendous explosion and a sheet of flame burned through the frost glaze of the window. They heard the machine cough and choke, slow, swerve and then go on. Then suddenly the car had halted. And with a great rattling of the bolts the door had been swung open and a gravel-voiced sergeant shouted: "All out. Stand to. Look lively, you bastards."

Michael clenched his teeth. The memory of that night swept through his veins like hot vodka. He clenched his teeth in raw, cold anger. They had been dumped out on the ground, he and the others. A short, dark-mustached officer stood beside a small log shelter, camouflaged with pine branches. He was apparently a Georgian and he had his greatcoat thrown over his shoulders like a Cossack cape. He stood beside the hut, picking his teeth with a sliver of pine. There was a heap of dirty white ponchos lying in the snow beside him.

"Line up," the officer ordered. The men formed a ragged line in the snow. One of them, an older man, probably in his early forties, suddenly bent over and fell forward. The sergeant kicked him in the ribs with his heavy boot. The man did not move. The sergeant kicked him again, this time in the head. Still the man lay quiet. It was obvious that he had lost consciousness. The sergeant kicked him again but the officer waved him aside.

"Here, you two," the officer said, designating Michael and the soldier next to him, a tousled-haired blond country boy. "Throw that fellow off the road."

The two knelt beside the older man. He was heavy and not easy to lift. They struggled with the body and finally half lifted, half dragged the soldier to the side of the road.

"Leave him there," the Georgian ordered, adding with an evil grimace: "Maybe a little rest in the cool air will make him feel better."

The Georgian briefly explained their mission. The main body was moving forward at dawn. It was a surprise attack. No artillery preparation. The squad would start ahead of the attack, moving forward along the line of the designated advance.

"A very simple job," the Georgian said. "Mine detection. If you find any—set them off so our soldiers can get through. You'll need no weapons for this task. The sergeant here will be moving along just behind you. He will carry a tommygun. If anyone gets too far ahead or too far to one side—the sergeant will put him straight— with a round from his gun."

The Georgian turned to re-enter the log dugout.

"Oh, yes," he said, "one more thing. You can wear the snow ponchos over your uniforms."

If there had been a survivor from that mission besides himself, Michael did not know of him. His own survival could only be considered sheer luck. Half an hour after the little band had started its tragic and inevitably fatal stroll across the open snow fields that separated the Soviet positions from the advance outposts of the Germans the blond tousled-haired farm boy, walking perhaps a hundred feet from Michael, had stepped on a mine. It exploded with a roar of black powder that shook the ground under Michael's feet,

167

and he felt himself hurled to the ground by a fierce slap against his thigh. The last thing he remembered was the roar of flame, the sight of the blond boy disintegrating before his eyes and the powerful blow that knocked him to the ground.

Hours later—or so he presumed, for it was now daylight—he felt himself jolting along the ground on a sled, excruciating pains shooting through his leg and hip. He had been picked up by a first-aid girl, a short, dark-haired girl clad in cotton-filled jacket and heavy army trousers. When she looked back and saw that he was conscious, she smiled slightly and said, "Hang on, soldier, we're almost at the dressing station now."

Then he had gone off again, only to awaken on the operating table. The operating room was a tent, lighted with a strong gasoline light. The surgeon stood over him, his gown smeared with blood like a butcher's. There were nurses about.

"You look like a lucky one, boy," the surgeon said, a tired man whose gray hair was not covered by his surgical cap. "We'll just probe a bit for pieces of shrapnel and then put a big splint on that broken thigh of yours and send you on back to the rear."

The wound had healed slowly. Twice after Michael had been evacuated to a rear hospital on the outskirts of Moscow infections developed. Once there was some talk, he knew, of the possibility of amputation. But his young and healthy body had thrown off the infection and after drainage the wound began to mend.

True, the muscles of the right thigh had never been a hundred per cent correct. When he was tired he walked with a suspicion of a limp. Exhausted as he now was, his whole right thigh ached and pounded. But, for all that, Michael smiled grimly. The wound was the most fortunate thing that had ever happened to him. For it saved his life. He was never sent back to the punitive battalion.

As soon as he was able to get about he had been permitted to join his mother in Leningrad. That, of course, was Orlov's doing. He had never been entirely certain of what he thought about Orlov. Or, rather, he had more than one opinion of the General and, as he was aware, they did not exactly coincide. Orlov was, he recognized, a fine man, a decent man, a good general certainly; a man whose instincts were right, a man who believed in honor and knew, or thought he knew, what honor was. And yet it had seemed to Michael that he was a man who fought without quite knowing what he fought for; a little like those knights of the medieval crusades. They had themselves a fine code of morals, the highest of ideals. And yet they served, sometimes, in the most shameless of causes, and their masters were monsters in their aims, ambitions and aspirations.

"You see, Michael dear," his mother had said to him, "Constantin Constantinovich is what I would call a pure man. That is, he is pure in his thoughts and pure in his own character. He does not merely talk of honor or of bravery. He lives it. And perhaps because of this, because of the cleanness of his own character and his own mind, it is very difficult for him to understand that others, particularly others whom he has been trained to respect and to obey—that these other men may use the same words that he uses, may speak of the same principles and yet, in their own lives, act at complete variance with them."

This had been one of the conversations, one of the many conversations, he had with her in these months that they spent together in Tashkent. There had been time for conversations in Tashkent and he was grateful for them and for the privilege—for so he counted it—of being with his mother in her last months. One thing she did not talk of—the war. She did not talk of her experiences nor did she ask Michael about his life in the Army. It was as though she had deliberately closed the door on a major chapter in her life. Once Michael, without thinking, had asked her what had become of her famous "End of War" group.

"I walked out of the studio with one suitcase, Michael, as you know," she said bitterly. "What I left behind I left behind. Please don't remind me of it."

Such outbursts, however, were rare. She was not well. Something had broken in her when she had been disgraced. The first time Michael saw her in Tashkent he had not been able to keep the shock from his face.

"Ah, Micky," she said to him, "I know what you're thinking. You are thinking that I look like an old woman. I know without your saying it. And I do too, Micky. I look like an old woman and I am an old woman."

He had put his cheek against hers and had told her not to talk like that.

"No," she replied. "No lies between us now, Michael. I have not got a long time to live. I know it and you do, too—or you will soon enough."

Sometimes she talked about the days long, long ago when she had been a little girl in St. Petersburg before the war. She told about the dancing school she attended on Vasilevsky Island and how there was a ball at Christmastime for all the youngsters.

"There was one boy," she said, "who was several years older than I. I was terribly in love with him. He was tall and slim and very handsome but a little bashful. The older boys really were supposed to dance with girls of their own age. But I was not going to let any girl dance with him. I considered him my personal property."

His mother had smiled a little at that point.

"I was almost the first girl to arrive at the ballroom," she said. "As soon as the boy came I walked right up to him. We had little white programs with red-tassel ribbons and white leather covers. I gave him my program and a little gold pencil and said: 'Write your name after each one of the dances.'"

Michael smiled. "Did he do it?"

"Of course he did." His mother laughed. "And we danced every dance together. At the end of the evening the dancing master spoke to my mother about it. And I was given a lecture. Well-bred young ladies, I was told, don't do things like that."

Michael had been working on a cotton farm not far from Tashkent when his mother was sent there. He was given permission after a few months to come and live in the city with his mother. They had two rooms, good pleasant rooms on a rose-scented court through which a small stream ran, two rooms in the mud-plastered house of a kind Uzbek couple in the old city. The rooms were cool and dark during the strong heat of the day, and in the evening they sat in the courtyard and smelled the strong scent of the roses and listened to the quiet noises of the city. In the distance there was always a mournful song, an Uzbek singing to his lover. It was peaceful and it seemed like another planet from Moscow and Leningrad.

He tried to persuade his mother to go on with her sculpture. "There are all these wonderful faces," he said, "just waiting for your hand."

She smiled gently. "No, Michael," she told him. "No more sculpture. My days as an artist are over. I am just waiting a little bit. Resting you might say. Then, I will go along. Let's be honest, dear. I'm not long for this world."

But she did find the hours hanging heavy on her hands with Michael gone all day. He had a job of sorts, working as a freight handler at the railroad station. It was hard physical work but his body was lean and strong after the months of work on the cotton farm. One evening he came back to the house in the old city. The Uzbek couple were sitting in the inner court, a charcoal brazier was burning and a teakettle hummed on it. His mother sat on a bench nearby, bent over something which she held in her lap. She looked up at Michael and smiled.

"I've gone back to work," she said, holding up a small embroidery frame. "I've joined the co-op. It's the first time I've done embroidery since I was a little girl and used to be taken to the Summer Garden by my nurse. So it will take me a little while to get the hang of it."

Actually, her embroidery was fantastically accurate and neat and her hand was incredibly swift. But she tired quickly and could only work at it for short stretches.

The bus, Michael noted, was slowing down to a stop. His head felt a bit clearer now and he got up and asked the sleepy girl conductor where they were. She glanced out the frosty window. "We're just coming up to the Kazansky Sabor," she said. He thanked her and a minute later, his right leg limping slightly, hopped off the bus. He looked up at the clock in the tower of the old Duma building. Eleven had just struck. The cold and the wind had driven everyone indoors and there was hardly a person on the Nevsky. He crossed the wide boulevard and hurried down the snowy pavement that bordered the Catherine Canal, walking as rapidly as his tired legs would carry him in the direction of the studio which he knew so well.

22

Ahead of Michael loomed the strange façade of the Alexander II Cathedral, somehow menacing and sinister in the cold glitter of the winter night. There flashed into his mind a picture of Zhelyabov and his little group, of their patience and their daring, pitting the strength of a handful of youngsters against the vast power of the Czarist state. He had thought of them often in these past days and now the image of the steel will of the young revolutionary band sent new strength into his own tired body. How tired they must have been as they worked, night after night, scooping out the tunnel under the roadway, scooping the earth up by the cupful, lest the noise of their excavation give them away. How often they must have been seized by panic, by fear, as their plans trembled on the brink of discovery. How close they had been to catastrophe when that inspector chanced to wander into the little cheese shop. Michael set his jaw firmly. He knew something of how they had felt. He knew the smell of fear and the salt taste of fatigue.

The wind seemed to have slackened for a moment and suddenly Michael had the sensation that someone was behind him. In fact, he felt that someone had been behind him for some time. It hardly seemed possible that anyone could have followed him through the bitter cold of the Leningrad night. True, he had not been entirely alone on the bus, as he had thought. When he rose to get off he noticed a red-nosed old duffer, apparently half-soused, slumped in the corner behind him. Now, although Michael did not turn his head, every instinct told him that somewhere behind him, following along the canal, was another human being.

At this point Michael was not going to take any chances. Just ahead was a gate that led into a courtyard and beyond this, Michael knew, lay a tangle of paths which ran between buildings and would bring him out into the park not far from the Engineering Castle. He was on his home ground now. Here was where he had played as a youngster. Every twist and turn, every old courtyard and fence, was etched in his memory. He edged into the shadows close to the buildings which faced the canal. When he came to the gate he ducked inside, concealing himself behind a small shed. Now he would see whether it was simply a chance passerby, coming late to his home after a long evening's work. Michael held his breath, his eyes glued on the narrow opening in the gate. A minute went by. He began to think he was mistaken. Then, across the small patch of semi-shadow the figure of a man passed, walking straight ahead along the canal. Michael's tired eyes could not be sure but it seemed to him that the late passerby resembled the old duffer he had seen slumped in the bus. He hesitated a moment, tempted to try for a better look at the solitary pedestrian. Then he shook his head. Ridiculous! If the man was following him he had been shaken off—or soon would be after Michael had plunged through the maze of back alleys which only a Leningrad boy could know. The important thing was to get away from this spot quickly before the fellow, if he was following him, discovered that Michael had given him the slip. This was no time for hesitancy. It had been a long road Michael had come these last few days and there must be no relaxation now.

The morning his mother had died Michael had made his decision. It was not a calculated thing. He had not planned it. How could he when death had struck so suddenly, so cruelly just when it seemed to him that she was looking a little better, taking a little genuine interest in life—not merely waiting for it to end?

They had sat drinking tea that evening. He had been working the night shift and did not get home until after midnight. It was cold and there was snow. Everyone said it was most unusual weather for Central Asia although, of course, they had snow almost every year. But there was a snap to the air and Irena had laughed when he came in, his cheeks rosy, with snow crusted in the fur of his sheepskin cap.

"Oh, how nice, Michael," she said. "Real snow. And cold. Almost like Leningrad!"

There was a sparkle in her eyes which he had not seen for so long that it brought a catch to his throat. He went quickly to her side and kissed her hastily. She moved her head just as he drew near and the kiss intended for her cheek landed on her forehead.

Irena laughed with mock despair. "Oh, not there, Michael," she said. "I'm not dead yet."

He kissed her again on the cheek. She poured out the tea and they sat for a while, not talking, just comfortable in their mutual silence. He finished his tea.

"You must go to bed," she said. "It's late now."

"What about you?" he asked.

"I'll just sit up a bit," she said. "And finish this design that I've started."

Michael had gone to bed soon thereafter and sunk into deep sleep. He had awakened about five in the morning. He did not know what had broken his sleep. Had he heard a sudden noise? Had his mother called him? He lay a moment, listening. The room was completely still and not a sound broke the intense silence. Yet a sixth sense told Michael that something was wrong. He listened to the quietness for a bit and then got to his feet, the conviction that something was amiss growing within him. He opened the door to the other room. His mother was still sitting in the chair by the light,

175

just as he had left her, her embroidery in her lap. At first he thought she had fallen asleep, but as he approached a tremor ran down his spine. Her head was slightly inclined to one side, her mouth half open. She was not breathing.

It was an hour before Michael was able to get the doctor from the clinic, but, as she said, it really had made no difference. The doctor was a woman, middle-aged and tired. She carried her medicine and instruments in a very worn black leather bag. She examined Irena Galina swiftly and then turned back to Michael.

"Well," she said, "as you see . . . it is the end. And, of course, it is not very surprising. As I told her when she came in to see me . . ."

Her voice trailed off as she saw the shock in Michael's face.

"I'm sorry," she said. "Apparently Irena Mikhailovna didn't tell you. She probably didn't want you to worry about her. But it was so. Her heart was bad. Very bad. I told her. But she had known it already. I gave her some medicine to take if she had a spell. But apparently it happened so suddenly—you heard nothing?"

No, Michael said. He had heard nothing. Unless it was some sound from her which had awakened him. And he had not known about the heart condition.

"Well," the doctor said, putting her stethoscope back into the worn bag. "It came very suddenly, you see. No one could have done anything for her. And perhaps it is better that way."

Michael offered her some tea but she declined.

"It's getting on to daylight," she said. "I'd better get back. There is a long day ahead of me."

The door closed behind the tired figure of the doctor and Michael was alone with his mother. He went over and lifted her in his arms—surprised at the slightness of her figure—and laid her gently on the couch. He crossed her arms on her breast and kissed her on the forehead, remembering suddenly that he had kissed her forehead only a few hours before. Then it was warm. Now it was cold as stone.

He sat on the table beside the lamp and looked at his mother, lying on the couch in the shadow, her face calm and pale. So, he thought. This is how it ends. Here in a mud-and-wattle hut in a God-forsaken Asian city. Two thousand miles from Leningrad, from the Neva. Far from everything that was near and dear to her. Far from the city and the country to which she had given her soul, her life, the bright spark of a golden talent. And why? What had she done? Who had sentenced her to die in this forlorn desert? For what crime? Had she damaged her country? Had she betrayed some great principle? Was she false to any man or woman? Had she done injury to the cause of the good and helped the cause of evil? Was she a coward? Was she a traitor?

He asked himself the questions and the fire burned stronger and stronger in his breast. Why should this be? How could this be? Was there no justice in this Russian land? He remembered once sitting very straight in a horsehair chair in his mother's studio while she talked with some of her friends and drank tea. Morozov was among them and he was telling about an experience he had had as a little boy—how his father had come back from the Bloody Sunday in Petersburg in 1905 and sworn a great oath that injustice and the trampling upon the weak by the strong must halt. But it had not halted. No. Despite a revolution, despite two revolutions. What went on? Cruelty stalked the land. Evil triumphed over good. There was not in all of Russia—indeed, not in all the world—a woman so filled with a passion for good, for the right, for a better world, for justice, for an end to cruelty, as his mother.

She had been beaten down in the end. She had been broken before she had arrived here in this distant Tashkent. The forces against her had been too great, too powerful. They had smashed her as though she were a fly between the rollers of their great machine. They had shown how weak, how impotent was the single woman, the lone individual, against the vast apparatus of the state. Resist? You will be crushed. You will be flattened. Oh, Michael knew the story—knew the story well. He had resisted. He had survived the punitive battalion—thanks to his mother, thanks to her friend. But it had not taken long for the state to crash down on him again. Of course, he saw now and had seen for some time that the blow, while directed against himself, had been really aimed at his mother.

The lesson was obvious. Take it. Submit. Thank God that you are alive. Count such blessings as you have. Keep quiet. Toe the line. Well, he was not going to take it. His life was not that important to him. And it was important to no one else. No one at all. He had no love for his father. He had refused to take Voronsky's name because of the way he treated his mother. But he did agree with him on one point. He remembered a drunken night when his father had been swilling vodka. Earlier, there had been friends at the studio but apparently they had all left. His father was standing beside his mother, a glass of vodka in his hand.

"There's only one way to live!" Voronsky shouted. "Only one way! Live so you can spit in the eye of any son of a bitch in the world. And if he slugs you—slug him back. Kick him in the belly and gouge out his eyes."

Voronsky threw back the vodka and hurled the glass across the room, roaring at the terrified little boy: "Do you hear that, Mishka? If any bastard tries to put you down—kick him in the balls! Hear me? Don't take it! Don't take it from anyone!"

Michael was no longer the eager-eyed youngster he had been when he volunteered for the Red Army. He was not the proud but naïve lad he was when he and his band of partisans hurled their caps in the air at the sight of their Red Army comrades.

He thought of the long trip East in the prison boxcar. It was late summer and the car had been stifling hot as slowly their train made its way east to the Urals, across Siberia, and then been shunted down into desert Uzbekistan. There was not much that he had not learned about the nature of the human animal in the course of that trip—the stinking hole in the floor that served as a toilet, ever more stinking as the journey progressed; the wooden tubs of slop which passed for food; the boy who had shoved open the door—and the amazed look on the boy's face when the guard's bayonet pinned his hand to the wood, blood spurting from the wound in tiny jets;

the grizzle-cheeked old convict, back to Siberia for the tenth time—or the twentieth—who leaned back, swigged a drink of *samogin* and sighed: "Only in Siberia can you really be free."

And slowly he had begun to realize as the weeks lengthened into months that there was more truth—more bitter truth in the old convict's words than he would ever have believed. In Siberia, in Central Asia, anywhere east of the Urals, it was a different Russia. God knows it was not the Siberia of the Decembrists, nor even the Siberia of the Bolsheviks in the days before the Revolution. But it was a world where you learned a new sense of values. For one thing you learned how little there was to lose. You could, of course, be sent from one hell hole to another even worse. You could be shifted from Karaganda to Yakutsk. You could be sent from Yakutsk to Kolima. But, after all, what difference did it make? A few less years to your life.

No, Michael told himself, here in the East a man could think, could reason, could learn the real meaning of life. The value of life and the value of death. And having at least begun to have some appreciation of real values Michael well knew that he was not going to sit by meekly and permit the memory of Irena Galina to be snuffed out as casually as you squash a bedbug against your forefinger. No, by God. He would not take it. Whatever the consequences might be the least he could do was to honor his mother—honor a woman who stood for everything in his life which was precious and meaningful. If there was not one other human being in all of Russia who would honor her he at least would do what should be done.

He made himself some strong tea. It was growing light now. He went to the brown imitation-leather suitcase which was under his mother's couch. He thought he knew how his purpose could be accomplished.

Opening the suitcase, he rummaged around until he found a small chamois bag. He drew it out and opened the drawstring under the lamp on the table. There fell into his palm a pair of diamond earrings, the large diamonds set in a beautiful pendant, circled by a myriad of smaller diamonds. They were, he knew, his mother's dearest possessions, given to her by Voronsky on his return from a wild, rollicking journey to Berlin, Paris and London. Where his father had acquired the diamonds had never been entirely clear to Michael. On the gambling tables at Monte Carlo! That was what Maxim Voronsky had shouted one night. But Michael knew from the indulgent look in his mother's eyes that this was just a story.

It made no difference now, Michael thought, looking at the gems sparkling in his hand. It made no difference where these bits of crystallized carbon came from. What mattered now was that from them he would gain the power to accomplish his purpose. He put one earring carefully back in the little chamois bag. The other he wrapped in his handkerchief. Then he tucked both into his trousers pocket, picked up his heavy sheepskin jacket, put his sheepskin cap on his head, felt in his breast pocket to be certain he had his passport and the death certificate left him by the doctor, went over once more and kissed his mother's brow and then quietly tiptoed out of the room, locking the door behind him.

23

It had all been astonishingly easy. The only real problem had proved to be old Azimov and his wife, the kindly Uzbek couple from whom they rented the two rooms. The Azimovs felt that it was sacrilege for him to move his mother's body without having it rest in mourning there in the house where she died.

"Really, Michael Maximovich," the old man said, his face wreathed in pain. "It's not right. Take your mother to Leningrad if you must. But first let her lie in state so that we who loved her can mourn her parting."

Michael felt like a criminal. He apologized as best he could but the Azimovs felt it was indecent that he was taking his mother away this very night. He had not really intended to tell them about his intentions but finally he was left no alternative.

"I am taking my mother's body back to Leningrad," he said, "so that she may be given the kind of funeral which her life and achievements merit."

Even this did not satisfy the old man. He kept asking questions: What sort of a funeral did Michael plan? Who would he invite? Where would it be? Michael came close to losing his temper. It was too much like a cross-examination, and for a moment a dark suspicion flared in his mind but he suppressed it. Azimov and his wife were simple people and it was unfair of him not to bear that fact in mind. Quietly and precisely he told the old couple exactly what he planned to do: the people whom he hoped to invite to the ceremony; how he hoped to carry out his intentions and why it was impossible to delay. Even then Azimov tried to persuade him to wait over a day or two.

Finally, Michael had to be firm. He simply could not wait. If his plan was to succeed, speed was of the essence. He had a permit to ship the body on the evening express. He had a permit to accompany it and to be absent from Tashkent for a total of ten days. It was remarkable good fortune that he had been able to obtain both permissions and to obtain them within a few hours.

For this good fortune he had paid. He had paid a small fortune. He had gone straight to the old bazaar. He knew he would find there a flinty-eyed Russian with whom he had dealt before when he had sold a few of his mother's possessions to get furniture for their rooms. The man was a Russian, but his face was so burned by the hot Uzbek sun and so seldom washed that in his green-striped *khalat* and his greasy *tubetyeika* he might readily have passed for an Oriental.

Michael entered a smoky *chainaya*, sat down at a table and ordered a glass of tea and a *bulochka*, a small roll. He saw the Russian, eating a herring sandwich and polishing off an early-morning glass of vodka with two friends. Presently, the two men rose, leaving the Russian alone.

Michael waited a few moments then casually sat down at the man's table. The Russian peered suspiciously at him and grunted: "What's your business?"

Michael sat silent a moment, then spoke. "Something I think you'd be interested in."

"What do you mean?" the trader asked, an evil glitter in his eye.

"Not here," Michael said. "Perhaps outside."

The trader pondered a moment. "All right," he finally said. "You go ahead. I'll join you."

Michael got up and strolled out of the restaurant. He walked along the street a few doors and then stopped to peer at a window. Presently, the trader joined him. They turned down a narrow alley and entered a small shoemaker's shop, passing through into a dimly lighted back room which served as the trader's "office."

"Let's see what you have," the trader said.

"Give me a little light," Michael said. "This is not a child's toy."

The trader rose and drew back a curtain which concealed a window. Michael stepped up to the light and pulled out the earring which he had wrapped in his handkerchief. The man could not restrain a gasp as the light caught the facets of the big diamond.

"It's real," Michael said, anticipating the trader's first reaction. "I even have a state jewelry store's appraisal slip."

He handed the trader the slip, meantime carefully holding the earring in his palm and keeping at arm's length from the man. He was taking no chances. The trader read the appraisal slip quietly, then said: "How do I know it is the same stone?"

"You know that it is," Michael said coldly. "What I don't know is whether you have the money to buy it."

The trader made a gesture with his shoulders. "How do you know I want to buy it?"

"Because," Michael said, "you're not a fool and because I am offering it to you at exactly one-half the appraisal value—take it or leave it."

He saw the light rise in the trader's eyes.

"No bargaining," Michael warned. "Take it or leave it. And the money must be ready one hour from now."

He put the stone back in his pocket and started for the door.

"Just a minute," the trader said. "At least I must examine the stone."

"In one hour," Michael said, "I will be walking through the park near the railroad station. If you want to do business meet me there."

One hour later Michael had the rubles in his pocket and was heading for the visa section of the Interior Ministry. The office was deserted, the window of the little cubicle was locked tight and there was absolutely no response to Michael's knocking. He knocked again. No answer. Then he took a note from his wad of rubles and carefully inserted it under the edge of the service window, keeping a firm grasp on the bill. A moment later a shadow appeared against the glass and he felt a tug on the note. When the window actually began to open Michael let go of the bill. By the time the head of the Lieutenant-in-Charge had appeared the note had vanished.

"I am sorry to trouble you, Captain," said Michael, noting the contented grimace with which the duty officer received this sudden promotion in grade. "The fact is I have a small difficulty which perhaps you might be kind enough to help me with."

He explained the permissions which he had to have.

"Quite impossible," the officer rejoined, starting to close the window. "Absolutely irregular . . ."

"Just a moment," Michael interrupted. "Please. Just look at my passport."

He passed over the document quickly, having stuffed another large note between its pages. The officer glanced at him, then went to one side with the document, returning a moment later with a frown on his face.

"Hmm," he said. "This is a very difficult matter. Especially on such short notice. I don't know whether it would be possible to get the Colonel's signature. And there are the forms to fill out."

"I understand that," Michael said. "If you would just let me fill out the forms. I know that it is a matter in which several persons must be involved and—well, you know the old adage—live and let live."

With this remark he ventured a quick wink and let the Lieutenant have a glimpse of the roll of bills in his hand. After that there was really no further difficulty. He filled out the forms, the authorizations were signed, the proper stamps were affixed, more banknotes changed hands and before noon he was out of the office and over at the railroad station, arranging for the transportation back to Leningrad.

At each step Michael had awaited a tap on the shoulder, a sudden summons to the prefect. When he handed in his papers and requested a railroad ticket he kept expecting to be called to the *Komendatura*. Instead, after a long wait the tickets were brought to him, fully in order and without comment. As he boarded the train he looked behind him, expecting to see a patrol at his heels, to hear his name called and a shout to halt. Nothing happened. The coffin was loaded into the baggage car, he took his seat in the "hard" car, threw his blanket down on the wooden bench and leaned back. Almost immediately he was on his feet again—too nervous to be quiet. He looked out the window. Nothing was to be seen but the hurrying crowds of people, the bored railroad guards, the flag girl with her rolled flag and lantern, mechanically looking from the forward end to the rear end of the train. He glanced at his watch. Two minutes to departure time. Would they come? He could feel the beating of his heart. One minute. Thirty seconds. The girl dropped her flag. The train began to move. The light in the compartment flickered. He was under way.

And so it had gone. At every station he leaped off the train and paced about, half anticipating that a railroad guard would come up, salute and order him to accompany him to the police. But nothing happened. His companions in the compartment, he knew, thought him more than a little queer. Perhaps he was. Half the time he rode not with them but in the baggage car, where he now was sitting with the guard, a tall, handsome old man with long Ukrainian mustaches, who had been in the railroad service since before the Revolution—Uncle Peter, the others called him. At first it had sent a stab through Michael's breast to see the old man casually seat himself on the coffin, pull out his pipe and leisurely stuff it with tobacco which burned so badly that Uncle Peter could never keep himself in matches. But so natural was the old man, so apparent was it that no gesture of disrespect was implied that Michael quickly lost his feeling. The coffin simply made a comfortable spot

185

on which the old man could rest his bones and expound the philosophy acquired in forty years of traveling up and down Russia on the iron rails that bound the land together.

The old man had his pipe going now and he began to talk as the train hurtled forward over the endless distances of the steppe. Uncle Peter knocked lightly with his pipe on the coffin.

"You see this, now," he said, gesturing to the coffin. "This has a meaning. One which it might be that the ordinary person would pass by. That is, someone who had not been connected with the railroads like myself. For the railroads are a great place to watch the history of our Russia unfold, roll by, as it were, past the windows of our cars.

"You take Central Asia now, for an example," the old man said. "Well I remember the day the Turksib line was opened up. What a day that was! You never saw such a thing in your life. Foreign potentates they had on that first train. Dukes and counts—and princes, too, I guess. No telling who they all were. But they came from the ends of the earth. From America and England, from France and Germany. Not that I ever did like the Germans. Never could trust them. Mean folk they were."

The pipe was out again and the old man vainly tried to get it going.

"Well," he said, "you never saw a train like that one in your life. At least I never did, and I have seen a lot of trains. Champagne, they had. Bottles in every compartment. Great buckets of caviar. And so much shashlik you were sick of it. I was, that's certain. They couldn't eat it all—the passengers couldn't and so we had to pitch in and help them."

That, said Uncle Peter, had been the first real achievement of the new Soviet regime.

"That hit 'em in the eye," he chuckled. "All those Europeans. They couldn't laugh that off. Here we had gone and built as fine a railway as anyone had ever seen—revolutionaries and Bolsheviks that we were. That showed that we were on our way. And it never has stopped. Not for a minute since then."

It was a long time—and Michael had begun to wonder whether the old man ever would get around to it—before Uncle Peter finally returned to his starting point—the coffin on which he was sitting.

"What I meant about that was just this," he finally said. "In the old days it was a bitter time when death came to a family. There was the priest to pay and the coffin to buy and the place in the cemetery. You had to have money—or else. And many is the family that spent their last kopek—and then some—just for a decent burial. And, if you didn't have it—poofff. Off to the potter's field with you. And many a good lad ended up there, as you know very well."

Yes, Michael agreed, that had been common enough in the old days. So he had heard.

"And then," said the old man in triumph, "we changed all that. We brought in the crematorium. A real triumph of our culture. It was cheap and it was dignified and what was the real difference whether you ended up in an urn in the wall or in a box under the soil? Fact of the matter, I always thought the urn was more dignified. Not to say more sanitary. And everybody could afford it. No problem at all."

"Some people," Michael ventured deferentially, "didn't like the crematorium."

"Now," said the old man, "that's true. And that is just what I was coming to. You see, we've made another real step forward. For those who want it—there is the crematorium. For those who want burial—well, there are boxes to be had and nice plots of land even if you have to go from one end of the country to another."

"What's the point of it? Why go to a lot of fuss?"

The interruption was made by Uncle Peter's helper, a squint-eyed young man, a substitute who had swung onto the train at the last moment when Uncle Peter's regular assistant failed, unaccountably, to show up for the run.

The assistant nudged Michael in the shoulder. "How about it?" he said. "Why the fuss? Isn't the ground out in Tashkent fancy enough for your taste?"

Michael's anger boiled over and he took a half step toward the surly assistant, but before he could act Uncle Peter had raised a restraining hand.

"Now," said the old man. "Everyone has a right to his taste. And a railway carriage is no place for an argument. There is a reason for everything but if we knew all the reasons there would be nothing left for us to find out. A dull world, in other words."

The old man's words eased the moment, but Michael glared at the assistant, who returned the look with an insolent stare.

So it had gone. The days passed quickly. It was a long cold journey, broken only briefly for a change of trains at Moscow. The nearer he approached Leningrad the higher rose Michael's inner excitement and tension. For the trip to Leningrad marked only the opening phase. What he now had in mind was infinitely more difficult, infinitely more complicated and, as he was naturally aware, infinitely more dangerous.

It was this element of danger, this possibility that as he neared the accomplishment of his purpose he might suddenly be thwarted, which had activated his senses tonight, exhausted though he was. It was this that had put him on the alert against possible shadowing.

Michael had successfully threaded his way through the back alleys, skirted the edge of the big Mikhailovsky Park and crossed the Fontanka by the Pantelemon Bridge. There was not a chance that any sleuth, no matter how skilled, had been able to follow his complicated trail. He was approaching the studio now and his heart was beating rapidly. It was very late, much too late, he knew, to be knocking at Nadya's door, but he could not help the hour. He had not been able to get there sooner. He hoped that she would be in. He hoped that she would not be disturbed. He hoped he would not be received as he had been at his last visit on Vasilevsky Island. The snow, he noticed, had slackened and the lights of the city glowed in reflection against the low overhanging clouds. He stood now before the familiar door but he did not knock. He stood quietly in the shadows, listening and peering intently in all directions. Even though he had obviously shaken off any follower, there was still the possibility that someone might be watching this building. He let the minutes tick by as he waited for any clue, any sign of human life. Every nerve in him was tingling. He felt that if anyone were watching, the nerve waves from his body would sense them out. All was quiet. Softly he stomped his feet to free his boots of snow and then knocked, a light, diffident knock. After a moment he heard a quick step and then a voice saying: "Is someone there?"

"Yes, Nadya," he said in a low voice. "It's me. Michael Maximovich. May I come in?"

24

Michael's body was racked by terrible sobs, dry sobs that seemed to have no end. He had hardly entered the room and gasped out word of the death of Irena Galina before he collapsed in Nadya's arms. The girl held him to her breast, stroking his forehead gently and saying: "There, Michael. There." She spoke the meaningless words again and again, her mind gripped by the fact of Irena's death. It did not seem possible. Irena Galina dead! How could this woman so possessed of the spirit of life be now lying cold and inanimate?

Nadya's arms were around Michael's quivering shoulders but she herself had gone back in time, back to another January, the January of 1942, when all Leningrad lay starving in frozen stupor. Nadya was a girl of fifteen at the Kirov works in those times. Her brother had been an engineer at the works, her father a superintendent. Even her mother had once worked in the plant. She was a Putilov girl and as proud of that as she was proud of being a Leningrad girl. In the aristocracy of Pietersky workers, of the men and women who had built the industry of St. Petersburg before the Revolution, the name of Putilov held first rank. Since Kirov's assassination in

1934 the factory had been called after the martyred Party Secretary. But to Leningrad it would always be the Putilov plant and the workers were still Putilov workers.

Nadya had been a Putilov girl since the day her brother joined his regiment in July, 1941, and she had not missed a tour of duty in the shop since. Nothing had stopped her. She was in the plant the August day when a Nazi tank was shot into flames outside the factory gates. She was there the October day when the shells rained down for ten hours without cessation. And now on this January day Nadya and her friend Lena, once a chubby red-faced youngster but now, like Nadya, leaner than a wolf, sunken-cheeked and yellow-faced, had been assigned to the emergency squad. The emergency squad was a fancy name. But its duty was very simple. Each morning two or three patrols of girls were sent out from the plant equipped with a sled, a pocketful of food and a short list of names. Their duty was to go to the addresses on the list—workers of the plant or members of their families. If they found someone alive and in need of help, they did what they could. If, as was likely, they found someone dead, they put the body on the sled and hauled it to the nearest disposal point. There was no burial in this month of ice and cold. The bodies were simply taken to the morgue on Marat Street, to one of the cemeteries, or, in plain fact, to some location near one of these points.

Nadya shuddered as she recalled those times. Once toward the end of the war some foreign correspondents had visited Leningrad. They wanted to know what it was like in the time of the blockade. She had tried to tell them but she knew it was hopeless. Unless you had lived through it no one could understand what life had been like.

"We all lived in the plant then," she said. "That is, those of us who were able to get there. Some persons were too weak."

They had huddled in a small shop. In the worst times of January no work had been done at all. There was no power and no one was strong enough to stand at the lathes. For a few hours a day a small fire burned in a little stove made from sheets of iron. They sat around in a circle, close so that their shivering bodies might communicate a little heat to each other. Sometimes someone told stories or read—but it was not easy to read in the poor light. There was no radio.

On this day in January Nadya and Lena had started out on their patrol. They had only a few addresses, none of them distant, but they were so weak they had to rest every hundred yards or so. At the first address they found no one. The apartment was open. No one locked his flat. In case of emergency they wanted it possible for someone to come to their aid. The girls inspected the apartment carefully. A week ago an older woman from the plant had been living there—ill and feeble but alive. No sign of what might have happened to her. The girls rested and went to the next address, the third floor of a building which had been half demolished by a bomb. They knocked and heard a faint voice. Inside they found a fourteen-year-old boy huddled in bed. He looked at the girls with wild eyes. On the table stood a kerosene stove and a pan with grits in it. They warmed the grits, heated water and fed the boy. Almost immediately he went to sleep. The boy was the brother of one of the girls in the shop.

"Last week," said Lena, "her mother and sister were still here."

A cloth had been stretched across one corner of the room to make a sleeping nook. Nadya pulled it aside and shrank back. The mother, her body drawn up almost into a ball, lay dead on a cot. Silently the girls covered the fragile form with the cloth from the screen. Then, making a cradle of their hands, they slowly and painfully carried the body down and placed it on their sled. It took them an hour to carry it to the nearest disposal point.

The next address was that of an old turner, a man who had worked at the Putilov plant since long before the Revolution. He was a favorite with everyone, a cheerful man who had insisted on trying to teach the girls the secrets of the turner's art, even though the temperature of the shop was below zero and there was no power to turn the lathes.

"You've got to learn my secrets," he insisted to the girls. "Otherwise who will carry on if something should happen to me?"

Lena and Nadya approached his flat with reluctance. Each hated the thought that the chipper old man might be lying there stiff and lifeless. The door of the flat was ajar and the girls pushed it open. They were met immediately with a gruff cry: "Who goes there?" Exhausted as they were, they could not help but giggle.

"Just a couple of Putilov girls, Grandpa," they said.

"And about time," the old man said. "About time for a report on how you're keeping the shop."

The old worker was seated in an armchair, wrapped in his coat, two or three blankets, a scarf and his fur hat.

"And how are you feeling, Grandpa?" Nadya asked.

"Not too bad," he said. "Not too bad. If only these legs of mine would hold up, believe me I would be out there with you."

The truth was that an ulcer had started in one of his legs—the first portent of fatal dystrophy—but this he did not let on, and they left him, having given him a small packet of sugar and a can of sprats which somehow had found its way into the plant commissary.

And so it had gone all day. Some of those they sought to help were alive. Some were dead. Some had vanished. One of the calls was in the building where Nadya lived. She dreaded the idea of going there. The apartment was cold and vacant. She had taken her mother's body to Marat Street a month ago. Her father had gone to fight on the approaches to the city in one of the Putilov workers' brigades. He had not returned. Only Nadya and her brother remained. Nadya had not intended even looking into the apartment, but as she passed the landing some impulse caused her to push open the door. In the mailbox she saw a piece of paper and pulled it out. It was a buff-colored postcard . . . The Commissariat for War begs to report that Vladimir Fedorovich Kaverin is missing in action and believed dead. She held the card in her hand and came out of the apartment. Lena stood waiting for her and the girls descended the staircase silently. At the doorway they found their sled and started to walk back to the factory. The wind blew strongly in their faces. They had almost reached the plant when Nadya spoke.

"Oh," she said, "by the way. My brother is dead. They sent a card."

Lena walked on, her back bent and the rope of the sled over her sagging shoulders. Finally she broke the silence.

"Well, yes," she said. "So it is. So it is."

By the time the girls got back to the plant dusk had fallen.

Nadya had tried to tell the foreign correspondents what it had been like, coming back to the plant after spending hours plodding through the Leningrad streets on "emergency patrol."

"The first thing you did when you got back," she had said, "was to look around the room. You looked around to see if all your friends were still there—to see if anyone was missing after you had been away all day."

And that evening she had followed the usual custom. When she came into the little room there was a flickering light from a crack in the door of the stove where a small fire was burning. She looked around the circle, counting off in her mind, and sighing with relief. Everyone was there. The circle was not broken. A day had gone by and the company had not diminished. All of her friends were still alive. No one spoke, and she slipped silently into a vacant place on the bench, her eyes going around the circle once again to be certain she had missed no one. Suddenly, her gaze halted. True, everyone was sitting in the circle. Everyone who had been there that morning. But directly across from her sat Valya—Valya, the spitfire, the dark-eyed girl from the Ukraine, Valya, who had been so pale this last week, Valya whose eyes had been so glazed this morning. Tonight Valya still sat where she had this morning. But Valya was no longer of the company. Nadya's mind slowly absorbed what her eyes told her—the peculiar way in which the girl's head was thrown back, the closed eyes, the leg twisted inward and the open mouth through which no breath passed in or out. Valya still sat in the circle but Valya was dead. Nadya looked away from the dead girl; her eyes fell on her own hand. Clutched in her fingers was a crumpled piece of paper. Puzzled, she brought it closer to her eyes. Oh, yes. She remembered now. Her brother. He was dead. Of course. Now, her family was gone. No one was left but her. How curious it was. And how strange that no one had noticed that Valya was dead. Perhaps they were all dead and only she was alive. She looked carefully at her companions. No. They were alive. Quite possibly they hadn't noticed Valya. In that case she would say nothing about it. There was no need to bother anyone now. In the morning would be time enough. It was very cold in the shop, and perhaps there would be no need to disturb anyone. Perhaps by morning they would all have joined Valya. It was very cold. Very cold and dark . . .

The next thing which Nadya knew was a strong hand behind her head and a firm voice saying to her: "Come, dear, drink this. It will do you good."

She opened her eyes and saw that she was lying on a cot with her head supported by the arm of a woman whose eyes were the most beautiful she had ever seen. In one hand the woman held to Nadya's lips a steaming glass which appeared to be tea. The girl drank a little of the steaming liquid. It *was* tea—sweet tea. She shuddered with delight.

"Who are you?" she asked in wonderment. "Where am I?"

The woman smiled. "Drink your tea and the questions can come later."

The woman was Irena Galina, Nadya quickly realized as her senses began to come back to her. Irena Galina had adopted the Putilov girls early in the siege. As conditions had grown worse and worse she had not abandoned them. She had arrived at the plant in a military truck a few minutes after Nadya's collapse and had taken matters into her own efficient hands. The truck was going right back to the city and the driver agreed to carry Nadya to one of the special first-aid centers which had been set up to treat persons collapsing of fatigue, cold and hunger. Irena went along. She gently removed from Nadya's clenched fist the notice of her brother's death and read it with an aching heart.

Nadya drank the tea and felt its warmth going into every part of her body. She felt her eyes closing and the drowsy drug of slumber creeping into her tired limbs.

"I know who you are," the girl said as she drifted into sleep. "You're my fairy godmother."

The struggle to save Nadya's life was longer and more difficult than the young girl could have imagined. She was far closer to joining the dark-eyed Ukrainian Valya than anyone ever told her. In the hospital to which she was transferred Nadya's life hung in the balance for weeks. Day after day Irena visited the girl, seeking to infuse in her the spirit to live again. It was almost, Nadya later thought, as though the older woman had been determined by sheer physical force to wrest her life from the grasp of death. Finally, the tide turned. Day by day, as spring strengthened in the northern city, Nadya's strength began to return. To give the girl something to do, something to which her interest might be attracted, Irena brought her paints and drawing materials. She encouraged her to draw, at first thinking of it only as a kind of therapy, but to her astonishment she found that the Putilov girl had a sensitive eye, a sure hand and a true talent.

One afternoon in late spring Irena was sitting with Nadya on a bench in the Summer Garden. It was a warm, pleasant day. Around them was a hubbub of activity. The park was being dug up for the planting of potatoes and cabbage. But where they sat it was quiet. Nadya was pale, thin and weak. But there was life in her eyes again and she smiled as she watched the clumsy efforts of some Leningraders whose hands, obviously, were more accustomed to wielding a pen than a shovel.

Irena was watching her with a mother's warm affection.

"Dear Nadya," she said, "I wonder if you would consent to do me a very great favor?"

"But, of course, Irena Mikhailovna," the girl responded. "I would do anything for you. Without you—well, I'd not be here."

"Now, none of that," Irena said. "You're here because you are a fine, strong, vital human being—and a talented girl besides. What

I want to ask of you is this—I am all alone now, as you know. You are alone too. Would you come to live with me? It would be very good of you."

"I'd love it, Irena Mikhailovina," the girl said. Then a shadow crossed her face. "The only thing is—well, the fact is I'm thinking about the other girls at the Putilov works. I can't let them down."

"No," said the sculptress seriously. "Of course not. So long as you are needed the plant comes first. But now that streetcars are beginning to run again you can keep up your work and, meantime, I want you to begin seriously on your art. This, too, is an obligation which you must not neglect."

Thus it had started. Nadya's fairy godmother became a godmother and more. She shaped the talent of the young girl, personally supervised her training, encouraged her to try sculpture as well as painting. And when Irena came to do her "End of War" group it was Nadya whom she chose as the model for the young virgin.

Now, thought Nadya, the woman who gave me life, the woman who became my mother when I was left alone in the world, the woman who touched the spring of my talent and started me on the long, hard, satisfying apprenticeship to art, the woman who had life enough to give to a whole generation of Leningrad is dead.

Gradually, she realized, Michael's body had become quiet, and now he raised his head and looked deeply into her eyes.

"Forgive me," he said. "I do not know how I could be so weak. I am ashamed that you should be the victim of my poor nerves."

Nadya returned Michael's gaze with frank and open eyes. She leaned forward and kissed him gently on the roughness of his thin cheek.

"Dear Michael," she said. "It is very difficult for me to believe that Irena is dead. But bless you, dear Michael, for coming here. It has been a long time. A very long time."

197

25

The dam had broken now and words were flowing from Michael's lips in a steady stream, the sentences tumbling over each other as he tried to tell everything at once, how his mother had died, how he had felt in that moment, what he had learned from life in the East, the plans he had made, how he had brought his mother's body to Leningrad, all that had happened on the way and all that had happened since his arrival.

How expressive his eyes are, Nadya thought. They are gray-green like his mother's and have the same yellow sparks in them. And how lined his face was and how dark the bristle of his chin and cheeks. What fire came into his eyes as he talked! How white his teeth and strong his mouth. Nadya caught herself suddenly. What was coming over her? What feeling was stirring in her breast? What impulse had compelled her to kiss this man? She gasped inwardly. It was this same man, this terrible boy as he was then, who had shamed his name, who had permitted himself to indulge in the cheapest scandal, who had brought suffering to his mother. Currency speculation! Trading in the street! How could he have done it? Nadya had been stunned when it happened. She had seen it all—the police coming to the studio, the search of Michael's room, his arrest and the spectacle of him being led away from the house. When the two investigators came out of Michael's room and she saw him standing between them her heart had leapt into her throat. It could not be. They could not do this. It was some terrible mistake. She started to go to him and then she saw the sick, guilty look on his face and the way he turned his eyes from her. She covered her face with her hands and ran into her room, locking the door and throwing herself on her bed, where she cried until she could cry no more. How could he? How could he? If he had no feeling for her at least he might have spared his mother. Finally Nadya began to bring herself under control. Sometimes, she said, a thing like this happens. Sometimes, a person whom you admire and trust violates that trust. This is life. It is hard but it must be endured even though the pain is great. Never again, she vowed, would she speak to Michael. Never again would she see him. Not even if he should come back. She would train herself not to think about him, to erase the memory of him from her mind. After all, she told herself, this was not the first time Michael had been involved in something bad. What the trouble had been in the Army she did not know exactly, but once she had come into the room where Irena was working and found General Orlov with the sculptress; they were talking about Michael. She had heard the General say: "Rest assured. I have gone over the record completely. There is no case against Michael. Nothing."

Was that really so or was General Orlov just trying to be kind, just trying to reassure Michael's mother? On the terrible day when the officers led Michael away she remembered Orlov's remark. She thought, too, of Michael's father—of the scandalous stories which had circulated about him, of the dreadful things he was supposed to have done. Reluctantly, very reluctantly, she told herself that Michael must take after his father rather than his mother. What made her so reluctant was that she had begun to be fond of Michael. She knew that in him there existed a vein of deep, deep bitterness, but she knew that he had gone through terrible experiences in the war—who had not? And when the bitter mood was not on him he had such a gay, mad spirit that he quite set her head spinning. Occasionally he would play the accordion, improvising songs as he went along, like the village boys. Except that Michael's songs were not tiresome and full of smutty puns. His songs were light and witty as the bubbles in a glass of champagne. Nadya and Michael had long talks together in the time when he was still convalescing from his wound. She told him about her dreams of someday becoming a sculptress like Irena Galina.

"I know you'll think that I shouldn't talk like this," she had said, "when I am just a beginner."

"No," Michael had said, and she could still see the faraway look in his eyes. "No. You should talk like that. Dream of the stars. Perhaps you'll not reach them. But then again you may. The road to the stars. That's the one to follow."

They had been lying in the long grass of the Botanical Gardens. The summer sun was hot and the grass smelled of a thousand flowers, a thousand perfumes. It was so tall and heavy that lying there together was something like being in a green cave with the blue sky high, high above them.

"I think you'll reach the stars, Nadezhda Fedorovna," Michael had said. And, listening to him, Nadya believed she would, too. And, in her heart, she saw Michael climbing up the road to the stars at her side. Looking into Michael's eyes as he talked, Nadya had another impulse in her heart. She wished in that moment that Michael would take her in his arms, hold her close to him and kiss her while the warm sun shone down on them.

But Michael's mind seemed to be concentrated on the future rather than the present. He did not, he told Nadya, want to follow an artistic career. He did not have his mother's talent, nor the poetic gifts of his father, either. Nadya had tried to persuade him that he was wrong. Perhaps he had not inherited his mother's ability but when he was improvising verses so freely, so gaily for his accordion there was more than an echo of Maxim Voronsky's wild, impetuous flow of words. But Michael brushed aside Nadya's arguments.

"No, Nadya," he said. "I know what I want to be. True, I have lost a great deal of time because of the war. But that is not unusual. That must simply be passed over. No, what I want to do is to go to the scientific faculty of the university. I think that a new world lies just ahead of us—a world which science is going to give us—one which will make this puny, dirty, stupid world of ours seem as backward as an African tribal village. Or one of our own poor villages out in the back country of the Volga—if we speak realistically. That new world is the one I want to live in. That is where I want to put my mind and my energies and what abilities I have. Into science. Call me naïve, if you wish, Nadya. But that is my road to the stars."

They had strolled along the canals of Leningrad, along the Fontanka and the Moika, discussing those questions which Russian young men and women have discussed since the time of Pushkin and Lermontov, discussing the nature of truth, the struggle between passion and conscience, whether man was noble and only made vile through environment or whether, as the religious philosophers held, there was in each man a born evil, a tendency to baseness which only his own struggle and the conditioning of a positive social system could overcome.

And, of course, they discussed love.

Love, Michael said, was not the simple emotion which many women seemed to think. It was an extraordinarily complex phenomenon. At its base was the ancient and eternal physical nature of man and woman, the need of each for the other, the need of each to find completeness in the other, and, of course, the social and economic characteristics which derived from the family. He sketched in the sociology and history of the family with broad gestures, even becoming a little pedantic, as though he were on the lecture platform at the Polytechnic. Nadya was amused although she took care not to smile. Suddenly Michael laughed at himself, saying: "What nonsense I talk, Nadya! Why don't you stop me when I get going?"

And he took her hand and gave it a swift, warm kiss.

"But why should I stop you, Michael," she replied, "when you are speaking so interestingly? I want to hear what you have to say—even if I don't entirely agree with you."

"Ha!" he said. "I'll bet you don't. No woman thinks a man knows anything about love. All of you are the same. Sometimes, I think you women imagine that you invented love."

"But of course," Nadya flared up. "Of course women know more about love than men do. After all, men have many things on their minds. We have more time to think of love."

"What a thing for a new Soviet woman to say." Michael laughed.

Nadya knew that he was teasing her. Nevertheless she persisted.

"No, Michael," she said. "I am serious. Very serious. Love is the very center of woman's life. We begin to study love when we are little girls. We think about it all during our girlhood. And then when we are women, or even before that, we begin to live in love. So, of course, we know more about it than men. And it is right that we do. You men know much more about other things than we do. And that is right, too."

So their talks had gone. Nadya had not stopped to analyze her feelings about Michael. There had never been time. They had walked together, talked together, laughed together, held hands, even kissed, a little shyly, a little hesitantly, a few times. Then from this, from talk of the nature of love, from dreams of the stars, suddenly to fall into the abyss. Cheating . . . deals . . . dirty foreign money . . . the police! How could Michael! How could he! Nadya had tried very hard not to let Irena Galina suspect how she felt about Michael. When Irena suggested that Nadya write to Michael, that it would help him over the hard time he was going through, that he would be so pleased to hear from her, Nadya made one excuse after another.

She had not written to Michael. Nor had he written to her—at least he had shown the good taste to spare her that. Nadya threw herself harder than ever into learning to be an artist. She was working in the Institute where Irena Galina conducted classes; she was studying the history of classical art; spending long hours in the Hermitage. There was so much to learn and so little time. It was only later that she began to realize how preoccupied Irena Galina was; how worried she was becoming.

One evening Nadya came home to find the sculptress sitting in the studio. It was long past six but there was no light. Irena was sitting in the dark on a small bench against the wall, her chin on her breast, deep in reverie. She obviously had been sitting there for a long time. Nadya was startled.

"Oh, Irena Mikhailovna," she said. "Is something the matter? Are you feeling all right?"

The sculptress looked at Nadya with tortured eyes.

"Nothing is the matter, dear," Irena said. "Nothing—or everything. Sometimes it is hard to know which. Sometimes it is very hard to understand what it is that one is trying to do with one's life. Or, perhaps, I should say what life is trying to do to you."

Nadya's face betrayed her troubled feelings.

"You are young, Nadya," Irena said. "Yet you have seen more of life than I at twice your age. Perhaps you will grow up a wiser woman than I—less prone to judge others, more charitable of the fact that we human beings are such imperfect creatures."

Nadya busied herself putting a teakettle on the hot plate. She had never seen Irena, usually so decisive, so optimistic, in such a mood.

"When you are young," the sculptress continued, "you are apt to be harsh with those whom you think have failed to measure up to the standards which you set for them. In the name of justice—or some other abstract ideal—you commit the greatest of crimes. And then as you grow older life teaches you a lesson. Life bends your back in its strong hands and you suddenly find that you, too, are not measuring up to those standards of your youth. But now as you begin to understand the true nature of charity—it is too late. The victims of your passion for justice no longer exist. Or have learned to live without your belated charity."

"But, Irena," Nadya protested, "how can you say such things?

You have done such great good to so many people."

"I wonder," the sculptress said. "I really wonder. Before the war I don't suppose I ever thought very deeply about questions of human conduct. It seemed to me that there was only one way to behave— the right way, the honest way, the straightforward way. I thought I knew what those words meant."

"You do, Irena," the girl interrupted. "You do."

"Perhaps, dear Nadya." Irena sighed. "Perhaps I know now. Having lived through a war in which I saw the best men and women I knew die. In which I saw beautiful children crying in pain or silently watching their life blood bubble out of a broken artery.

"One day I was walking on the Nevsky. I think it was in November of 1941. There was a boy just ahead of me, a thin, ragged, dirty boy of twelve or perhaps fourteen. A woman came out of the bakery with her ration in her hands—a hard black piece of bread the size of your fist. The boy grabbed it from her but she caught him by the shoulder and started to rain blows on him.

"The boy paid absolutely no attention to the blows—they were hard blows, too. He just put the bread to his mouth and tore off hunks with his teeth. The woman kept crying: 'He stole my bread. I'll starve. I'll starve. Help me.' And the boy kept eating the bread, not even feeling the blows she hurled at him."

"How terrible, Irena," Nadya said.

"Yes," said Irena. "It was terrible. The boy had no ration card. Without the bread he would starve to death. The woman had a ration card. But without her bread she would starve to death. Where was right? Where was justice? Where was the truth between the starving boy and the starving woman?"

Irena was silent a moment.

"The boy was like a young wolf. The woman was like an old wolf. They were two animals, fighting like animals, living like animals," she said. "Why? Why? This was the question that tortured my mind. It was not the boy. It was not the woman. It was all of us who permitted the world to exist in such a shape, who fashioned our society in such a way that, sooner or later, we became animals.

All of us. Myself included, dear Nadya. And so I resolved to fight that world, to fight that society. To do what one woman could with what strength she had to change this system in which we live and die as beasts in human form."

"Oh, Irena," Nadya cried, "we will build a better world. We will. Everyone says that we will."

Irena put her head in her hands and rocked back and forth, overcome by the force of her emotion. Finally she rose, shaking her head and clenching her teeth.

"I do not know, Nadya," she said. "I really do not know whether we can or not. We are such animals. Such animals."

What specifically had put Irena Galina into this mood of deep pessimism Nadya never knew. But it was only a short time thereafter that she was denounced—denounced, disgraced, exiled. Three words, but they had marked the division in Nadya's life from girlhood to womanhood.

Irena had called Nadya to her one evening. Her face was white as paper but her lips were set and her eyes were clear.

"I want to tell you something extremely serious," she began. "A meeting of the Committee on Art will be held tomorrow. It has been summoned to act under a decree which the Party has already approved. This decree has as its subject—myself. Soon, perhaps within the week, I shall be sent away from Leningrad."

Nadya broke into tears.

"No, Nadya dear," Irena said in a firm voice. "No tears, please. This is much too serious for tears. There are two things which it is important for you to understand. In the first place, the crime which I have committed is the creation of my 'End of War' group. This, they say, is an artistic crime against the state. To be against war, or at least in the sense in which I oppose war, is said to be against the interests of the state. Please do not forget this."

Nadya nodded solemnly.

"The second thing, Nadya dear," Irena said, "is that I do not want you or anyone who has been close to me to be involved. Do not—if you love me—say or do anything. This is my business. Not yours. You will only make life more difficult for me if you become involved."

"But, Irena Mikhailovna," the girl cried, "this is cruel. This is unjust."

"Please, Nadya," the sculptress interrupted. "Please. Do not talk of justice. If you wish to help, if you wish to give me some small comfort, be silent. Remember me. Do not forget me. But—for now —be silent. Work at your art. Become a fine artist. I believe you can become a very great one. Do this and try to be true to life and true to what you believe in."

Irena had sent her away. Had flatly refused to let her speak. It was their last real conversation. The next few days passed like a nightmare. Even now Nadya could not think of them in any coherent fashion. All that she was certain of was that within a fortnight she had been left alone. There was a great iron padlock on the studio. Irena had been permitted to take only a suitcase of personal things. The studio was sealed. Indeed, to this day it was still padlocked and unoccupied. The police had come and questioned Nadya. They had been polite, and when the inquiry was over she was told that she might continue living in her room.

"We are sorry to have had to put you to this trouble," one of the plainclothesmen told her. "It's really only a formality. Now you go on about your work just as though nothing had happened."

The men had politely touched their caps and stepped out of the room, leaving Nadya to go to school every day, to spend the afternoon in the Hermitage, the evening in the library, and return at night to make herself a lonely glass of tea, passing each time she went in and out of her door the great padlock on the entrance to the studio.

All those resolutions she had made long ago about Michael— somehow, they did not seem to make any difference to Nadya now. All that seemed to matter was that he was here, sitting beside her, talking, talking, talking, and she, she suddenly realized, had been lost in thought and hadn't heard half of what he had said.

206

"Oh, Michael," she said, "I don't know what has come over me. I have been letting you talk, and never thinking about how you must feel. You're so tired. I must get you some tea. This minute."

Michael looked at her as she sprang to her feet and went over to the electric hot plate on the table. He smiled and then rose slowly and followed her.

"Thank you, Nadya," he said. "That would be very good. It's been such a long day and the night is more than a little frosty."

She turned to him and he drew her into his arms, holding her close and putting his bristling cheek against hers. She felt herself melting against him. Their heads moved and his lips, warm and firm, touched her own.

26

Suddenly it seemed to Nadya that she must apologize to Michael for turning her back on him when he was arrested. She felt a surge of guilt in her heart as though she had in some way forsaken him. She knew in this instant what she had not known before—that Michael had done nothing wrong, that he could have done nothing wrong, that what had happened had been done against him.

"Oh, Michael," she said to him, her brown eyes dark with tears. "I have been so terrible. I have acted so badly to you. Please forgive me."

Puzzlement spread over Michael's face.

"But, Nadya," he said gently, "I don't know what you are talking about. Certainly you have done nothing against me."

"Oh, yes, I have," the girl insisted. "You just don't know. You don't know what I did—what I felt—when you were arrested and taken away."

She put her hand shyly on his arm.

"I must tell you, Michael, how bad I was," she went on slowly. "You see, I was such a fool. Just a stupid fool. When the police came I thought you had done something wrong and it shocked me so that I lost my sense of judgment. I don't know why it was, Michael, but when I saw the expression on your face—you looked, well, you looked ashamed and guilty. And I felt you had betrayed me. And I was hurt and angry."

Michael was looking at her with a mixture of compassion and wonder. She forced herself to go on.

"I decided, Michael," Nadya said, "that I would never speak to you again. Nor see you—if you ever came back. That's—that's why I never wrote you. Even though your mother asked me to."

Michael took her face in his two hands and looked Nadya straight in the eyes. He looked so long and so deeply that her head began to swim.

"You are so good, Nadya," Michael said. "So good that you do not even understand how good you are. I am the one who should be asking your forgiveness."

He walked away from her, into the shadows at the edge of the room, and then returned, his face deep in thought.

"I was arrested," Michael said, "on a charge of trading in foreign currency. Of buying dollars from a speculator. The charge, unfortunately, was true. The fact that many others did the same is incidental. It was, perhaps, not a serious crime in ordinary circumstances. But because someone wished to treat it seriously it became a serious matter."

Michael resumed his pacing and then went on.

"I was a silly and thoughtless youngster, Nadya," he said. "You should understand that. I jeopardized my mother's position, I brought pain and distress to you and, at least in one sense, ruined whatever prospect I had for making some use of my life."

Nadya interrupted him.

"Don't be unfair to yourself, Michael," she said. "I don't care what you say. I know perfectly well you did nothing bad. Admit it —you were not going to do anything bad with the money."

Michael made a wry grimace. "No, Nadya," he said. "Nothing very bad. A boy I knew at the Institute of Electrophysics had a chance to get some technical manuals—American and English ones they were. The man insisted on having dollars. I knew a fellow who had some dollars so I sold him a few things I didn't need. That was it."

Nadya looked at him triumphantly.

"So you see, Michael," she said, "there was nothing wrong with what you did. And yet I behaved as though you were a great criminal. You see how stupid and unkind I really am. Your mother once said—it was one of the last talks we had together—that when you are young you are often cruel and unjust—thinking that you are being just. And I have been unjust. Terribly unjust."

Michael sighed. "Would that there were in the world no more injustice than you are capable of creating, Nadya. What a fine world it then would be. You have no idea."

Then he returned to his point.

"You see, Nadya," he said, "regardless of whether or not I was guilty of the crime of speculation I was guilty of a greater crime—that of exposing persons whom I loved to the retribution of cruel, remorseless enemies. That was my crime. And I hope that I have learned my lesson."

Nadya squeezed his hand tenderly.

"It was no accident, Nadya," he said, "that I looked guilty and ashamed when I was arrested. I knew then how guilty I was. I had had one chance already to learn what the world was about—to learn what kind of blind and desperate forces lie in wait for us. But I did not learn my lesson. I was young and confused. I could not believe that what had happened to me was really true."

"You never spoke to me about this," Nadya said.

"No," Michael replied. "I didn't know what to say because I didn't really know what to think."

He told Nadya about his wartime experience, how he had become separated from his comrades while on patrol and had wandered about for two days, trying to find a way back through the German lines. Three times he had almost been captured. Once he literally stumbled over a German on outpost duty but the man was asleep, or possibly drunk, and in the dark Michael managed to escape.

Finally, he had attempted a wide circuit of the lines, through a deep swamp. It was here he encountered the partisans.

"There were only a dozen of us," Michael said. "We kept thinking our troops would break through and we could rejoin them. But the lines got pushed back and we had to fend for ourselves, like it or not."

Fortunately, there were peasants in the area who kept them supplied with food. The group was too small to think of attacking the Germans, but a few weeks later the detachment grew to about forty men when some prisoners on a work detail managed to make their escape.

"We carried out several pretty good operations," Michael said. "Once we knocked out a truck column and blew up some ammunition. Another time we raided a camp and stole some machine guns. We killed five or six Nazis that time. And lost two of our lads."

When the Red Army finally advanced the partisans were able to rejoin their comrades. "We threw our caps in the air," Michael said. "We literally did. We hugged each other. Oh, how happy we were!"

But the partisans were herded into a special camp, treated like prisoners of war, interrogated, sometimes beaten, kept without food and water.

"Some of the boys said, 'See—why did we bother to fight the Nazis? We should have given up. Nobody believes us anyway.' But I didn't agree," Michael said. "I said it was a mistake. That perhaps the Nazis had infiltrated some agents into the partisan groups. That special precautions had to be taken."

Even when he was put into the punitive battalion Michael had tried to convince himself that somehow there was no bad intent lying behind the grim mechanism in which he found himself trapped.

"The other lads said I was a silly kid," Michael recalled. "They said if they had a chance they would run away to the Germans. 'There's one chance in three that we can surrender without getting killed,' one of them said. 'That's better than staying here where the chances are three out of three.'"

"My poor Michael," Nadya said, putting his head against her breast. "No wonder you were sometimes bitter."

"I was bitter," Michael said, "but I had not learned the lesson. I was still trying to tell myself there was something unusual about what had happened. Not until the officers came to arrest me for currency speculation did it begin to penetrate my mind that none of these things were accidents; this was life; this was what it meant to live in Russia; this was the system which we had fought to preserve; this was not bad luck; this was the way things were planned to be."

The tea was long since finished and Michael suddenly rose.

"I'm forgetting entirely about the time," he said. "I must go on."

Nadya looked at him in wonder. "Where are you going?"

Michael for the first time seemed confused.

"Well," he said, "on my way. It is late. You are tired and I must be up early in the morning. I have much to do."

"Yes," Nadya persisted. "But where do you propose to stay, Michael?"

He frowned and Nadya quickly added: "You are going nowhere, Michael. You are staying here tonight. Don't try to think up some lie for me. I know perfectly well that you have no place to go."

Michael looked around the room. On one side was the couch on which Nadya obviously slept. Across the room was a large upholstered settee. He smiled at Nadya.

"Well, of course," he said, "you happen to be quite right. I've been so busy that I forgot to think about a room for the night. But before I accept your offer there is one thing which I want you to understand."

Michael sat down again, placing Nadya by his side.

"I want to tell you what happened just before I came here tonight," he said. He explained how he had made the long trip to Vasilevsky Island, seeking out Katerina.

"I was sure that she would want to know about my mother," he said. "And I was sure Mother would want her to know."

He had knocked at the door and a little girl opened it. He asked if her mother was there and she ushered him into the room where Katerina sat nursing a fat, husky baby. He was a big-headed, blue-eyed boy and already he resembled his mother. Katerina did not rise. She did not recognize Michael, and when he told her of his mother's death she did not seem to understand exactly what he was talking about.

He stood near the door and said again to the woman: "I am afraid you do not know who I am. I am Michael Galin, the son of your friend Irena Galina. My mother has died and her funeral is tomorrow. I thought that you would like to know."

As he was saying this he watched Katerina rise, suddenly looming large in the room. She set down the child on the chair and advanced upon him with blazing eyes.

"What do you mean coming here, you scum," she said, raising her hand and striking him full on the cheek. "I don't know what you're talking about and I don't want to know. Get out of here before I throw you out. Get out!"

"How could she have done that?" Nadya interjected. "What came over her?"

"Nothing," Michael said grimly. "She is a wise woman and a prudent mother. When I staggered out of the room my head was in a daze. I thought for a moment I was going mad. But I understand Katerina now. She is a woman with a family, a woman with two fine children and a husband. She doesn't want to get involved in anything which would threaten them. I think that she thought I was a provocateur. She reacted with the natural instinct of a primitive mother, defending her young."

"But that's ridiculous, Michael," Nadya said.

"No," he replied. "I am a danger to her and I am a danger to you and this you must understand. It is a miracle that I have gotten as far as I have. But this kind of miracle is going to come to an end. Perhaps they will not interfere with the funeral tomorrow. Perhaps

213

they will. I do not know. You realize that, don't you?"

Nadya nodded her head.

"For myself," Michael said, "I don't care. I know what I am doing and I am prepared to pay any price that is exacted of me. I have told those who I thought should know about the funeral. I have tried to tell all of the persons who played some important part in my mother's life—her friends, her enemies. I even have invited the Security Chief, Chaikovsky, and Party Secretary Ivanov. Perhaps this seems strange to you. But these are the people who I—the son of Irena Galina—think should honor her memory. And so I have asked them to come tomorrow. These people understand what is involved. They are not children. It is their decision whether they come or not. I spoke, incidentally, to some of the students at the Art Institute. That is how I learned that you were still here. I told them of the funeral, too. But I warned them that it was serious business."

"But, Michael," Nadya began to protest.

"Now Katerina obviously thought that even my coming to see her might be a danger," Michael said. "And I am not so sure that she was not right."

Michael told Nadya of his suspicion that someone had followed him after he left Katerina and was on his way to the studio.

"Of one thing I am certain," he said. "No one tracked me here. No one knows that I am here. No one knows that I have seen you. And no one is going to know. I will leave in the morning, quietly as a cat, and if you do not come to the funeral not only will I understand but I will respect your good judgment and wisdom."

Nadya looked at him aghast.

"That was a cruel and unthinking remark, Michael," she said. "You know that I am going to the funeral and you know that I am going with you in the morning and I am going to help you in every way that you can be helped."

Michael looked at the slim figure of the girl, so solemn, so determined. He looked at the set of her mouth, the calm conviction of her brown eyes and the firmness of her hands, clenched into white fists.

He put his arm around her shoulder.

"Yes," he said. "I suppose you are coming to the funeral. And I will not try to halt you in that. But you are not going with me in the morning. I have things to do. And while you may get into trouble for coming to my mother's burial, I do not think you will get into serious trouble if you do not come with me. Come with the other students."

Nadya argued hotly and bitterly. But Michael was inflexible. He insisted that he would walk out of the room into the cold night unless she gave him her promise that she would permit him to leave quietly, circumspectly and unseen in the morning. He made her promise, as well, that she would come to the funeral with the students and that if she were questioned ("And, dearest Nadya, you will be questioned. I can assure you of that") that she would not mention that he had come to her and, naturally, that she would not say that he had spent the night in her room.

"And now," Michael said, stifling a yawn, "it is time that we were getting some sleep. I must be up very early. You have no idea of the number of things I must do."

But, of course, that was not the end of it. Not by any means. Tired as Michael was, tired as Nadya was, their minds were too much astir, the excitement of their reunion, the sensation of being together, of being alone and secretly alone from the whole world, were too much in their blood to let them quietly drift off into dreamless slumber.

Michael took off his heavy boots and stretched out on the settee, covering himself with his overcoat. Nadya came and sat on the floor beside him, taking his hand and holding it to her breast.

Michael began talking about life in the East.

"Do you remember, Nadya dear," he said, "how I used to talk about reaching for the stars?"

"Oh, yes," Nadya said. "I've never forgotten that. The road to the stars."

"That's right," Michael said. "The road to the stars. I used to tell you about the new world that science was going to build and how I wanted to be part of that world. I don't know now. I'm not so sure that science is really going to make over this old, stubborn, cruel, ignorant society that we live in. I just don't know whether society is going to permit science to substitute new for old and good for bad."

"But what will happen, Michael?" Nadya asked.

"Lord, I don't know," he answered, his forehead creased with frowns. "But one thing I do know. That is that out there in the East, in Siberia, or Kazakhstan or the Uzbek country, a man can begin to think, to think about the really basic things of life."

"But you can do that here," the girl said. "You thought about life. We talked about it."

"True, Nadya, true," Michael said. "We did talk and we thought we were talking about life. But I don't believe we had really begun to understand it. You know I met a very interesting man out there. He turned up at the cotton plantation where I was working."

The man was a tramp. He appeared one autumn evening just at dusk, an old man, probably in his seventies, but spry in his limbs, a man who walked with upright back and a spring in his pace. He was clean-shaven except for a tiny fringe of a beard. His eyes were pale blue like a baby's and his cheeks were tanned and ruddy from years of exposure to wind and weather. He wore an old belted Russian blouse, the wide pantaloon trousers which the Urals miners still favor and soft leather boots, very soft and very worn.

He came up to the barracks just as the men were lining up for supper and asked for something to eat. Someone handed him a bowl and a spoon, he joined the line, took his bowl of soup and hunk of black bread and sat down on a wooden bench. Michael sat next to him.

"Have you been out here long?" Michael asked. Something about the man excited his curiosity. He had a feeling that the stranger had something to tell him. What it was and why he had this feeling he did not know.

"Oh," said the man, scratching his silvery hair, "I'm an old one. I've traveled these roads since I was a boy. I'm what you might call a real *brodyaga*—a real old-fashioned tramp. Why, back in the days before the Revolution I walked all the way to Siberia in one of the old *katorga* parties. And I've been walking the roads of Siberia and the East ever since."

He had come, he said, originally from Petersburg.

"I was a wild one," he said. "Always getting into trouble. Of course, I could say that it was political and some of it was. But, to tell the truth, more of it wasn't. It was just wildness. Wildness and youth."

And had he never been back, Michael asked.

"Aye," he said. "I went back to Petersburg. Petrograd it was then. After the Revolution. But it was not for me. I couldn't stand the feel of pavement under my boots. Nor the voices of men telling me: Do this. Do that. Work at this. Think of that. No, that was not for me."

He had, he said, been sent East again.

"Well, it wasn't the *katorga* this time," the old man said. "It was the new Soviet power. I fought for the Soviet power in Siberia. But that didn't seem to change too much. Once you've had a taste of being a free man—well, it does something to you. People say that Siberia is a terrible land—a land of pain and suffering. Well, I say Siberia is a land where a man can be a man. It's a hard life. Sure. But life everywhere is hard. And not many places is it free."

The old tramp had rambled on and on.

"You know," he said, "Siberia gets into your blood. I've seen it time and again. A man comes out. Let's say he's sent out. Like yourself, if you don't mind my saying so. He hates it. It tears his life to pieces. He is separated from his family. He loses his place. His job. He comes out here and he's like all the rest of us—just a clod— a clod on the great Siberian continent. Sure, he has to work. But no one cares too much what he does, how hard he works. If he wants to go into the forest, into the *taiga*—well, who's going to work up a sweat looking for him? Let him go, poor devil. He'll come back soon enough. Or he'll starve. One or the other. And they're right. Comes the winter, the fierce Siberian *burya*. What happens? Well, he either survives, finds a way to live, or he comes back to the camp—if he can make it. Otherwise he dies. But it is his own free choice. No one makes him do it."

Like the convict in the railroad car the old man was convinced that Siberia was the land of true freedom.

"People think that they are free," he said, "when they are back in Moscow. Or in Leningrad. They think that Siberia is a jail. But what is the truth? The truth is that in Moscow or Leningrad you are chained to a desk, chained to a factory, chained, God forgive you, to a wife and a family. And what about Siberia? Free. Free as a breeze. Go where you want. Do as you please. Who cares? It's all a prison anyway so what difference does it make? The difference between Siberia and the rest of the world is that here we are all prisoners and all free. And in the rest of the world you are all prisoners and all slaves."

"The curious thing about it is," Michael said, growing more and more excited as he talked, "the curious thing about it is that this upside-down, topsy-turvy philosophy of the old man has a strange truth about it. Out there you'll find that men are more free. They are more brave. They do speak their minds. They think in a way that we have almost forgotten back here."

Nadya looked up at him. There was pure adoration in her eyes.

"Out there in the East," Michael said, "I began to understand those things that had puzzled me so—the punitive battalion, the way we partisans were treated, the arrests for currency violations and all the other violations that may or may not be serious, depending on whether someone wants to consider them serious, and, of course, the campaign against my mother, the necessity for destroying her; indeed, the inevitability of her destruction. These are the mechanisms which have turned Siberia into a prison. But they are also what make Russia the antechamber of Siberia."

Michael clenched his fist.

"Does any of this sound familiar to you?" he asked. "Does any of this sound like the Russia we thought our fathers had destroyed, once and for all? When I began to realize what a diabolic thing had been done to my mother my mind was made up. There was no longer any choice. I am her son and if no one else in the world believes in her and still I believe in her, then I must act— or the belief is meaningless. Perhaps you think I'm just a Don Quixote. Just an adolescent . . ."

"No, Michael," Nadya cried. "No."

"If we march, generation after generation, grumbling a bit like sulky children but keeping step, minding the drill sergeant," he said, "doing what we are told because we are afraid to do otherwise, then we should at least understand that the inevitable goal is extinction—moral or physical. And I can't see that there is much difference between one and the other. I am just a young man and my life has no meaning. But perhaps by sacrificing it I can give it some meaning."

Michael looked at Nadya. She smiled sleepily at him. Gradually the fierceness died from his eyes. He sprang from the settee, picked Nadya up in his arms and carried her over to her bed. He laid her down gently, pulled a blanket over her, kissed each of her eyes tenderly, pressed his lips lightly against her own, ran his hand over her soft brown hair and retreated to his own bed, saying softly: "Sleep, little one. Sleep. Soon it will be dawn."

27

Fortunately, Smirnoff knew precisely where General Orlov lived —Room 233 at the Hotel d'Angleterre, more recently called the Hotel Leningrad since the publication of a feuilleton in the local paper, commenting sarcastically on the name as a "survival from the bourgeois past." The General had moved into the hotel when it was taken over by the Army at the start of the war and had grown fond of his big old-fashioned room with its view of St. Isaac's Square. When he was offered a flat in the new building which the Defense Ministry was putting up on Stalin Prospekt, he declined. "My place is comfortable and convenient. Let one of the men with families have that flat."

Smirnoff shaved himself with special care. He hated to use a razor and ordinarily went to a barbershop. He liked to have the man fuss over him, massaging the slack muscles of his jaw and dousing him with fragrant toilet water. But he could not wait this morning. It was vital to catch Orlov before he left the hotel.

"Goddamn it!" Smirnoff exclaimed. His hand was not steady after the events of the night and he had managed to nick himself badly, just under the chin. Blood flowed freely until he finally tore a corner off *Pravda* and applied it to the wound.

What should he wear? Smirnoff always gave particular consideration to his dress. In part this was petty vanity but in part it reflected
private fears over his appearance. Because of this he constantly
sought to dress in the precise manner appropriate to a given oc-
casion and won the reputation of being more of a fop than he
actually was.

In truth Smirnoff had acquired his respect for and interest in
clothes from his father, who at the time of the Revolution was the
proprietor of a haberdashery and clothing establishment in a little
Volga town not far from Kazan. This was the darkest secret of
Smirnoff's past. In fact, he had almost wiped recollection of his real
father from his mind, so assiduously had he applied himself to telling the story he had invented—of the father who had worked as a
laborer on the Volga, a genuine *batrak*, sweated in the summer,
frozen in the winter, beaten and starved, summer and winter; how
he turned against his masters, fought in the Red Army and finally
was killed in the bitter battles against the Cossacks down in the
Don country. His mother long since dead, Smirnoff had been left
an orphan, making his way to Moscow. He got a job as a sweeper
boy in a big foundry, was recognized as a bright youngster by the
Party agitator, sent to the *rabfak*, then to another school, and finally
emerged as a writer, first of newspaper sketches and then of literary
works.

Part of this story was true. Smirnoff had been orphaned and he
had made his way to Moscow, gotten a factory job, been spotted
by a friendly Party worker and the rest had followed, more or less
as he told the tale. What he had almost succeeded in forgetting was
that his father was not a revolutionary. Indeed, he came from an
ambitious, greedy peasant family. Smirnoff's grandfather acquired
not a few rubles by squeezing his fellow peasants, enough so that
Smirnoff's father, just as greedy and just as ambitious, had managed
to set up in business in the little town. He was a kopek-pinching,
miserly man whose pride was to dress himself in a fine black frock
coat with a silk kerchief, fawn-colored spats and a gold-headed

cane and promenade along the dusty main street of the town on feast days. When revolution came to the little town, the merchants put up their iron shutters and bolted their doors, but the mob had little trouble tearing down the shutters and breaking into the establishments. Most of the merchants were in the street, watching what was going on, more or less philosophically. "Well, that's what revolution is!" old man Barazov, the owner of the grocery store, said, as he watched the hogsheads of liquor being broken open and the sacks of flour being carted off.

Not so Smirnoff's father. When the mob came to his store, he was inside with a pistol. Smirnoff, just twelve, and his brother, a few years older, were there, too. Smirnoff was terrified. He was a roly-poly boy, intelligent, quick with his lessons, sensitive about his fatness, often teased because other boys discovered his sensitivity, and invariably comforted by his mother, who loved to buy him special little cakes, particularly those made with hazelnuts and whipped cream. The boys were at their father's side to help him see that "those pigs do not break in."

"Don't try to break in," his father shouted to the crowd. "We are inside with weapons. And we are ready to shoot."

A raucous howl went up from the mob.

"Once a kulak always a kulak!" someone shouted, hammering on the door. Smirnoff crouched behind the counter, shivering in fright. His father called again: "Stand back or I'll fire." Another roar went up, then the sharp crack of a pistol. His father had fired, Smirnoff realized, as his nostrils caught the acrid stench of powder.

"The son of a bitch!" came a yell from outside. "He shot Kolya. Let's give it to him, lads!"

There were a rain of blows and a rattle of shots. Smirnoff heard his father cry out and a wail of pain or terror from his brother. That was the last he heard. Scrambling like a monkey on all fours, he managed to get out the rear door of the shop and into the alley, running blindly he knew not where until he found himself at the railroad yards. A long train of freight cars was resting on a siding and the door of one car was slightly open. He crawled inside, into the darkest corner, and huddled there, shaking with fright. Hours later he felt the train moving but he did not stir from his corner. Thus, he left his Volga birthplace. A year or two later he met in Moscow a boy from his home town who told him what had happened to his father and brother. His father's shot had killed one of the mob leaders, and when they broke down the door and found both Smirnoffs wounded but still alive they had sacked the shop in fury, and then, binding the two to a counter, poured kerosene on the floor and shelves, touched a match to it and stood by jeering as the flames crackled louder and louder, drowning out the cries of the dying men.

No matter what inner scars remained to torture his subconscious, Smirnoff had erased from his recollection these memories of earlier existence, and the only trace which seemed to have survived was the persisting care which he devoted to every detail of clothing himself.

He decided this morning to wear his olive-drab army breeches and his old tan Party blouse with its leather belt, a subtle way of emphasizing the Party's traditional superiority to and authority over the Army.

Smirnoff reached the hotel just before nine and went directly to the General's room. To his knock there was the instant response: "Come!" followed a moment later by the opening of the door by the General himself. His military greatcoat with its gray caracul collar lay on the bed. Obviously, Orlov was about to depart. A little nonplused, he shook hands with Smirnoff and waved him into the room.

"I must ask you to forgive me for approaching you in this informal manner," Smirnoff said hesitantly. Now that he was actually in the General's presence, face to face with the austere, commanding officer, his confidence faded. He began to speak rapidly and emphatically, as much to reassure himself as to impress the General. He told of his meeting with young Galin, not noting the General's involuntary start at the mention of the name.

"I know you're surprised, Comrade General," Smirnoff said, "that young Galin came to see me. But the fact is, in spite of what later happened, his mother had once been a good friend of mine. A very good friend."

The young man, he said, apparently had lost his mind.

"It is my only explanation, Comrade General," he said. "I am convinced that he has gone mad and in his madness he thinks that he must destroy everyone who once was associated with Irena Galina. He holds them responsible for her death. It seems to him to be an act of vengeance."

Smirnoff was relieved to see that the General was following the account with closest attention. Perhaps this was going to turn out all right.

He sketched his version of the boy's threat to Orlov, delicately showing his sympathy but, at the same time, revealing that he was aware of the blackmailing potentialities of the letter which he said Galin possessed.

"I tried to get it away from him," Smirnoff said warmly. "But he was too quick and refused to let me have it in my hands."

In ordinary circumstances, he suggested, the case would be a simple one for the police. But in the situation it was a most delicate matter. The boy in his insanity was quite prepared to destroy others regardless of the consequences.

For the first time Orlov intervened.

"One moment," he said. "Supposing all this to be true—what is your purpose in coming to see me?"

Smirnoff looked squarely at the General. This was the critical moment. There must be no suggestion of self-serving in what he was about to propose. The General must feel he was a man's man, talking in the language of the world.

"Comrade General," Smirnoff said, "I am going to speak very openly. Perhaps too openly. But I am a blunt man. The Galin boy is headed for destruction. The only question is whether he is destroyed before—or after—he brings others, innocent persons, down to destruction. I see no reason why we should sit idly by and let him carry out his lethal intentions. We are adults and we can speak plainly, man to man."

Smirnoff felt the sweat standing in his pores.

"Fortunately, Comrade General," Smirnoff said, "you are a military man, a commanding officer with great power. A word from you and this unfortunate young man can be eliminated. I have no doubt that he has committed violations of the military statutes. In any event he certainly could be required to submit to inquiry. He is armed—of that I have no doubt. The arresting party would certainly have orders to shoot to kill at any sign of resistance."

Smirnoff paused. It was out now. He had cast the die. He watched the silent General, whose face had set like rigid concrete as the writer's tongue moved faster and faster. Suddenly fire blazed in the General's eyes and before Smirnoff could move Orlov's long arm lashed out, grabbing him by the collar and drawing him up to his tiptoes. The General held Smirnoff a moment, fighting for control of himself, then he spoke in a voice so low and tension-charged that Smirnoff's spine tingled.

"You bastard," the General spat. "You slime of a sow's litter. I should kill you with my own hands. But that would be too easy. I wish we were on the steppe. I'd handle you the Cossack way. I'd tie you to a stallion's tail, pour a little turpentine in his ass and watch you die with pleasure."

A paroxysm passed over Orlov's face. He tightened his grip on Smirnoff's collar until the writer was red and choking, then released him with a violent shove that sent him to his knees.

"Get out of here, Smirnoff," the General said. "Get out of here or I'll shoot you in the belly and pull your yellow guts out with my own hands, meter by meter."

Smirnoff staggered out the door and into the dark corridor. He started down the circular staircase but caught himself at the top, almost fainting. An old porter was methodically polishing the floor, rhythmically shuffling his feet back and forth with the heavy polishing brushes.

"What is the matter, sir?" the old fellow asked politely. "Are

225

you ill? Can I get you something?"

Smirnoff looked wildly at the man's plain peasant face and stumbled down the staircase, through the lobby and out into the street. His heart was pounding and his breath came in gasps. Another moment and Orlov would have strangled him. He had seen the blood rage in the tall man's eyes. Never had he been so close to death. Never. He shuddered. No. That was not exactly true. Once before he had felt such terror but when it had been he could not say. Long, long ago. He swayed down the street. His mind was numb. He saw a clock. It was only 9:15. How could that be? Hours had passed. Perhaps the clock was wrong. No. The day was still dark. The sun was still low under the heavy banks of snow clouds. It was beginning to snow again and there was a dampness in the air that would bring fog. Smirnoff inevitably found himself on the Nevsky. The sidewalks were filled with black-coated men and women. What to do? What could he do? Should he try to brazen it out? Hope that by some rare chance the finger of fate would not point him out?

Smirnoff sighed heavily. He was not a fool. Not completely a fool. True, he had made a mess of the Orlov affair. He had thought the General, no matter how puritanical his exterior, would, like any human being, be interested in preserving his own skin. What other move could he make that offered any possibility? He might as well face the reality. His cause was desperate. He had sent too many people to disaster not to recognize the fatal momentum which the Galin affair would acquire. It would carry him with it—of that there could be no doubt.

Well, he told himself, there is one more card to play. Only one. This might not work and even if it did the consequences might be almost as disastrous. But a drowning sailor does not pause to see whether the raft he clutches is made of good pine wood or bad.

There was a taxi stand beside the Hotel Europa. Still trembling, Smirnoff opened the door and seated himself next to the driver.

"Where to?" asked the driver with a sullen glance.

"The Ministry of State Security," said Smirnoff. "And hurry."

28

Orlov remained in the center of the room, his hands clenching and unclenching. He stood motionless for a moment, then walked quickly to the window, peering out at the scene. An old woman with a gray shawl was tossing bits of bread to the pigeons on the steps of St. Isaac's. Light snow was beginning to sift down. He saw a man lurching down the street. A drunkard. He looked again. No, by God. Not a drunkard. Smirnoff! The General shook his head. He could feel the blood throbbing in his temples.

"Why," he said aloud, "I could have killed him. In fact, I almost did."

He looked at his hands again. Perhaps he should have killed him. Perhaps he should not have permitted the habits, the self-control, which years of training had given him to stay his hands at the last moment. But immediately he felt the conviction rise in him—personal vengeance was no answer. What real difference was there between strangling the man with his own hands and Smirnoff's callous proposal—that they conspire to murder Irena's son? If honor had any meaning—and his life was founded on the proposition that it did have—surely it did not possess a bill of exceptions which permitted you to ignore its general rules because of personal feeling or sudden passion.

Orlov sat down in his armchair, torn by his thoughts. Perhaps his code was wrong. Certainly something was wrong somewhere—something terribly and fatally wrong. He was not a political innocent. Indeed, he probably knew more about politics and political forces than most persons supposed. He had been close to Zhdanov during the war. He respected Zhdanov. Indeed, he admired the Party Secretary. He knew the pressures under which Zhdanov worked and he knew the compromises which had to be made. They were made in the name of "military necessity," a principle which he understood, reckoned with and could live with. In the name of "military necessity" he had himself done terrible things. He had tortured men, or ordered them tortured—prisoners from whom it was vital to get information and get it quickly. He had been cruel when he felt that only cruelty would serve his purpose—which was the defense of Leningrad, the survival of Leningrad. He had shot a man—actually, he was little more than a boy—who had stolen another's ration. He could still see the unbelieving, brown, fawnlike eyes of the boy as he drew his pistol. He supposed he would always see those eyes and that this was the price which he had to pay for the responsibility he carried.

He knew that when Zhdanov cut the bread ration, cut it again, cut it a third time, cut it a fourth time, cut it almost to zero, the Party Secretary understood perfectly well that with each decree he was signing the death warrant for 100,000, 200,000, 300,000 lives. This was military necessity. But was there no end to military necessity? Was there no limit? No terminal point? Once started down this road did you not come to a kilometer mark, a road sign and say: Enough. It ends here.

This was where he had diverged from Zhdanov—not that he had made it a matter of dispute between them. He was a military man and very conscious, some would have said overconscious, of the separation of military and civil responsibility. Political matters were in Zhdanov's sphere. Military affairs were his. But was there

228

not some point when personal honor compelled him to speak? After all, honor was not like a certificate in the state loan, a sheet of green paper to be held a few years and then turned in for a new certificate with the process being repeated ad infinitum into the future. No. It was a general code of life, a contract which you made with yourself. It was either fulfilled or not fulfilled. If you fulfilled it—you had honor. If you did not—then, no honor. Just as simple as that. And, while he was a military man, he was also a human being. What kind of honor did he possess if he permitted a scoundrel, a monster who should have been strangled at birth, to live and flourish while a woman like Irena was driven into disgrace and death?

And, as Orlov saw it, the question was even larger. It was not merely the matter of personal honor. What might one say about the "military necessity," the "Party necessity," the "state necessity" of a system under which the Smirnoffs flourished and the Galinas perished?

It had taken life with its jagged edges, its abrasive surface, its cruel knives to bring Orlov to this point in his understanding. When the Party decree against Irena had been issued he was outraged, frantic—and irrational.

Irena had looked at him and said: "Constantin, this is not like you. You are thrashing about like a small boy who has been sent up to his room for breaking the vase which the cat knocked over. You are so hurt and so angry you are not thinking straight."

And Irena was right. She was right in forbidding him to resign and attempt to accompany her to the East. The matter was far too basic, far too complicated for such a gesture. He would simply have been cashiered and sent to a labor camp. They would never have seen each other again anyway, and nothing would have been changed or improved. Irena's instincts, as ever, were sounder than his own. He remembered how he had followed her to Paris at the time of the Exhibition. It had taken no little wangling to get the assignment to consult with the Soviet attaché in Paris, and the first thing he had done after arriving was to look up Irena. He had seen her only a dozen times in Moscow, always in company of someone else (usually Cheprikov), had talked very little with her but had fallen hopelessly and completely in love.

They had met at the Café de la Paix because it was one of the few places in Paris which he knew how to find.

He was terribly nervous when Irena appeared. He had gotten to the appointment twenty minutes ahead of time, had ordered a lemonade (because he was afraid the waiter would make him go away if he didn't order something) and was sitting watching in all directions when Irena came up.

She greeted him warmly.

"I am so happy to see you," he told Irena. "It is such a lucky coincidence to come while you're here."

Irena pursed her lips.

"Constantin Constantinovich," she said, "I am very fond of you and I think I am going to be more fond of you. But let me tell you one thing. Never tell me a lie."

He started to interrupt.

"Don't interrupt, Constantin Constantinovich," she said. "In the first place you can't tell lies. You are such a truthful person that it shines right through your face. In the second place I know you too well already. And I'll know you better soon."

He smiled like a schoolboy caught with a Latin pony in his desk.

"So." She smiled. "Let's start again. It's just wonderful that you thought enough of me to pull all the wires you knew how in order to come to Paris and meet me here. Isn't that a better way to put it?"

They laughed together. He took her arm and they sauntered down the Paris boulevard. And that had been, quite literally, the last untruth he had ever told Irena. It had been almost—but not quite—the same with her. She was completely honest with him but once or twice she had said: "Please, Constantin Constantinovich. Don't ask me about that. I don't want to talk of it." He had respected her occasional silences although he did not always understand them. In Paris—they were not there long, only a week or ten days—one night they had gone to a café near the Sorbonne. Not one of the big places on the Boulevard St. Germain. A little one on a side street. They had just become lovers. That very afternoon in her hotel room with the sun slanting through the slats of the shutters and casting black and white stripes across their bodies, and now they were walking about Paris with a special intimacy which had turned the whole world into an enchantment, devised just for themselves. They sat in the café with small glasses of some sweet liqueur in front of them and held hands. Orlov was hardly aware of anything that was going on around him, so completely was he absorbed in the physical presence of Irena. Suddenly she clutched his hand with something akin to terror and whispered hoarsely: "Quickly, Constantin. Get me away from this place. Immediately." He asked no questions, took a handful of bills, shoved them under the saucer, drew an arm around her and in five seconds they were walking down the street. He felt Irena's shoulders trembling under his arm. By the time they had returned to her room she seemed to have recovered—or almost. She was gayer, more lively than usual, probably trying to drive out of her mind the memory of what had terrified her. So Orlov thought. She never explained what it was and he had never asked her. But in the swift moment in which they left the café he had noticed, sitting to the rear, a lone figure, apparently a Frenchman with a small gray mustache and an opera cape carelessly thrown around his shoulders, who was staring at Irena with the beady intensity of a falcon. Who he might be and what he might represent in Irena's past the General had never learned.

Orlov had asked Irena to marry him. She refused.

"Had we met ten years ago," she said, "perhaps I would have married you. But if we had met ten years ago I don't think I would have been ready for you. Nor you for me."

He did not protest because he recognized the truth of what she said.

"Now, dear Constantin," she said, "we have met and we are ready for each other's love. It will endure—this love of ours. You have a passion for order in your life. You live by a code, by a set of principles. I admire all of this in you. But I do not believe in shackling love with paper chains. I trust you. You trust me. We will not betray each other. That is better than any signature in a registry office."

And so it had proved.

It was time that he was getting to his headquarters. He was just as precise in his habits as Irena had said. Perhaps more so, with the passing years. Every morning he walked the few blocks to his office, arriving right on the dot of nine o'clock. But this had not been an ordinary morning. He picked up his greatcoat and drew it on. His mind was clear now and his pulse had gone back to normal.

What had he said to Smirnoff? He had not talked that way since he was a subaltern in Büdenny's cavalry army during the Civil War. In fact he had not talked that way even then—but he had heard sergeants and commanders who did. And he had seen a deserter once tied to the tail of a stallion and trampled to death under the cruel hoofs of the enraged animal.

He put on his fur hat and took his gloves in his hand. The effrontery of the man. The worst insult was his bland assumption that he, Orlov, was the kind of person to whom you could make this kind of proposition. If any further evidence was needed of the low price at which codes of honor were now being hawked in the market place Smirnoff's conduct had provided it.

Well, said Orlov, opening the door of his room and striding briskly down the corridor, it is time for action. Past time.

29

When Dmitri Chaikovsky was angry, twin lines, almost knife-thin, appeared on his brow and stayed there as long as the emotion was with him. Only persons who knew him very well and had observed him very closely were aware of this sign. The lines creased Chaikovsky's forehead now and had from the moment he came into his office and thumbed through the Galin reports. That idiot, old man Glukhovsky, had lost Galin last night. It was incredible that so experienced and skilled a sleuth could be guilty of such a childish mistake—but guilty he was. Somewhere along the Catherine Canal Galin had given him the slip and it wasn't even apparent whether Galin had done it deliberately or the whole thing was an accident. One thing could be said for Glukhovsky. He was honest. He was proud of his profession, as proud as an actor, and had many of the actor's tricks of make-up. He had been an "angel," as sleuths were called in the trade, for many years, and his record was good enough so that he could afford to admit an error when he made one. The boy had simply vanished beside the Catherine Canal, not far from the church. Glukhovsky had back-tracked, trying to discover where Galin might have turned. He found a gate with marks in the fresh-fallen snow but the footprints became confused in the courtyard and there was no telling where they might lead. He had spent a couple of hours walking up and down small lanes in the vicinity, hoping to turn the boy up by chance. But no luck. Galin had been picked up again this morning by the man assigned to the morgue, but whom he might have seen after leaving Vasilevsky Island and where he spent the night was a mystery.

Normally, such a minor slip would not have affected Chaikovsky one way or the other. In his business such things happened. Sooner or later such small mysteries resolved themselves and, if they did not, it made little difference in the end. But the situation this morning was not the normal one. Sitting across from Chaikovsky was a sandy-haired young man with two gold front teeth, a generous sprinkling of freckles on his nose and cheeks, and a wayward lock of hair that dangled over his brow in the immemorial style of the village Don Juan. He was about half Chaikovsky's sixty-three years. His name was Galpert, Chaikovsky had never seen nor heard of him before and he was in charge of the special detail which Moscow had sent to help on the Galin case. Galpert was one of those superficially easy-going types who would have his arm around your shoulder inside of five minutes and sought to give the impression that, as he was now saying, "My chums and I are entirely at your disposal, Dmitri Trofimovich. You just say the word—and we will carry it out."

The truth was, as Chaikovsky could see in an instant, that this young fellow was out for blood. His eyes were everywhere. His "innocent" questions were of the most penetrating and oblique kind. He had not, as yet, thought to ask for a look at the reports of Chaikovsky's angels. But when and if he did and he discovered that Galin's whereabouts for eight or nine hours had been unknown to the Leningrad security detail, he would be certain to magnify the fact in such a way as to insure that Chaikovsky drew a sharp reprimand from Moscow if nothing worse.

For the moment the two men sat in the office, fencing with each other. Chaikovsky had taken the lead, hoping to draw Galpert away from the sensitive subject of Galin's personal activities.

"Our detail is already out at the cemetery," Chaikovsky said. "Do you happen to be familiar with the location?"

Galpert was not familiar with it. He was a Moscow man and had never chanced to be in Leningrad before.

Chaikovsky heaved an inward sigh. That was a small blessing— if true. It would be just like this bastard to pretend he had never been in Leningrad when he actually knew the city like the back of his hand.

Actually, Chaikovsky's arrangements were quite simple and quite efficient. He was accustomed to working with small details. He didn't believe in showy operations. He had assigned enough personnel so that men would be on hand at every phase of the proceedings. But he had not replaced all of the grave diggers, cemetery workers and attendants with police agents. That would simply flutter the pigeons. There were too many old women idling around the cemetery whose tongues would begin to wag if they saw so many unfamiliar faces. Chaikovsky's men would sift into the cemetery from several directions. Some would move on parallel paths. Some would join the funeral party. Some would be waiting for other funeral parties. There would be enough men to take care of any contingency. He had taken into consideration the Galpert detachment and Galpert's men could be blended right into the proposed layout. Young Galin had made the arrangements for the funeral with the cemetery foreman yesterday. He had the number of the plot which had been assigned. It had cost Galin plenty—five thousand rubles as a matter of fact, because the boy wanted a good location—but the foreman had been privately told to go along with Galin's request in the normal manner.

Galpert chuckled. "Is five thousand rubles the 'normal' bribe for burial at the Volkhov cemetery?"

Chaikovsky shrugged his shoulders. "The foreman said business is business and he might as well get what he could while the getting was good."

"Your arrangements sound perfect to me," Galpert said, putting

235

a finger in his mouth and probing for a bit of sausage that had become imbedded in a rear molar. He dug for a moment, produced the bit of meat, looked at it closely and casually snapped it off into space.

"Tell me, Dmitri Trofimovich," said Galpert with studied casualness. "There's been no sign of anyone getting the wind up about this business? None of the pigeons look like flying the coop?"

Chaikovsky screwed his mouth around a bit. "No," he said. "No one has flown the coop. Not yet, anyway. But some of the people seem to be rather nervous. Of course, that's perfectly natural."

"Hmmm," Galpert responded. "Yes. I rather guess so. I think you and I might be a little on edge under those circumstances—eh?"

He laughed and Chaikovsky grinned feebly. He didn't for the life of him see anything to laugh about.

At that moment Chaikovsky's assistant, a brisk young man with a rather military bearing, entered the room.

"May I?" the assistant said, nodding imperceptibly in Galpert's direction.

"Lord, yes," Chaikovsky responded with apparent joviality. "We have no secrets from Comrade Galpert."

"Well," said the assistant, raising his eyebrows, "it's just this, sir. The writer Smirnoff has turned up. Says he must see you on a most urgent matter. He won't tell me what it is and he says it won't bear waiting on."

With no apparent pause for thought Chaikovsky responded: "Let him wait outside a bit. Don't tell him I'll see him. I'll buzz you when to send him in."

Galpert winked and smacked his lips in appreciation of the deftness of Chaikovsky's technique. "That'll warm him up," said the Moscow man.

"Yes, indeed," said Chaikovsky, his mind working like lightning. Damn this man Galpert! There would be no getting him out of the room while he talked to Smirnoff and he could not put off seeing the writer without arousing Galpert's suspicions. The last thing in the world that he wanted at this point was to have to talk to this tricky, slippery writer in Galpert's presence. Any doubt that Smirnoff wanted to see him about the Galin case was almost immediately removed when one of Chaikovsky's agents telephoned to report that Smirnoff had had a stormy conference with General Orlov and had left the hotel, seemingly in a state of shock.

"This fellow Smirnoff," he told Galpert, "is very much mixed up in the Galin business. He was more or less responsible for Irena Galina being denounced and sent out to forced residence."

"Ah, yes," Galpert responded, shaking his head as though this were news to him. "I seem to remember about that."

You bastard, Chaikovsky said to himself. You know every word of Smirnoff's connection with this case, including a good many which I've yet to find out about.

"What does he want to talk to you about?" Galpert asked.

"Specifically," said Chaikovsky, "I don't know. But I would say from experience that when someone like this shows up on the eve of an expected event they usually want to make a little deal, trade a little knowledge and, if possible, save their skin."

I wish I did know what Smirnoff wants, Chaikovsky thought. I would feel a lot more comfortable.

"So Smirnoff may be ready to spill the beans, eh?" Galpert said cheerfully.

"We'll soon find out," Chaikovsky replied, pressing the buzzer.

The man who entered the room was the shell of the self-possessed, sophisticated bon vivant who a few hours previously had stepped so blithely to the door of his apartment and flung it open to admit, as he expected, the young poetess whom he planned to put into his bed.

Smirnoff seemed to have changed overnight to a haggard old man. His hands worked nervously, his eye twitched, his face hung in folds, the scar from his morning's shaving looked angry and red and he was hastily stuffing his mustard-colored muffler into the pocket of his overcoat.

He muttered a greeting to Chaikovsky, nodded vaguely to Galpert, and stood silent, apparently uncertain whether to proceed or

237

possibly waiting for permission from Chaikovsky.

"Good morning, Comrade Smirnoff," Chaikovsky said in his colorless official voice. "My secretary tells me you have some urgent information to impart."

"Yes, it's true," Smirnoff said, so agitated he hardly seemed to be aware what he was saying. "It's very important, indeed. It has to do with Irena Galina, the sculptress, you know. Or rather with her son, young Galin. She's dead, you know. Died out in Tashkent."

Galpert was watching with interest. Smirnoff paused so long that Chaikovsky said: "Yes, well now, Comrade Smirnoff. Just what was it in this connection?"

"You see," Smirnoff said, "the boy came to me. God knows why. Perhaps because I had known his mother slightly in the old days. He told me some long story. I couldn't make head or tail of it. Something about a plot—a plot against his mother. All sorts of prominent people involved in it. He mentioned names. Said he was going to get his revenge—on all of them."

Smirnoff picked up the water carafe on Chaikovsky's desk, poured himself a glass and drank it greedily.

"Did he name you as one of his victims?" Galpert intervened suddenly.

"Yes, he did," Smirnoff said. "Of course he's crazy. Crazy as a loon. But he claims he has papers, documents, evidence. You can imagine what it amounts to."

Chaikovsky looked genuinely puzzled. "But what was the urgency of all this?"

"Oh, yes," Smirnoff said, rubbing his finger on his nose. "That was it. The urgency. I almost forgot. You see he is having Irena Galina buried this morning. At the Volkhov cemetery. And he threatened to read out all these charges, all this evidence, at the grave."

Smirnoff hesitated and then went on: "I thought, Comrade Chaikovsky, that perhaps you could stop it some way. Perhaps arrest him. For his own good, of course."

Both Chaikovsky and Galpert were silent for a moment. Then Galpert suddenly asked: "So you know who the persons are who are involved in this—these prominent persons? Did the Galin boy tell you who they were?"

"Yes," said Smirnoff. "That is, I know some of them. I don't suppose I know them all."

"Well," said Galpert with an air of satisfaction. "It seems to me that Comrade Smirnoff may have some interesting information—very interesting information, don't you think so, Dmitri Trofimovich?"

Chaikovsky cleared his throat. "Yes, indeed," he said. "I should not be at all surprised. I think we had better go over this matter very carefully."

"But," interjected Galpert, "don't you think it would be better to discuss this all after the funeral—rather than before it? Then we will have the whole picture more clearly before us."

I see what you are driving at, Chaikovsky said to himself. You're putting a little bird lime on this miserable Smirnoff's claws. You are lining up a canary to do a bit of singing later on. Well, why not?

"Comrade Galpert is right," Chaikovsky said. "We will have a long talk about this. But not until after the funeral."

"After the funeral?" Smirnoff asked.

"Yes," said Chaikovsky. "Just go ahead and attend the ceremony as though nothing had happened. You needn't even mention dropping by here. Later on we will contact you and go into the matter with the greatest care. You can be assured that the matter is in good hands."

Smirnoff backed out of the office. Chaikovsky almost expected to see him touch his forelock and bow to the floor like an old peasant.

Galpert rubbed his hands together gleefully.

"There's a frightened canary for you," he said with satisfaction. "We'll have that one singing for us in short order, eh?"

Chaikovsky's secretary reappeared.

239

"Comrade Ivanov's secretary called while you were occupied," he said. "Comrade Ivanov is dropping by here on his way to the funeral and will give you a lift in his car, if you like."

Chaikovsky could not refrain from frowning. Ivanov really must be sweating if he was going to try to pump him in person.

"It's not possible—" he started to say to his secretary, but Galpert smoothly intervened.

"Wait a minute," said the Moscow man. "Don't you think it's better to let him come by? Perhaps he, too, has something interesting to tell you. And, as for the ride, don't bother about me. I'll find my way to the cemetery without any trouble."

"Good enough," said Chaikovsky to his secretary. "Tell Ivanov's office that it is all right."

Then he turned back to Galpert. "I think you're on the right track," he said. "I'll ride out with Ivanov and you can take my car. We'll come back together."

"Good," said Galpert, digging the wax out of his ear with his little finger. He looked at the wax with some interest, then rubbed it between his thumb and forefinger and wiped his hand carefully on the side of his breeches.

"Very good," he repeated. "We're going to get along just fine, Dmitri Trofimovich. I feel sure of it."

30

It was still dark when Michael slipped out of Nadya's room. He drew on his boots quietly and donned his coat without disturbing the sleeping girl. She lay on her back, one arm at her breast and the other outside the cover. He leaned over her and brushed her lips with his own. She stirred slightly but did not awaken as he softly opened the door and departed. He made his way by crowded bus down to Nevsky to the Moscow station. There he retrieved his bag, washed, shaved, put on his only white shirt, took under his arm a small parcel containing the black silk dress in which he was going to bury his mother, returned his suitcase to the checkroom and headed for Marat Street.

The room in which his mother's body had been placed was No. 9. It was in the basement of the building off a rather wide but ill-lighted corridor, paved with cement, cold, drafty, and already bustling with people. Everywhere there was the overpowering stench of carbolic acid and the festering smell of drains to be found in the depths of old Russian buildings.

Michael discovered the door to Room No. 9 locked. Someone had scrawled the word "Galina" on a piece of brown paper with a blue pencil and stuck it in a crack in the door. It was some time before he located a crone in a dirty hospital smock who consented to open the door.

"It's not required, young man," she grumbled. "It's not required to open the door. The porter is supposed to see to that."

At first he started to protest but then he realized she was simply complaining so that he would be sure to give her a tip.

Room No. 9 was a cell-like chamber, perhaps fifteen feet long and ten feet wide. A naked electric bulb dangling from the ceiling provided illumination. There was a small window let into a recessed grating but since the room was below the level of the street little light came from this source at any time and none, of course, during the winter. The only furniture was a deal table, just large enough and strong enough to support a coffin and, against a wall, a single wooden chair with a spavined back.

Room No. 9 was one of a dozen which the morgue provided in which bodies could lie in wait while relatives and friends gathered for a last look at the beloved one. Most of the bodies laid out in these rooms were taken directly to the crematorium, incinerated and the ashes returned to the family in a small urn to be placed in the cemetery wall.

Michael had arranged for his mother's coffin to be brought to the room so that the body could be prepared properly for burial. Now he lifted the lid from the pine box and put it to one side. He found it hard to believe that Irena had been dead for five days. The whole trip had been made in sub-zero weather and there was not a sign of change in her features since he had placed the lid on the coffin in Tashkent. He solemnly kissed her white brow, surprised to find he was crossing himself as he did so. From what unremembered alcove of the past had that gesture sprung?

The crone was hovering around.

"Perhaps you could help me," he told her, showing her the dress in which he wished his mother to be buried.

"Just leave it all to me, dearie," the old woman said, her character softened by the tip and expectation of another. "Death is woman's business. We know what to do. Just you go out in the corridor and I'll take care of your mother for you."

Michael left the room and began to pace up and down the dark corridor. There was much coming and going, doors were opening and closing, he could hear weeping from some of the rooms; but in some of the dark corners there was scuffling and unmistakable giggling.

At one end of the corridor the body of a young woman, possibly twenty-three or twenty-four, lay on a narrow shelf. She was clothed in a figured print dress in a splashy design of wine-colored flowers. Her hands were crossed upon her breast and her legs looked trim in good silk stockings and neat black leather shoes.

About her clustered three women, obviously peasants, for they wore dark woolen shawls around their heads, heavy cotton-padded jackets, wool skirts and high *valenki*.

"Come now," the oldest woman said, "help me with the stockings."

As Michael stood there the woman wrenched off the girl's shoes, pulled back her dress, carelessly exposing her marbled thighs, and began cautiously to work the silk stockings off each leg.

"Come, Masha," the woman said. "Lift her hips a bit. I don't want to get a ladder in these stockings. They are too nice."

She managed to get the stockings off, and then paused.

"It's a pity to leave that good slip on her," she sighed. "It's got a bit of lace on it, too. Would just about fit you, Masha."

"Oh, Olga," the younger girl said. "Let it go. It's too much trouble now."

"Well," said Olga, "I suppose you're right. But it is a shame. Not as though she'd ever miss it."

She put an old frayed pair of cotton stockings on the girl's legs and some battered felt slippers on her feet. One slipper had a big hole in it and Michael could see the girl's foot, naked and white, through the hole.

The woman called Olga stuffed the good stockings and shoes into her bag and straightened the girl's skirts.

243

"Where is that old fellow?" she asked impatiently. "The one who said he would take her to the crematorium. Go find him and tell him she's ready to go."

An old man in a white porter's apron appeared, pushing a cart on which rested the body of a middle-aged man.

"You were supposed to take us next," Olga said angrily.

"Wait a minute until I take this one in," the porter said, hurrying along. The sheet which was covering the body caught in something and slowly began to pull off, exposing a sunken chest and body covered with curly white hairs.

Michael turned abruptly, almost colliding with a blond girl, not more than eighteen, who carried in her arms a small cardboard box containing the mummy-wrapped figure of her dead infant. It seemed to Michael that he had ventured into some sub-department of hell. This was the way life ended! Human carcasses being trucked this way and that, in and out. So life ended in Leningrad. In wartime it had been horrible. Yes. He knew all the macabre tales about Marat Street. The corpses that piled up in the streets around. The corpses with missing thighs and calves. The rats . . .

He could not bring himself to think of the ghastly things he had heard. But that was wartime, when the whole city was dying. And this was supposed to be peacetime in a city whose culture was known in the very ends of the earth. Michael wiped his brow, drew a cigarette from his pocket, climbed the staircase and went outside. It was snowing a little and the air felt unpleasantly raw and damp. He smoked his cigarette, drawing deep breaths of tobacco into his lungs until his nerves gradually quieted. The sky was overcast and he noticed a curious halo where a feeble sun was trying to break through. Strange weather.

The old woman should be finished by now. Michael descended the staircase and made his way down the corridor to Room No. 9. He knocked.

"Just a few minutes more, dearie," the old woman rasped. "Don't be impatient."

Michael stamped out his cigarette. For the moment the hall was quiet except for the weeping behind the door of the adjoining cubicle and a contralto chuckle in the shadows.

"Now, Kolya, quit it," he heard a girl say. "Not here."

There was a nudge at his elbow.

"There we are now, my dear," the old woman said. "Come and look at her. She is a real lady. Just like she was lying there asleep."

He went into the room. It was true. His mother looked beautiful. The old woman knew her business. She had combed Irena's hair and fluffed it gracefully. Her hands rested like white doves against the black silk gown with its high collar. Again Michael kissed his mother's brow.

"Thank you," he said, pressing a note into the old woman's hand. "You have been very good to me. I just don't know what I would have done."

"Never you mind, young man," the woman said. "What must be must be. Now you will bury her as it is fitting and proper to bury a good Christian woman."

Michael was left alone in the bare room. He sat down on the spavined chair and looked at his mother. It was true, as the old woman said. She did not look dead. She looked as though she were just resting. A feeling came over him that if he closed his eyes and opened them again she would not be dead. He let his eyelids drop and it seemed to him that his mother was beside him, was speaking to him, but he could not quite grasp her words. What was she saying? What was the message? If only he could understand. There was a knock at the door. He shook himself and strode over to open it. Two men stood there, wearing greasy fur caps and chauffeur's sheepskins.

"We've come with the truck," one said. "Are you ready to move her now?"

"Yes, I suppose so," Michael said. "Just wait a moment."

He closed the door, went back and seated himself. "We'll be quiet just a moment, Mother," he said aloud. "And then we will start the journey."

245

He sat silently for a minute, observing the ancient Russian custom going back to God knows what ancient superstition, of remaining seated in silence for a moment before starting on a journey.

Then he rose, kissed his mother, made the sign of the cross over her and placed the lid on the coffin. He opened the door and motioned to the men.

"Very well, we can go now," he said. "Be careful how you handle the box."

The two men spat on their hands, took the coffin by the head and the foot, and started down the long, badly lighted corridor. Michael followed in the rear, his cap in his hands and the sound of the weeping in the adjacent room still in his ears.

31

Nadya awakened with a start. She was late for something but momentarily she could not think what it was. Then it all rushed back to her. She looked across the room. Michael was gone and it was past nine already. She started to rise and then drew back, knitting her brows in deep thought, going over in her mind all that Michael had said—about life, about the East, about Siberia. For possibly twenty minutes she did not move, resting on one elbow, her eyes open but unseeing, her mind grappling with a series of complex problems. Then she rose, rapidly dressed in a neat, serviceable and not very becoming blue serge suit and pulled out from under her bed a small black wooden suitcase. She packed this, taking some paints, brushes and drawing paper from her desk and most of her small wardrobe. There was no lock on the suitcase but she neatly tied it with stout cord and then shoved it back out of sight under the bed.

Nadya then went to a large portfolio of drawings that had been tucked behind her desk. She laid the portfolio flat on the desk and leafed through it, selecting a small black-and-white pencil sketch of folio size. There were two or three framed prints on the walls of her room. She held the sketch up to each until she found a frame that matched its size, removed the print and slipped the sketch into its place. She wrapped the framed sketch into an old copy of *Pravda* and looked at her clock. Almost ten. She must leave in a few minutes.

She understood Michael's reasoning perfectly and had realized there was no point in arguing further with him last night. It would simply have driven him out into the snow with no place in the city to rest his head. But she would be with him, especially this morning as he went through the painful last moments before his mother's burial. What was going to happen as a result of the ceremony she could not very well imagine except that Michael was risking grave trouble. It was all right for him to say that he had made up his mind to face the consequences. Perhaps he had. But she had a responsibility too. If her mind had not shown that to her before her heart showed it to her now. Nadya was a Russian girl and when her heart spoke her mind obeyed. Her place was at Michael's side. Others might keep her from that place—but certainly not Michael.

She put on her coat, tucked the newspaper-wrapped parcel under her arm and went out into the street. Although it was midmorning it seemed almost like dusk. There was snow in the air and a wet wind blowing fog in from the Neva estuary.

Nadya hurried to the bus stop. She just had time to get to the art school before the other students would be leaving for the cemetery. It would never do to be late.

She thought of her mother as she entered the bus and took a seat on the side. "A woman's place is beside her man," her mother had always said with just a hint of stubbornness. She usually made that remark when she was talking about how she had worked in the same shop with her husband at the Putilov works. Her father's eyes twinkled when the conversation took this turn.

"Really, now, Maria Ivanovna," he would say. "You know you don't believe that. A woman's place is in the home."

And so the argument would flow back and forth until finally

her mother would put her hands on her hips and say angrily: "Now, Feodor, stop teasing. It's not fair."

And her father would put back his head and laugh and, sometimes, give her mother a friendly pat on her amply rounded rear, saying: "Of course I'm teasing, Maria Ivanovna, of course I am. And wherever you are—in the home or in the shop—we are shoulder to shoulder, you and I, and that is how it should be and must be."

The cause of her mother's death had been dystrophy—or whatever it was that everyone in Leningrad died of that terrible winter. But Nadya had always known that it wasn't disease germs, not cold nor even hunger that had killed her mother. It had been word of her father's death at the front with the workers' battalion.

She had been just a girl, hardly more than a child then, working all hours in the plant and bound up with her new tasks. She hadn't been with her mother as much as she should have been. It wasn't possible in those terrible days. But, even so, she had seen the light fade out of her mother's eyes, had seen the spark go out of her soul, had seen her become listless and uncertain, careless of herself, uninterested in anything that was going on.

Yes, thought Nadya, when her mother said that a woman's place was with her man she meant it literally. It was not a figure of speech. And when her man had died she had begun to die, and not even the thought of her children had been able to arrest the course of the fatal illness of her heart.

So we Russian women are, thought Nadya, a little proudly. This is our nature and it is right that it should be so, for men are not men without their women beside them and women are not women without the men whom they love.

Nadya smiled to herself. How great was her love for Michael. She could feel it welling up in her breast and she knew that it must be disclosed by her face. There was an old man sitting across from her on the bus, probably a professor judging by his carefully brushed overcoat, his carefully trimmed beard and the careful manner in which he turned the pages of the book he was reading. He lifted

249

his eyes and smiled at her, a pleasant smile like that of an old friend bidding her good morning. Nadya smiled back at him. It seemed wrong at such a time yet she was glad to be alive on this snowy, foggy Leningrad morning.

32

It had not been Gregory Ivanov's intention to try to pump Dmitri Chaikovsky for further details of the Galin case. He realized that the chances of getting anything more out of the close-mouthed security officer were slight. Yet, he felt a certain satisfaction—mingled, to be sure, with lingering apprehension—as the big Zis limousine carried them through the streets of Leningrad. He had offered Chaikovsky the place of honor next to his chauffeur but Chaikovsky with perfect etiquette had declined. So Ivanov rode in front while Chaikovsky shared the rear seat with Ivanov's personal deputy.

As the car rolled along Ivanov kept up an intermittent conversation while his mind busily picked over what fragmentary clues the visit to Chaikovsky's headquarters had provided.

"Curious weather, isn't it?" he observed. "A good deal of fog along with the snow."

"Typical," Chaikovsky observed laconically. "Typical Leningrad winter weather."

Ivanov's purpose in seeking out Chaikovsky this morning had been devious although his objective was simple enough. He was playing his chosen role of the peasant bumpkin, stumbling over toes, acting in a manner calculated to be embarrassing yet doing nothing which could open him to specific criticism. He was behaving like the valet who drops the collar button, lets the hot water run over in the tub and forgets to put out the shirt studs—in order to divert his master's attention from the fact that he was caught last night in bed with the chambermaid. The difference was that in Ivanov's case he hadn't done anything wrong (so far as he knew) but he was afraid he was going to be accused of something very serious.

His wife had been surprised to find him asleep on the sofa when she got up this morning. Usually, he dropped in for a few minutes later in the day. Or, sometimes managed to have lunch at home. She was instantly concerned.

"What's wrong?" she asked. "Have you been fired?"

"Don't ask silly questions," he snapped. Her remark rubbed his nerves the wrong way. Actually, he had come out of a reluctant sentimentality. If anything did happen he felt he would like to have a quiet hour with Nina Sergeyevna. And, in general, the visit fitted into the peasant characterization which he was so heavily under-lining.

"Things are dull," he said. "I thought I'd get a few hours of comfort at home."

His wife brightened immediately and began to scurry around. She put the teakettle on the hot plate, found some sausage and cheese in the "icebox" between the double windows, set out the salmon in jelly that she had been saving and even asked Gregory whether he wouldn't like a small glass of vodka to start his blood circulating more briskly.

Ivanov ordinarily did not drink at breakfast except, occasionally, when he was out in the country or at a village meeting. However, the suggestion struck him as good. He downed a shot and the warmth in his stomach took the edge off his feeling of concern.

He sat down at the table and ate with good appetite. His wife began to tell him about the magnificent new wardrobe which their next-door neighbor, the chairman of the City Council, had just acquired.

"It was only twenty-four hundred rubles," she said. "But of course she got it because the head of the factory wanted to do something nice for her husband."

"How do you know?" Ivanov asked. He knew that what his wife said was true.

"I know perfectly well, Gregory, and so do you," she said. "It does seem to me that you might use your influence once in a while. You know how badly we need something for our clothes. We just have that old chest of drawers."

After an hour of this kind of domestic discussion Ivanov was glad to escape back to his office. He had been thinking about his next move and decided to see whether he might not compel Chaikovsky to associate himself, willy-nilly, in making a joint appearance at the funeral. This, Ivanov felt, would take a good deal of the onus off his own presence, but he hardly imagined that the crafty Chaikovsky could be tricked into it.

Yet here they were riding in Ivanov's limousine to the cemetery. It was a little too good, Ivanov thought. In fact, going back over the conversation in Chaikovsky's office he got the definite impression that the Security Chief himself was a bit at sea.

This Moscow man, Galpert, obviously was calling the tune. And Chaikovsky could hardly be expected to like that very well. Ivanov had taken an instant dislike to the Moscow man, which he concealed under a layer of heavy cordiality. He inquired effusively about the young man's comfort, whether there was any facility which the Leningrad organization might provide for him, offered felicitations to the young man's chief in Moscow and, in general, behaved like a house serf, tendering bread-and-salt to the returning *barin*. Not that any of this would soften Galpert's heart. No, indeed. But Ivanov did hope that his behavior would cause Galpert to rate him as a fool, a stupid man who could blunder into trouble but who would never have the wit to play a leading role.

"This Galpert," Ivanov said to Chaikovsky, "have you worked with him before?"

"No," said Chaikovsky, getting the word out so quickly he almost bit his tongue.

Ivanov sighed. There was no drawing Chaikovsky into conversation this morning. He had not failed to notice when he produced the information that General Orlov was going to attend the funeral —his ostensible excuse for stopping by to talk with Chaikovsky— that it was Galpert's interest that was whetted, not Chaikovsky's. Of course, Chaikovsky had known about Orlov all along. But then presumably Galpert knew it, too. Yet Chaikovsky had greeted the announcement with a morose shake of his head while Galpert immediately brought forward a whole series of questions as to the relationship between Orlov and Irena.

The morning air had certainly not improved the atmosphere, Ivanov thought. They were pulling up to the gates of the cemetery now. It was a peculiar day, Ivanov observed, the snow continuing while the fog seemed to be growing heavier.

"Excuse me," Chaikovsky said, descending from the car and going directly across the street to a peasant who was standing with padded jacket and sheepskin cap beside a pile of pine boughs which he had obviously brought to sell to funeral parties.

Chaikovsky had a quick word with the man and then rejoined Ivanov.

"Everything in order, Comrade Chaikovsky?" Ivanov asked heartily.

"We're a little early," Chaikovsky said, moving off toward the cemetery gates.

33

The most curious thing about it all, thought Morozov, is that the whole apparatus of this most powerful state should have been mobilized to crush a single woman, her ideas and her ideals. And more. These ideas and ideals were, in reality, hardly known to more than a handful of people.

Morozov had debated with himself whether to come to his office before going to the funeral. He finally decided that he would stop in for a few minutes. At least he would have a chance to greet Ludmilla, perhaps for the last time. As it happened she had not yet arrived and he was alone again at the desk in the room overlooking Hertzen Street.

The truth was, he thought, rising and strolling slowly over to the windows, that Irena's "End of War" group had never been shown, never been exhibited, and no one in Russia even knew of its existence outside of a small circle that was comprised almost exclusively of Irena's closest friends and, no doubt, a few of her students.

This was the reason why the Party Decree of 1946 had caused a certain amount of bewilderment, particularly in the lower echelons.

But, of course, the habit of obedience was so well instilled and the fear of becoming suspect if any questions were asked was so great that no one dared voice doubt of the justice of the action.

There was no little boy to tug at his mother's skirts and exclaim: "Why, the emperor isn't wearing any clothes!" There was no one in this fourth decade of the great Revolution to ask: What is this crime of which Irena has been convicted? So far as the general public knew the "End of War" group simply had no existence.

Everyone knew Irena had done *something* but no one knew *what*. Nor was this the end to the contradiction. Irena was not a flaming revolutionary. Her passion was strong, her conviction deep but, Morozov felt certain, she had not intended directly and deliberately to throw herself headlong against the Party. When it became obvious to her, as it did very soon (he did not know precisely why and how but he presumed she had shown the group or told of it to Zhdanov or one of the other Party men), that the climate was not suitable for public exhibition of her work she had been willing to wait, at least for a while, until the signs were a little more propitious. She had covered the group with a big canvas and kept it in her studio.

"Naturally, Georgi," she told him one afternoon, "there can be no question of exhibiting the group so long as the war is on. That is obvious, even to me. Once the guns fall silent it is a different matter."

But the time for public exhibition never arrived. So far as he knew she had never shown the statue to any outsider. No. That was not quite right. There was one exception that he recalled. Just after the siege was lifted in January, 1944, a group of foreign correspondents had come to Leningrad. Some of them visited Irena's studio and she must have shown them the "End of War" group because there had been mention made of it later.

What a strange evening that had been! What a mixture of people! The surviving intelligentsia of Leningrad, or a cross-section of them—writers, poets, painters and even an architect like himself. Some of the military. Orlov was there. Some of the Party people.

Ivanov. The Mayor. A few editors and about fifteen foreign correspondents, mostly Americans and Englishmen. There were vodka, champagne, brandy and wine to drink. And more food on the banquet table than anyone in Leningrad had seen in three years—mounds of caviar, great hams, butter, white bread, sturgeon in jelly, roast turkeys, fresh tomatoes (they must have been flown in from the Kremlin hothouses), meat pasties—he couldn't begin to enumerate the rich dishes. The Leningraders had eaten till they could eat no more. The journalists had drunk a good deal more than their capacity. So had the Leningraders.

The gathering was held in the House of Scientists on the Palace Embankment, a lavish nobleman's residence of the late nineteenth century.

When the toasts finally began, the vodka, rich food and international good will combined to cause incredible confusion. He remembered an American Negro correspondent imbued with racial pride who proposed "one minute's silence" in honor of Pushkin. When this was translated into Russian as "one second's silence," bewilderment was general. There were at least a dozen toasts offered to Zhdanov. One tipsy American—to Irena Galina's intense embarrassment—proposed a toast "to that gallant citizeness of Leningrad who has so brilliantly dedicated her talents to a crusade that may end future war." Another correspondent who had lived in Russia for some years offered a toast in Russian to "the day when the Northern Palmyra once more will reflect its imperial grandeur." Orlov and Ivanov had both spoken, thanking the Americans and British for the aid they had rendered Leningrad during the siege. "Someday," Orlov had said, "we hope to repay you in full measure." Ivanov had been equally cordial. By the end of the evening some of the Americans had to be carried out the front door and some of the Leningraders had been tucked away in a second-floor dormitory to sleep it off.

He had taken Irena Galina home that night. It was very late and she was upset.

"I never should have shown those foreigners the group," she said.

257

"They don't understand at all. I was so embarrassed when they started talking."

He tried to reassure her.

"They mean nothing wrong," he said. "It was just the effects of all that vodka. It is our fault. We shouldn't work so hard to pour it down the throats of our pleasant guests."

"No," she insisted. "It isn't just that. They don't understand. It isn't *my* crusade. Not just me alone. I am only the instrument of the feeling which all women—not just Russians, not just Leningraders, but all women everywhere—share. Those men didn't understand anything about it."

So far as Morozov was aware this single half-drunken reference by an American newspaperman was the only public mention which had ever been made of Irena's work—until the Party Decree (and even that was so deliberately vague that unless you understood what was meant you would not be aware of the exact target of the criticism).

He heard the door open behind him and turned. It was Ludmilla, a guilty frown on her face—because she was late and because he was there to see that she was late.

"I'm so sorry, Georgi Alexandrovich," she exclaimed. "I had to stop at the store and there was such a queue."

He stepped over to her and swiftly embraced her, kissing her gently—something he seldom permitted himself at the office.

Ludmilla pressed him to her breast with a little sigh, saying shyly: "Is everything all right, Georgi Alexandrovich—do you feel better today?"

"Much better," he said. "I got in early because I have to go out for a while. Tell Andrei he can go down and start the car. I'll be with him directly."

He sat down at his desk, leaned back and immediately let out an involuntary cry.

"That damn lion's head!" he exclaimed.

"How many times have I told you—" Ludmilla began.

"I know, I know," Morozov said. "I should put the chair out for visitors and take the other one for myself."

"But," continued Ludmilla with a smile, "it is the symbol of your authority and uneasy lies the head . . ."

"That's right." Morozov grinned. "So go and tell Andrei to warm up the car."

Ludmilla left and he was alone again. He rubbed the back of his head reflectively. It had been quite a while since he'd been so careless with the lion.

"A good lesson for you, Georges," he could hear his father saying. His father would have loved the lion's head and would never have failed to underline its significance and to warn against the danger of becoming too slack, dropping one's guard, forgetting the limits of one's authority.

A good lesson. Sound morality. And, he thought, as he rose somewhat wearily from his chair, excellent philosophy in a world in which society is guided by more or less well-defined standards. But not much use in a jungle where the law of the beast is to eat or be eaten. His father had believed in Revolution, believed in it deeply because he was a moral man and was so repelled by the shameless degradation produced by the society in which he lived. He thought that if the evil of the old could be swept away, man would create a bright new world, founded on reason and justice and respect for human dignity. And he himself, Morozov thought, had shared the dream of his father, had believed like so many of his generation that he was going to help to build a new Russia that would rise white and gleaming from the dirt and misery of the old.

What a blessing that his father had not lived to see the world turned upside down, to see the Revolution glorifying lies in the name of principle and institutionalizing degradation as the chosen way of life.

He drew on his coat, casually exchanged a smile with Ludmilla and walked into the hallway. The packing cases were still standing there and probably would continue to stand there for some weeks. As he walked down the staircase he paused a moment before the figure of the Mongol warrior in his armor. It was so easy to blame

259

the Mongols, he thought. So often it had been done—by Russians and by Western historians. Russia is backward—it's because of the Mongol conquest. Russia is uncultured—she missed the Renaissance. Russia has no code of justice—the concept was extinguished by the Mongols. Russian tyranny, Russian despotism, Russian cruelty, Russian ignorance, Russian filth, Russian backwardness, Russian servility—blame the Mongols.

I wonder, he said to himself, if that isn't a little too easy. I wonder if we haven't had enough centuries since the Mongols departed to begin to act like men and women, to show each other a little kindness, a little humanity.

Andrei was listening silently to the motor, which, as usual, was sputtering a little. Sometimes Morozov felt that he ought to present his chauffeur with a stethoscope, for never had a man dedicated himself more completely to the aches and coughs of a piece of rather dilapidated machinery.

"The Volkhov cemetery," he said. It was, he noted, a curious day. Snow gusts were falling, a thin fog had made its appearance and the feeble sun looked like a yellow coin wrapped in gray gauze.

34

Morozov walked over to the gates of the cemetery, carrying in his arms a white azalea plant, cumbersomely wrapped in newspaper. He knew that the delicate blossoms would quickly be seared by frost, but when he saw the white flowers in the shop he could not resist buying them. Irena had loved azaleas. The first winter they spent together he had gotten a white azalea for her name day. It was dreadfully expensive and he'd had to sell his French edition of De Maupassant to get the money for the flowers, but he could still see the stars in Irena's eyes as she tore the wrappings off the package and saw the pure white petals and the green leaves.

"Oh, Georgi," she cried, putting her face against his. "You are so smart. You know exactly how to touch my heart."

And then she had sniffed the blossoms, wrinkling her nose like a dog.

"Now," she said, "it will be spring all winter long."

Within the cemetery gates Morozov found a little party already gathered. He bowed stiffly to Secretary Ivanov. He had not expected to see him here and he was startled to perceive Chaikovsky, the Security Chief, talking to an unpleasant-looking young man with freckled face. The presence of Chaikovsky was more than startling. It was unsettling. Immediately, Morozov's premonition of disaster was reinforced.

He looked about for Michael but saw no sign of him. To one side stood a wooden platform, apparently to rest the coffin on, and about it were gathered a dozen cemetery attendants, black-shawled old women, men in breeches and some with muddy boots—obviously grave diggers.

Snow was falling persistently now and the fog was drifting lightly over the cemetery, foreshortening the long allées which radiated from the entrance and casting a vague aura of mystery over the quiet, everyday scene.

Morozov was about to exchange a polite word or two with the Party Secretary but Ivanov chose that moment to join Chaikovsky and the unknown man. Morozov had no desire to get any closer to the Security Chief than he could help. He set his bulky parcel down and began to stride back and forth, swinging his arms to strengthen the circulation. The damp wind cut through to his bones and he felt a chill coming on.

Morozov knew the Volkhov cemetery well. His mother and some of her family were buried here. And he remembered his first visit to the cemetery as a child. It was a sunny Sunday afternoon in early autumn. The leaves were golden on the birches and the pines were dark as night. His father had brought him to see the "Little Literary Bridge," the spot where so many of Russia's great writers, Belinsky, Dobrolyubov, Chernyshevsky and Turgenev, were buried.

"When I was a student in the university, Georges," his father had told him, "we came several times to the Little Literary Bridge. We held a demonstration on the anniversary of Dobrolyubov's death. Once a gendarme arrested me and I was held at the police station until my father came and got me out. Some of the other students were not so fortunate."

They had stood before the simple stone shaft over Belinsky's grave and his father had told him how Belinsky had been buried here, in this remote and swampy corner of the cemetery, because he

262

was so poor and his friends had no money to bury him in a better place.

All this time one question had burned in Georgi's mind and finally he could repress it no longer.

"But, Papa," he said, "where is the bridge? I don't see it anywhere."

His father had smiled.

"Well, that's so, Georges," he replied. "I hadn't thought of that. The bridge hasn't been here for many, many years. Once there was a little stream and you crossed over by the bridge but now they have drained the marsh and the bridge has been taken down."

His father looked up and down the quiet allée. Men and women were promenading in the afternoon sunshine. Some were sitting on the benches, their heads buried in books.

"You know, Georges," his father reflected, "there's a lesson in this for you. Don't take names too literally. Sometimes they mean something entirely different from what they sound. There is no bridge at the Little Literary Bridge, for instance. And we often speak of 'Holy Russia' but we seldom stop to ask why it is 'Holy' and, if it once was so, whether it is still 'Holy' today."

As a little boy Georgi had not quite understood his father's remark, but in later years it had often come back to him. Like so many of his father's small lessons it had an enduring quality.

Morozov had always been fond of the Little Literary Bridge. Once, near the end of the war, he encountered Irena unexpectedly as he was walking away from the General Staff Building. Her face, so often harassed and worn, shone with some kind of inner light.

"What have you been doing?" he asked.

"I've just spent the afternoon at the cemetery—at the Little Literary Bridge," she said. "Just sitting there on a bench. You don't know the peace that it brought to my soul."

But he did know because he could see it written on her face. It was, he thought, fitting that Irena was to be buried here. Here she would be at home. Here she would lie beside the other men and women whose genius had made the city of Peter.

A group of young people was entering the cemetery. They looked like a sleigh-ride party, their cheeks red and snow crusting the collars of their coats and glistening in the hair of the girls. How unexpected! Then Morozov saw Nadya among them and realized that these must be young people from the Institute, young artists and sculptors, former students of Irena's who still held her name dear. Somehow he had not thought to see anyone not of Irena's own generation—and his—at the burial.

It was incredible how young Michael had arranged all of this. In Morozov's preoccupation with the fact of Irena's death and its significance, he had, he must confess, rather ignored the actual situation. He had not questioned Michael as to how he had got permission to bring his mother's body to Leningrad nor how he had arranged for the burial to be held nor how he had gotten word of the ceremony to the people who were appearing.

Nadya came to him. She was wearing her fur cap and heavy jacket and looked to Morozov hardly a day older than when Irena had rescued her from the Putilov works and painfully nursed her back to life.

"Good morning, Georgi Alexandrovich," she said gravely, shaking hands in a formal manner.

"Good morning, dear Nadya," Morozov said. "It's so pleasant to see you even at this sad moment."

"Where is Michael?" Nadya asked with concern.

"I haven't seen him this morning," Morozov said, glancing at his watch. "But I am sure he will be here at any minute."

Nadya started to turn away and then whirled back and spoke to Morozov in very low tones: "Do you think it is going to be all right? That they won't interfere?" She nodded imperceptibly toward Ivanov and Chaikovsky.

"Dear Nadya," Morozov said very soberly, "I wish I knew. I don't think there will be any trouble until after the burial. But then —perhaps. Who knows?"

"That's what I told the students," Nadya said earnestly. "But some of them think Michael may have been arrested already."

"We'll soon know, dear," Morozov said. He was nervous himself but there was absolutely nothing to do. The premonition of tragedy which struck him so strongly when Michael appeared last night in his office had returned with full strength.

"Good God!" Morozov exclaimed involuntarily. Nadya followed his look.

"Why," she said, "it's that awful Smirnoff!"

Smirnoff had walked through the gate. Perhaps swayed was a better way of describing it. He did not weave but he was moving with the careful imprecision of a man who stands on the verge of drunkenness. His dark green velours hat with the wide brim which he thought added a touch of Montmartre to his appearance was askew. His mustard-colored scarf bulged out of his half-buttoned coat and he carried in his hand a spray of palm leaves which seemed to have been cut with a jackknife from a potted plant.

Smirnoff walked straight to Chaikovsky and threw back his arms, obviously with the intention of embracing the Security officer. Chaikovsky avoided the embrace by a neatly executed waltz step which put Ivanov's solid figure between himself and the writer.

"Good morning, Comrade Security Director," Smirnoff bellowed. "And good morning to you, Comrade Ivanov."

Smirnoff turned to the third member of the group, the freckled-faced man whom Morozov did not know. Freckle-face smirked at the writer and extended his hand.

"Why," sputtered Nadya, "that man is drunk. How dare he come here!"

She angrily rejoined her young companions. Morozov saw them glaring at Smirnoff and for a moment thought they might be preparing to throw him out. But their attention was diverted, first, by the arrival of General Orlov, tall and handsome in his soft gray fur hat and his long gray coat, and immediately after him by Michael, who drew up with the truck carrying his mother's coffin.

There was a general stir as the cemetery men carried the coffin in and put it on the wooden stand. Michael looked about frantically, his eyes quieting when he saw Nadya with the other young people.

It was snowing harder than ever now and Morozov realized that the crowd had grown considerably. Most of the faces were unknown to him. But he saw an old woman, very neatly garbed in black cloth coat and a black cloche hat which certainly dated to the mid-twenties. She was, he knew, an aunt or cousin of Irena's. He recognized two or three painters or sculptors. Who the others might be he had no idea.

Morozov approached Michael now and pressed his hand.

"Is everything in order, Michael?" he asked.

"Yes, I think so," the boy replied quietly. "Will you help with the coffin?"

He nodded agreement. In a moment the small cortege was formed. There were six to carry the coffin—himself, Michael, Orlov, one of the students, Orlov's aide and the painter Trepelov. Two grave diggers, their long-handled shovels over their shoulders, walked ahead to lead the way. The mourners walked behind. An old woman pushed a handcart with some of the flowers and wreaths. There was no funeral band and the coffin was decorated not with the traditional black-and-red but with fresh-cut boughs of spruce.

The walk seemed endless. Snow fell steadily and the fog had closed down so that the grave diggers repeatedly paused at cross walks to get their bearings. The monuments of the cemetery faded into the cotton-wool background. Suddenly, a tall mausoleum loomed up black as a monolith in an arctic waste. The branches of the trees were encased in hoarfrost and the long paths led into nowhere. It seemed to Morozov that they had entered a new world— a world of white and black, black and white. Black tree trunks. Black grave stones. White branches. White grave stones. Iron fences enclosing vague ghosts. Trees bereft of their tops. Grave shafts resting on banks of mist. A world without life, in which only the procession to the grave was moving. The snow on the footpaths muffled all sound, and Morozov had the sensation of walking forward into white emptiness. It was a region in which the senses of sight and sound had lost all significance. He felt his shoulder and the arm which bore the coffin growing stiff. His chill had been

266

replaced by sweat, which stood on his forehead like winter rain on the edge of the eaves. On and on they walked. Where were they going? Where would it end? Did anyone know their destination? Or was this walk something like life itself—a matter of putting one foot down after the other, endlessly moving past objects whose purpose you could not fathom and whose names had no meaning— moving, moving, moving, through a fog which lifted only occasion- ally to disclose a small clearing whose walls faded into infinity, but still not halting though your shoulders ached, your arms grew stiff and your body weary, walking from nothingness into nothingness, a coffin on your back and a grave digger for a guide.

Finally the grave diggers turned to the left. They passed through a narrow opening in a curved wrought-iron, blue-painted fence and suddenly came upon the open grave—the earth thrown up yellow and angry against the snowbank, red sand newly sprinkled on the approach. They knelt slightly and rested the coffin at the graveside.

Morozov stepped back. He had no idea where he might be. There was a moment of confusion. Two of the girl students were sobbing quietly. Michael stood looking down at his mother's coffin as if he were seeing it for the first time. The thought flashed through Moro- zov's mind: No one knows why we are here, where we have come or what to do next! He saw Ivanov standing, very ill at ease, still next to Chaikovsky, who looked serious and concerned. The freckled-faced man had vanished. So, apparently, had Smirnoff.

Then Orlov, tall, grave, hat in hand and right arm across his breast, walked up to the coffin.

"My dear friends," the General said. Instantly there was quiet— a quiet that seemed to be enfolded by the white wall of the snow and the fog. "My dear friends, we have come together to spend a final moment at the side of our beloved friend and comrade, Irena Mikhailovna Galina."

The General paused and one of the girls choked back a sob.

"I need not tell you that Irena Galina was a woman of courage and talent—a woman of Leningrad, a true daughter of our mother- land.

"So long as the language of Russia endures her name will glorify it. But we need not speak of Irena Galina today. History and the world will speak of her. Today, my dear comrades, we must speak of another matter. Not of her who gave her life to her country and her people and to humanity. We must speak, instead, of ourselves.

"There is no one who hears my voice who does not know the fate of Irena Galina, who does not know how she fell in battle, who does not know the cause in which she is a casualty."

The General's simple oratory brought tears welling from Morozov's eyes. He clenched his teeth to dam back his feelings. He saw Ivanov standing a little bit to the rear and sensed that behind the mask of flesh in which the tough Party Secretary's face was encased that he, too, had been caught up by Orlov's words.

"My dear comrades," Orlov continued, "for her glory Irena Galina has done everything that need be done. But to us the loss is greater than can be counted. For in her burned the deepest and most noble of desires—the desire to bring to all people peace. Irena Galina believed in peace. She hated war. She hated the men who make war and who make war possible.

"I ask only one question: Irena Galina died for the cause in which she believed. What did we do to help her? What have we done? Nothing . . . nothing . . . nothing."

The General bowed his head until his chin rested on the edge of his collar. He stood in silence as the snow flicked down, sifting over the coffin.

He raised his head and, speaking so low that Morozov had to crane his head to hear, added: "Shall this be all? Shall Irena Galina have died in vain? Let us answer now: No. No. No."

Two tears started from the General's eyes and slowly descended his face as he stood motionless. Then he stepped back a pace and put on his hat, not bothering to brush from his hair the snow that glistened there.

The General's words had set the chords of Morozov's soul vibrating like a cello. There was in them a faint echo of the past, as though in some previous incarnation Morozov had heard them

268

spoken before. Suddenly he realized what it was. Consciously, or much more likely unconsciously, the General had paraphrased the famous words of Chernyshevsky at the funeral of Dobrolyubov, words spoken only a stone's throw from this very spot—the words which were the summons to battle, the cry to arms of the "men of the sixties," the generation of the last century which had set the Russian stage for the overthrow of the old regime.

These words were not merely a tribute. They were not merely a set piece of eloquence. Morozov honestly did not know whether the General appreciated every implication of what he had said. He had put the question softly. He had spoken with his usual parsimony of phrase. But he had, as clearly as had Chernyshevsky, assessed the guilt for Irena's death, assessed the measure of her belief and called for action in the name of her cause.

Morozov stepped up to the General and silently took his hand. Orlov, he thought, I am proud of you and proud to be at your side.

One of the students came forward. He held a visored student's cap in his hand and wore a threadbare dark blue cloth coat. His blond hair was long and tangled. His face was almost as thin as Michael's and his eyes had the same hawklike stare. He stood beside the coffin and began to declaim in the somewhat melodramatic Russian fashion.

Morozov's eyes fell on Nadya. Her whole attention was fixed on the young speaker, her hands clasped at her breast, her eyes wide and round. Young Galin stood beside her. There was something instinctively protective in the posture of his body, the inclination of his shoulder to hers.

What was it that the young man was declaiming? Morozov turned his attention on the speaker. Of course! Maxim Voronsky's "Ballad of a Poster Maker," one of his rabid, early revolutionary declamations. Not a poem to Morozov's taste. How well he remembered Voronsky on the platform of the hall on Litenny Prospekt. He had taken Irena to hear him recite his poems soon after her return from Paris. She had never heard him before.

Voronsky was all Greek fire that night—his hair like a stallion's mane, his eyes ablaze, stalking about the stage, posturing, raging, laughing, fuming, flaunting his force, playing with the crowd like an animal tamer in the lion's cage.

And, of course, "Ballad of a Poster Maker" had been the climax of the evening. . . .

> Tear down the placards from the walls
> And you will find the words
> Graven in stone.
> Burn the paper and the smoke of the fire
> Will be stench in your nostrils
> To the grave.
> Tear the paper to bits and cast it to the seas—
> A thousand years from now it will
> Litter the beaches of history.
> I am the poster maker. I deal in paper and words.
> Perishable products. The wind blows them away
> But you cannot escape them.
> I am the poster maker. I have no gun, no weapon.
> My bullets are made of paper. They can do no harm
> To ordinary men and women.
> But, messieurs and gentlemen, I tell you no lie—
> My words can shake a mountain, destroy an Empire
> And kill a Czar.

The hall went wild when Voronsky shouted his final words. Morozov felt Irena's hand grasping his arm like a steel vise. For a week the claw marks of her fingernails remained on the flesh of his muscle. She was shouting: "Bis! Bis! Bis! Bravo! Bravo!" And she went on shouting until her voice was hoarse.

"Oh, Georgi," she cried to him. "What power! What strength! He shakes you to the depths!"

She clung to him as they hurried home through the cold night, holding his arm to her breast, and when they reached the little room off the Haymarket she had thrown her arms about him, had crushed her lips against his, had pulled him down on the bed, crying: "Please, Georgi. Please, Georgi. Hurry. Hurry. Hurry."

The youngster had come to the finale: "I am the poster maker. I have no gun, no weapon." Morozov felt the hairs on the back of his neck begin to tingle. He did not like the poem. Truth to tell he hated it. But Voronsky's words reeked of revolution and, spoken by this young voice, by this young man whose face burned with passion, spoken across the grave of Irena Galina on this strange day in which snow and fog had enclosed the funeral party within a white island, they set the adrenalin pumping into Morozov's veins.

My God, Morozov thought. It sounds like a declaration of war! And it is intended to be one. He looked across at Ivanov. The Party Secretary stood like a stone image and Chaikovsky was his twin.

There was silence. The boy had finished the poem. Morozov heard a snarl of voices just beyond the circle around the grave. It was Smirnoff, suddenly appearing. He looked even worse, as though he had taken several more long pulls on the vodka bottle.

"Let me through," Smirnoff was saying in slurred tones. "Le' me through. I gotta pome to read. Let me through."

A shudder went through Morozov. Orlov's body stiffened. But Smirnoff's voice was cut off in the midst of a sentence. Morozov saw the freckled-faced man step beside him, put an arm around his shoulder and say something in a soft voice into Smirnoff's ear. God knows what it could have been but Smirnoff's face blanched and he lapsed into silence.

The time has come for me to speak, Morozov thought, and I do not know what to say except that the only woman I have ever loved lies frozen, still and forever silent in this plain box, resting on the new spaded earth. He moved forward and turned to the small circle around the grave. He stood a moment. How pale their faces and how few they were, how few of all those who had known Irena, who had loved her, whom she had loved, how few have come to be with her in this moment, thought Morozov.

"My dear friends," he said. "I have but one word to say. I loved Irena Mikhailovna from the first day I saw her, a little girl in Petersburg, long before war and revolution changed our city and our motherland. All my life I have loved Irena Mikhailovna and that love has given my life its only meaning. Our Northern Palmyra has had many glories but only one Irena Galina. Her death casts a shadow upon all our lives. It leaves my own life empty and at an end."

Morozov halted. Somehow it did not seem to him that he had said anything that was in his heart. In his heart was the golden image of Irena. He saw her as she ran down the leafy allée of the Summer Garden to join her governess the first time they had met. He saw her as they played on the beach at Reval, her pink cotton skirt tucked up around her thighs to keep the waves from splashing it. He saw her as he had held her in his arms the first time they had made love, the soft warmth of her body melting into his, her eyes slowly opening, the shadows deep as a well, the lazy stretch of her arms like a white-and-yellow cat, the red of her tongue, flicking from her full lips. And he saw, too, the fire of her eyes, the anger of her nostrils as her words crashed in his ears, telling him of the bomb which had exploded next to the hospital wall, the raging blows of her fist as she beat on his chest and swore that she would give her life, if need be, to halt the stupid, animal slaughter of man by man.

What could he say? How could you put a life that had as many sides as a crystal into a few sentences? How could you capture a dream in words or paint a passion in gestures?

He realized that he had been silent for a long time—just how long he could not say.

"I'm sorry," he said. "I do not know how to speak of Irena Galina. It seemed to me that she held life in her hand like quicksilver, gleaming and running faster than the eye could see or the mind could think. Now the quicksilver is gone . . . I'm sorry . . ."

Morozov put his hand to his eyes. He could not help it. It was a miserable thing but he had not even said what he had promised Irena he would say—that she had survived war but had died fighting for peace. How badly he had spoken. And how badly he felt. Perhaps he was going to be ill. For the first time it swept over him that Irena was gone, that he would never see her again, and with that feeling it seemed to him that the world had grown dark.

Michael was speaking now, his hands thrust into the sagging

pockets of his worn sheepskin. Fatigue lines creased his face. With his high cheek bones, his thin lips, his wind-weathered face, Morozov thought he looked like an Indian from the pages of Fenimore Cooper.

"My name is Galin," Michael was saying. "I am proud of my name because it is the name of my mother, Irena Galina, and I am proud of my mother. She died far from this city which gave her birth, the city to which she gave her life. She believed in peace. She died for peace. Indeed, her very name was peace. You have come here today, to this place which she loved, to honor her. As the son of Irena Galina I thank you."

Michael looked about. Everyone stood silent in the semicircle. Then two of the cemetery workers quietly lifted the coffin into the grave. Michael reached down and threw a handful of earth into the pit. Nadya did the same. The others came forward to the edge of the grave and tossed a little dirt into the hole as the grave diggers rapidly shoveled, the earth rattling on the lid of the coffin and then the rattle ceasing as the wood was covered and the excavation filled.

The men with shovels neatly heaped up a shallow mound over the coffin and stepped back, wiping the sweat from their brows and resting on their shovels.

Snow carpeted the new earth as the old woman scattered pine boughs over the grave and set the flowers and wreaths among them. The white azalea glistened with unearthly pallor against the snow. The students had brought handfuls of red, blue and yellow paper flowers, which they twisted into the green boughs, like a midsummer carpet. Orlov's aide carefully placed in the center an ornate wreath of artificial laurel with a red silk ribbon on which Morozov was surprised to see inscribed in Latin characters the words "Semper fidelis."

Nadya unwrapped the newspaper parcel which she had held under her arm throughout the ceremonies and set within the circle of the big wreath a framed picture. It was a crayon sketch of Irena's "End of War" group, done either by Irena herself, or, perhaps, by Nadya. Morozov could not determine from the style. It was, however, a striking sketch that had caught in bold relief the power of Irena's terrible concept.

Well, thought Morozov, and so it is all over. At an end. He looked around him. The funeral party was beginning to drift away into the white world of the fog and snow. He saw Orlov's tall figure moving down the path into the dimness of the distance and turned to follow him. I want a word with Orlov, he thought. I want to thank him for saying what had to be said about Irena. Morozov turned up his collar and pulled down his cap a bit. It was really getting cold. The snow was thicker than ever. He could hardly see Orlov down the long allée ahead of him.

35

The man was like a leech, Chaikovsky thought. He attached himself to you and there was no getting rid of him. From the moment they had arrived at the cemetery he had tried to separate himself from Ivanov but the Party Secretary had stuck to his side as if his life depended on it. Chaikovsky was perfectly aware of what Ivanov was doing. The old man was in a blind funk and he thought that if he stayed cheek-by-jowl with the Security boss it might save his skin in the end. How naïve could Ivanov be, Chaikovsky wondered. Surely, the Party Secretary had been around long enough to know that if his number was coming up it would come up and there was nothing to do about it. He was sorry for Ivanov because, as he now knew, Ivanov's number *was* coming up. But there was nothing to do about that. Chaikovsky couldn't change the situation. It wasn't his fault and he felt no sense of personal responsibility. It was just the run of the cards. Ivanov had held good hands for a long time. Now he was drawing the black ace. What could you expect? If you lived on caviar and shashlik long enough, you had to pay the bill. That was the law of life and so far as Chaikovsky knew it was not much different here in Russia than it was anywhere else.

Now with the funeral drawing to an end Ivanov was an embarrassment. It had been bad enough having to ride out in the same car with him. Not that this had been his idea. No, indeed. But with that freckled-faced bastard Galpert breathing down his neck he had no alternative.

He must say he had seen Moscow do some strange things but the way it had handled this Galin matter set a record. Of course, it was not without precedent to send in a special detail on an important case and certainly, as was now obvious, Moscow regarded this as a most important case.

What was mystifying and, Chaikovsky admitted, a little frightening, was the "embroidery" which was being worked into the affair. In the normal run of things, Chaikovsky knew, his instructions would have been very simple. Just place Galin under arrest as soon as he appeared in Leningrad. But nothing so ordinary had been proposed. And, to go back of that, why had he been permitted to come to Leningrad in the first place? Chaikovsky was not born yesterday. Someone had begun to spin this web a long way back. Obviously, there had been a tip-off. Moscow had known that Galin was returning to Leningrad and, in general, what the young man hoped to do. Galin must have told someone in Tashkent of his plans before he left—someone who had communicated instantly with Moscow. Nor was that all, Chaikovsky thought. By coincidence the plans of young Galin to bring his mother's body back to Leningrad and to bury her with public ceremony had happened to suit Moscow's complicated purpose. The only possible explanation was that the Kremlin had been waiting to take action in Leningrad and saw a chance to achieve its ends by permitting Galin to act as a kind of unwitting decoy or catalytic agent. The scheme reeked of the deviousness so typical of Moscow but would be nonetheless deadly in its consequences.

Certainly it had been no accident that Galin was permitted to run all over town, to invite anyone he wanted to the funeral, to assemble them here, and on this spot, of all places, not a stone's throw from the Little Literary Bridge. And why, incidentally, had not Chaikovsky been told that Galin had bribed the superintendent to give him a site right next to the place where all the prominent writers and revolutionaries were buried? Why, in God's name? All he had received was the number of the plot. Of course, when he heard that Galin had to pay five thousand rubles he knew, automatically, that it must be a good location. But Moscow's word had been: Don't interfere. So—what? He had interpreted it too literally, he supposed. But he would get hell for this. He could feel it in his bones. He could hear the questions now: "And, Comrade Chaikovsky, why did you think that the funeral should be conducted in the most prominent place in the cemetery? And, Comrade Chaikovsky, were you not aware of the political implications of this action?"

Indeed, the more Chaikovsky thought about the Little Literary Bridge, the more worried he grew. By God, he thought, I could be sacked for that. Why hadn't he been told? He could guess. It was because that thieving superintendent wanted to keep the big bribe. That superintendent was going to be sorry. Chaikovsky would see to that.

There was a bad aura about this case anyway, Chaikovsky thought grimly. One thing going wrong after another. The agent losing Galin last night. Galpert had not got onto that yet—but he would. Never fear.

And he still had the problem of separating himself from Ivanov. When the funeral party had begun to move from the gate he had lingered behind to talk to Galpert. But Ivanov stuck to him so closely that eventually he had had to move along.

Of course, he would not have gotten himself into this fix if Galpert hadn't kept him on tenterhooks to the last moment as to what move they were going to make. He had his agents on the spot, well deployed. Everything had gone smooth as clockwork. Galpert's men had been meshed into the operational scheme without the slightest trouble—on that score, at least, Moscow would have to give him full credit. Almost half the mourners were his men. He had them distributed among the attendants. The old woman who trundled the handcart was his operative. One of the

277

art students was an undercover agent.

There was only one drawback which was beginning to worry Chaikovsky. This was the weather. The combination of fog and snow made things a little tricky. It was hard to find your way around the cemetery, for instance. Even the grave diggers had had their troubles. Thank God, he thought, that I was smart enough not to replace the whole crew with my men. We never would have gotten to this spot.

Concerned as he was with his own problems, Chaikovsky had missed the first couple of sentences of Orlov's remarks. Then, his ears suddenly pricked up. Well, he had thought, now I begin to see why Moscow was so interested in this affair. When the General's brief speech came to an end he had stolen a cautious look at Ivanov. He saw Ivanov's Adam's apple bob up and down. The Party Secretary had swallowed—swallowed hard. He was repressing an emotion. What it was Chaikovsky could not be sure. Fear? Quite possibly. But it was just as likely that he had been moved by the General's words. Ivanov had a soft spot in his heart for Irena Galina, Chaikovsky knew. Not that this was surprising. He, Chaikovsky, had a special feeling for her too. She had been a real woman. Let the rest of them have their politics, he thought, a real woman is the thing that counts in life.

It was at that moment that Galpert had returned and signaled him with a lift of the eyebrow. Chaikovsky moved over to the Moscow agent.

"I have the word now," Galpert whispered. "We will move in as they leave. Nothing at the graveside. Pick them up as they walk down the allée toward the entrance."

"Okay," said Chaikovsky. "I'll pass the word to my men."

"One minute," said Galpert quickly. "That's not all. We will only take the principals and we will try to manage it so that the others do not notice."

"I understand," said Chaikovsky. "We'll manage that, I think."

"Now," said Galpert, "as for the principals—that means only the following: the speakers—that is, Orlov and the others. The pallbearers—Morozov, the General's aide, the boy, that painter Trepelov; Smirnoff, of course."

"Okay," Chaikovsky had said again. He was impatient to get to his lieutenant and pass the word along. It would be a little tricky taking these people into custody without the others noticing what was happening.

"Let me just check over again," said Galpert with a bland smile. "We don't want to leave anyone out."

Galpert's eyes roved over the crowd, then he suddenly snapped his fingers.

"I knew it," he said with a smirk. "Almost overlooked the biggest fish of all."

Chaikovsky frowned. "Who?"

"Oh, you know," Galpert said, putting his lips close to Chaikovsky's ear. "Our former friend, the Party Secretary. You've noticed, I'm sure, how closely he got himself tied up with these people."

So, there it was, thought Chaikovsky. Just as big an affair and just as dangerous as he suspected. What it amounted to was a clean sweep—a clean sweep of the whole top Lenigrad leadership, political, military, ideological; Ivanov, Orlov and Smirnoff, plus a mixed lot—students, artists, God knows who. He could not say that this was a bolt from the blue. Any experienced observer had known, since Zhdanov's death in August, that there was bound to be a shake-up. The only question had been when and who and how big. But Chaikovsky shook his head as he watched Galpert fade away again. This was no ordinary changing of the guard. This operation had ramifications which even his well-trained mind could not follow. If the Kremlin had determined to carry out a purge and not merely a shuffling of personnel then, thought Chaikovsky, what is happening here at the Literary Bridge, this glorification of a woman who long since had been declared ideologically corrupt and banished as a state criminal—all of this could be placed by Moscow in a new context. It could be viewed not as the personal and political willfulness of young Galin but as a deliberate, calculated challenge to the state by a group of high officials.

279

As to why the Kremlin had determined to carry out a new purge in Leningrad, Chaikovsky long since had trained himself to turn his eyes away from the motivations which underlay the orders he was called upon to execute. Yet he could not halt his thoughts at an arbitrary line. He knew as well as any insider that Moscow did not trust Leningrad. He knew as well as any insider how easy it was to stimulate the Kremlin's uneasiness. He knew a good deal about the inner mechanics of the Kirov case; more, perhaps, than he would ever admit. He knew, for example, that Moscow had hinted at a private and generalized "concern" about the Leningrad situation long before young Nikolayev so fortuitously appeared on the scene with his grievances, his threats and his mutterings. And the thought that he knew why Nikolayev had chanced to slip through the security barricade and accomplish the assassination of Kirov; and why the Leningrad security chiefs were first congratulated—and later purged. Sometimes, Chaikovsky thought, people supposed that history could not repeat itself. After a lifetime in police work Chaikovsky was prepared to swear that history was much more likely to repeat itself than not. What had happened before almost certainly would happen again—especially in Russia. Right now it was repeating itself before his eyes in Leningrad.

Chaikovsky was only too familiar with the process which started with suspicion and swiftly blossomed into conviction—the process whereby a man was, at first, only suspected of a crime and how, often without his being aware that he was suspect, he provided the ever-vigilant observer with evidence that if not yet guilty of the crime he possessed inherent tendencies which someday might cause him to commit it. Chaikovsky had carried out in his time a goodly number of "preventive arrests" and now, if he was not mistaken, something like this was going to be applied to all or most of the Leningrad hierarchy.

Thank goodness, Chaikovsky thought, that I am considered part of the Moscow apparatus rather than that of Leningrad. Otherwise, he might be going the way of Ivanov. Well, he still had the problem of breaking away from the Party Secretary. He had done callous things in his life but, if he could help it, he did not want to be with the Secretary when the arrest was made. Not only would it be embarrassing personally but it would not be astute politically.

The way this case was shaping up he fully expected to be put on the carpet before it was over. He did not want his inquisitor to wind up with the question: "And how, Comrade Chaikovsky, do you explain the fact that it was in your company that the state criminal, former Party Secretary Ivanov, was arrested?"

No, indeed. Friendship was friendship but business was business. It would not help Ivanov one iota to be arrested in Chaikovsky's company. And it might harm Chaikovsky considerably. He had passed the word along to his chief lieutenant about the operation but he could not leave the scene and, for the moment, there was nothing to do about Ivanov.

Chaikovsky had listened glumly to the young student and his poetry. Students! They were all alike. So far as he was concerned the country would be better off if they closed the universities. All they did was stir these young fellows up so that they started spouting their heads off—a lot of fancy words and flashing eyes. Where did it get them? The same place it was going to get this brilliant young orator—Siberia. After all, what was the point of it, anyhow? These young fellows never seemed to learn. One generation after another. It had been the same under the Czars. Chaikovsky had watched them for years. There wasn't a single season when he had not had to pick out half a dozen—sometimes more—from the leading classes of the university. Off they went every year to Siberia. And then the next year a new crop, like the first dandelions in the spring. What compelled them to talk? Why did they have to complain? Some kind of youthful disease, he supposed. But if they would enroll them in trade schools, put them in the factories, send them to the farms and give them good, healthy work to do they wouldn't get these fancy ideas. He sighed. Well, he supposed it was part of the price you paid to have a cultured society. Science, art, music, things like that—they were the frosting on the cake. You had to pay for them because without the frosting the cake tasted flat.

Not that it was his problem, thank goddness, and if the students provided him with a few cases every year—well, what was a police department for? If people didn't violate the rules he'd have nothing to do.

He recognized "Ballad of a Poster Maker," but it did not move him. He had never cared for Voronsky's flamboyant style. Yessenin—there was a poet after his heart. The real feeling of the village. Russia as it was, as it always will be. Funny thing how all those poets wound up killing themselves—Yessenin, Mayakovsky, Voronsky. Must be something in their blood. Went to their brains.

The grave diggers were filling the hole in the ground. The time was approaching to give Ivanov the slip. Imperceptibly, Chaikovsky edged to one side while Ivanov moved with the rest of the crowd to the grave. Chaikovsky faded off to the left a few paces. The plot where Irena Galina was being buried was a small one, but a granite tombstone on the next plot half shielded him from Ivanov's vision.

Chaikovsky watched the group of mourners. This was the critical moment, for now they would drift back down the long avenues to the entrance to the cemetery. It was along these avenues that his agents were posted with instructions to slip out quickly, pick their man and slip away before anyone realized what had happened. Half a block beyond the entrance in a little side lane there were several blue-painted Security police vans waiting to take the victims away.

Chaikovsky put his finger to his nose. His assistant standing at the entrance to the small plot caught the gesture. It was the agreed signal that the exodus was starting. The fog was heavier than ever and Chaikovsky hoped it would not lead to confusion.

Ivanov was looking about now, obviously trying to place Chaikovsky. Fortunately, Ivanov assumed that the Security Chief had gone toward the pathway and walked in that direction. By the time Ivanov had reached the allée his figure began to blur in the haze.

At least, thought Chaikovsky, I am spared the look from his eyes.

He glanced at his man standing by the fence. The man inclined his head a fraction of a degree. Good. Everything was still okay. But where was Galpert? He wanted him to witness how smoothly the operation was going. His eyes swept the crowd—Galpert had vanished and so had Smirnoff. Well, probably Galpert had taken Smirnoff off personally. Smirnoff had almost created a real scandal. He had to admit the Moscow man handled that deftly.

The crowd had thinned now. Not many left. The boy, Galin, one or two of the students, the old woman in the black costume, who must be a relative. One girl seemed to be sticking very closely to Galin. Perhaps there was a relationship which should be investigated. He would put a man on that as soon as he got back to the office—and he still had the question of where Galin spent the night. It would be very convenient if that little fact could be wormed out of Galin before Galpert got his hands on him. Then, the back track could be covered.

The last of the mourners were going now—all but Galin and that girl. They stood beside the grave, her arm in his. Yes, there was something between them beyond doubt. The snow was coming down more heavily. It had quite obscured the carpet of evergreens. Only the red and yellow and blue paper flowers stood out, their blossoms still above the white blanket. The white azalea plant would not last long in this temperature, Chaikovsky thought. Well, just a moment more and we will be finished with this phase of the operation. What next, of course, was hard to tell.

Chaikovsky saw a man at the gap in the fence. It was Galpert, returning. The fog was so heavy he had been invisible until he actually arrived. He came up to Chaikovsky with a loose smile on his lips. Just at that moment Chaikovsky noticed Galin and the girl turn their backs on the grave and start to move straight ahead, away from where he stood. They were going not to the allée but across the adjacent burial lot in the opposite direction, the direction that led to the Literary Bridge.

Chaikovsky turned to Galpert and started to speak but the words froze in his throat at the sight of the crooked grin which was spreading over Galpert's freckled face.

By God, the thought flashed through Chaikovsky's mind, this son of a bitch is going to arrest me!

Galpert suddenly clapped his hand to his side and brought up a small blue-steel snub-nosed revolver, which he pointed at Chaikovsky's abdomen.

"Officer Chaikovsky," he said, "I have the honor to inform you that you are under arrest. Please raise your hands above your head."

Slowly Chaikovsky's hands went above his head. The bastard! The little Jew bastard! Galpert leaned forward and deftly extricated Chaikovsky's revolver from the holder under his shoulder. Chaikovsky's jaw fell slack and for one instant he thought that he was going to faint. The fog had closed in all about them like a curtain.

Two of Galpert's aides stepped up behind Chaikovsky. One seized him by either arm.

"Let's get along now," Galpert said. "We've got them all. This was the last."

Chaikovsky began to move forward, his eyes on the ground. He saw his boots lift, one after the other, leaving black marks on the fresh snow. Words, questions, stumbled through his mind but none of them made any sense. Nothing made any sense. Why me? His mind asked the question again and again. Why me? What did I do? It was some terrible mistake. This fellow Galpert, who was he anyway? Who had told him to make the arrest? Someone in Moscow had gotten the whole thing mixed up. There were such cases. Like the time they executed the wrong fellow. There had been hell to pay for that. He, Chaikovsky, had delivered the reprimand in person— three months loss of pay, reduction by two grades and a transfer to Khabarovsk. Moscow didn't forgive mistakes. No, indeed. After all, what had Comrade Dzerzhinsky called the Security service— "The good right arm of revolutionary justice." No, there was no toleration of blunders. And this man Galpert had blundered. Had gotten the thing all mixed up. Of course, Chaikovsky must admit he had made a couple of slips in this case. He was ready to concede that. He could be held accountable for permitting the ceremony at the Literary Bridge. That was his responsibility. He should have known about that. So let them deliver a reprimand. But that was no grounds for arresting a man. Not after twenty years of devoted service to the GPU, the OGPU, and the NKVD. After all, he was a senior worker. He had six medals. You didn't treat a senior worker like that. He did not claim that his record was perfect. He had made a mistake on the cemetery to be sure. But he had organized the rest of the operation very well, had he not? He had carried out every instruction about the Galin boy right to the letter, had he not? Oh, God. No. There was one other slip. And he had made it and he would accept the responsibility for it. He would even admit that he had tried to cover it up. He had lost track of the boy last night. For eight or nine hours Galin had disappeared. But just let him have fifteen minutes with that boy and he'd worm it out of him. Yes, sir. He, Chaikovsky, knew how to make a pigeon sing.

They had come to the end of the path. Chaikovsky saw pavement under his feet instead of the snow carpet.

"Step up now," one of the plainclothesmen said.

Chaikovsky stepped up. It was the blue-painted police van. He entered its murky depths and slumped on the wooden bench, his eyes still looking down.

He was puzzled. He had been going to mention something to Galpert; it had been on the tip of his tongue and just at that moment Galpert had drawn his gun. What was it? Something about young Galin. And now it had gone right out of his mind. Something Galin had done. No. Something he was doing. That was it. Of course. The scene came back to him now. Galin and the girl. They had walked away from the graveside—but in the wrong direction. They had walked toward the center of the cemetery, toward the Little Literary Bridge, instead of back toward the entrance. And Galpert hadn't seen it; hadn't seen it because he was so busy drawing his gun and announcing Chaikovsky's arrest.

Chaikovsky spat on the floor. Well, it would serve the bastard right if they slipped through his fingers. He threw back his shoulders and leaned against the wall of the van. The car had begun to move and he swayed a little. He lifted his gaze from the floor. Someone was sitting directly across from him. His eyes started with the man's black leather boots, followed the trousers up to a heavy overcoat, then up the line of the overcoat to the man's face. It was a face which was almost as familiar to him as his own—that of Gregory Ivanov, Party Secretary—former Party Secretary—sitting straight on the bench and staring at him with blank eyes from a wooden face. So far as you might judge from Ivanov's expression he had never seen Chaikovsky before.

Well, thought Chaikovsky, that's the way life goes, life in Russia.

36

The train for Sverdlovsk left at five minutes after midnight. Michael and Nadya stood in the dimly lighted corridor, looking out the frosted window to the station platform. It was still snowing and the last strains of the national anthem had just died away on the loudspeaker. Just past midnight. They held each other's hands and their breath seemed to come in unison. In a moment the yellow flag of the bosomy train girl was going to fall, the lantern would swing and the train would begin to move. At the end of the car the *provodnik*, a small wiry woman with more than a trace of a black mustache, was fussing with her little stove, trying to get the samovar going for tea. The scent of the smoking pine chips mingled with the heavy odor of *mahorka* and the stench of generations of passengers which was engrained in the walls of the "hard" car.

The train began to move now, almost imperceptibly, but definitely moving. The overhead light flickered out. Michael and Nadya turned to each other and quickly kissed in the dark, pulling away like children stealing a swift embrace in the parlor.

"It's moving, Michael," Nadya said, her head close to his and her eyes watching the platform through the round hole in the frost which they had melted with their warm hands.

"And it will keep moving, too," Michael said.

They smiled almost invisibly in the murk of the train. Exactly how they had gotten here, Michael thought, would be hard to tell anyone. Certainly he had not expected this to happen. Neither had Nadya—well, maybe that wasn't exactly right.

As they stood side by side at his mother's grave Nadya had said in a whisper: "Michael, I must talk to you about a very serious matter."

Michael looked into her warm brown eyes and knew that she was speaking from her heart. Her words brought him out of the almost somnambulant state into which he had fallen since leaving the morgue with the truck bearing his mother's body. He had arrived at the cemetery in a kind of iron daze, his muscles moving automatically, his body responding to his will, his voice speaking. But it was another set of muscles, another body and another voice. He heard General Orlov's tribute to his mother as if through a glass wall. When young Romanov recited "Ballad of a Poster Maker," Michael could feel the words rattling on the bones of his skull like hail on a roof, but they had no meaning to him. He knew that he had himself spoken. What he had said was a mystery.

Now, however, he was aware that he stood beside Nadya. The snow was drifting over her face. At his feet the green blanket of fir boughs was turning into a comforter of feathery down. Somehow, he did not know why, everyone seemed to have melted away. Only he and Nadya were still there. He pulled himself together, jerking himself into consciousness.

"Yes," he said. "We must talk—somewhere, away from the others. But where?"

He glanced about them. They seemed to be walled in by the snow and fog.

"I know," he said. "Just beyond here. I was there yesterday—the Literary Bridge. There are benches. A big fir tree. No one will bother us."

He took Nadya by the arm and, turning from the graveside,

swiftly moved forward, slipping between a gap in the fence, along a narrow path between two large sarcophagi, and into a larger plot which was separated by a boxwood hedge from the approach to the spot called the Literary Bridge.

They squeezed through the hedge and walked down the allée to an enormous overhanging fir tree whose limbs, weighted with snow, hung low over a bench. As they seated themselves their arms went around each other and Michael buried himself in Nadya's face, his lips pressing against hers. For a long moment they remained in a breathless embrace.

"Oh, Michael," Nadya said.

"My dearest Nadya," he replied, kissing her again. This time she broke away from him with a nervous gesture.

"Michael," she said, "perhaps we haven't much time and there is something I want to tell you—something you may have guessed. I love you and I'm not going to be separated from you. Whatever happens to you will happen to me and you must know that."

Michael put his hands on her shoulders.

"And I love you, dearest Nadya," he said. "And because I love you I will not permit you to share my fate. It must not be. This is the end of the road for me. The next stop—one way or another—is Siberia."

"I don't care," the girl said. "I have thought and thought about this. The place for a woman is with the man she loves. I love you, Michael. And that gives me the right to be with you. Not only the right—the duty. If you go to Siberia—I go with you."

"But you can't," he said.

"I can," she said. "And I am going with you. You love me, Michael, and you cannot keep the woman who loves you from going at your side. You have a duty to me, too."

"But, Nadya dear," he protested, "they are liable to arrest me at any moment. You know that. I am not going to have you arrested. I love you. You don't know what it means to be a prisoner in the East."

Nadya drew herself up proudly.

289

"I am a Russian woman," she said. "We Russian women have gone to Siberia with our men since the time of the Decembrists. If you are arrested, I will ask to be arrested too, so that I may accompany you."

Michael smiled. There were stars in Nadya's eyes, her cheeks were flushed as roses and dewy snowdrops sparkled in her hair. The deep green fir leaned over them, its arms protecting them like those of a great bear. They might have been in a cave for all the wind that reached them here. Outside, the wall of white was unbroken. They could barely make out the monuments in the fog.

"And why do you think you will be arrested, Michael?" Nadya said suddenly. "You have done nothing wrong. You had permission to come to Leningrad to bury your mother. What crime have you committed?"

He sat silent a moment, running over possibilities in his mind.

"I'm all packed, Michael," Nadya said. "Ready to leave this minute. I tied up my bag before I left my room. All we need do is stop by and pick it up."

Michael's mind was working at top speed now.

"I wonder," he said aloud. "I just wonder."

He turned to her again, encircled her with his arms, drew her face to his and pressed his lips against her soft lips. His face had lighted up and his eyes were clear. Excitement was gripping him.

"My dearest Nadya," he said, "my darling, my strange, wonderful, beautiful, pure, lovely woman. We are going to go to Siberia. There probably is no other place in the world where we could go. But I have a curious feeling that it is not impossible to go to Siberia, and that we even may be permitted to pay our own way."

But it was not to be an easy thing. In the first place they got lost—completely lost. Michael thought he knew how to get back to the entrance but the pathway which he chose led them endlessly through a world of fog and funeral markers and finally to a dead end. They started back but took a different turn and walked for half an hour without seeing a soul or passing any recognizable spot. Michael grew more and more nervous.

"I'm terribly sorry, Nadya," he said. "We are lost. This awful fog has twisted things every which way. The worst part is that we haven't any time to spare."

Finally they came to a small red brick building. They could see a faint light in the window and within there was the steady sound of a workman's hammer.

They opened the door without knocking and found a cheerful young man with a mallet and saw busily putting coffins together. A stack of a dozen of them, piled one on the other, reached almost to the ceiling, and he was hammering away at another.

The young carpenter halted his pounding, took a handful of nails from his mouth and said in a cheery manner: "Well, folks, I hope you've not come here in search of a coffin. They're in mighty short supply these days and every one I've got—and more—is on order."

"No," Michael interjected hastily. "It's not that. We seem to have lost our way. Could you direct us how to get out of the cemetery?"

"Well," the young man said, "that's a good deal less of a problem than a coffin, I'm telling you. It's easier to get out of the cemetery than it is to get in in these times, I'm telling you. You have no idea the trouble people have—no coffins, no plots for the graves. Headaches, headaches. Life is not easy, as you will be finding out, and death is no easier."

The young man led them to the door.

"You are a good long way from the main entrance," he said. "Which is, I suppose, the way you came in. The quickest way out is right here—just beyond the shed there you'll find a small door in the wall. That puts you right out on Volkhovsky Prospekt, where the tram line runs."

They caught a streetcar and rode back to the center of town.

"The first thing to do is to get your bag," Michael said. "Then we will go to the station and see what we can do for tickets."

They entered her room and again embraced—embraced quietly, silently, saying nothing and separating breathlessly. Nadya immediately reached under her bed and pulled out her bag, neatly bound with cord. Michael took from the bed a comforter and an old army blanket of gray wool. He rolled the comforter inside the wool blanket and bound them to Nadya's suitcase. Then the two of them stood looking about at the room.

"Let's sit a moment, dear," Michael said, "before we start on a long journey."

For a minute they sat in silence, drinking in each other's presence. The room was absolutely still and not a sound reached them from the street.

Michael rose, grabbed the bag with one hand and opened the door. Neither of them turned a head to look at the entrance to the studio, still barred by the big padlock.

"We are going to do this in the simplest and safest way," Michael said. "I'm not going to bother to reclaim my suitcase. There is really nothing in it anyway except a couple of shirts and my razor. Everything I have of any value is in my pockets and they might be watching for me at the checkroom. But there is one thing which I think you will have to do."

He explained that Nadya would have to buy their tickets.

"We are not going to go to Tashkent," he said. "All that is behind. We will strike out entirely on our own—straight to Siberia. First, we'll go to Sverdlovsk. Then we'll change for Novosibirsk and from there, if we are still lucky, we will push on out to the real East. To Irkutsk and Baikal."

There was a long, long wait in line but the plan worked without a hitch. Nadya's passport was in perfectly good order. She bought two tickets, for herself and her brother, hard class, to Sverdlovsk. She didn't have her brother's passport, he was coming down that evening from Petropavlovsk, he would bring it and show it when he came. She was trying to squeeze a tear into her handkerchief when the tired woman at the window said: "Oh, never mind, dear, I trust you. You have an honest face. Nobody would want to go to Sverdlovsk unless they had to go there."

She handed the tickets over to Nadya and in a moment she had joined Michael, her face wreathed in smiles.

"Now," said Michael, "we had better get out of the station until it's time to board the train. There are too many angels hanging around. One of them might spot me."

Nadya left her bulky suitcase in the luggage room and they went out into Revolution Square. The snow was still falling and the fog had not lifted. It was long past dark and the street lamps glowed like golden halos vanishing into infinity. They walked as if in a dream, and their feet inevitably took them from the square directly into the Nevsky. The sidewalk was crowded, the snow had melted into slush and people moved slowly and sullenly, tired after a long day over lathes and benches, weary at the thought of the queues in the stores, the long ride home in the sardine-packed bus and the angry clatter and eternal argument of the communal flat.

They found a little restaurant down one flight of stairs, opened the door and were met by a wave of hot, moist air, fragrant with the smell of onions, garlic and frying meat. It was a small *pelmeniya,* a café dedicated to the succulent Siberian meatballs which Michael loved.

He took Nadya's hand in his.

"You will have to get used to *pelmeni,* my little Siberyachka," he said tenderly. "That's all we eat out there, east of the Ob and the Yenisei."

She smiled. "Michael, dear, you shouldn't hold my hand in public. People will think we're not cultured."

Michael laughed. "Let them! Let them think! The fact is we are not cultured. We are free Siberian citizens and we make our own rules and do as we please."

He ordered a glass of wine for Nadya and a glass of vodka for himself. "Just one," he said. "To toast our betrothal!"

Nadya blushed in embarrassment and delight.

Michael started to talk.

"I don't really know what has happened today," he said, a little puzzled. "Someday you will have to tell me about it. But not now. It is a very curious thing. I came all the way back to Leningrad to bury my mother, as she should be buried. And I did do that, but now it seems to me that what I came here for was to find you, to find you again."

He told her that he had often thought of her during the long months he spent in the East.

"But I didn't really ever hope to find you," he said. "I felt ashamed. Felt that I had left you in the lurch, as it were."

Nadya's brown eyes smiled at him.

"I didn't know how much I had missed you until you came back," she said.

Michael talked about the future. It was not going to be easy. Somehow he felt that they were going to be able to reach their destination, to get to Siberia without being stopped by the police.

"It all depends on tonight," he said. "If they don't find us on the train—well, there is a good chance they never will."

Once they had arrived—let's say in Irkutsk—there would be no problem.

"Nobody out there worries about who you are," he said. "If you are in Siberia it means that you've been sent there—so why ask questions."

"But won't there be trouble with the police?" Nadya asked. "When we register—won't they want to know where we came from?"

"Nadya, dear," Michael said, "the police don't care where you come from—not in Siberia. They only care if you are trying to leave Siberia. Surely, there might be a question or two. But, if we say we lost the permit to transfer from Alma Ata to Irkutsk and we need a new one—well, it's just a matter of a hundred-ruble bill slipped into the sergeant's hand. What difference does it make to him?"

They ate leisurely and strolled for a final time on the Nevsky—bade farewell to the great Klodt stallions and the austere columns of the Kazan Cathedral, and walked almost to the end of the avenue for a last glimpse of the Admiralty spire. Then they slowly returned to the station and found their train ready for boarding.

Now the train was moving through the night and they stood

294

for a while peering from the window. Already Leningrad was behind and in the uncertain light they could see that they were
passing through forests of white birch, pine and spruce. Here and
there in the distance gleamed a tiny light—a little hamlet surrounded by snowy fields and dark woods.

This is the endless Russian forest, Michael thought. As far east
as we travel we will be passing through it. Birches and pines, lakes
and streams, glades and meadows, end without end, all the way
across Russia, across Siberia, right up to the cold gray waters of the
Bering Sea.

Nadya pressed closer to him. The train was swaying from side to
side and the cars passed over the rails with a rhythmic click-click-
click.

"This is going to be our world, dearest Nadya," Michael said.
"This is going to be our life. It will not be easy but nothing in
Russia has ever been easy. It will strain our backs and tire our
souls but in the great forest we can live and breathe and still
dream of the future—of that road to the stars."

Nadya pressed his hand.

"And if we don't climb that road, dear Michael," she said, "perhaps our children will find the way."

Michael's arm tightened around her.

"Our parents," Michael said, "thought they had cleared away the
debris and rubbish so that we could climb up that path. They
thought they had smoothed the way for us. But they were too
optimistic. The task is harder than they ever imagined. We are
violent people but nothing changes rapidly here. The dark forces
of our Russia are stronger than a single generation. This is what we,
their children, have learned. Life has taught us that if we are to
find the road to the stars we must keep our feet firmly on the
ground—ground that is slippery, muddy and often covered with
filth."

"But, Michael," Nadya said, "what is going to happen? You
risked your life to honor your mother. We all gathered beside her
grave. General Orlov spoke. That boy, Romanov, spoke. Everyone

said that Irena Galina must not have died in vain. And now what happens? Do you suppose everyone may be arrested? And what of ourselves? We go to Siberia. We start a new life. Will all that Irena Galina stood for be forgotten?"

Michael was silent for a while, looking out the window, staring straight ahead as if he had not heard.

"The window is frosting over," he finally said. "Soon we will not be able to see anything outside. So it goes. No, Nadya dear, the words that were spoken today beside my mother's grave are not like drops of water, falling into the sea, mixed and diluted and lost. They will live forever. Just as she will live. Just as all the brave men and women who have died for Russia, for a better Russia, still live. No one has forgotten Belinsky. No one has forgotten Zhelyabov. No one has forgotten young Alexander Ulyanov. And by dying none of them lost his power to inspire us. Each new generation of Russians worships the same heroes. Each new generation strives for what the older generation failed to attain.

"It is true what you say. Perhaps General Orlov has been arrested. Or soon will be. I imagine that he understood this might happen before he spoke. It may be that he even welcomed this. And you are quite right, Romanov probably will be arrested. No one could listen to 'Ballad of a Poster Maker' this afternoon without understanding what he was getting at. Maybe, in fact, everyone who was at the funeral will be arrested. Certainly I think everyone who came understood that was a possibility. And, I imagine, these people may be sent to Siberia, just as we ourselves are going to the East. It is even conceivable that worse may happen."

"But, Michael," Nadya said, "that is terrible."

"True, dear," Michael replied. "It is. And do not forget that you and I, if the police lay hands on us, will not face a very pleasant fate."

Nadya clutched his arm. Michael was silent a moment and then went on.

"But suppose all this happens, Nadya," he said. "Suppose all of us are scattered to the ends of the earth. Will memory of us and what we believe, memory of Irena Galina and what she believed, will all that vanish like a handful of dust tossed into the air on a windy day? No. There will always be one Russian alive who knows what Irena Galina believed in and died for, who will keep a candle burning at her ikon, who will pass this faith on to others and from others it will spread out over the land, enriching the soil of Russian minds, helping by its example to strengthen the new generation that comes along."

"And this is our task, too, Michael," Nadya said.

Michael gravely nodded.

"We will build our life anew in the East," he told her. "It will not be a wide life. The horizon will be limited to a dusty town, a muddy road, a small wooden hut, a clearing in the grove. And you, dearest Nadya, will bend your back at the marshy pond, washing clothes, instead of painting beauty on a canvas, and my hands will grow thick with calluses, from swinging my ax against the tough fiber of the trees, and we will sink down to sleep at night exhausted.

"Many times we will wonder, you and I, why we have done this. Was it really necessary to turn our backs on the canvas and the marble? Did I have to abandon the test tube and the laboratory? Was it worth it? Why did we do it? And every time, looking at the baby sleeping in the crib, looking at the red cheeks of the little girl bending over her exercise book, we will quietly nod to each other—yes, it was necessary, yes, it had to be thus. And through our eyes the new generation will see Irena Galina and with our voices they will hear her voice, just as we have heard those which have gone before us.

"Did the death of Pushkin still his voice? Did the death of Mayakovsky? Did the exile of the Decembrists cause them to be forgotten? Did the execution of the young people of the Narodnaya Volya halt the cause of Revolution?

"No, Nadya. Death or exile has never extinguished the flame of Russian spirit. It has nourished it. Siberia, our Siberia, the land which will become our own, this is Russia's seedbed, and each generation comes to it, time and again, fertilizing and refertilizing, planting and replanting."

Michael fell silent for a moment.

"That was a long speech, my dear," he said. "And you are tired."

"No, Michael," Nadya said. "It was not long. It was beautiful and true. I am proud of you and proud that you love me."

Nothing was heard now but the music of the rails. The overhead light swung dimly. There had been other passengers in the aisle, warmly dressed, sturdy men and women in *valenki* and sheepskins —just like Nadya and Michael. It was a train for Siberia. The people looked like Siberia—robust, healthy, hardy and ready for cold and hardship. The *provodnik* came up to them.

"Would you like some tea now?" she asked. She had a pleasant, tired smile.

"Thank you," Michael said.

They took the two glasses and sat on their bunk. Already the passengers on the other bunks were curled up, asleep and snoring. Only Michael and Nadya seemed to be awake. They sipped their tea silently, Michael leaning his head against Nadya's breast. Presently, Nadya looked at Michael. His eyes had closed and his breath was coming in long even drafts. He was sleeping.

Nadya shifted her body slightly, so that Michael was resting more easily against her, her arm cradling his shoulders and his breath gently touching her hair. She felt tired but at peace. This was her world from now on. And this, she thought, is how it should be, how it must be. Feeling Michael's body warm and resting against hers there was within her a deep contentment. Whatever the future might bring she would find it beside this man. She would comfort him and nourish him and he would protect her with his strong hands and cherish her with the warmth of his heart. She sat quietly in the dark as the train roared on through the night eastward, kilometer after kilometer, toward Siberia.

37

Galpert leaned back in the chair, cradling the telephone in the hollow of his shoulder. He was sitting in Chaikovsky's office waiting for Moscow to come on the line. Before him on the desk was a small pad of paper on which he had scribbled a series of hieroglyphics. The reason for the delay on the telephone was that Moscow wanted to put a secretary on an extension line to take the conversation down stenographically. Galpert ran his hand over his forehead, pushing back the village lovelock. His forehead was creased by deep fatigue marks and he looked much older than he had appeared while conversing with Chaikovsky and Ivanov in this room just before the funeral.

Finally everything was in order, and a moment later he heard the soft, rather musical voice of his superior saying: "Well, Comrade Galpert, what do you have to report?"

"Things have gone extremely well, Pavel Pavlovich," Galpert said. "As you know we faced some serious difficulties but I am pleased to report that we have overcome the obstacles and can consider our task accomplished in all its main essentials."

"Our Chief will be extremely pleased to hear this news," the

Deputy in Moscow said. "There has been great concern that this matter be cleared up—not only swiftly, but efficiently and smoothly."

"From this standpoint," said Galpert firmly, "I can assure you that everything is in good order."

The greatest difficulty, Galpert said, had arisen from the fact that it had been necessary to leave all of the physical details of the security arrangements in the hands of Chaikovsky.

"This gave us some anxious moments," said Galpert, "but once I had his operational plan I was able to place my men strategically so that the danger of 'accidental' slip-ups was held to a minimum. With a single exception—for which Chaikovsky was completely to blame—we were able to take into custody all of the persons whom it was desired to arrest."

Making check marks against his hieroglyphs, he listed those who had been seized, beginning with General Orlov, Secretary Ivanov and Chaikovsky and winding up with the writer Smirnoff.

"I can see that you have been operating with your usual efficiency, Comrade Galpert," the Deputy said. "Now what have you learned of the conspiracy itself? Have you been able to find evidence which supports the hypothesis which was outlined to you before you left for Leningrad?"

Galpert smiled knowingly to himself.

"I have extremely good news on this score," he said. "I now have a full account of the conspiracy which confirms in every respect the version which I received in Moscow. I have obtained this account from one of the principal plotters himself—a man who has been in the midst of the affair from the very beginning and who had long been able to conceal any suspicion from himself by a series of most deceptive actions. Repeatedly he had brought denunciations against various individuals—even including some members of the ring itself—in an effort to throw dust in our eyes."

"Who is this witness?" Moscow inquired.

"The man is the well-known writer Smirnoff," Galpert said. "He told me, for example, that the charges which he brought against the state criminal Galina were simply a blind. The members of the conspiracy agreed that someone had to be sacrificed because suspicions were beginning to be aroused. Galina volunteered to make the 'sacrifice' and Smirnoff, accordingly, arranged to 'denounce' her."

"Very clever," the Deputy said, his voice smooth as silk over the Moscow line. "Very clever, Comrade Galpert. The Chief will appreciate your working out this angle. This is the kind of thing which is most helpful. Have you been able to determine who was the principal figure in the conspiracy?"

"The principal, Pavel Pavlovich, as you correctly indicated to me before I left Moscow, is dead," Galpert said, running his hand again over his forehead. "Following his death last August the leadership appears to have been assumed by a troika: Chaikovsky-Orlov-Ivanov. The most active figure was, of course, Chaikovsky. He made Ivanov his tool. At no point have we been able to determine—at least in preliminary examination—that Ivanov did more than obediently carry out orders passed on to him by Chaikovsky."

"Has Ivanov shown a desire to co-operate with the State Prosecutor?" asked the Deputy.

"Yes, indeed," said Galpert. "He has said that he is prepared to make a full confession and is ready to testify against his fellow members of the conspiracy. However, I have delayed accepting his offer until I consulted with you as to the precise details to which you might wish him to testify."

"But he will be available for such use as we wish to make of his testimony?"

"Quite correct, Pavel Pavlovich," Galpert replied. "He says that he is a simple man, accustomed to obeying and carrying out orders. He received these orders up until last August from his immediate Party superior. Since that time his instructions have come from Chaikovsky. He said, for example, that his presence at the funeral this afternoon was explicitly at Chaikovsky's orders. I foresee no difficulty in getting whatever testimony we need from Ivanov."

301

"I suppose," observed the Deputy, "that you have not been able to obtain much in the way of co-operation from General Orlov."

"No," said Galpert, ticking off another hieroglyph. "He refuses to answer questions of any kind. But some of his remarks reflect directly upon our Party and its leadership. There is no question about his deep hostility and long-standing antagonism to the Soviet state. His speech at the funeral this afternoon made this only too plain."

"Ah," said the Deputy. "Then our Chief's suspicion that this plot directly imperiled the security of the state has been thoroughly confirmed."

"That is correct," said Galpert. "It is apparent that the vital defenses of our northern frontiers and the security of the second-greatest city of the country have been endangered. But this is not all. There is foreign involvement in this conspiracy."

"So we had suspected, you will recall," the Deputy said with obvious satisfaction. "So our Chief was convinced from the very start. I well recall him saying to me, 'Pavel Pavlovich, where there is smoke there must be fire. It is incredible that a conspiracy of such a scale could be carried out without a connection with foreign intelligence agencies.' "

"Thus far," Galpert said, "we have only the general outlines. It remains to fill in the details. But from the testimony of Smirnoff it seems evident that the first contacts with foreign intelligence were made as early as the period of the Great Patriotic War. You may recall that through the negligence of the Leningrad military, Party, and security apparatus, agents of foreign intelligence, in the guise of correspondents of newspapers from the United States, England and other countries, were permitted to visit Leningrad, to inspect the city's defenses, to meet and have contacts with representatives of the conspiracy during the wartime period."

The first formal contacts, said Galpert, apparently had been made just after the lifting of the Leningrad blockade in January or February, 1944.

"The conspiracy," he said, "probably had its origin during the very first days of the war, during the period of the Nazi assault on Leningrad. At a moment when our fatherland was in direst danger, when Comrade Stalin was calling upon every citizen to stand firm, the jackals of Leningrad were already conspiring to deal a treacherous blow in the back to our fatherland."

"I know that it will be hard for our Chief to believe," said Galpert, "but on the testimony of Smirnoff this conspiracy assumed a definite form during the siege winter of 1941-42. It is not yet certain whether the plotters planned to turn the city over to the Germans but this is not impossible. It is also possible that they deliberately took precisely the opposite actions to those necessary to prevent suffering in the city. Thus it was suggested by Smirnoff that they might have deliberately set fire to the Baldaev warehouse in order to starve the city to death. He suggested that Ivanov might have carried this out at the orders of the Party Leader. He also suggested that we investigate the actions of General Orlov in that period, to determine whether he had not attempted to open the way to the city through the eastern approaches. There is also the possibility that Chaikovsky deliberately permitted theft and sabotage of food supplies in order to destroy the morale of the city."

"Outside of the testimony of this Smirnoff," said the Deputy, "do you have any other evidence to support the existence of the conspiracy at this early phase?"

"Indeed, there is such evidence," said Galpert. "Some of it we found in the possession of Smirnoff and some of it is to be found in the city archives. For example, we have found a rather full account of a meeting in January of 1942 at which one of the defendants, Morozov, obviously acting as a go-between for the military and the city authorities, made the first mention of the plot. As a cover for the nefarious intentions of the conspiracy it was described as a 'housing' project. This enabled them to carry on their discussions in public without the possibility of disclosure since the cover name was meaningless except to those actually involved in the plot. The first objective of the conspirators, I might say, was to transfer the capital back to Leningrad from Moscow."

"They were obviously prepared to go to any lengths," said the Deputy.

"That is correct," said Galpert. "In connection with the January,

1942, meeting we have a record of declarations made by almost all of the principals pledging their full support to the scheme. We have similar documentation available of the meeting at which the formal contact with the representatives of British and American intelligence was carried out. The meeting was even held in one of the most prominent places in Leningrad, the House of Scientists. Again, almost all of the plotters were present—including Orlov."

Galpert interrupted himself a moment to glance at a note which had just been placed before him by one of his aides.

"Yes," he said. "Pavel Pavlovich, I want to report a further development. We have just carried out a raid upon the Leningrad Museum for the Great Patriotic War. We have sealed the museum and taken the documentary materials into our hands. Among these documents are reports of both of the meetings which I have described to you as well as many other useful items of evidence in support of the general charges. We have, for example, copies of an almanac which was issued in 1942, utilizing the cover name of the conspiracy. This was used as a vehicle of propaganda and communication by the plotters. For example, it has a sketch of the so-called 'End of War' statue which the woman Galina prepared. It is quite evident from the testimony of Smirnoff that the Galina statue was designed as an instrument of propaganda to undermine national patriotism, to arouse opposition to the policies of the Soviet state and to make difficult if not impossible the defense of our motherland against attacks from abroad. Thus, it was designed to create the psychological preconditions for the carrying out of the aims and intentions of the group."

"Have you had any success with Chaikovsky?" the Deputy asked.

"I'm sorry to report, Pavel Pavlovich," said Galpert, wiping the sweat from his brow, "that we have made no progress whatsoever during the preliminary questioning of Chaikovsky. It is quite obvious that we will have to shift to other methods of interrogation before his co-operation can be secured."

"There can be no doubt that he was in the center of the affair, can there?" the Deputy asked.

"None whatever," said Galpert. "As you are well aware, he provided complete and full protection to the conspirators at all times. You will search his files in vain for the slightest suggestion that any plot existed. We have found evidence that he intervened at one time in behalf of the state criminal Galina in connection with her deportation to Uzbekistan. There is also evidence that he was intimately acquainted with her. His relations were extremely close with Ivanov. He had cleverly avoided public contacts with Orlov, obviously fearing that conclusions might be drawn from any unusual association between the military and the Security agency."

"Hmm," said the Deputy. "This is shaping up excellently. As soon as the necessary confessions have been forthcoming we can, I hope, go forward to the final liquidation of the conspirators. Have you been able to get any clue as to when they had intended to strike?"

"This cannot be said with assurance as yet," said Galpert. "It may be that we will not be able to get an outline of the final plans until Chaikovsky begins to talk. However, we do have one clue of great value. A meeting of most of the plotters was held only last night. Obviously they felt that time was growing short and probably they had been told by Chaikovsky that we were closing in. The customary 'cover' was employed. The project was discussed in guarded tones. Orlov agreed to the liquidation of one of the most important and highly secret defense installations in Leningrad. This was to be carried out in the guise of its 'removal for a housing development.' This would have crippled the city's defenses and left our industrial centers open to enemy assault at any moment. Ivanov apparently was to act in a liaison capacity. When agreement was reached upon the general program he offered to act as co-ordinator between the military and the Party and, what is most important, specifically announced that he would obtain 'Moscow's approval' for the plans.

"Thus, it seems obvious that the plotters have an alternate center, that they were preparing to act not only in Leningrad but also in Moscow. Thus far, we have not been able to obtain the names of their collaborators in Moscow."

"Ah," said the Deputy. "This is extremely vital information. It fits in precisely with that which has been developed by the Chief and, I might say to you in strictest confidence, that we have not been idle in Moscow. We have already moved against the 'alternate center.' A number of individuals have been in contact with Leningrad and some of them had been sent to infiltrate the Moscow organization—men who were very close to the late Leningrad leader."

"I'm gratified," said Galpert, "that the Security forces once again in timely fashion have been able to eliminate a danger to our beloved fatherland."

"To return for a moment to Chaikovsky," said the Deputy. "It seems to me you mentioned certain difficulties in connection with the arrangements for the arrests."

"That is correct, Pavel Pavlovich, there were certain difficulties," said Galpert. This point worried him but he tried to keep the worry out of his voice. "It was obvious that he was trying to cause us to lower our guard and relax our vigilance. He tried ostentatiously to disassociate himself from Ivanov. He attempted to distract my suspicions from Smirnoff, probably fearing that Smirnoff might give the plot away. He deliberately arranged, you might say, for the funeral to be held at the Little Literary Bridge, hoping to create a sensation in the city and arouse support for the conspiracy among the proletariat. However, fortunately he was thwarted in almost all of his designs. We were able to limit the attendance at the funeral to the plotters themselves, and a very small group of others, including a few misguided students. He did achieve one small coup, however, which it is necessary to mention.

"By a clever ruse which we are still investigating he permitted young Galin to get away, having carefully created a hole in the net for the fish to slip through.

"However, I am certain that we will catch this fish without too great delay."

"Hmm," said the Deputy. "This one might better be described

as a minnow, don't you think? The minnow with which we baited the hook for catching the pike and sturgeon. What is important in this connection is that we have safely netted the bigger fish—and Chaikovsky among them."

"Well, Pavel Pavlovich," said Galpert, "I trust that I did not take too literally your instructions to concentrate my attention on the big ones—especially the biggest of them."

"You have carried out a difficult assignment precisely according to your instructions," said the Deputy. "I think that you will without question receive the congratulations of the Chief. So far as this one small sardine is concerned—well, it will require a little thought. But for the moment perhaps we will just let him swim around in the big sea. Once the bait has been taken there is really no further use for it. Yes. In fact, just between us it does not seem likely that we need that kind of flavoring for the stew we are preparing, eh? Suppose we just leave it at that. If he turns up you can let me know and we might have another look at the situation."

"Thank you, Pavel Pavlovich," said Galpert, putting a hand over the receiver to cover the sigh of relief that escaped him. "Do you have any other instructions at this time?"

"I think not," said the Deputy. "Oh, one thing—just a matter of curiosity. What was the cover name which the conspirators employed?"

"Oh, yes, Pavel Pavlovich," said Galpert, daintily inserting his little finger into his right nostril and probing high in his nose. "Yes, well, the cover name. I meant, of course, to tell you. It was 'Northern Palmyra.' They called their affair the 'Northern Palmyra' project. And that permitted them to carry on public discussions of it and to make public references to it without danger that their designs would be understood by the organs of state security or anyone else not privy to their secrets."

"I see," said the Deputy. "Well, I think that covers everything for the moment. I think of no special instructions at this time. Carry on with the interrogation. Don't worry too much about that sardine. And, as you suggest, it might be just as well to try other methods with Chaikovsky. He is a tough nut and it will not be too easy to crack him."

"Very good," said Galpert, replacing the receiver on the hook. He removed his little finger from his nose, inspected the nasal debris with care, and wiped it on the underside of Chaikovsky's desk.

He pressed a buzzer and his assistant instantly appeared, a young square-headed blond built like a gymnast.

"Okay to go ahead with Chaikovsky," he said. "The Chief's orders. Let me know when you have him ready to sing."

Chaikovsky was an old police officer, Galpert mused. He should understand that the time inevitably comes when you are ready to confess whatever your interrogator desires. Why not do it now and save the pain and agony, not to mention the interrogator's patience, time and energy. Ah, well, thought Galpert, there's no fool like an old fool. He knows as well as any one of us the Chief's instructions in difficult cases: "Beat, beat, beat!"

38

She was a large woman and her face was red from walking a long distance against the cold wind that was sweeping down from the north, blowing the snow and carving it into sculptured drifts. She walked with her shoulders slightly bowed, a man's sheepskin cap on her head and a man's sheepskin jacket obscuring the outlines of her powerful torso. Her feet were clad in peasant *valenki* and a drab black wool skirt protected her powerful hips and thighs.

She walked down the long allée with the plodding walk of the peasant who has come many miles and has many more miles to go, the walk of a woman who knows what it is to trudge through the deep frost and the deep snow with a burden on her shoulders, trudging from the distant *izba* to the village market before dawn and back home again after noon.

In her strong hand she clutched a handful of brightly colored paper flowers—large imitation poppies they were—and these were the only color in a landscape that was all white and black and gray.

So cold and stormy was the day that she seemed to be almost

the only person abroad, and she walked with purpose and resolution, a woman who knew where she was going and what she was going to do.

Presently, she left the allée, made her way through a snowdrift, through a small blue-painted wrought-iron fence and stood before a new-made grave, almost obscured under the fresh fall of snow and the billows heaped up by the wind. She knelt a moment, placing the paper flowers on the grave, and then, brushing off the snow with a casual hand, seated herself on a small bench, her head sinking in meditation and her lips moving as though in prayer. She sat silently thus for a few moments, then sighed and rose, saying audibly: "God bless you, dear Irena Mikhailovna. Forgive me. Forgive me."

As she turned away from the grave an ancient figure in worn burlap robes with long white beard, a thick stick in his hand, and his white hair flowing in the wind approached her, silently questioning her with his eyes.

"God save me!" the woman cried suddenly, pressing a bill into the priest's hand. "Say a mass for Irena Mikhailovna Galina, please."

The priest bowed his head slightly, clasping his hands together, and asked: "And in whose name shall the mass be said?"

"No name," said the woman, her eyes burning with a fierce light. "No name. Just a mass for a woman in the name of a woman."

She turned from the priest and walked back down the allée, her head slightly bowed, striding sturdily into the wind, the snow streaming in her face.

The priest stood motionless until the woman vanished in the distance. Then he turned in the other direction.

"So be it," he murmured. "So be it."

ABOUT THE AUTHOR

Harrison E. Salisbury has been a writer since his college days at the University of Minnesota. He became a newspaper reporter while still an undergraduate, and the newspaper profession has been his field ever since.

Mr. Salisbury has spent many years in Russia as a correspondent, first for the United Press and then during the last of the Stalin years and the early post-Stalin era for *The New York Times.*

He has traveled widely in the Soviet Union, visiting almost every part of the country, including Siberia, the sub-Arctic, Central Asia, the Volga country and the Ukraine.

His first visit to Leningrad was paid in January, 1944, when the 900-day blockade of that city was ended. He has revisited Leningrad many times.

Mr. Salisbury was awarded the Pulitzer Prize for international correspondent in 1955 for a series of dispatches on the Soviet Union published in *The New York Times.*

The Northern Palmyra Affair is Mr. Salisbury's sixth book and first novel.